# Wish
# You
# Were
# Her

*Other books by Elle McNicoll:*

Some Like it Cold

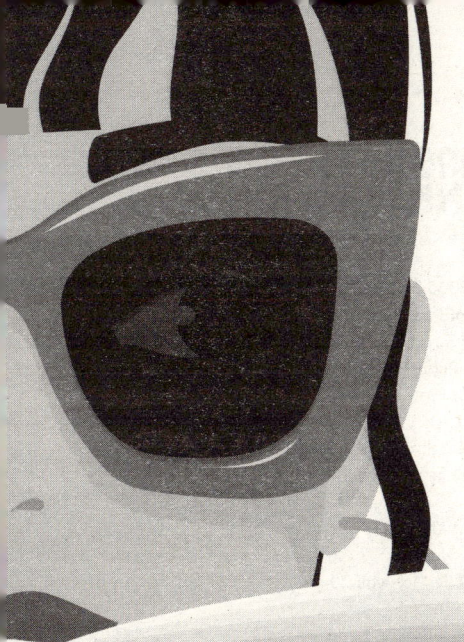

# Wish You Were Her

## Elle McNicoll

**FIRST INK**

Published 2025 by First Ink,
an imprint of Pan Macmillan
The Smithson, 6 Briset Street, London EC1M 5NR
*EU representative:* Macmillan Publishers Ireland Ltd, 1st Floor,
The Liffey Trust Centre, 117–126 Sheriff Street Upper
Dublin 1, D01 YC43
Associated companies throughout the world
www.panmacmillan.com

ISBN 978-1-0350-2787-3

Copyright © Elle McNicoll 2025

The right of Elle McNicoll to be identified as the
author of this work has been asserted by her in
accordance with the Copyright, Designs and Patents Act 1988.

All rights reserved. No part of this publication may be reproduced,
stored in a retrieval system, or transmitted, in any form or by any means
(electronic, mechanical, photocopying, recording or otherwise),
without the prior written permission of the publisher.

Pan Macmillan does not have any control over, or any responsibility for,
any author or third-party websites referred to in or on this book.

1 3 5 7 9 8 6 4 2

A CIP catalogue record for this book is available from the British Library.

Printed and bound by CPI Group (UK) Ltd, Croydon CR0 4YY

This book is sold subject to the condition that it shall not, by way of trade or otherwise,
be lent, resold, hired out, or otherwise circulated without the publisher's prior consent in
any form of binding or cover other than that in which it is published and without a similar
condition including this condition being imposed on the subsequent purchaser.

*To the booksellers and the book festivals.*
*Thank you for all of it.*

*And to Josh. True love, best friend and bodyguard.*
*You're every male lead I write.*

*'A Star is Made!' And she is every bit as unapproachable as a star in the heavens. Allegra Brooks is a supernova, make no mistake. But what is actually beneath the glittery, polite veneer? I'm afraid, reader, this journalist was unable to find out.*

Julie M. Atkins writing for *The Eyewitness*

*I'm waiting in the front entrance of Balthazar when a waiter comes over to discreetly tell me that my lunch date is already here. I must look surprised and in truth, I am. I've interviewed many a sleb in recent years, and they all come in a number of different designs. Some like clean diets of lemon juice and raw vegetables (which is code for weight loss, drug usage and aesthetic surgeries), others are addicted to spending every waking moment in the gym (or rather, taking videos for social media of their workouts in activewear they've been sent by a sponsor). I've met musicians who chain smoke, influencers who collect Pomeranians like they're designer purses and celebrities who escape their families by obsessively working. There is only one quality that they all have in common:*

*Lateness*

*So I am inordinately stunned as the waiter leads me to a dark and quiet corner of the restaurant. Waiting for me is none other than my interview subject: Allegra Brooks. It seems I am the last to arrive, for once.*

*I ask about her family background. Her mother, Roxanne, works in publishing and her father, George, runs a bookshop in a small town. She tells me he's prepping for a big book festival there, one that he hosts every summer.*

*'I have a whole summer off. I'm not sure what to do with it yet. It's the first little bit of freedom I've had since I started working.'*

*This young woman's screenwork may be extraordinary but getting behind the dark glasses is like squeezing blood from a stone. There's something off about her. Something strange. I've seen stars rise, I've seen them fall. None have seemed as inhuman as this girl. It's uncanny. She's not doing anything disturbing. Her stunning smile is there. But the beautiful naturalness that she has on camera seems so unnatural in person. I feel both attracted and almost entirely repelled . . .*

*Continued on page 75 . . .*

Search Results for 'Allegra Brooks':

@lunadeclare
I don't know who needs to hear this but Allegra Brooks is highly overrated.

@morrisey1983
Allegra Brooks used to respond to fan letters and DMs but she hasn't answered any of mine since winning at the Globes. So, screw her, I guess.

@mira2335
Allegra Brooks bought out a whole movie screen for some autistic kids in my neighbourhood and they had the most amazing time and I'm kinda mad that no one is talking about it tbh. I only know about it because my dad works there. Why don't the papers report that?

@JJ4765442
Dear Allegra. You still haven't responded to my messages. I will take drastic action if you continue to ignore me.

@marzipanlight
Allegra Brooks won't see your mean comments about her body but your curvy friends will. Be nice. @AllegraBrooks #BeTheChangeYouWantToSee

Top News Stories for 'Allegra Brooks':

Showbiz News: Allegra Brooks leaves *Court of Bystanders* after-party early. Could break-up with ex-frontman be getting to the young starlet?

Update! Director Bon Michaelson claims Allegra Brooks could be 'the next Marilyn Monroe' – if not for her lack of eye contact and quiet manner on set.

Source Tells *Private Lives* that Allegra Brooks will take summer off. Has overnight success become too much for Hollywood newcomer?

# Chapter One

By eighteen, Allegra Brooks was used to hearing her name from the mouths of strangers. She was accustomed to people speaking excitedly to her without introducing themselves. She was even used to the occasional grab and shove.

But she never quite acclimatized to being pulled apart by people she had never met. She watched fans become her biggest critics, all because her boundaries had angered them.

'Stop scrolling. Put that phone down.'

The words were whispered to Allegra by Natalie, her publicist. Natalie was twenty-six and the hardest working person Allegra had ever met. She would often ask herself 'what would Natalie do?' before forcing herself into a party she had been terrified of going to, because the woman's professional courage and work ethic put everyone else to shame. The two of them were in the back of a hire car – they were due to appear at a swanky benefit for literacy – and the tinted windows offered a brief respite from the outside world.

'Nat,' Allegra said, her voice shaking a touch, as she swapped her dark glasses for her regular ones. 'I'm not—'

'Forget that stupid article. Stop reading those comments. It's basically self-harm at this point, Allegra. Enough,' Nat said firmly. 'Being loved on a massive scale means being disliked and misunderstood just as much. It all balances out. Wear the dark shades, there are tons of photographers. You'll get overstimulated.

Don't think about that stupid hack of a writer. I never should have agreed to her.'

'I must have done everything wrong for her to have written that,' Allegra remarked, as they waited for the car to stop. 'I feel like I'm not playing the fame game very well.'

'Nonsense, you're perfect. It's a clickbait tactic. The snarkier and meaner they are, the more people will read it. You were trending on socials because it created so much discourse—'

'I hate discourse,' breathed Allegra, rubbing her palms and trying to find some calm.

'But the best people are on your side, kid. Don't you stress. Now, come on. Chin up. Let's go.'

Allegra let Natalie propel her out of the car and the flashes started. People yelled out her name and she pretended that they were calling for someone else. Some other eighteen-year-old girl who had just set the world on fire.

One successful open call audition at the age of thirteen, and she was now the owner of two Emmys and one very shiny Golden Globe. She had been made a household name by her most recent and most famous role to date: Clera in the globally acclaimed television adaptation of fantasy series *Court of Bystanders*. It just didn't feel like a name she recognized any more. She had been cast in a revival of the musical *She Loves Me*, but the director's dubious past had been made public and the whole thing had been cancelled. So now she had a free summer for the first time in years.

She was almost afraid of the open calendar.

At that moment, Allegra noticed a young woman filming herself at the main door. When she spotted Allegra, her eyes widened and she leapt into motion.

'Allegra? Allegra! Oh, my God! I need a picture with you!'

Allegra smiled instinctively but she saw how anxious her eyes looked as she stared at herself on the girl's phone screen.

Once inside, Allegra felt a bitter taste under her tongue when she looked around at the glitz and sparkle: this was a *charity luncheon*. There was a vast ballroom full of tables with guests milling all around. A large screen played slides full of information about the people they were supposedly there to help, but nobody paid attention. Attendees buzzed from table to table, all trying to find the most socially beneficial beehive. Allegra had made a sizeable donation and had hoped, in the car, that the event would highlight the underprivileged children the charity was trying to help.

Now it seemed like yet another soulless gathering for the people who had decided she was going to be one of them. Well, if she behaved.

'This is not my world,' Allegra said, too quietly for anyone to hear. 'I don't belong here.'

Natalie was a human battering ram against the crowd of photographers. Some attendees nodded at Allegra in greeting, others looked her slowly up and down. Almost all of them whispered to their companions as she and Natalie passed by.

Allegra had been working steadily for years, hacking at the tree of acting and making little dents with every artistic pursuit. Then one day, the tree just fell. All those years of working on its trunk had paid off and the towering thing hit the ground with enormous shockwaves.

And there was no standing the tree back up.

Natalie found their place settings at their table and Allegra moved to turn off her phones – one for work and one for herself.

Natalie had wrangled the personal number from her so she could reach her late at night, but otherwise only the odd co-star and her mother got in touch on the personal phone.

So she was surprised to see a little red number one looking up at her from its barely used inbox.

People were still filing into the room. She opened her inbox to find an email from Brooks Books, her father's bookshop; a reply to an email she had sent, intending it to reach her father:

**westendgirl@gmail.com**
**to: shopfloor@BrooksBooks.com**
**Subject: Summer Book Festival**
Hello!
Hope it's okay for me to email here. I called the shop but no one answered. Can I double-check the dates of your book festival? You don't have a website and I can't find it on socials.
Lots of love!

**shopfloor@BrooksBooks.com**
**to: westendgirl@gmail.com**
**RE: Summer Book Festival**
Dear Mysterious Reader who did not leave a name,
Apologies for our lack of technological advancement. Alas, I have implored George Brooks, my fearless leader, many times for a website but he is an adorable curmudgeon about such matters. The festival preparations have begun and it's already taking years off my young life. We open on 28 July and the last

night is 23 August. Only two months to go.
Wish an overworked bookseller luck!
Warmest wishes,
Said Overworked Bookseller.

Allegra smiled. It danced on her lips and then grew into something wide. She started to type a response.

**westendgirl@gmail.com**
**to: shopfloor@BrooksBooks.com**
**RE: Summer Book Festival**
Dear Said Overworked Bookseller.
So sorry to have added more to your to-do list. For some reason, I thought Mr Brooks was manning this email address but I should have known better. Consider me scolded.
Thank you for the festival dates, it's gratefully received. The twitter account only has this email address in its bio and no one has tweeted in this calendar year. Appreciate speediness of response via email.
Best,
Mysterious Reader.

Allegra sent the email and switched both of her phones off, before sliding them into her clutch bag. It was a gift from an up-and-coming designer. She so rarely chose her own outfits any more. She had become a canvas for other people's art.

She found herself daydreaming for most of the luncheon. She

knew so little of her father's small town, Lake Pristine. Her mother had always spoken of it with great fondness and her father would send beautiful pictures of it at Christmas (physical Polaroids in the post because technology unnerved him). His bookshop was his pride and joy and Allegra could imagine it, in the sunny picturesque town where everyone was as friendly and funny as the bookseller on the other end of their email exchange.

She had begged to visit as a child, imagining it to be a place of mermaids in lakes and fairies in the woods. But her father had always chosen to visit them in the city instead. The drive was too long for her, her parents would say, and as a child prone to travel sickness, she believed them. Now she wondered if it was just hard for the two of them to be there together – in the place where they had first fallen in love.

When Allegra's acting career had taken off, her life had become one of trailers and hotels. No time for any kind of home.

Now Lake Pristine suddenly felt like an escape portal. The kind of world she wanted to fall into, even if only for a short spell.

'We need to discuss the summer,' Natalie finally murmured. 'Have you decided what you'll do with your time off? I can pull together a schedule if you want to keep working. You won't be needed for press until August though.'

Allegra turned her personal phone back on.

She could feel Natalie watching her curiously. 'You're staring really hard at that thing. Not reading any more trash opinions, I hope.'

'No,' Allegra said. 'I – just emailing a friend.'

'A friend?'

'Don't sound so surprised.'

Natalie blushed. 'I didn't mean it like that. I just know work's had you a bit . . . isolated.'

'I'm emailing a *new* friend.'

Natalie gave her a look of approval and held her hands up, as if to assure Allegra that she would let the actress draft these emails on her own and would not pry or spy.

And she did.

**shopfloor@BrooksBooks.com**
**to: westendgirl@gmail.com**
**RE: Summer Book Festival**

Dear Mysterious Reader,
I feel you're less mysterious now, though I obviously don't know who you are. A book lover, I hope!
No scolding intended, I assure you. I don't think you live in Lake Pristine, or you wouldn't have emailed. People who live here don't believe in polite contact – they just come and bang loudly on the front door if they want something or have a question. Most of our festival patrons receive a posted programme, and descend on the town when the festival starts. I sometimes forget people might look for us on social media. I avoid it all now, too divisive. Or I'll get caught in a rabbit hole of some weirdly specific drama, usually not related to anyone or anything that I know, and then my evening has gone and I'm cold with shame.
Love,
Ashamed ex-Twitter addict.

Allegra blurted out a laugh. Someone at the next table threw her a look of suspicion and her mask slipped back on without a moment's hesitation. She sighed. Being perceived took away the precious things and made them feel cheap.

'What's wrong?' Natalie asked, looking up from her own phone. Perhaps she so rarely heard Allegra laugh, she had mistaken it for a noise of distress while focusing on her own alarming inbox. The publicist's emails replaced themselves like a shark's teeth. There were always more waiting.

'I know what I'm doing over the summer,' Allegra said decidedly. 'I'm spending it with my dad.'

'Your dad? At the bookshop? The whole summer?'

'Yep.'

'Which is where again?'

Allegra slipped her dark glasses on and smiled. 'Lake Pristine.'

# Chapter Two

'Aha! Got it. These wretched customers will NOT defy me!'

Jonah Thorne shouted the words from atop his ladder in Brooks Books. He had deduced that a customer had been moving some of the books around earlier that morning and his suspicions had just been confirmed by a classic that was covering up a stack of self-help manuals. He stared down at the copy of *Heart of Darkness* by Joseph Conrad. It was one of those rare books, where he actually preferred the movie version: *Apocalypse Now*.

'Lake Pristine,' he said under his breath, and only to himself. His best impression of Martin Sheen. 'I'm still only in Lake Pristine.'

'Huh?'

'Nothing. Found it!'

'Why do they do that?' asked Simon, his fellow bookseller, from the bottom of the ladder.

'Might be an author?' Jonah replied. 'Around festival time, they show up and start moving things around. Putting their books out front and centre, and their enemies in the back.'

'That's cracked.'

Jonah leapt down onto the shopfloor and sneezed. 'Though Joseph Conrad has been dead for some time now so perhaps not. It's dusty as well, man. We need to get up there with a dry cloth.'

'Well, if you weren't always lurking around the computer, you could do it.'

There was only one computer in the expansive bookshop and it was older than the booksellers who worked there. A large, chunky thing sitting on the cash desk. Jonah had a tempestuous relationship with it and its slow speed.

But after some recent, pleasing email exchanges, he was growing fond of the old thing. The last week had been full of sweet missives from a stranger and he now found himself looking forward to checking the work inbox.

'Jonah?'

'Yes, Simon? Speak while helping me open this delivery, please.'

Simon joined Jonah by the large blue boxes full of new books and helped his friend to scan them into the system, all without losing his enthusiasm.

'Heard the boss's exciting news?'

'Nope. He barely speaks to me any more.'

Jonah did not mean for the words to sound embittered, but that's how they came out. He had been working in Brooks Books since the age of sixteen. Almost three years on, and his once warm relationship with the bookshop owner and general manager, George Brooks, had cooled.

He did not know the reason, and he had never been skilled at reading other people and their changing emotions.

'His daughter's coming here for the whole summer.'

Jonah could feel himself making a face. 'Didn't know he had one.'

'Not just any old daughter.'

Jonah looked up at Simon, who was positively salivating. 'You're being weird. What's wrong?'

'It's just too good, Jonah. I can't believe he's never milked this or even mentioned it. His daughter is—'

The shop door opened and their employer came striding in. He had a newspaper tucked under one arm and, in a first since Jonah had met him, he was humming.

'Morning,' Jonah said.

'Morning, lads.'

'I was just telling Jonah that your daughter's staying with you this summer, boss.'

The words were volleyed with sunny familiarity. Jonah had always marvelled at that talent of Simon's. Whenever it was just the two of them – and they had been friends since they were kids – Jonah saw all of Simon. Savvy, sarcastic, sometimes a little bratty. When he was around other people, he turned into sunshine. It always took a little while for people to see the real Simon, and George still got the sunshine version five days a week. Jonah wished he could do the same.

The bookshop owner smiled and looked younger in the process. 'Yes. She had a break in her schedule so she's coming home.'

'Home?' Jonah said. He had never even heard George refer to Lake Pristine as home, let alone a mysterious daughter that none of them had ever seen.

'Well, she's never visited here before. But it's always home for her if she needs it,' George clarified. 'Which is a good segue to this: I want her to enjoy the festival. I thought she might like to work it alongside the both of you.'

That was enough to stamp out all of Jonah's good humour and curiosity. 'Our festival? The one we've been planning for months. That festival?'

'Yes, Jonah,' said George, a little curtly. 'She's smart. She'll be an asset.'

'Definitely an asset on the PR front,' Simon said, a joke laced into his voice that Jonah did not understand.

'We have a packed programme! We don't have time to train someone new,' Jonah insisted. 'And when I say "we", I mean me, because Simon doesn't know the half of what I do.'

'When it comes to this place, true,' Simon conceded. 'To life outside of it? You're an old man and you need me.'

Jonah smiled. He and Simon were the same age.

'She won't need any training. Books are in her blood and she's a hard worker. She's taken on more than a small-town book festival in her life, son. She'll be fine.'

The use of the word 'son' softened Jonah's irritation and he decided to drop his protestations.

'Right,' said George. 'I'll be in the office. She's arriving this afternoon.'

Jonah watched his employer vanish through the door with a 'staff only' sign at the back of the shop, then yelped as he found himself being grabbed by the collar, Simon dropping his professional act completely now that George was gone.

'Dude, relinquish your creepy possessiveness of the work computer and let me google something for you.'

Jonah grumbled but allowed his friend to drag him over to the ancient computer. It took an embarrassing five minutes for Google to load and then Simon was typing furiously while Jonah, who was far taller, peered over his shoulder.

*Allegra Brooks.*

Google knew what Simon wanted before he had even finished

typing the fourth letter of her name. Millions of results appeared, from an IMDb page to multiple articles published in the last twenty-four hours.

'She's, like, freakishly famous. Not just small-town famous, *globally* famous. She just won all the awards for . . . acting and shit.'

Simon was breathless with excitement but Jonah was barely listening. He was staring at the three pictures of Allegra Brooks that had appeared at the top of the search page. One was from a modelling shoot for a magazine he had never heard of, and the other two looked as though they were from film premieres.

She had the most voluminous hair and large, incredibly kind eyes. She was smiling in one of the pictures and Jonah had to remind himself to breathe.

'Oh, God,' he said shortly. 'She's coming here?'

'Yup,' said Simon. 'And I am going to be the one doing the training, my guy, make no mistake. You just relax.'

Jonah said nothing. He moved swiftly away, leaving Simon to the computer, and began sorting the books from their latest delivery onto his trolley. His brain categorized them by cover and genre, his hands moving with a quickness that only years of practice and a touch of brilliance could achieve. He sorted through the boxes of new books, and started wheeling his trolley to the appropriate shelves.

Simon glanced up from his scrolling to peer over at his friend. 'You okay?'

Jonah moved to the next box of books. 'Fine. Never better.'

Simon's brow furrowed but he did not question his friend's strange shift in mood. 'Want me to do the morning emails?'

'No,' Jonah said quickly. 'I'll do that.'

'Thank God,' Simon said with a relieved exhale. 'I'm going to start on the window.'

They swapped positions, Jonah moving to stand by the old monitor while Simon wheeled the trolley over to one of the shop windows so he could begin constructing a new display. Jonah went to close the internet search but paused, staring once again at the images of Allegra Brooks.

He closed the search and opened the shopfloor email. He instantly spotted a reply, one he had been hoping to find, so he saved it as a reward for getting through his professional obligations. He replied to people about pre-orders, author events and the upcoming festival and once they were all cleared, he finally opened the one he had been waiting for.

**westendgirl@gmail.com**
**to: shopfloor@BrooksBooks.com**
**Subject: Twitter Recovery**
Dear ex-Twitter addict,
Please accept my apologies, I did not intend to bring up a sore subject. I hope your recovery is going well. I'm so envious, however, because I have to do social media for work and I loathe it. I understand your need to cut yourself off from the rubbernecking. Are you in a group? A programme?
In all seriousness, social media is addictive and makes people way sadder than they realize and so I'm glad you're free. Feel bad for the rest of us.
Yours,
A friend from out of town.

'Why are you smiling? Is someone asking where to find something on Amazon again?'

'I'm not smiling,' Jonah said, answering Simon with a forced expression of neutrality. He moved the email to a folder he knew Simon would never check – the handover notes – and started drafting a response.

**shopfloor@BrooksBooks.com**
**to: westendgirl@gmail.com**
**RE: Twitter Recovery**
Dearest friend from out of town,
Still mysterious, but slightly less so now that I know you work in social media. What a career. I'm secretly thrilled to work for a man who hates the internet, it makes my recovery so much easier. What does your job entail? Do you get lots of trolls? I once tweeted from the bookshop account that audiobooks are valid and absolutely the same as reading a physical book and a man in his sixties threatened to come to the store and hit me over the head with a copy of his novel.
I'm not part of a group but I am enjoying these emails. They're tiding me over, so I won't dive into social media looking for human connection.
So, it would be really awkward at this stage if you turn around and tell me you have millions of dollars to give me, I just need to send you a fee to cover the wire transfer.
I'm usually a pretty disgruntled bookseller but if there

is anything else I can do for you, I'm at your disposal.
Yours,

Jonah felt the urge to sign his name. He had been enjoying this email exchange since its random arrival in his life. Everybody knew everybody in Lake Pristine and so it was pleasant to have a little contact with the outside world.

'Jonah?'

Jonah smacked 'send' out of sheer panic of being perceived, as George poked his head out of the backroom door and called over to him. The email disappeared into the ether without a moniker.

# Chapter Three

Allegra's mother, Roxanne, came to collect her daughter from the airport and, as the eighteen-year-old slipped into the front passenger seat of the old Vauxhall, her mother became slightly tearful.

'Ma, don't,' Allegra said, her voice full of incredulity.

'Well, I'm sorry,' her mother replied, laughing. 'This is the first time I've seen you properly in months.'

'I saw you at the *Bystanders* screening.'

'For five minutes, Ally.'

'I know, I'm sorry. It's been busy.'

'Well, anyhow,' her mother sniffed as they hit the long, runway-like road that would lead them to Lake Pristine, 'I get to boast about you at the office but it's not exactly the same as seeing you.'

'It's been a wild year.'

'You're just everywhere,' her mother said, glancing at her daughter with a touch of worry. 'I watch one episode of the show and then you're every recommended video on my phone. Your press tour was . . . a lot, Ally.'

'Well, I'm done with the show now,' Allegra reminded her. The relief and satisfaction was very evident in her tone. 'Unless they find a way to un-drown my character.'

'Your dad hated that scene.'

Allegra was surprised. She didn't know that he had been

watching the show. 'It was a mess to film.'

She had become hypothermic. The director had been told he was only allowed to film in the cold water for fifteen-minute intervals, but he had been annoyed at the 'suppression of his art'. So, Allegra, despite her protests, had been sent into the cold water for long stretches.

Which resulted in pneumonia. Her agent, Maria, had screamed at the producer for over an hour as Allegra was wheeled off to get an X-ray.

Now, almost a year later, she was weaker in the lungs and desperate for sunshine. She had never been to Lake Pristine but her mother had assured her that it was at its most beautiful in the summer. As the car sped closer and closer, the pale grey clouds turned to iridescent blue skies.

'If it weren't for the nosy busybodies, I'd consider moving back,' Roxanne said. 'Or at least staying with you this summer.'

Allegra wondered how true that was. Her mother was very happy in the city, far from the small town she had grown up in. But Allegra still believed that old ghosts were the reason Roxanne stayed away.

'I'm going to be normal for four whole months,' she said softly.

Roxanne kept her eyes on the long stretch of road ahead, which was baking in the sun and casting illusions of water. She reached over to squeeze her daughter's arm.

'Don't you worry about "normal",' she said, just as softly. 'Not a good enough word for you.'

Allegra tried to smile. 'Ma? Did you read the *Eyewitness* piece on me?'

Her mother scoffed derisively. 'I did. Then I looked up

the journalist's background. Her parents are both giants in the newspaper world and she was fired from a previous job for plagiarism. I don't know where she found the audacity—'

'Should I tell people I'm autistic?'

Roxanne pulled her car over to the side of the road. She turned off the engine and shifted her body to face Allegra.

'Ally, where has this come from?'

Allegra stared at the long road ahead of them and all of the cruel comments people had been making about her heaved into her mouth. 'I'm not like other people. And they're starting to work it out, Ma.'

'Tough. It's not their business.'

'I keep thinking, maybe it should be. Maybe I should, I don't know, come out of the library, so to speak.'

'Do you want to?'

Allegra thought about what her publicist would say. Natalie firmly believed that telling the world would only narrow her opportunities and force her into the unwanted role of a spokesperson. 'I don't know. I want people . . . I want them to know there is a reason why I do things the way I do. That journalist called me cold. I'm not cold.'

At the end of the article, Julie M. Atkins had quipped that a summer of rest was probably 'too much warmth for the frosty, unapproachable, impenetrable Miss Brooks'.

That closing line lingered in Allegra's memory. It had burned into her sense of self with a sticking quality that kind compliments never seemed to achieve.

'If you're going to be public about it I want you to be completely ready and happy,' Roxanne said carefully, and Allegra could tell by her mother's expression that there was no fear over her daughter's reputation or public image, just her mental health. It felt like a balm. 'Once you give private parts of your life to the press, it's out of the box for ever.'

Allegra had learned that fans could get obsessed by the smallest details. She had been in the industry for years but landing the role of Clera had changed everything – the public attention on her had tripled. Her horoscope had been hotly debated by early fans, until her birth chart was made public by a stranger. Her fashion was discussed and dissected on daytime talk shows. If she was dating somebody, their whole identity would be put on trial to decide which one of the pair was unworthy. The slow burn had become a wildfire because of one little golden idol.

Allegra sat back. 'Well. It's something I'm considering.'

'Okay,' Roxanne said, gently starting the car again. 'Are you sure you don't want to pal around with me in the city all summer? We can do pedicures every day!'

Allegra was rarely ever at home with her mother. Her jobs were filmed all over the world, and although she had a flat in the city she was never there. She felt piercing guilt at her mother's hopeful tone. But she was craving the anonymity of a small town, where people were too busy worrying about a festival with lots of famous authors to care about one little actor. She would be George's out-of-town daughter, not a cover girl.

Her father would always tell her stories about the eccentric townspeople of Lake Pristine. Maybe it was one too many luncheons or benefits or after-parties, but something in Allegra needed to experience the eccentricity for herself. She wanted the mundane. The habitual. The antithesis of la-la land.

'I want to be as far away from multiple smartphones and large crowds as possible. I'm going to give Lake Pristine a shot.'

'Well, I'm always on the other end of the phone.'

'Yup. As is Maria. And Natalie. And the studio. And—'

'And me, more than anyone. I mean it. Do they want you doing anything or are you allowed the whole summer off?'

'I have a premiere in August. Other than that, it's mostly Zooms.'

'All right. You need a proper break, Ally. I've told your father that. I know you want to help him with the festival, but if you need a day by the lake with a glass of something sparkly, that's just what the doctor ordered and he has to allow it. And! If you're able to snap a picture of one of my authors' books while lounging by the lake, that would be great, too.'

Allegra laughed. The only time her mother took advantage of Allegra's fame was when one of her authors needed a boost on social media. She was an editor and she had a history of publishing writers who were famously averse to social media. So, Allegra had become her de facto publicity assistant.

'Also, not sure if Dad can allow or disallow anything any more,' Roxanne added, more for herself than for Allegra, it seemed. 'You're eighteen. You can do what you want now.'

The words were spoken with an air of disbelief. Allegra knew why. It had happened quietly the previous October. Her mother had been at the Frankfurt Book Fair and Allegra had been on a press tour. They had spoken briefly over the phone. Then Allegra had spent her eighteenth birthday alone in a hotel room.

'All those sanctimonious mothers when you were growing up,' Roxanne murmured. 'So smug because you would run away from school or because you needed extra help. Where are their amazing offspring now?'

'Stay humble,' Allegra chided, but it was with the smallest, proudest smirk.

'You are the greatest kid on this earth. Even if you're barely a kid any more.'

There were enough things weighing on Allegra's mind to make her feel like an adult. She had a schedule and a team and a public image.

Now, she just wanted a fun summer. It was owed to her, after years of call sheets, invasive questions from journalists and no friends.

It was funny. As a child, she had dreamed of glamour and glitz and glimmering people. Now that she had seen those things up close, she wanted something real.

She shook away the thought and focused on the road ahead. Woodland had started to appear and the trees held a green colour that she had only ever seen in the glorious technicolour of her movies. A large, clean sign waited for them and it was no mirage.

*Welcome to Lake Pristine.*

Allegra found herself snapping pictures on her phone of the little town as her mother pulled into Main Street because she knew a dozen set designers who would find it so inspiring. It looked like something from a movie. They found a parking space by a shop called Vivi's Cupcakes. Allegra stared through the window at the creative concoctions, cakes with pastel-coloured icing and famous faces made out of confectionery. There was a vintage clothing store, a haberdashery, a sweet little cafe and a laundry, all on the corner where Allegra and her mum were standing by the car.

The sun was so bright, it made the streets of Lake Pristine glisten. They gleamed in the aftermath of a small summer rainstorm, more welcoming to Allegra than anything she had seen in months.

People were heading towards the woods, in the direction of the actual lake that the town was named after (Allegra had seen it briefly on their way into town: a large, emerald body of water that the mid-thirty-degree heat called for) and as Allegra watched them in their swimwear, carrying their coolers and deck chairs, she felt suddenly at ease. Already it was everything she had imagined.

'This is exactly what I need,' she said quietly.

An elderly couple on the other side of the street looked over at them. 'Roxy!' the woman called. 'You're back. Good to see you.'

Allegra stifled a laugh as her mother grimaced but offered a polite wave back. 'Good to see you, Ginger. Doug.'

'How's the city job?'

'Good. Fine.'

'I didn't like that crime author you published. Too gruesome.'

The woman was yelling from the other side of the street, with no self-consciousness.

Allegra watched as her mother turned back into a teenager. 'Sorry to hear that, Ginger.'

The couple moved on, either indifferent or oblivious to Allegra.

'Oh my God, Ma.'

'Don't say a word,' muttered her mother. 'You'll be dragged into this small-town nonsense soon enough.'

Allegra, laughing, moved to the trunk of the car and retrieved her old suitcase. Across the town square, connected to Main Street, was Brooks Books. It was one of the larger shops in town, and she knew her father's two-bedroom flat was located just above it.

'Well, that's you for the next four months,' Roxanne said gamely. 'Within walking distance of books, beach and cupcakes.'

Allegra closed the trunk and beamed at her mother. 'Perfection.'

Jonah felt as though he had been on the phone to this customer for as long as he had been alive.

'It's kind of an annual tradition,' he said into the phone, and it was the fifth time he had uttered this sentence. 'People rent out their spare rooms, the one tiny inn fills up, and everyone else comes in on these shuttle buses. The whole town's population triples over the summer. It's . . . nice.'

He did not exactly care for the sudden influx of people himself, but it was wonderful for business. It set them up until Christmas and so it was his duty to promote it.

'But I've called the inn for a booking and they wouldn't give me one!' barked the man on the other end of the line.

'Yes,' Jonah said, shocked at his own patience. 'Most people book really far in advance. We open soon. Most readers have booked accommodation already.'

'Then where the hell am I supposed to stay? You haven't even announced the programme yet!'

'I know, sir,' Jonah said, pinching the bridge of his nose and exhaling slowly. 'Our festival-goers are very committed. But as I say, shuttle buses from the city run twice every hour. There are loads of hotels in the city.'

'I don't want to be stuck on a bus with idiots!'

Jonah almost put the phone down, his wrist straining as he forced himself to stay on the line. 'Okay. But as I say, if the inn is booked up, you may have to rent a room in town from one of the locals, or shuttle in from the city. Our programme will be announced in two weeks. Thank you for your interest in the Lake Pristine Book Festival.'

He slammed down the receiver and let his elbows drop onto the cash desk. 'Simon?'

'Yup?'

'Can I take my break?'

'No way. People are heading this way.'

'You didn't hear this guy on the phone. My blood pressure is skyrocketing.'

Simon threw him a look of sympathy. 'Give me the phone next time. You always say the wrong things to people, Jonah.'

Simon was in the window, finishing the display. He was making a rainbow out of books, coordinating by colour. His blonde hair was starting to moisten and he was wearing dark glasses to combat the heat. People waved at him and smiled in appreciation as they passed by outside and he would throw them a salute in greeting. Jonah swallowed and glanced down at his hands. He loved Simon but he envied him, too. He made everything look so easy.

'Fine, but you man the desk. I'm dusting those top shelves.'

Jonah was atop his ladder and removing books from the top shelf when the shop door tinkled and opened.

'Don't let the air conditioning out,' Simon quipped, throwing the visitor a winning smile.

Jonah glanced down at the customer, a well-dressed woman in her forties with a sunny smile. She wore a maxi dress and a sun hat, with sandals and a large tote bag. She was obviously a book lover.

Simon would have no trouble with her.

Jonah returned to dusting.

'Sorry to be crouched in the window like a ghoul,' Simon said to the customer, getting to his feet. 'Can I help you?'

'Hello,' she said in an airy, cheerful voice. 'Is George about?'

'He's just stepped out to see if he can buy another fan. Is there anything I can help you with?'

'No, I'll wait, it's fine.'

The door tinkled once more and someone else entered the shop. From his vantage point, Jonah could only make out the top of her head. She was young, tall and wore a baseball cap, sunglasses and a fabric mask.

'You doing okay up there?' the older woman asked, calling to Jonah with a pleasing smile.

'Oh, fine,' he called down. 'Just dolling the place up a bit.'

'It's almost festival time,' Simon added, returning to his window. 'And we have a celebrity on their way to town, so we can't have a mucky shop.'

Jonah continued to clear the shelf. He kept his back to the customers. Simon was always good at keeping people busy so that Jonah could do the cleaning and the organizing.

'What kind of celebrity?' the older woman asked Simon.

'A famous actress. It's the talk of the town.'

'Surely there are better things to talk about.'

'Well, that's exactly what I think,' Jonah said matter-of-factly, wiping clean the now empty top shelf with ferocious speed. 'She's probably going to take one look at this place and bail.'

'You think?' asked the younger woman, taking off the cloth mask covering the lower half of her face.

'Yes, I mean, this place makes the town in *Footloose* look like Sodom and Gomorrah,' Jonah went on, still focused on the bookshelf.

'Oh, really?'

He threw her a cursory look. She was taking off her shiny, purple baseball cap and had started to unpin her hair.

'She's probably stuck-up too, that's how she looks in her pictures. Spoiled and snooty,' Jonah said, more to himself than to the customer. 'Hollywood type. She'll hate it here.'

'I can't imagine why, you're all so welcoming.'

Something in her tone made Jonah glance down and his expression went from curious to horrified. The young woman fluffed out her long, wavy hair and removed her oversized sunglasses to look up at him with amused sea-green eyes.

'Oh, God,' Jonah croaked.

'Nice to meet you,' the beautiful young woman said. 'I'm Allegra. Do you need help up there? I think the dust may have affected your manners.'

# Chapter Four

Allegra felt a little stab of satisfaction at the bookseller's mortification, and then several things happened at once. The affable blonde boy in the window leapt to his feet and rushed at Allegra, as if she were a long-lost love, and the shop door burst open to reveal her father, George Brooks, holding a brand-new fan still in its box.

'Ally,' he yelled. He darted towards her, as though wanting to scoop her up, and then composed himself. He dropped the fan by the door and quickly kissed her mother on the cheek, before turning to Allegra.

'Great to see you, kid,' he settled on. 'You're so . . . tall.'

'Well,' said Allegra, who felt suddenly awkward and unsure, 'I was thirteen when I last saw you in person.'

Her career had meant family and friends falling by the wayside and the guilt, while always present, was suddenly loud and stifling. The years had sped by while she flew all over the world and spent months on location in Ireland or Croatia or New Zealand. Their video chats were always harried and rushed, usually from cars or airport lounges.

'Well, I see you on the small screen every Monday,' he reminded her. 'I watch all of them. Reruns, too.'

Allegra smiled shyly. 'Thanks.'

She wanted to say that people never looked like they did on

television but she was highly aware of the two boys her own age standing close by.

'So, these are my two trusty booksellers. That's Simon,' George said, gesturing to the blonde by the window, and then to the one on the ladder, who had dark eyes, dark curls and a dark mood, 'and this surly one is Jonah.'

'Thanks, fearless leader,' said Simon and Allegra's eyes shot to his face.

Hadn't she heard that expression in one of the emails?

'Welcome to Lake Pristine,' Simon said warmly.

So here he was.

Allegra gave him the smile she reserved for red carpets and thanked him. She wondered if he knew, too. If he had worked it out. His enthusiastic greeting had been such a blast of warmth, it made her feel like they shared a delicious secret. He was good-looking, too. Especially as he wore such a sun-filled smile. The other bookseller wore a face full of thunder.

'Right!' Her father clapped his hands. 'I think we should close up for an hour and have lunch out the back on the terrace.'

The five of them – two parents, two booksellers and one global superstar – sat around the outdoor dining table with a huge salad and a couple of takeaway pizzas. Allegra felt like a little girl again as she watched her parents. She chewed on a slice of chicken pizza and analysed every move they made. Her mother had remarked on the town being almost exactly the same and George had shrugged and quietly stated that it was better and brighter now that Roxanne was back.

Allegra held her breath but Roxanne merely smiled at the

compliment and then looked away.

'How was the journey in?' her father asked her mother, quickly masking any disappointment he felt.

Allegra knew they would occasionally meet up while she was on location but she had never been able to fully analyse or label their relationship.

'Pretty good,' said Roxanne. 'How's the festival coming along? Surely it's not just the three of you running things?'

'Not any more. George caved and hired a PR firm two years ago and that's what we do each summer,' Simon said.

Allegra had to admire how at home Simon felt with two complete strangers.

'So, how long have you both worked for George?' her mother asked the two booksellers.

'This is our third summer,' Simon answered. 'Mary and Nick come in on the weekends to help, but it's mostly been us for the last couple of years. We both used to hide here after school.'

'How old are you?'

'Eighteen,' Simon said, answering for Jonah too, who Allegra noticed was facing away from the group and staring into the distance.

'Going to university in September?'

Simon glanced at Jonah, clearly checking in with him and making space for him to join in. When he remained silent, Simon spoke once more for the both of them. 'Me, yes, him, no.'

'It's going to be a hunt to replace Simon,' George said.

The look of surprised delight on Simon's face made Allegra wonder how often her father praised them for their work.

'I just have to say something,' Simon said, after everyone had eaten a little more of the food. He beamed at Allegra. 'It is . . . surreal to be sat across from you right now.'

Allegra allowed a small, polite smile. People always thought this kind of fawning was enjoyable for her. For a while, maybe it had been. Now it just made her feel panicky.

'She's just in need of a nice, chill summer,' Roxanne said, with only the tiniest note of reproach in her voice.

'Yes, no leaking Ally's location, boys,' George said firmly. 'She's here for a break. Leaks will be a sackable offence.'

'Unrelated, but you need to get a mobile phone,' Roxanne told her ex-husband with a disbelieving laugh. 'You have been impossible to get hold of these days. You only have the old landline in the shop, and you never answer it. We were praying the voicemails got to you.'

'The boss can't cope with technology,' Simon interjected. 'I even have to do your emails, right, George?'

Allegra smiled at that, while George shrugged and looked at her mother.

'You can always write me a letter, Roxy.'

Allegra watched her mother soften and look away.

'I should probably open the shop back up,' Jonah said, speaking for the first time, his voice deep and detached.

Allegra watched the dark-haired bookseller stalk back into the shop with a touch of dismay. She had tried to be funny about the little social blunder from before but he seemed extremely vexed. His pride was clearly wounded.

'I don't think I've made a very good first impression with him,' she told the rest of the group.

'Oh, don't worry about Jonah,' Simon said, edging his chair

closer to Allegra. 'He's only ever all about books. He's actually pretty great, you'll warm to him. Now, I have a million questions about filming *Court of Bystanders*!' He stopped as he read the changing expression on Allegra's face, her sudden withdrawal at the mention of her job. He changed tactics. 'But you're here for a break, so I'm going to be totally respectful of that. So, Allegra Brooks, totally average teenager in Lake Pristine, what's your favourite book?'

As Jonah reopened the shop he tried to focus on anything other than his visceral embarrassment. He was used to saying the wrong things to the wrong people, but this was one of his worst offences yet. It had been almost too unbearable, sitting there with everyone who had witnessed it.

Allegra, more than anyone.

At the table he had found his acute embarrassment morphing into complete rudeness. He'd found it difficult to look at her, and it didn't help to watch Simon turn on his customer service mask. Allegra and her mother were already halfway-charmed.

He busied himself with Simon's abandoned window display and when a familiar face tapped on the glass with a smile, he gestured for them to come inside.

'Hey, Grace.'

Grace Lancaster, his former classmate and friend from Lake Pristine High. She had recently celebrated her eighteenth birthday and had, after getting a little tipsy on her older brother's beer, forced Jonah to do karaoke with her. He laughed fondly whenever he heard Stevie Nicks and remembered their terrible duet of 'Blue Denim'. She peeked round the door with a hat over her dark curls and a denim jacket covering her dance leotard, and Jonah knew exactly why she had come.

'Is she here yet?' Grace asked. She smiled at Jonah knowingly. He knew she could read his irritation over all of the fuss.

'Who?' Jonah said, playing the fool. 'The big movie star?'

'Of course the big movie star,' Grace chastised him, as she fanned herself in the shade of the bookshop. 'Is she here? Is she beautiful?'

'She's having lunch with Simon and her parents in the back,' Jonah said, moving to the computer.

'And you were made to stay here?' asked Grace, a laugh in her voice.

'No, I . . . I offered. She's not my kind of book.'

It helped Jonah to think of other people as books. Sometimes they came in genres, just like novels.

The beautiful, romantic kind. The history-obsessed. The zany and particular. The pretentious and dull.

Sometimes they were recommended to you by other people. Their covers didn't always match the contents, and the ones with plenty of praise thrown their way were often the ones Jonah had the most trouble reading. He had the disquieting sense that Allegra Brooks was the kind of book everyone raved about and adored and that fact alone made him want to avoid picking it up.

So, he wouldn't read her. She clearly had enough people turning her pages, she didn't need another.

He opened up the shopfloor email. He smiled in spite of himself as he noticed a reply from the anonymous pen-pal. He was on the keyboard in an instant, pouring out the frustration he was enduring after such a weird afternoon.

> **shopfloor@BrooksBooks.com**
> **to: westendgirl@gmail.com**
> **Subject: New Arrival**
>
> Dear Friend,
> I think I can call you that now, strange person who only wanted to know about festival dates. You have now been coerced through your own politeness into being my pen-pal. Sorry.
> There's a glamorous new arrival in Lake Pristine and I just made a complete fool of myself in front of her –

Jonah paused, his fingers hovering over the keys. He deleted the sentence and started again.

> – and my colleague just made a complete fool of himself in front of her, so I'm dying of second-hand embarrassment for him. Nice to see our fearless leader so happy, though.

He didn't want to be uncharitable to Simon, but his friend was far too enchanted by fame and it irked Jonah. Surely even Allegra could see through the boy's flattering and toadying, even if Simon himself was oblivious to the fact that he was doing it.

> Stay tuned to see how else my co-worker can make a spectacle of himself.
> Kindest and fondest regards,
> Bookseller.

Before he could send it, Grace's voice pierced his concentration.

'Hey, Simon.'

Jonah glanced up to see his colleague jogging into the shop, looking all lit up. He ignored Grace's greeting. 'I need the computer.'

'Why?' Jonah felt the urge to wrap himself around the old thing.

'I want to memorize her IMDb page and look at all her socials.'

'Oh, Simon,' said Jonah, looking at him with distaste. 'Don't be that guy.'

'Sorry.' Simon tried to elbow Jonah away from the computer, which prompted the latter to press 'send' quickly on his email. 'That's the girl I'm going to marry.'

Grace snorted and Jonah finally relented and gave up the computer to his friend. 'Do you need anything, Grace, or are you just here to stare at her?'

'I'm just here to stare at her, and don't make it sound so sordid, this is the most exciting thing to happen here in a while.'

'This is not a zoo,' Jonah heard himself say, eyeing the pair of them with stern disapproval. 'This is a *person*. George's family. You can't just hang about and gawk at her. Enough.'

Simon and Grace exchanged a look, the former raising his eyebrows in an attempt to make the latter smile. But Grace was duly chastised. She offered her friend an apologetic smile, which settled the matter in Jonah's mind.

Simon made himself busy on the computer and Jonah was halfway up his ladder once more when Allegra and her mother finally emerged. Jonah watched Allegra smile at her phone and inwardly rolled his eyes.

She probably loved that she was a hot commodity online. (And everywhere else.)

'Sending emails?' she asked Simon airily.

Jonah watched Simon quickly close his browser. 'Yup. No one tells you how much emailing you have to do in the book world.'

Allegra smiled as if he had said something much more adorable and Jonah scowled at his shoes. Grace nudged him as she stepped forward to address Allegra.

'Hi.' Grace tucked her hair behind her ears a little self-consciously, and held out her hand. 'I'm Grace. Your dad mentioned you might like a tour, so here I am!'

Jonah looked up to see if Allegra was horrified at the suggestion. Was she far too above the residents of Lake Pristine to accept their company? But the actress was beaming. 'I'd love a tour. Thank you.'

# Chapter Five

'I am literally a phone call away, like I said,' Roxanne whispered in her daughter's ear as they hugged goodbye. 'Promise. If your dad gets too hyper-fixated on the festival, and you need someone to vent with, call me. I can get out of any meeting. We're on summer hours at the office, Fridays aren't even a real work day any more. I promise, anything!'

'I'll be fine,' Allegra assured her. 'Honestly. I'm good. Now leave so I can start having fun.'

Her comment had the desired effect because Roxanne laughed and slipped into the driver's seat. She wound down the window as the engine started. 'Love you, kid.'

'Love you, Ma. See you in the fall.'

'I can come get you any time. Or Natalie can. Or Maria. Or David, or Sanchez—'

'Go! I'm fine.'

Her bags had been taken in by an overzealous Simon and as Allegra waved goodbye to her mother, she felt bittersweet. When the car was long out of sight, Grace Lancaster crept out of the bookshop and smiled meekly at her.

'My mum is always coming and going,' Grace said, in an obvious bid to be supportive. 'You guys seem close?'

'I haven't seen my parents in ages,' Allegra said honestly. However, that was all she revealed, as she was feeling private. 'So!

Show me Lake Pristine.'

The two girls set off into the heart of the town and Allegra slipped her cap and dark glasses back on.

'Can I be brutally honest about something?' Grace asked a little mischievously.

'Sure.'

'The cap and sunglasses may be a good disguise in the city, but they make you stick out like an apple in an orangery here.'

Allegra had to laugh. 'Okay, I'll lose the hat, but the glasses have to stay.'

'A good compromise.'

Allegra regarded Grace. She looked fresh-faced and perfectly at home, with a quiet confidence that made her small frame seem larger and her walk more purposeful. She was pretty.

People waved to her with genial smiles as they passed. She was obviously a beloved member of Lake Pristine. Everyone knew everyone here, it seemed. Everyone was famous. Which, in a wonderful way, meant that nobody really was.

'So, this is Main Street?'

'Yes! So, this is where you come if you want cake, coffee, books, groceries, fabric or to sit in this lovely romantic bandstand. Church is up that little road, and Mrs Montgomery's dance studio is over there. The festival usually sets up all its tents around the maze – there – and the woodland over there. Then, right up ahead, is the jewel in the crown.'

'Oh, yeah?'

'My brother's Arthouse!'

Allegra gazed up at the large picture house and nodded. 'Impressive.'

'It is since it's all been redone. Come inside?'

The girls moved into the cinema and Allegra couldn't stop herself from gasping in awe at the interior. They were greeted by a marble lobby with art deco design and beautiful green flashes on the walls, plus a chandelier that would have been at home in a fine hotel. The concession stand made the large, impersonal cinemas where she had attended premieres look like dumpsters. None of them had the panache of this small arthouse.

'Art! Come and meet Allegra!'

Allegra found Grace's vigour sweet, but she secretly hoped she wouldn't have to meet too many new faces on her first day in town.

Grace's brother, in a white tee and jeans, was lifting a crate of champagne onto the back counter of the concession stand. He was objectively handsome: tall with dark hair and a serious expression. He waved politely at Allegra and then did a familiar and comical double-take.

'I've seen that face on my screen a couple of times,' he said.

'She's a massive name, Arthur, don't be weird,' Grace said, rolling her eyes at the bemusement on her brother's face.

'Hi, I'm Allegra,' Allegra said, forcing herself to sound casual in the hope that it would read as a cue for Grace's brother to be normal.

'Nice to meet you, Allegra,' Arthur Lancaster said, reading between the lines beautifully. 'Hope you like it here.'

Then he carried his crate into the back of the cinema as if nothing untoward had happened.

'He seems cool,' she said to Grace, and it was true.

'He is,' Grace said, as they left the cinema and set off back towards the centre of town. 'I have an even older brother, too. He works for the council.'

'And are you in school?'

'I'm hoping to get into dance school. I had my call-back last week. Just waiting.'

Allegra watched the other girl pick at her fingernails as she said this. She knew better than anybody how awful it was to await the results of an audition.

'Oh, wow. Good luck. I'm sure you'll get it.' It was said out of politeness, but Grace gave her a smile of appreciation anyway.

'Thanks.'

As an appropriate silence fell between the two of them, Allegra realized how long it had been since she had last done this. All of her social interactions for the last few years had been in auditions, rehearsals, read-throughs, interviews and after-parties. At these, there was always a shorthand, an understanding running through each transaction. Should anything become too overwhelming she had trailers to escape to and a team to save her.

Now she was just a girl walking along Main Street.

'Grace, could we see the lake?'

As soon as Grace and Allegra headed off towards Lake Pristine, Jonah watched Simon rush back into the heart of the bookshop, where he released an obnoxious yell of triumphant joy.

'God, what?' snapped Jonah, returning the last book to the top shelf before climbing back down his ladder.

'She is so hot. Like, biblically. I cannot believe this is all actually hap—'

'Can you, like, do some work?' Jonah asked bluntly. 'I've done almost all of the deliveries, I've done stock, I've cleaned. Please do something.'

'Why? This is *fun*, Jonah. You know this town gets, like, one new person every six years. Live a little.'

'To live, I must work. Same for you. So get to it.'

'She's super nice. She'll totally forgive you for that bad first impression.' Simon's voice softened as he said it. He regarded Jonah with a look of sympathy.

'Unlikely,' muttered Jonah, but he did soften towards his friend. 'I was bad, even for me.'

'I need you to get on with her. Cannot have you feuding with my future girlfriend.'

Though Jonah knew his friend was joking, the remark still turned his stomach.

'That's so unbelievably gross,' muttered Jonah. 'I'm going to work on the mailing list.'

He moved into the back of the shop and knocked on George's door.

'Enter,' called his employer, sounding thoroughly distracted.

Jonah stepped inside. 'George? There's definitely an increase of people calling the shop, confused about the festival. If we're not going to have a web—'

'We're not going to have a website,' George said glibly, not looking up from his ledger.

Jonah let out a slow breath. 'As I say, if we're not going to have a website, someone needs to update socials regularly. And the Lake Pristine Tourist Board need to put more information on *their* site.'

'I thought you were on socials?'

'No, you took me off for arguing with trolls.'

'Well, I'll call Courtney.'

'At the PR place?'

'Yeah, she's a bit of a whizz, you know. She can handle all of that.'

'Well, okay. I just thought hiring a social media person might not be a bad idea. It's a full-time job. I think your generation underestimates it.'

He thought of his friendly virtual friend and her job in social media management. He briefly fantasized about being able to offer her a job in Lake Pristine. He acknowledged it was a very strange way to feel about someone he hardly knew.

'Do you know any full-time social media managers?' asked George dryly, finally looking at Jonah.

'Not exactly,' Jonah said, 'but I can have a look around.'

'Courtney can handle it,' George said, his tone reflecting his desire for this conversation to end. 'Thanks for checking in.'

Jonah took the dismissal with a touch of sadness. Months ago, George would have been warm about the whole thing. He would have asked Jonah questions about his personal life. He would have asked what he was reading. Now, nothing. He left the room without another word and returned to the computer.

But to his delight, there was something waiting for him.

**westendgirl@gmail.com**
**to: shopfloor@BrooksBooks.com**
**RE: New Arrival**

Dear Friend (I'm happy with that salutation, if you are.)

How thrilling! A glamorous new arrival in your town!

You'll be too distracted to converse with me now, I'm sure. Who are they, what are they like? Nice to hear you'll have some excitement. Maybe I'll get to meet you all at the festival. I can't wait to see Lake Pristine. Keep me updated, I don't want to feel left out. I would really love to keep finding emails from you each time I glance at my phone.
Curious regards,
Your Friend.

'You're smiling at your phone; are you telling your friends how silly we all are?'

Allegra jerked in surprise at Grace's question.

The two girls were sitting by the actual lake in Lake Pristine and Allegra had slathered her long legs in sunscreen. The Lake Pristine beach was not vast, sitting at around two hundred yards long. But despite its smaller scale, everyone seemed able to find a deckchair and a small space of their own. It was not cluttered or overcrowded. The sand was like caster sugar, and the lake of Lake Pristine was large enough for people to imagine they were really sitting by the ocean.

Allegra felt like a different person as the sun shone down on her skin. It felt pleasant, rather than overstimulating. The cool water of the lake called to her like a comforting balm, promising cool relief should anything become too intense. There was a small stall at the other end of the beach, serving ice cream, chilled bottles of pop and free drinking water. Children splashed in the shallows of the lake. Two older men lay side by side in their swimwear, eyes closed behind their sunglasses, their hands entwined. A man and woman were pretending to bury their older child, who giggled delightedly at the game.

Allegra considered the townspeople gathered on the sand. No one stared at her for too long. They all looked away when she caught their eyes and she liked to think that they were just looking out of curiosity rather than recognition.

She looked away herself and caught sight of a grand house on the other side of the lake. There was a whole row of such houses, but one sat in the middle and stood out from the others. Grace caught her staring and said, 'That's the Montgomery family home.'

'It's massive.'

'Yes. That family are . . . they do all right for themselves.'

The words made Allegra's eyes drop to her phone, and she wore a smile she hadn't worn in a long time. She suddenly felt the urge to share her secret.

'Grace, I think I'm email-flirting with someone.'

'You *are*? Fun!' Grace was so instantly intrigued and engaged that Allegra almost adored her for it. She had been massaging her ballerina feet by the water, but now stared at Allegra, completely spellbound. 'I can never be cute over text and email.'

'It's someone in town.'

'How? Who? You've been here all of fifteen minutes!'

The delighted outrage in the other girl's voice made Allegra snort as she attempted to take a sip of her drink, cold soda almost coming out of her nose. They both suddenly broke out into laughter.

'Can't say yet, I only worked it out today. Can I run something by you and will you tell me if it's too sociopathic?'

'Sure. I'm a great litmus test for monstrous behaviour.'

Allegra laughed at that and angled her body so the two of them were almost forehead to forehead, now completely in each other's confidence.

'I know who they are, but they don't know who I am. Is it horribly manipulative of me to carry on the anonymity until I know them better in life?'

Grace considered the question and Allegra realized she liked that.

'I think, as long as you don't play games with them, it's okay. As long as you don't set them up to fail or make fun of them, or get too much of a kick out of them not knowing. I mean, you're famous. Like, super famous. I've never felt so exposed in this town before. Everyone looks at us – and by "us", I mean you. They're only leaving you alone because they're scared of George's wrath.'

Allegra nodded. She knew that fame brought a power imbalance, but hearing Grace say it so casually made her feel a little nauseous. She wondered if she had been fooling herself in regards to her low profile in town. Maybe people were just very good at disguising their notice.

'So . . .' Grace continued. 'You, more than anyone, deserve to get to know someone, and have them get to know you, without any of that stuff getting in the way and complicating things.'

'Sorry if it's weird to tell you this,' Allegra added, her voice catching and breaking. 'I'm . . . not great at judging when something goes from polite to personal. Between people, I mean.'

Allegra's idea of small talk was asking people she had just met what they would tell the whole world if they suddenly had a direct line to seven billion people, but she had learned the hard way that this was not preferable to discussing the weather or remarking on the traffic.

'I don't mind,' Grace said. 'I like it. I like that we're sort of in cahoots now.'

'Yes, please don't tell anyone I have a secret pen-pal,' Allegra said, smiling. 'But it's been sort of nice. My job is really lonely and the emails have perked me up a bit.'

'Now, you're not going to make me feel sorry for you. You're a supernova.'

Allegra laughed. 'Well, nothing's lonelier than outer space.'

'How does it feel, knowing that everyone in this town is frantically googling you right now?'

'Not good,' Allegra said, without a moment's hesitation. 'Besides, not everyone. That other bookseller at Dad's certainly isn't.' She didn't know what had possessed her to bring him up.

'Who, Jonah?'

'Are you friends?'

'Yeah. We were in the same year at school.' Allegra felt Grace glancing at her before adding, 'He's a good guy. He just shows it really badly.'

Allegra decided to keep her opinion to herself. 'What about the other one, Simon?'

They both chose that moment to recline into two suddenly available deckchairs. The sun was just right for Allegra, not too overstimulating. A nice brush of heat to a neurotypical could feel like a burn to her.

She closed her eyes for a moment, as Grace answered her question.

'I don't know Simon very well; he was way more popular than Jonah and I were at school. He's nice, though. Maybe a bit immature but he's a good sort. He's always nice to my mother, and she's not an easy lady to be nice to. He throws the best parties, too. He was a big deal in school because of that.'

Allegra made a small sound of envy. 'I haven't been to school since I was thirteen. Not one with other kids, that is.'

She thought about the horrible luncheon where she and her pen-pal had first emailed. Perhaps parties suddenly became more enjoyable when you had someone facing them with you.

'Shut up!' cried Grace. 'Is that true? God, that's a stupid question, I've seen bits of your show. It's been on for years.'

'Yeah, you can't really film all that *and* do press *and* school. I had a tutor on set.'

'Is your mother in the business?'

'The business?' teased Allegra.

'I don't know,' muttered Grace with a blush, but she was smiling. 'Do they still call it that?'

'She's in publishing. *Court of Bystanders* did a lot of open call auditions. I queued for hours with a number on my shirt and got it.'

'That's so cool. Not a nepo baby.'

'No. But, like, ninety per cent of the industry is.'

Allegra was used to sitting in green rooms with the children of models, actors, directors and producers. She didn't really mind. They were always a little insecure but often sweet underneath all of the bravado.

'Your secret pen-pal is safe with me,' Grace reiterated. 'Small towns aren't the best at keeping things discreet. But you can trust me.'

Allegra hoped she would not regret it.

# Chapter Six

**shopfloor@BrooksBooks.com**
**to: westendgirl@gmail.com**
**Subject: Wish You Were Here**
Dear Friend,
Please find attached a picture of *Emma* by Jane Austen outside the Lake Pristine haberdashery, a place Emma and Harriet would happily frequent, I think. It's sunny and I wish you were here!
Yours,
Bookseller

Allegra woke up in her father's spare bedroom feeling positive. She felt even more so when she opened up a new email from the bookshop. As promised, her pen-pal had attached a picture of a beautiful new hardback of *Emma* by Jane Austen. It was propped up in the early dawn daylight against the large green door of the haberdashery. Allegra smiled in delight at the message and leapt out of bed.

She showered and then applied moisturizer and SPF. She rubbed body butter all over herself, blow-dried her hair and brushed out the long waves. She put on mascara and a soft pink lipstick.

She had no work engagements to attend. This was just for her. And it felt incredible.

She threw on a yellow and green polka dot sundress and moved into the reception room of the small flat. Her father was at the breakfast table, looking tired and a little stressed.

'Morning,' Allegra said, blazingly aware of the lack of routine between them. There was no comfortable, familiar way to be – they were practically strangers.

'Your mother told me that you don't like to eat too much in the morning, but I can make you anything you want,' George said, speaking rapidly and with a worried look in his eye.

Allegra swiped a piece of brown toast and the jam knife. 'This is fine. Thanks!'

They made their way down to the shop for ten o'clock and she noticed Jonah waiting by the entrance. While her father turned on the lights and brought the till trays through from the office, Allegra went to unlock the front door. She smiled politely at Jonah but he quickly looked away. She sighed and let him in.

'Welcome to the Saturday morning meeting,' she said cheerfully.

He merely grunted.

A table was set up in the middle of the shop, one that would normally hold a lot of books with reduced prices, but was now prepped and ready for a meeting, with water jugs, pens and paper, all arranged by Allegra. Mary arrived shortly after Jonah, ready to man the desk in case of customers, and Simon and Courtney, the publicist from JCPR (the publicity firm hired to help out) joined just after ten.

'I brought you a doughnut,' Simon said triumphantly, presenting it to Allegra with a flourish.

'Oh!' Allegra said, delighted by the charming gesture. 'Thank you.'

She gingerly took the doughnut box and placed it in front of her. She felt a little awkward, being the only one to receive a gift of baked goods. If it were more than one, she would give them to the whole table, but Simon had bought her a single doughnut with pink icing and hearts made out of sprinkles.

'Can I just say,' the publicist spoke in a soft voice, full of wonder, 'what an honour it is to meet you?'

Allegra gave her a tight smile. 'Thanks. Ditto.'

'I mean, I've watched that adaptation of *A Little Princess* so many times with my daughter, you were such a wonderful Sara Crewe.'

'Wow, that's an early one,' joked Allegra. 'Thank you.' It had been her second acting project and her first time at the top of the call sheet. She had loved playing Sara. A little girl who missed her father.

Her eyes flashed to George and she hoped that Courtney would leave the conversation at that. Acting had always been her escape. Her way of making order out of chaos. Discussing and dissecting it seemed to taint it.

'Shall we start?' asked Jonah, pouring himself some water from the chilled jug. 'We have a lot to get through.'

'Well,' said Courtney. 'I'll start by letting you all know that the box office is set up with the Lake Pristine Tourist Board and I'm in contact there with Sajid and Kate. We'll be keeping an eye on ticket sales as soon as the programme is live. People can book through their website or over the phone.'

Allegra watched Jonah make excessive notes, his brow furrowed in concentration. Simon was observing her and smiling eagerly every time she made eye contact with him. He was like a golden retriever, determined to be friends, so she always smiled back at him. Mary was reading at the cash desk and George was listening intently to Courtney.

When Allegra spoke, everyone looked surprised.

'Because Dad refuses to get a mobile, I'd like to volunteer myself as his stand-in should anyone need to get in touch with him directly about matters to do with the festival.'

'That would be exceedingly helpful,' Courtney said frankly. 'Thank you, Allegra.'

As Jonah took notes on the meeting he tried to avoid looking at Allegra. Everyone else around the table was staring at her as if she were an angel from heaven and it gave him enormous second-hand embarrassment. He queried Courtney on the programme announcement and asked Simon about mailing out brochures. He put questions to George about cost and transportation and ordering more stock.

He lived for the summer book festival. He liked being surrounded by people who loved and appreciated books. And he liked that his days were filled with so many tasks to do. Everything always went down to the wire, and although this would be his third year with festival, many things were still unpredictable and it was what he worked for all year. Now, his mentor was giddy about handing over a ton of responsibilities to his daughter, someone who was all about film and not books. Someone who had not earned a place at the table.

'There's only one thing really worrying me at present,' Courtney said, as the meeting began to draw to a conclusion. 'Quentin Morrison as the . . . sort of . . . big author event?'

'Yes?' George prompted her to go on and Jonah could tell by

his boss's expression that he knew what was coming next.

'Well,' Courtney was clearly trying to be tactful, 'he's famously... not the easiest to work with, and his agent still hasn't confirmed if he will be doing his festival event in August.'

'He appeared for us two summers ago,' Jonah said, a tad defensively. 'He likes leaving things to the eleventh hour.'

'Is he that big crime writer?' asked Allegra, and Jonah forced himself to look at her.

'Yes. Three hardbacks a year. He's quantity over quality, but his shows always sell out.'

'Wow, harsh.'

Jonah frowned. 'What is?'

Allegra looked surprised by his challenge, but she shrugged and smiled so winningly he was almost distracted. 'I'm sure *he* doesn't think his books are not "quality". Nor his readers.'

A tense hush fell over the table before Simon quietly whispered, 'Oh, here we go.'

Jonah fixed her with a hard stare. 'Have you read any of Quentin Morrison's books? Because let me be the one to assure you that they hold no artistic merit.'

He watched her release a resigned sigh but she stood her ground. 'No. I don't really read crime novels.'

'You don't? Shocker.'

'I read novels where people fall in love.'

'Well, romance is just like crime. Same tropes and formula, over and over again.'

'You say that like it's derivative and not the foundation of the genre. The whole point of romance, and crime, is that the reader has some sort of expectation of the formula. It's not classified as a romance novel if they aren't together at the end, it's not a whodunnit if there's no body. The genre is a genre *because* it has tropes and repeated patterns.'

'Authors should re-invent.'

'Yes, but not the wheel. And the wheel is the genre. Authors re-invent with their own voice. Marginalized authors, for example, do you think if they set a novel in a stately home or on a train or on the Nile, they don't know that they're referencing Agatha Christie? Of course they do, but they're not a dead white woman, so it's a brand-new lens.'

Jonah stared in astonishment. The mature part of his brain told him that he needed to ease up and do better with this girl, but the embarrassment begged him to stay cold, to hold on to a little dignity. In the end, all he could do was mumble, 'Well . . . he's a rich white dude, not a marginalized author. And his books aren't any good.'

'Then why invite him?' demanded Allegra, arching a perfect eyebrow and staring him down.

'Because he's a sell-out. Literally. Everyone buys a ticket. He brings in a lot of money.'

He watched Allegra consider his words and he could see himself going down in her estimation. 'I suppose I'd rather be the kind of bookseller who can appreciate that there are all kinds of books in the world, than someone who can only make money from someone else's art,' she said. 'Sorry. Their lacking-in-quality art. Art that they don't respect.'

Simon released a low whistle and Courtney's lips twitched. Jonah looked to George, but his employer was gazing at his daughter with all of the burning pride Jonah had been craving from him over the last few years.

'I'm a bookseller,' Jonah said finally. 'I don't care about making money, this is not the job for that. I care about people finding quality prose.'

Allegra leaned a little more towards him and he grew suddenly nervous. 'Then ask for authors you actually like and want to read. Maybe other people will feel the same. And get a more diverse line-up. In every sense, including genre. There should definitely be more romance writers on the programme. More new voices. More women who write non-fiction. And children's authors.'

'Write that down!' George said, turning to Courtney with a fizz in his mannerisms, one that Simon and Jonah had not been able to inspire of late.

Jonah got to his feet, a little jarringly. People started and stared at him in bemusement. He marched towards the bookshop door.

'I need some air!' he said flatly, as he made a hasty exit. 'Carry on without me.'

'Don't mind Jonah,' Simon said to Allegra, as she watched her sparring partner exit. He gave her a genuinely sympathetic smile and spoke with understanding. 'He's one of those booksellers who doesn't like people touching the books.'

For the briefest of moments, while they'd passionately debated books, Allegra had entertained the idea that *Jonah* was the bookseller emailing her.

But Simon was light and friendly and funny, just like his emails. Jonah was . . .

Not.

'I think I was a bit rough on him,' Allegra said begrudgingly.

'Don't let him upset you,' Simon said, nudging her in an overly familiar fashion.

'I'm not upset,' she replied, and it was the truth.

'He doesn't really like anybody. He tolerates most of us, but books are his only love.'

'And good luck to him.'

She broke off some of the doughnut and offered a piece to Simon, who gladly accepted.

'Hey, a bunch of us are going to the arcade tonight for drinks. You are totally welcome to come along.'

'There's an arcade? Grace didn't mention that on the tour.'

'It's just off one of the dirt paths, beyond the maze. It's one of the few places in town that stays open late and serves more than lemonade.'

'I don't drink, I'm afraid. Still allowed?'

'Of course.'

'And who's "us"?'

'Me and my friend Skye. Jonah, unless you've scared him out of town.'

'What about Grace?'

Allegra noticed Simon's face flicker slightly with distaste. 'Grace Lancaster?'

'Yeah. She was super nice, squiring me around town. She can come too, right?'

Simon hesitated and Allegra wondered if there was some deep, dark reason behind his reluctance. She didn't like to think it could be snobbery – that Simon thought of Grace as someone who was beneath him.

'Sure, she can come.'

'Great, I'll text her.'

'Wow, lucky Grace,' he said with a grin, picking up the empty doughnut box and dropping it in the bin.

Allegra smiled, curiously. 'What?'

'First person in town to secure your phone number.'

Allegra didn't know what to do with her face so she just shrugged and said, 'One of my numbers. I have too many.'

'Well, can I have one of them? Or your email address?'

Allegra almost told the truth. She almost revealed that she was the person he had been emailing but then a familiar, ever-present thought interrupted her.

Just because the emails were starting to mean something to her, it was no reason to believe that they meant anything to him. She was an all-in kind of person. But that was not the rest of the world.

So she held her tongue.

'I'll be there,' was all she said.


When closing time arrived, Jonah was alone in the shop with George.

Courtney, Allegra and Simon had all gone to a meeting with the Lake Pristine Tourist Board and Jonah appreciated the quiet they left in their wake. He sold an economics book to a visiting tourist and some picture books to frequent customer Mrs Heywood for her grandchildren and then began to cash up.

'Jonah?'

George's voice sounded from the office door and Jonah froze by the till. 'Uh-huh?'

'Can you take it just a little easier on Allegra? Please.'

Jonah looked over at his boss. 'I didn't realize I wasn't.'

The lie fell flat and they both knew it.

'She's new to town, she needs a bit of a break. Just be nice, son. She has a mad life. And I know the festival is your project, you do so much for it and I'm grateful. But she's only helping out. She's not taking anything away from you by just helping out.'

'I know,' Jonah said stiffly, avoiding eye contact and busying himself with receipts. 'Sorry if I seemed . . .'

'It's all right, son. She's only here for the summer. I'm sure she makes lots of boys nervous, you won't be the only one. Can you just pretend to be nice for a summer?'

Somehow, the word 'pretend' irked Jonah. He felt prickly about it. 'Fine.'

'I can do all of this. Go and meet Simon. It's Saturday night.'

Usually Jonah would protest and stay to show his commitment, but when George dismissed him, he made swift work of grabbing his things and leaving the shop behind. He walked to the arcade for Saturday Night Debrief with Simon, trying not to get worked up about George's gentle reprimand.

Simon was usually a little hard to handle when he was with their other friends from school. It rekindled the immature side of him, in a way that Jonah struggled to find amusing.

At eight o'clock, the sun was still out in Lake Pristine and as many people were heading out to the beach as returning from it. The lake was a constant source of distraction during the hot summers in town. People were shutting up their shops and running with great urgency, desperate to cool off in the water.

Soon the marquees for the festival would be arriving, and before long the maze would open for its summer season.

Jonah felt some of the day's stresses slipping away as he reached the arcade, which was already filling with Lake Pristine's younger crowd. He heard Simon before he saw him and gravitated towards the sound of his laugh.

Simon was in their usual booth with his friend Skye, and her friend, Kerrie. The latter hurriedly fiddled with her hair on noticing Jonah.

'Evening, troops,' Jonah said.

He was about to slide in next to Simon when his friend held up a hand.

'Someone else is coming, sit next to Kerrie.'

Jonah exhaled wearily. He knew exactly who Simon was anticipating.

'I'm really nervous to meet her,' Kerrie said conspiratorially.

'I'm not,' scoffed Skye. 'That show she's on is pretty terrible.'

'They killed her off,' Jonah offered.

'Yeah, well, I'm not surprised. She wasn't very good on it.'

Kerrie frowned anxiously, glancing at her friend. 'You said yesterday you've never seen it.'

Skye stalled but rallied in an instant. 'Yeah. I stopped watching. It's a drag, Kerrie. Lots of people think so.'

Jonah was about to roll his eyes but as he perched on the edge of the booth there was suddenly a presence next to him. Allegra had obviously gone home to change, because she was no longer wearing the sundress from earlier. Instead she was in denim shorts and a band shirt, with her hair scraped up. She looked effortlessly chic.

'What's a drag?' she asked, with an impish, knowing smile.

Skye, if she had been a different kind of girl, could have laughed off her own insecurity and taken the moment as an opportunity to make an interesting friend. But she was not a different kind of girl.

'Just talking about a TV show,' she said, looking Allegra up and down, slowly.

The latter didn't mind. She continued to smile sunnily and then turned to hold her hand out to Kerrie. 'Hey, I'm Allegra. Nice to meet you.'

Jonah watched Kerrie's hand tremble as she reached out to take the one being offered to her. 'I'm Kerrie. It's . . . it's literally so cool to meet you.'

Jonah saw what felt just like his own annoyance flash across Skye's face and he was surprised by how distasteful it looked. He wondered if he seemed as bitter when he reacted to the sycophancy.

'I love your rings,' Allegra said to Kerrie, nodding at the girl's fingers and smiling.

'Oh, my God, you can have all of them,' Kerrie babbled, laughing a little too hard.

Allegra slid in next to Simon, who was gesticulating frantically for her to do so. Jonah felt another familiar pang of irritation.

'I've told Grace we're here,' Allegra said to Simon.

Before he could respond, Kerrie leaned over with a tentative smile.

'Can I just say something?'

Jonah wondered how many times Allegra would hear this over the summer. 'Of course.'

'I follow you on Instagram and you always look so amazing. Just so beautiful. Like, every picture.'

When Kerrie stopped to take a breath, Skye smirked and said, 'That wasn't a question.'

'Skye,' Kerrie said softly, sounding slightly betrayed. But she soldiered on. 'I am being so serious right now, Allegra, I don't want this to sound offensive. Not even a bit. But . . . you're . . . I mean, one of the reasons I love you so much is because you're so beautiful but you're not, like, this skinny girl? If you know what I mean?'

Allegra forced herself to keep smiling. She was proud of her curves but it would never stop being strange, having people openly comment on her body and her looks within moments of meeting her.

'It's just nice to see a mid-size girl getting loads of attention, you know?' Kerrie concluded, her eyes searching Allegra's face for approval. 'And you're going to be a princess in that new Disney movie. I saw an article about it online!'

'Just her voice,' Skye interjected, before taking a long slurp of her glass of blue slush.

Allegra paid her no mind. She could see Grace had arrived and was talking to a woman who looked like management. They seemed friendly and relaxed with one another and then the woman pointed Grace in the direction of their booth. Allegra waved her over.

'Can we budge up a bit for Grace?' she said to Simon and Skye.

'I don't remember inviting her,' Skye said with a thin smile. Simon, too, seemed reluctant to let Grace in, but eventually did so when Allegra looked at him, forcing a pleasant smile onto his handsome face. She was a little dismayed by this new show of social snobbery.

'Who was that?' Allegra asked Grace as she sat down next to her.

'That's Hera. She runs this place.'

'Do you come here a lot?'

'Sometimes. With my brother and sister-in-law.'

'Sister-in-law?' Skye let out a piercing laugh. 'Your brother isn't married.'

Grace narrowed her eyes at Skye, not the slightest bit afraid of the other girl. 'Not yet, but he will be.'

'You're that desperate to be able to say you're related to Jasper Montgomery? Whatever floats your boat.'

'At least Jasper knows my name,' Grace said, with enough spice in her tone to make Allegra smile. She wondered who the mysterious Jasper was. 'You're just some girl who could never get into her mum's ballet school. Didn't your dad even try calling them one winter?'

Skye's mouth dropped open and she made a choking sound of disgust. 'You can't afford to be this rude to me, Grace Lancaster.'

'Hey, now,' Simon said, nudging Skye. 'Stop. You started it, she finished it, we don't need an encore. Be cool.'

'How's the festival planning going, Jonah?' Kerrie asked, pushing some of her hair over her shoulder and smiling hopefully at the bookseller in question.

He shrugged one shoulder. 'Fine, thanks.'

'It's keeping you busy.'

Allegra wondered if Jonah knew this girl was keeping an eye on his availability.

'I'm so over the festival,' Skye said wearily. 'The whole population tripling. Completely random people rocking up in town. People who don't belong.' She cast a sideways look at Allegra, which only made the latter want to choke down a laugh. She was curious about the small-town dynamics that were currently at play, but she could see how annoyed Grace was. Even Kerrie looked disturbed. So Allegra got to her feet and smiled a civil smile at the table.

'Not really my vibe in here. Grace? Kerrie? I'm going back to the bookshop flat if you want to join me. I make really good virgin cocktails.'

'I'm there,' Grace said, without a moment's hesitation.

'And me,' Kerrie said, almost clambering over Jonah to get out of the booth. She turned back to throw him another expectant smile. 'You staying here?'

Allegra watched Jonah nod in reply. He was clearly oblivious to the way Kerrie's voice softened when she spoke to him.

She wanted to tell Kerrie that he wasn't worth it, that he was far too cantankerous, but she refrained. It was none of her business, after all.

# Chapter Seven

Jonah watched Simon look displeased as Allegra and the other two girls left the arcade. While Simon was foolish around Allegra, he obviously had enough dignity to suppress the urge to chase her out of the building. Instead he sank back into their booth in a sulk.

'She's harder work than I thought.'

Jonah was used to Simon chasing girls. He had chased a lot of the people Jonah had had crushes on during school. When they would start going out, Simon would profess complete horror at the thought of stealing anyone away from Jonah. And the latter would always forgive him.

Still. It was refreshing to watch Simon work hard for once. Clearly Allegra wasn't quite as taken in by Simon's charisma as others had been.

Jonah regarded his friend. 'You thought a global superstar was going to be easy to win over?'

'I kinda did, yeah. I mean, there's got to be a real reason she came to spend the summer in this small town. I reckon she's on the rebound.'

'That checks out, actually,' Skye said. 'Apparently she was going out with that musician from Paisley Shine.'

'Terrible band,' muttered Jonah.

'Where'd you hear that, Skye?' asked Simon.

'Online.'

'I have *got* to do more research if Skye is ahead of me.'

'That wasn't very nice of you. Treating Grace like that,' Jonah found the courage to say to Skye, albeit quietly. 'And being rude to Allegra, too.'

'You're one to talk,' Skye said, her guard finally coming down a little, now that she was the only girl at the table. 'You're not very nice to her. What's going on there?'

Jonah scowled. 'Nothing.'

'This is too serious,' Simon said, laughing. 'Right! Come on, Skye, I need your expertise. What else do you know about her?'

'She has four-and-a-half million Instagram followers, but she—'

Jonah spat out the water he had just sipped and started to gasp for air. When he regained his composure, he stared at the two of them in horror. 'That's, like, almost all of Scotland!'

'Can I finish?' snapped Skye. 'God! Anyway, yes, four-and-a-half million, but she hardly posts and when she does it's always weird, arty stuff.'

'Such as?'

'Lots of bookish content, to be honest.'

'Don't say that like it's a bad thing,' Simon said, affronted.

Jonah blinked. 'Who does she read?'

'Oh, for God's sake,' Skye said, fishing out her phone and opening the app in question. She didn't need to type Allegra's full username, as it came up as her most recent search. 'Like . . . that.'

Jonah snatched the phone before Simon could. It was a black and white picture of Allegra sitting on what looked like a hotel room bed in an oversized baseball shirt. It had been posted over a month before, and she was sitting with a stack of books and a plate of fries. The caption said, 'Feminists and French fries'.

The pile contained Toni Morrison, Curtis Sittenfeld, Nora Ephron and Tamora Pierce.

Jonah's gaze was locked onto the picture and his thumb gently brushed her face on the screen.

'Don't *like* it!' shrieked Skye, snatching back her phone before Jonah could accidentally double-tap the photo. 'God, Jonah, don't you know how to lurk?'

'Jonah was never an Instagram guy, even when he was on social media,' Simon informed her. 'And I doubt Allegra notices every account who likes her pictures, not with that many people watching her every move.'

While the two of them huddled together to cyberstalk Allegra, Jonah slipped away. He googled Paisley Shine as he left the arcade, scowling down at a picture of the pretentious-looking frontman.

'Dick,' he said gruffly, taking a sudden dislike to a man he didn't know.

He went home. It had been a massive change in routine, watching Allegra glide into their festival meetings with her water and her smile and her almost ethereal aura.

He entered the stairwell that led up to his home. It was the flat above Vivi's Cupcakes and his mother, the famous Vivi herself, usually left the front door unlocked.

'Home,' Jonah called to her as he entered. 'Do you need me to grab you anything from town before I take my shoes off?'

'Nope,' his mother's airy voice called from the living room. 'Take them off and have a sit.'

He joined her on their large, squishy sofa. 'What're we watching?'

'A terrible reality dating show that makes any faith I had in the existence of true love shrivel up and die.'

'Well, that's why I read novels.'

He could feel his mother watching him. 'Jonah?'

'Yes?' he replied, his eyes fixed to the television screen but taking in none of the content. He knew what that anticipatory note in her voice meant.

'Did you meet her? What's she like? Oh, God, I went on a YouTube binge and saw every interview she's ever done. She's gorgeous. So humble and sweet. But just so stunning, I can't get over it.'

'Yeah, well.' Jonah felt exposed around his mother and less able to mask. 'Hair and make-up, I guess.'

'Nope! I watched her do one of those "get ready with me" videos for *Vogue* and she is *beautiful* without make-up. I'm so excited to meet her, I hope she comes into the shop. So, what was she like?'

'She was fine,' said Jonah. 'She was . . . I don't know.'

He wanted to tell his mother that she was normal. Just a girl from out of town who was enjoying Lake Pristine and the book festival for a summer. He wanted to tell her that she was dull or mousy or not even that pretty in person.

His ego wanted to say she was rude and unpleasant.

But he couldn't say any of those things because they weren't true.

'I didn't see much of her,' was all he managed to get out.

His mother muted the television and patted the palm of his hand, as the two of them sat side by side. 'Ah, Jonah. I hope you're not letting her make you nervous. Because when you get nervous, you get mean.'

'I wasn't mean,' Jonah said, feeling defensiveness rising up inside of him. 'If anything, *she* was mean.'

'Oh, really?' she asked, delighted and intrigued.

'Well. No, she wasn't. Skye was mean and Simon was stupid and Allegra walked out.'

'I like her already.'

'I'm just curious!'

'Trust me,' Allegra told Kerrie as she started making the three of them soda floats in her father's tiny kitchen, 'you don't want to see them. It's like staring into Pandora's box.'

'I get, like, one direct message a day,' Kerrie insisted. 'I have 427 followers. I want to see what it looks like if you have millions.'

Grace laughed a little hesitantly and Allegra forced herself to join in. 'No, honestly, it's a mess. I can't go in there any more.'

'Oh, please, Allegra,' Kerrie begged. 'I know I'm massively overstepping here, but I'm so, so nosy!'

Allegra glanced at Grace, who was eating a spoonful of ice cream and said, 'I'm also pretty curious, I'm afraid.'

Allegra was faced with a fork in the road – likeability or setting a boundary. It was easy to theorize about which route to take, but she was so desperate for a smooth ride over the summer. 'Fine.'

She let Kerrie open up one of her message request inboxes. Both Grace and Allegra watched as Kerrie's facial expressions moved from delightedly curious to surprised, to genuinely horrified.

'Yup,' Allegra said quietly.

'This is,' Kerrie continued to scroll, her face showing more and more disbelief as she did, 'a lot.'

'Why, what are people saying?' asked Grace, glancing unsurely between Allegra and her phone. She moved over to stand next to Kerrie, reading over the other girl's shoulder. Allegra found it almost comical to watch, as Grace's face also morphed into one of bewilderment and revulsion.

'So, there are the super sexual ones,' Allegra said, holding up one finger. 'Then the ones asking for money or favours, or just general acknowledgement.' Another finger. 'Then the sweet ones, who just want to say kind things.' Third finger. 'Then the really frightening ones.'

'Yeah, I'm reading one of those now,' Kerrie said. 'This person says that because you wore a wig in *Court of Bystanders* instead of your natural hair, you should be violently—'

'Ah, yes, the wig menace,' Allegra said, almost fondly. 'He's gone after me a few times. My co-stars, too. Called our agents. He only targets young women, weirdly enough.'

'This is so scary.'

Allegra shrugged. 'You get used to it.'

She remembered taking the first flurry of horrible messages to her team. They had told her it was part of the job, and that confronting the trolls or speaking publicly about the abuse would only encourage them to continue, and at a greater volume.

'I thought they'd be more fun,' Kerrie admitted, handing the phone back to Allegra. 'But that was really grim.'

Allegra smiled wanly. 'Admiration is calm and quiet, obsession is loud. Obsessed with love or hate, it doesn't matter. It pushes to the front of the line, either way.'

The three girls stood in silence for a moment and Allegra wished the whole thing hadn't happened. She poured the drinks and laid out the snacks, but she could tell Kerrie and Grace were shaken.

'So, what are the less awful parts of the job?' Grace finally asked, easing a little of the tension.

'A lot of it's fun,' Allegra said, wondering why she felt the need to reassure them. 'I have a premiere in a couple of months. I could invite you guys, if you want.'

'Would Jonah come, too?' Kerrie asked, without a moment's hesitation.

Allegra grimaced, but forced her voice to sound encouraging. 'Sure. We'll have a whole entourage.'

Both girls shrieked in spontaneous elation and it made Allegra laugh. They swept her up in a hug and the giggling became so loud that George poked his head out of his room. His face creased in a smile as he watched Allegra dance around the kitchen with the other two girls and he quietly slipped away again.

**@spicyn342**
Hey, Allegra.
You haven't responded to my last few stories so I guess you're not who I thought you were.

**@regretrien**
Allegra, you look so ugly in this picture, ngl. love you, though.

**@camelot55**
are you neurodivergent, Allegra? I saw you stim in an interview and I thought maybe you might be. also, are you bi? I saw those pictures of you and Calista at the Met Gala. pls tell me, I need to know you're not queerbaiting. ily.

@caseyvontrapp

I love you so much, you don't understand, jfc, you are my life.

@johnbacon1

Hate you and your incessant need for attention. Die.

> **shopfloor@BrooksBooks.com**
> **to: westendgirl@gmail.com**
> **Subject: Wish You Were Here!**
>
> Dear Friend!
>
> Today's book is *Heartburn* by Nora Ephron and I've left it in front of the pharmacy. Why, you ask? Because they sell neck creams. If you're a true connoisseur, you'll get it, which I know you will be. It's still stunning weather. The water has never looked more beautiful and it's still nice and quiet. Not too many out-of-towners.
>
> Still. Wish you were here.
>
> Yours,
>
> Bookseller friend.

# Chapter Eight

Allegra and Jonah were like two embittered old rivals as they worked alongside each other in the bookshop. If Allegra made a pyramid display of certain titles, Jonah was there five seconds later to redo it in a manner he found appropriate. If Jonah was on his ten-minute break, Allegra was flying through as many sales as she physically could so that she could beat his position on the system as highest seller.

If anyone had asked why the two of them didn't like each other, they would have snapped. Allegra resented his lack of apology for their first meeting and Jonah was frustrated by how easy everything seemed for the young screen goddess. Their resentment had bubbled over into their working relationship and the bookshop had become a battleground for a cold war that was ever heating up. The two would occasionally blame the boiling sun over Lake Pristine for their testiness, but no one believed them.

A customer was examining a book over by Allegra's new romance table when Jonah approached.

'I can find you a better edition of that novel,' he told the woman who was browsing. 'You'll have to forgive my colleague. She put out the copies with the film tie-in cover, not the classic jacket. Quite tacky. I'll find you a better option.'

The customer looked up at him in surprise but Allegra had already flown across the room from the cash desk.

'And what of it?' she demanded of Jonah, as the would-be buyer stood in between the two glowering booksellers. 'It's the same story, the same text, under that cover, Jonah. So, what of it? Maybe she likes the movie.'

'I do like the film,' the customer said quietly. 'It's what made me want to read the book.'

Allegra gave her a warm, dazzling smile while Jonah made a noise of disgust. 'And that's exactly what's wrong with consumerism right now. People only feel inclined to dip into the classics because they like some actor who was in the adaptation.'

'That's not—' the woman tried to defend herself, but Allegra was already there.

'You are an outrageous snob, do you know that? Now, I never knew Jane Austen—'

'Obviously, Allegra.'

'—but I bet she would have *loved* for her novels to live on through moving pictures. The Brontës, too. So, there's no point getting all high and mighty about defending their art from wicked adaptations, because there's nothing wrong with bringing great stories to wider audiences.'

'Austen, maybe,' snapped Jonah. 'But not the Brontës. Oh, no, they were radical to the bone; they would have hated movie tie-in covers.'

'Sentences I never thought I would have to listen to for one hundred.'

'I might just get it online,' the woman mumbled.

'No!' both Jonah and Allegra shouted at her, before turning back to each other.

'Reading is supposed to be an act of pleasure,' Allegra said silkily. She sidled up to Jonah until he was backed up against a bay of books. 'Fun? Enjoyment? Pleasure! Do these words mean anything to you?'

She was already walking away before he could catch his breath and fire back an answer. Instead, he resorted to snatching a book from the fantasy table and held it up for the whole shop to see.

'What do you think of this tie-in cover?'

It was *Court of Bystanders: Volume One* by Pamela H. J. Wilcox. Allegra scowled at him. She was one of the actors on the jacket of the book.

'I think it looks like it was author approved,' she said sharply.

'As if,' Jonah replied. 'Wilcox is a recluse, she hates the entire world. She's been writing volume six for ten years. There is no way she endorsed this hideous cover.'

'She likes it, you jackass.'

'There is no way you've met Pamela H. J. Wilcox.'

'Met her? I've had dinner with her! Who do you think had the final say over whether I got to play Clera or not?'

The customer had scuttled out of the bookshop, her potential purchase now abandoned on the table. Jonah threw the book he had been brandishing onto its former spot and glared at Allegra.

'Leave the hand-selling to the booksellers,' he snarled. 'You've scared away a sale.'

'Oh, I scared her away? You don't think maybe it was you acting like a lunatic and shaming her for watching a decent adaptation of a book?'

'It's not a decent adaptation. No one said the word "ex" in a romantic context during the eighteenth century, that's an unforgivable anachronism.'

'I am going to the computer,' Allegra said slowly, in a deeply threatening voice. 'And if I find one single reference to the term "ex" being used in the eighteenth century, you are done. You hand over all the best jobs with this festival to me.'

'I'll take that wager, because you won't find any evidence. Because that is a deranged use of language and the screenwriter should be arrested.'

Simon entered the shop with some lunch for everyone while Allegra was at the computer. Jonah watched him glance around, seeming to pick up on the frosty atmosphere despite the sweltering heat outside.

'Everything okay?'

Jonah and Allegra ignored him.

'Ha!' shouted the latter, from her place by the computer. 'First documented use was 1827.'

Jonah stormed towards the cash desk and slammed his hands down on the counter. 'That's the nineteenth century!'

'Everyone knows language is used liberally and regularly among the masses before it's documented.'

'Okay, so they start saying it in 1825 and someone writes it down in 1827. Ten years after Jane drops dead at the age of forty-one. Probably from total abject fear as she realizes that her work is going to be fundamentally misunderstood and appropriated for the next three hundred years!'

Allegra's eyes narrowed. 'Simon, where's the stapler?'

'Okay, okay.' Simon stepped between his two colleagues and held his hands up. 'Let's cool off, it's the heat that's making the two of you fight, I'm guessing.'

'Sure, the humidity goes right to my lady brain,' Allegra said stiffly.

'No,' Jonah retorted. 'I hate movie tie-in covers during all seasons, three hundred and sixty-five days a year.'

Simon laughed under his breath, but Allegra was already braced to retaliate. 'Is there anything you don't hate?'

The question threw Jonah as he stared at Allegra. He was rarely able to look directly at her. He found eye contact fine when he was listening to another person, but less easy when he was speaking, and it was sometimes hard to stare at Allegra Brooks because she looked the way she did. She looked like the kind of girl he would dream up in his head.

'I don't hate Pamela H. J. Wilcox. Not her books anyway.'

He meant it to be pointed but it came out far more cruelly than he intended. It was harsh and nasty and he didn't like himself for saying it. He opened his mouth to say as much but Allegra's face silenced him. She was regarding him with disappointment and a heavy sadness.

'You've been mean since I got here,' she said, matter-of-factly.

There was something about the word 'mean'. It felt so personal. He recalled his mother's words, about nervousness making him mean, and Allegra's words were at odds with how he saw himself. He wasn't a hateful person. He just had very finite tastes.

But Allegra made him so nervous. He was unable to name the reaction he had to her, but he knew it got twisted during the journey from his brain to his heart and it came out all wrong. He didn't intend to be so coarse and harsh with her; more often than not, he felt completely out of control whenever they conversed.

'Hey, Allegra,' Simon pounced when Jonah was unable to respond. 'We're having a game night at my house tonight. Werewolf.' When she looked slightly unsure, he clarified. 'Social deduction game. Loads of us will be there and you can be the guest of honour.'

'Only if Grace and Kerrie are invited.'

Simon placed a hand over his heart and smiled charmingly. 'Of course.'

'Then sure.'

As she moved away to eat lunch with Simon, Jonah took her place at the computer. He felt awkward and embarrassed. He quickly closed her search window and went to the bookshop inbox. He had always been better about his feelings when they were written down, he always liked himself more through the written word. So, he started drafting to the only person who seemed to have any patience for him any more.

A person he didn't even know.

**shopfloor@BrooksBooks.com**
**to: westendgirl@gmail.com**
**Subject: Messing Things Up**
Hey,
You first got in touch to ask about the festival dates and I just want to say, if you're near Lake Pristine or intending to come here soon, please pay me a visit in the bookshop because I'm losing friends left and right. I've been an asshole. I keep saying and doing the wrong thing. Nothing really new there.
Sorry for rambling.
A remorseful bookseller x

★

Allegra was still hot with annoyance as she ate with Simon. She ignored Jonah with intense determination, only looking up when she heard him go into the back office. She exhaled and shook her head slightly, furious with him and with herself for continually letting him goad her into a fight.

'You okay?' Simon asked softly.

She was touched by the seriousness in his usually buoyant voice. 'Yeah. He just gets to me a bit.'

Simon glanced at the closed office door, his brow slightly furrowed and his eyes coloured with concern. 'He doesn't mean to. Trust me. He's a good guy.'

'Just not with me.'

'He just loves the festival. And your dad, too. George has been such a big deal to Jonah, giving him a job, responsibility and stuff, you know. He might be a bit threatened by you and he just can't get on top of it. Honestly. I'm usually the super immature one between the two of us, he's always been the good example.'

Allegra offered up a wry smile.

'Sorry, by the way,' Simon added, still speaking softly and with a grown-up tone Allegra really liked hearing him use. 'I sometimes say stupid shit. Just to get your attention. It's cringy and childish and I know I need to stop.'

She handed him a napkin and gestured to a tiny drop of sauce on the corner of his mouth. She was glad to hear an apology. His immaturity had been a dampener on her mood and she was starting to grow tired of giving him the benefit of the doubt. 'That's okay, Simon. You're all good.'

He smiled appreciatively, wiping away the speck of red. 'Think you can extend that compassion to Jonah? He's genuinely a good person. I swear.'

Allegra said nothing for a moment, crumpling up the paper sandwich wrapper.

'I'll see how Werewolf goes.'

Simon chuckled and helped her to stand. 'Ominous last words.'

# Chapter Nine

**shopfloor@BrooksBooks.com**
**to: westendgirl@gmail.com**
**Subject: Wish You Were Here**

Dear Friend,

Sorry for morose last message. Please find attached *The Picture of Dorian Gray* by Oscar Wilde, taken in one of the finest houses in Lake Pristine.

Wish you were here!

Your friend.

Allegra met Grace and Kerrie at the lake before they walked around the perimeter to the collection of fine houses on the other side. As they made their way through the woodland on the edge of the gleaming water, Allegra nodded at a large and impressive-looking lakehouse, right on the shoreline, that stood solitary by the small pebble beach. She had seen the house from the other side of the lake, when she and Grace had lounged on the hot sand and sipped cold beverages. The vast house looked to be two or three storeys high and the ground level overlooking the lake was almost utterly transparent, with glass from floor to ceiling. It sat in isolation between the lake and the emerald wilderness of the woods, like a great, solitary keep. Allegra found herself extremely drawn to it.

'Who lives there again?' she asked Grace, as the latter seemed to know everything that went on in Lake Pristine.

'The Montgomerys,' Grace reminded her, and there was a glow in her eyes as she said it. 'Howard and Andrea Montgomery. They're one of the oldest and most respected families in town. Their youngest daughter is going to marry my brother.'

'Oh, wow,' Allegra said warmly. 'That's so cool, is she nice?'

Both Kerrie and Grace let out well-natured laughs.

'Is Jasper Montgomery nice?' Kerrie broached the question, sharing a knowing glance with Grace. 'No. She's, like, way more than that. She's the best. She's the queen of this town.'

'Ah, okay, the famous Jasper I've heard so much about. Well, would she join us for a game night?' Allegra ventured. 'We don't have enough for a good go at Werewolf, according to his Lordship Jonah Thorne.'

'I'll text her. My brother will probably want to come too,' Grace said, sounding giddy. 'He hardly sees her now that she has a fancy job.'

When they reached Simon's house, Allegra let out a low whistle. It was a large, impressive brownstone. The first apartment she and her mother had lived in could have fitted inside three times over. Kerrie let herself indoors with a confidence that told Allegra she visited regularly. Grace was texting as she and Allegra followed.

Simon's mother Tania welcomed them in the foyer and led them downstairs to the basement, which had been converted into a game room. It had a soft, cream carpet and dark maroon walls with a small chandelier in the centre of the ceiling, surrounded by smaller circular lights. It was fancier than any basement Allegra had seen before, even in famous circles. The furniture had been pushed to the side of the room and Simon was standing next to a dimmer switch on the wall. A boy Allegra presumed was his little brother clumsily poured himself a soda, while Tania took requests from the girls. Skye was sharing a leather chair with another girl and there were lots of people Allegra had yet to meet, all milling about.

The far wall was lined with tall brown bookshelves and Allegra squinted, recognizing one of the books facing outwards. *The Picture of Dorian Gray* by Oscar Wilde. She smiled and checked her email surreptitiously. The email that had pinged into her inbox fifteen minutes before her arrival, a missive she had read very quickly as she and the girls had made their way there, showed the exact book in that exact spot.

*Wish you were here.* It was how he signed off all his little book-spotting posts around town. She nodded at the book, making sure to look completely innocent. 'That's a good 'un.'

Simon glanced at it and smiled. 'Sure is. Let me just put him back where he should be.'

'In the attic.'

Simon laughed at that and Allegra felt a triumphant flare of elation.

'Allegra Brooks, in my house,' Simon's mother said proudly, while handing Allegra a lemonade. 'Now *you*, I just have to talk to before everything gets hectic and they all start murdering each other.'

Allegra smiled meekly and thanked her for the drink. 'Okay.'

'Can I take a picture?'

Allegra had been vehemently warned against general celebrity behaviour while on holiday in Lake Pristine. Natalie had been extremely clear. However, she was too shy to deny the older woman her selfie. 'Sure.'

'Just for the group chat,' Tania said, as if reading Allegra's mind.

Allegra smiled in gratitude and then posed for the photo.

The flash went off and, as it cleared, Allegra spotted Jonah and the woman who was probably his mother on the other side of the large room. The former rolled his eyes at the scene but the latter broke into a broad grin at the sight of Allegra and stepped forward with a refined hand outstretched.

'Allegra?'

Allegra kept the social mask firmly in place as she greeted the ballerina-like woman before her, who was frail and wearing lounge clothes made of soft fabric. 'Hello.'

'I'm Vivienne,' she said. 'You are just so like all of your pictures. Oh, my word, you are just so *exciting*.'

'Thank you,' Allegra said, deeply uncomfortable. She had learned to just say 'thank you', no matter what people said. It was pointless to try and return the compliment, they would only burst into another flattering remark and nobody appreciated it when she denied their praise.

'I've been watching everything you've ever done since hearing about your arrival in town,' Vivienne said and Allegra watched her tall son flinch at her words. He probably thought so little of Allegra, imagining that she would hold disdain for his mother and her enthusiastic fawning. Whatever version of Allegra that existed in his head, it was someone she probably did not want to be.

'Did you watch the terrible sci-fi I did right after *A Little Princess*?' Allegra asked in her most self-deprecating voice. 'I thought I had managed to get all copies destroyed.'

Vivienne laughed a little too loudly, as did a few other people in close proximity. When you were famous, every public meal, every party and every conversation would have a little bubble of people around it, all listening in and waiting for their chance to jump in.

'Jonah, isn't she just a delight?' Vivienne asked, hauling her son to stand next to her.

Allegra looked up and his dark eyes were staring down at her. A deeply uncomfortable pause fell between the two of them and Allegra could not stand it.

'I haven't quite mastered Jonah's system of bookselling yet, Vivienne,' she said, forcing her tone to be light and playful. 'So, I don't think I'm his favourite person.'

She wondered why a part of her secretly wanted him to agree with his mother's assessment.

But as Jonah opened his mouth to say something, Simon suddenly clapped his hands and the bustling room fell silent.

'All right, players. We're waiting on a few stragglers and then the game will begin. Does anyone not know how to play?'

Allegra hesitantly raised one hand. 'I've got an idea but I've never played.'

'They don't play games in your trailer between scenes?' Skye asked, and the girl beside her spluttered out a laugh which she quickly suppressed.

'That's not funny,' snapped Grace Lancaster.

'I agree,' Vivienne said shortly and Allegra felt grateful for both of them.

'Okay, it's super simple,' Simon said, manoeuvring his way around people so he could reach Allegra. 'I'm hosting, so I don't play. I just moderate and narrate what's happening. Everyone else picks a card and they don't show anyone what they have. We have a bunch of "villagers" and usually a couple of werewolves. You can have a doctor but we've given up on that.'

Simon began to shuffle a special deck of cards as he spoke.

'Once everyone has their part and their card, the game starts,' he went on. 'We'll have our first night phase. This is when I turn off the lights and the werewolves make their first kill. Everyone has to close their eyes, while the wolf or wolves pick their target. I will put the lights back up and narrate the night phase. The victim is out and the rest get to vote on who they think is a werewolf. We keep playing until everyone is caught, or the werewolves are discovered.'

'Got it,' Allegra said confidently and people made noises of appreciative anticipation.

'This is just one way to play, but it works for us,' Theo, Simon's little brother, said with the cheerful authority of his twelve years and it made Allegra smile.

'All right, everyone find your spot in the room and I will start handing out the cards!' Simon decreed.

This charmed Allegra. She liked how social he seemed. How unapologetically keen he was to engage the whole group in a shared bit of fun.

She sat on the floor by Grace and Kerrie, and her hands felt full of electricity. The only social gatherings she had attended over the last couple of years had been wrap parties, and she had always been chaperoned. Everyone else had solidly been an adult. She had done ten-hour days on set, disappearing occasionally to be tutored. People her own age were strange, exotic creatures that she had always watched from afar.

Now she was in the scene, and very worried about getting her lines wrong.

In Lake Pristine, everyone seemed to know each other so well, age was not a factor. Simon's mother was one of the group, as was Jonah's. They were both chatting to Skye's older brother, introduced earlier to Allegra as Carrick. The slightly surly but handsome cinema manager Arthur was there, too, with some of his friends. They were talking by the makeshift bar. One was a girl with lots of piercings, and she was holding hands with Hera, the woman who ran the arcade.

A card was handed to Allegra and she covertly checked it.

*Werewolf.*

'Keep your cards hidden,' Simon instructed, moving over to the dimmer switches on the wall once again. 'Werewolf or Werewolves, be ready to choose your first kill of the night. Everyone else. Close your eyes.'

The room fell into near darkness. 'Werewolf and werewolf only, open your eyes.'

Allegra did. She found herself staring into Jonah's eyes, as he was the only other person in the room whose head was not bowed. They glared at one another as the realization hit; they would need to work together.

'Werewolf, choose your victim,' Simon instructed, as Allegra and Jonah continued to regard each other from their opposite sides of the spacious room.

Jonah pointed to Skye but Allegra quickly shook her head. That would be far too obvious, and her siblings would extract revenge on her behalf. She pointed to Grace's brother. Jonah considered Arthur Lancaster and then nodded, albeit a little begrudgingly. Simon silently pointed to Arthur, too, to confirm their choice.

'Lights up! Wake up, townsfolk.'

Allegra used her best skills to pretend she was also opening her eyes with all of the others. She avoided looking at either Jonah or Arthur Lancaster, their oblivious victim.

'Townsfolk, something dreadful happened in the night,' Simon declared and people smirked, enjoying his melodramatic narration. 'An esteemed member of our community was brutally slain by the werewolf (or werewolves) at large.'

Allegra watched Simon hold court. She certainly found his charm attractive. She enjoyed spending time with him. She *loved* his emails. Now that she had been in Lake Pristine for almost a week, the online exchanges had become more and more frequent, and she was loving the adorable book cameos. They had discussed books, movies and music, all without Allegra giving too much away. She still had an air of mystery, something he regularly teased her about. He would also end every email now with the words 'wish you were here' and whenever Allegra responded, she was tempted to say that she already was.

The emails were a side of Simon she struggled to see in person. But his good-natured leading of the Werewolf game was promising – and that made Allegra hopeful, because the emails had become some of her favourite things to read. She had to get to know their author better, no matter how selfish or immature he might sometimes seem.

'Who was brutally attacked?' Hera, the arcade manager, asked gamely, in pantomime voice, drawing Allegra back into the game and away from thoughts of secret emails.

'While everyone was asleep in their beds, one of you got up to go for a midnight stroll. You made your way through the square, down Main Street and ended up at the bandstand, where you closed your eyes. You were waiting to meet someone. Someone who was late.'

Allegra grinned, along with most of the room. Only Skye, her sister Star and Jonah remained stoic. Arthur, the unknowing werewolf victim, Allegra noticed, kept glancing towards the basement door.

'While this person was waiting on the bandstand, they were hunted. Then caught. Perhaps the werewolf was jealous.' Simon did a full spin of the room, his arm outstretched. 'The first bite was to wound, but the second hit him square in the heart. I'm so, so very sorry.' Simon's finger landed on the bemused cinema manager.

'The werewolf got you, clean, Lancaster. Right in the heart.'

'Oh, no,' Arthur said, in a flat, deadpan voice that made Allegra stifle a laugh.

'Villagers,' Simon said. 'While the victim leaves the game, time for a town meeting! Who could have done this? Who are the secret werewolves among us?'

This signalled the start of a discussion, Allegra realized, as people leapt into speaking.

'I vote Grace,' Skye's sister, Star, said frankly.

'No chance,' Allegra heard herself retort. 'She wouldn't do in her big brother.'

'Don't let her angel face fool you,' Arthur said, laughing.

Arthur dutifully left the game and stepped to the back of the room as the accusations continued to fly. Skye nominated Allegra but no one took her seriously. Most people ended up focusing in on Grace, who didn't seem to mind the suspicion. She took great, theatrical joy in proving everyone wrong by revealing her civilian card and people cursed their own assuredness.

And the lights went off once more.

# Chapter Ten

Jonah was surprised that when it came to hunting people in a game of Werewolf, he and Allegra worked rather well together. They silently and curtly picked out their victims and maintained shocked but innocent expressions while fingers were pointed afterwards. Jonah was nominated by Kerrie but he talked his way out of it. He surprised himself by cutting a few people off when they turned their suspicion towards Allegra.

He had no reason to keep her in the game, but he did it anyway.

As Werewolf neared its end, the older members of the party began to drift away. Arthur, Odette and Hera left to go to the only bar in town. Jonah's mother gave him a quick kiss goodbye before disappearing to the upstairs den with Simon's parents and a few other older townsfolk who had stopped by.

When only the teenagers remained in the game room, Skye snatched the Werewolf cards out of Simon's hands. She had been voted out in an earlier round and was clearly sick of sitting against the wall with Star.

'I'm bored of this game. Let's play something better,' she declared to the remaining members of the party.

'Well, who are werewolves out of those of you left?' Grace asked.

Jonah glanced over at Allegra. She smiled demurely as she revealed her werewolf card to the rest of the room.

'Knew it,' Skye muttered. She had accused Allegra plenty of times, but nobody had agreed with her.

Jonah slid his onto the carpeted floor. 'What do you want to play instead?'

Skye's eyes glinted as she scanned the room. Her gaze landed on Grace, who was talking to two of her friends from her dance class.

'Truth or dare.'

There were shrieks of delight throughout the room but Jonah felt his pulse quicken ever so slightly. He knew, as the one who was ever sober, that this game always ended in tears. He looked to Simon, hoping to send his friend a wordless plea that would encourage him to call an end to the idea, but Simon was grinning at Skye.

'All right. Spin the bottle style?' he said.

'Yes!' Star said, grabbing an empty wine bottle from Simon's basement bar. 'Whomever the bottle lands on has to tell the truth or do the dare set by the spinner.'

It was decidedly simple, compared to the role-play they had all been partaking in just moments before. Jonah loved games like Werewolf. Catan. Monopoly.

Truth or Dare and Spin the Bottle always operated with secret, hidden rules that he could never uncover. And the price for breaking an unspoken instruction was always high.

Everyone arranged themselves in a circle. Jonah looked over at Allegra, who was looking unsure and a little anxious. She quickly masked it and slid gracefully into a sitting position between Kerrie and Grace.

'In or out, Thorne?' Simon called over to him.

Jonah reluctantly sat, too, with a great and heavy feeling of dread.

'I'll spin first,' Skye said jauntily. The bangles on her wrist clinked as she leaned across the carpet to touch the wine bottle. Everyone watched, but she refused to actually spin it, instead merely turning it so that its neck was pointing directly towards Allegra.

'Truth or dare?' Skye asked her.

'You have to actually spin and let the bottle decide,' Jonah heard himself say, but he was ignored by the group. Only Allegra's eyes briefly flashed towards him. She raised her chin and smiled politely at Skye.

'Truth.'

'How much money do you have?'

Simon hollered at Skye's question. Everyone else laughed also, albeit a little more nervously. Jonah was the only one glaring at the remark.

'I make enough,' Allegra said quietly.

'What was your last pay cheque?' Star asked, joining in with the interrogation.

Allegra smiled a barely-there smile. 'My last one? Three seventy-five.'

'Thousand?' demanded Hillary, one of the other ballet girls. She looked awed at the prospect, eyeing the fellow eighteen-year-old with reverence.

'No. Just three hundred and seventy-five. My dad pays us weekly at the bookshop.'

Jonah found himself grinning at that, while Skye glowered in distaste.

'Is it my turn then?' Allegra asked, reaching for the bottle. She spun somewhat clumsily and it landed . . .

. . . on Jonah.

'Dare,' he said, before she could ask.

She regarded him for a moment. 'I dare you to say something nice about every person in the group.'

There were audible reactions to this command, people hooting and hollering at the dare, while Jonah found himself wondering how he had so swiftly managed to convince this girl that he was an uncharitable person. The kind who never gave compliments.

'Fine,' he said, suddenly determined. He glanced around and his eyes locked onto Simon. 'Simon is . . .'

Everyone waited.

'Oh, God,' Simon said, squinting at his friend. 'Jonah's got the memory of a computer. He has so much bad stuff on me.'

Jonah snorted, despite trying to look pensive. 'Simon is a good friend. I'd do anything for him. He's the one who made school bearable.'

There was a beat of silence. Simon gently bumped his friend on the bicep, with a small smile servicing as thanks.

'Next,' Jonah pushed ahead. 'Grace Lancaster. Best dancer I've ever seen.'

Grace blushed and when Jonah stole a glance at Allegra, she was smiling almost smugly. She was also clearly triumphant at the forced generosity her dare had created.

'Skye.' Jonah could hear the strangled desperation in his voice as he tried to muster up something nice about one of the meanest girls in Lake Pristine. 'Skye is very . . . confident. Oh, and she's also a really good baker. I couldn't have asked for a better partner during that cooking class they made us take in school.'

Skye smiled, but Jonah's difficulty in settling on a kind remark had been noted by some of Grace's dancer friends, as they exchanged knowing looks.

Jonah fired off the last of his required compliments with diligent conviction.

'Kerrie is nice to everyone.'

'Hilary is . . . also a good dancer.'

'Eva has really great taste in books.'

'Lucien is the best football player in town, if you care about stuff like that.'

'It's not a compliment if you add "stuff like that",' Lucien said, but he was laughing.

Jonah smirked, then looked to Skye's sister. 'Star is . . . smart? You always won a lot of prizes in high school.'

Star shrugged one shoulder, unashamed of her academic prowess.

'Only Allegra left,' Simon prompted.

Jonah forced himself to look at Allegra. Her expression was unreadable but she gave him a small nod, almost as though she were giving him some kind of permission.

'It's okay,' she said, her tone jovial. 'I know you don't have anything in the compliment bag for me, wizard. I'll let you off with what you've given.'

'No,' Simon insisted, ignoring Jonah's obvious discomfort. 'Jonah, give Allegra one, too.'

Expectant faces looked between Jonah and Allegra, while they stared at each other in discomposure.

'You don't have to,' Allegra finally said quietly, when the

silence had stretched for far too long. 'I know we haven't exactly hit it off—'

'I think you're the most beautiful girl I've ever seen.'

Allegra was good at analysing different kinds of silence. It was a skill lots of performers possessed. There were awkward silences, silences of condemnation, sympathetic silences, silences of awe, silences of derision. Punishing silences, designed to make someone deeply uncomfortable and unwelcome.

And there were silences of complete shock, where everyone was suspended in time.

As Allegra stared at Jonah, she could see he was as astonished by his own words as everyone else, and she suddenly felt guilty for bringing this part of the game to life.

She felt other things too, but they were beautifully coloured potions inside her that she couldn't identify – and was perhaps too cowardly to drink.

It was a silly, unfashionable thought, but when she had been diagnosed, by doctors who had looked at her as though she was an alien they had watched fall from the sky, she had felt all of the heavy unwantedness of the world. Girls like her were studied, not admired. They were diagnosed, not loved. They were the subjects of academic papers, not great paintings or love stories. They were spoken about, not spoken to. They were projected onto. They were whispered about. They were sometimes shunned for being too different or ignored for being too good at camouflaging.

It didn't matter how many jobs she secured, or how many awards she won, a part of her still felt that unwanted sting. That burden of being 'other'.

So, when Jonah Thorne, someone who didn't even like her, called her 'beautiful' – not attractive, not hot, but beautiful – she felt the brushstrokes of being human on the canvas of her face for the first time.

She was, of course, unable to say any of this.

'Your turn to spin, Jonah,' Skye finally said.

Jonah readily pushed the bottle into motion and the game clunkily carried on.

Allegra's attention dipped in and out as the evening progressed. She felt her work phone vibrating in her pocket and each little trill sent a ripple of anxiety through her. Her team had promised not to contact her over the summer. She had made the case to her management and agency, telling them that it was essential for her to be a normal eighteen-year-old for a few months and Natalie had been her valiant second, supporting her all the way.

When the buzzing became noticeable to other people, Allegra excused herself. As she stepped into the lower ground floor corridor, she glanced at a large clock on the wall in the shape of a pig. It was getting to be quite late in the evening, and she was horrified at the thought of her team still working.

She called Natalie, who answered after the first ring.

'Everything all right?' Allegra asked.

She could hear that Natalie sounded tired.

'Hi, darling. Sorry to call you, I know you're out of the office for the summer, but this couldn't wait.'

Allegra sat down on the carpeted floor and listened while Natalie told her about a director who wanted to meet with her.

'Glory will be in the city when you're up for the premiere.'

A premiere for a huge, big-budget movie Allegra had wrapped

the year before. Her part was small, the ensemble cast had been enormous. The producers had stuffed the three-hour picture with as many famous names as possible. Allegra's part had practically been a walk-on, which was why she had done it. No expense had been spared in production.

Except when it came to the writing.

Allegra was not particularly proud of the film but she was still obligated to appear on the carpet.

She was eventually able to persuade Natalie to put everything into an email to her personal account, which she promised she would read.

'Can I give Glory your number?'

'Sure,' Allegra sighed.

'Amazing. Thank you, sweets. Go back to your holiday, have a great time.'

As Allegra hung up the phone, she listened for the sounds of the group next door. She could hear Simon animatedly shouting about something, while Lucien argued back jokingly. The others seemed to be all laughing and joining in.

Somehow, life with her peers had always felt like this to Allegra. She was the one sitting out in the corridor, or in a bathroom stall, while the fun carried on happily without her. She had never enjoyed walking into rooms. She always felt a little unwelcome.

Becoming famous had done nothing to change that. Her world had, ironically, shrunk. The bigger your name becomes, the more strangers will start to use it. Then one day you realize you haven't heard a loved one say it in for ever. They've given up trying to be heard over the din of the crowd.

The dramatic switch from being the girl teachers and other

teenagers treated like a burden to international superstar had been enough to break her neck.

She heard Simon bellow something that sounded uncharitable at Grace's friends and it made her wince. He was so different in the emails. Opening up the latest one made her smile again.

*Wish you were here.*

Perhaps he regretted his abrasiveness. He had said as much, in one of his emails. She certainly said and did things in social situations that had her lying awake late at night, wishing she could negotiate with the weirder parts of her brain.

'Answer the question!'

As Allegra re-entered the room, she frowned at the scene that greeted her. Grace Lancaster was squirming under Star's fierce gaze.

'Can I do the dare instead?' Grace asked, her voice becoming very small.

'Fine, I *dare* you to answer the question,' Star said fiercely.

'What question, what have I missed?' Allegra asked, sitting down next to Grace in the circle.

'Not much, I think this game has definitely run its course,' Jonah said. He sounded matter-of-fact but when Allegra looked at him, he looked nervous. Perhaps even a little distressed.

'I don't really want to answer,' Grace said, to the question Allegra was yet to hear.

'Well, that's not the game,' Skye said coldly, backing her sister.

'She wants to know if I've ever—'

'I don't need to hear,' Allegra told the other girl when she began to explain. 'If you don't want to answer, you don't have to answer.'

'Yeah, this is getting boring,' Kerrie said brightly, getting to her feet. 'I'm heading back into town if anyone wants to walk.'

'I do,' said Allegra. 'Grace, you too?'

'Yes,' said Grace quietly. Her two friends from the ballet also stood up.

'Grace, you don't have to be so serious all of the time,' Skye said with a disingenuous smile. 'This is all very unserious; you don't need to get worked up.'

Allegra watched Grace experience a tumult of emotions before she finally levelled Skye with a withering stare. When Grace spoke, it was with calm conviction. 'You're rude and mean to people because you know in your heart of hearts, you're boring. And you'll be stuck here for ever.'

The remark landed like a glove being thrown down. Skye's face suddenly looked years younger, as she stared up at Grace Lancaster. She seemed unable to formulate a response.

Allegra whistled. 'I don't know, you guys. Lake Pristine could give any audition room a run for its money, this place is lethal.'

She made for the door, offering Grace her arm. The latter gladly took it.

'I'll walk you home, Allegra,' Simon volunteered, jumping to his feet. 'If you want some proper company.'

She gave him a small smile, still trying to remember his endearing email persona. 'I'm good with the girls, thanks. See you at work.'

She left his house, hoping that she would start to see more of the Simon she was getting to know from their emails.

She liked that version so much more.

# Chapter Eleven

'What was she asking you, Grace? Do you feel okay telling me?'

Allegra asked the question softly once she and Grace had dropped off the others and were the only two left walking home. They were on the woodland path that would eventually link up with Main Street and the air felt warm, but not soupy. It was a pleasant balm against their skin after a lively evening and sudden exit.

'She was asking if I've ever had sex,' Grace confirmed, her tone forgiving and resigned all at once. 'Don't worry about me, Allegra. I'm used to people like that. I'm a lot tougher than I used to be.'

'Yeah, I can believe that. But it's still gross. Nobody's business. Some things are off limits, even in a game.'

'Hey.' Grace examined the other girl. 'It's honestly fine. This is small-town stuff. This is just what it's like here. Nothing ever really happens so people have to make drama out of nothing.' They reached the main square of town and passed the dance studio. Grace brushed the outer wall of the building with fond familiarity. 'Skye graduated high school at the beginning of the summer, just like me. But I'm going to school. I'm going to dance. She has nothing. I don't care if she's a bitch, I feel bad for her. This is all she has. You don't have to defend me.'

Allegra felt slightly embarrassed. 'Sorry. I . . . take things too personally. I would have been really upset.'

'That's because you're an actress. I bet people are always overstepping. Even when they're being nice.'

Allegra was taken aback by the accuracy.

'I appreciated you standing up to her, though,' Grace said. 'You reminded me of my sister.'

'Your sister?'

'Well, Arthur's girlfriend Jasper. She's a sister to me.'

'I thought I wanted the normal, pre-university summer experience,' Allegra said, as they reached the town square. 'But I'm a massive fish out of water here.'

'I think people are just intimidated by you.'

'Grace, can I tell you something?'

'Of course.'

The town was partially lit up in firefly-like lights, the sun having set, and it was still summertime warm. The kind of evening that made walking home a pleasure. Grace was heading towards the Arthouse and it shone out ahead of them. Allegra stopped walking so she would have more time to explain.

'Remember I mentioned my secret pen-pal?'

'Yes,' Grace said. 'I haven't told anyone.'

'I think it's Simon.'

'Shut up!'

'Yeah. I've been emailing a bookseller from the shop since before I arrived, only he still doesn't know it's me.'

Grace's mouth dropped open and she made a delighted sound of surprise. 'Seriously?'

'Yes.'

'You and Simon?'

'Yes.'

'Wait, you definitely know it's him?'

'Well,' Allegra winced. 'I'm not one thousand per cent sure. He never signs his name. But I've caught him at the monitor seconds after receiving an email and sometimes he sends pictures of books, and one of the pictures was from his den. I worked that out tonight. Also, he uses a lot of the expressions from his emails in real life.'

'But how can he not know it's you? And what kind of emails, Allegra?'

Allegra laughed at the pointed curiosity in the latter question. 'Friendly ones. I emailed the shop from my private email, intended it for Dad as I thought he was the only one with access to it. Simon replied. We started—'

'Flirting?'

Grace retraced her steps so she and Allegra were inches apart. Allegra appreciated the closeness, she didn't want any eavesdroppers.

'No. Maybe. I don't know. We talk more than anything else. About anything.'

'But you never told him you were you?'

'No.'

Grace blinked and crossed her arms. Allegra watched her try to piece together the whole story in her mind. 'Who does he think you are?'

'I have no idea! Some out-of-towner who's interested in the book festival. He kind of assumed I work in social media, and I didn't correct him. But the emails are sweet. They're charming and they made me realize how lonely I was and how much I needed a break.'

'But it's Simon?' Grace pointed out, seemingly a little baffled.

'Yes,' sighed Allegra. 'He's . . . different in his writing. Self-deprecating. Funny. Kind.'

'So, why does he act like such a . . .'

The girls shared a knowing look.

'I guess it's just peacocking?' Allegra finally suggested.

'Yeah,' Grace said, though her attempt at enthusiastic agreement fell a little flat, and her scepticism was clear in her face. 'I'm sure he's different behind closed doors.'

The girls walked with excruciatingly slow speed towards the Arthouse once more before Grace was the one to stop.

'Why did you tell me about your pen-pal? I mean, I'm so glad you did. But why?'

Allegra was a girl with scripts always at the ready in her head. She was always a work in progress, a girl in rehearsal who was trying to play the perfect neurotypical. But when Grace so frankly asked the question, Allegra wanted to be honest.

'I don't have anyone else to tell.'

She retrieved the phone in her pocket and showed it to Grace. 'This is one of three phones I have. One for personal use, one for work and a back-up one for work that isn't even out of the box yet.'

Grace raised both eyebrows and nodded at the phone in Allegra's hands. 'Which one is that?'

'Personal. But look!'

Allegra showed her the messages and call log.

'Who's Natalie?'

'My publicist from my management team. Then there's my agent. There's the odd group chat from productions, but they die off when people move on to their next project.'

'Wow,' Grace said, her voice a combination of amazement and sadness.

'The last true friend I had? The only friend I had in school, we went to drama club together. She told me she couldn't be my friend any more. She said my success was too painful.'

Grace gasped and Allegra realized that this was the first person she had told about her painful friendship break-up with Ana. She had tried to ignore the ghosting at the time. She had sent text after text, left voicemails and mailed postcards. Then when she had finally got in touch, Ana had spat out the words.

'I'm happy for you, but it was my dream, too,' she had said over the phone, while Allegra's world lost colour and brightness. 'I can't watch you do it. It's too hard.'

Allegra had tried to set up meetings, arrange castings for Ana, but her ex-friend had changed her number by then. It had felt like withdrawal, and Allegra's autistic sense of justice and sensitivity to rejection had led to numerous shutdowns.

No break-up with a lover had hurt nearly as much.

'That's awful,' Grace said and her serious voice and pained expression made Allegra feel lighter. She had gaslit herself into believing she was needy and desperate and weird.

When all she really felt was hurt.

'I don't really have any close friends,' Grace admitted softly. 'I pal around with the girls from ballet, and I know Kerrie from school, but . . . I've always found it hard to make friends. I love Jasper but she sees me as a little sister; she would never share with me like you just did.'

Allegra was grateful for the vulnerability. It felt like a gesture of solidarity.

'I want to be your friend,' she told Grace, smiling the smile she always saved for the final take, the one she knew they would be forced to use in the cutting room, despite what came before.

Grace blinked and returned the smile, utterly moved by her words. 'And I promise not to tell Simon. But when are you going to come clean?'

'Not sure,' Allegra replied. 'I can tell he likes the actor version of me that he has in his head.'

'Yes, he's not exactly being subtle.'

'But I want to make sure he likes *me*. Me, me. Not masked me.'

'Then it takes as long as it takes,' Grace said, her aura cheerful as they prepared to part ways. 'And I'll not tell a soul.'

George and his booksellers sat around their small table for another festival meeting, while the odd customer drifted in and out of the shop, browsing around the team and occasionally stealing glances at Allegra. She worried with every glance that someone might leak her location, but no leaks ever came. Simon's mother had kept her word by only sharing their selfie with a closed group. People stared, but didn't run to the nearest phone to report a sighting. So she surmised that every newcomer in Lake Pristine probably received this level of inspection.

'We've run into a bit of a snag,' George told his small team. 'Most authors are confirmed and in the log, but Quentin Morrison is asking for more money. We may have to cut someone.'

Jonah's head snapped up. 'Cut someone? Because he wants more cash?'

George took a sip of his black coffee and avoided Jonah's stare. It was something that he was doing more often of late. 'We can bump a couple of poets.'

'No!' Jonah stared at his employer in disbelief. 'No, we can't just "bump a couple of poets". The whole point of festivals like this is to let local talent, and writers without gigantic marketing campaigns, meet readers and find an audience. We can't hurt the up-and-comers because some old white man wants to take us for all we're worth. What about the marginalized authors? What about the disability in fiction panel, who are travelling all the way here? We can't look them in the face and say we value their input if we're paying some hack more money than them.'

He suddenly realized that he sounded like Allegra.

'He'll probably be most of the ticket sales, Jonah,' Simon said gingerly. Jonah hated how he was trying to sound reasonable.

Jonah frowned at that. 'Women and marginalized authors can bring in loads of money, too, they just need the same level of support.'

'Fine,' Simon allowed. 'But we've booked him. He's expected. And the press will want to ask him to talk about cultural issues, and that will make all the Arts sections.'

'Oh, great,' Jonah snapped, his voice becoming darker by the syllable. 'Another millionaire going on about cancel culture in a huge, three-page spread with lots of exposure while our real artists can't afford the bus ticket here. And none of us are allowed to point out the hypocrisy of it all. God! We're better than this, George, we can't have the festival associated with this crap. These summers used to mean something to people, real people, not the pretenders who think a book's only worthwhile if their publishers can pay enough to put it on a billboard.'

'That's enough,' George said, weary of it all. 'You're getting passionate about something that hasn't even happened yet. We'll remind him that, while we're far more popular than we once were, we still cannot afford to pay some writers more than others. And we'll go from there.'

Usually, George's answer would have been enough to pacify Jonah but he was so restless. There was something out of place when it came to George and the bookshop now. What had once been a place of familiarity and comfort was now a constant gnawing of insecurity, a feeling that he had overstayed his welcome as a bookseller. Once, it had been normal for George to ask Jonah about his notebook, the short story or novel he was working on. The two of them would talk about what they had been reading. Now, Jonah was lucky if he received a greeting in the morning and a farewell in the evening. He didn't understand why.

'Jonah, you've got to relax,' George went on, finally looking at his most loyal employee. 'It's just a book festival.'

The words slithered about in the air, serpent-like to Jonah in their audacity and contradiction.

'It's *not* just a book festival,' Jonah said, a little brokenly. 'How can you, of all people, say that, George? You, who started this whole thing. To bring books and events to Lake Pristine, to put it on the map.'

'Pretty sure the weird carnivals and the Valentine's Day Ball put Lake Pristine on the map,' Simon said, his voice full of a levity that did not belong in the conversation. 'This is a town for hopeless romantics, most of the year. The Summer Book Festival is the only time we can get people to actually use their brains.'

'I'm happy to talk to Quentin's team again,' Courtney interjected. 'I'm sure we can remind them that the festival has a collective nature to it and that we want all artists to be paid the same. His book sales will be enormous.'

'I'm sure his advances are better than most,' Jonah said bitterly. 'More than the poets, and the children's authors and the debut novelists. He can take it or leave it.'

'Excuse me,' George said, stepping away from the table to make sure no customers were listening to their meeting, 'I make the final decisions here. Jonah, you're acting like—'

'What if I can help?'

Allegra's voice cut through the tension. George stopped speaking at once, seeming to remember that she was there. It was the first thing she had said throughout the entire meeting. Jonah stared at her. 'What?'

'What if I can get an even bigger author to come? One who'll bring in more sales but won't mind taking the same fee as everyone else?'

'Who did you have in mind, Allegra?' Courtney asked. She put her glasses back on, poised to take notes. The whole room now regarded Allegra, awaiting her solution.

# Chapter Twelve

Allegra swallowed down all feelings of doubt. The chances of her only author acquaintance coming to the festival were as likely as her and Jonah becoming friends, but she had to try.

'Pamela H. J. Wilcox won't come here,' Jonah said quietly, knowing exactly what she was plotting. His heart didn't even seem to be in the denial, though. 'It's too remote, too small. She doesn't even do major cons. Why would she come here?'

'Because I'm going to ask her to,' Allegra replied.

She watched Jonah wipe a tiny speck of sleep away from the corner of his eye and grimace. 'And that's all it takes, is it?'

He finally looked at her and they regarded each other, both with the same amount of icy consideration.

'I'll try,' Allegra finally said, and it was as if there was no one else in the room.

Somehow Jonah Thorne's principled stance on the festival had touched something in Allegra. The film business was full of people who were happy to step on their colleagues if it meant more of the spotlight for themselves. Jonah had, at first, seemed indifferent to Quentin's presence, but his indignant dismay at the man asking for more money had brought out a better side to him.

'If she were to join the programme, we would need confirmation pretty swiftly,' Courtney said gently.

'I'm on it,' Allegra said, doubling down.

'I have complete and utter faith in you, Allegra,' Simon suddenly said.

'Me, too,' her father added, but he was slightly paler. 'Uh, Courtney, why don't we head to the tourist board for a debrief. The kids can manage the shop.'

'I can help,' Jonah said, and Allegra saw in his eyes something boyishly unsure and nervous.

'No,' George said curtly. 'Thanks.'

**shopfloor@BrooksBooks.com**
**to: westendgirl@gmail.com**
**Subject: Not Myself**

Dear Friend,

Have you ever watched yourself from above, like a helicopter pilot flying over a war zone? I mean, as though the real you is high above and all the stupid parts of you are down below. You watch your ego and your pride say completely inane things to decent people, and you're screaming down from the ladder, 'please stop' but they don't. I mean, you don't. You have to watch yourself botch a social situation so badly, you don't think you deserve saving. I'm sure this is a completely foreign situation to you, but it's been happening to me a lot lately.

Anyway. The festival seems to be in a bit of a shambles, but I'm still hopeful that you'll come. And that we can actually meet.

Wish you were here.

Yours,

Sad Bookseller.

Allegra reread the email during her break, which she spent on the shopfloor in the tiny romance section. She smiled at the remorseful words and glanced over at Simon, who was reading the blurb of a political non-fiction hardback. She was relieved to read that he was perturbed at the two versions of himself, because she felt the same.

A loud thud made her glance over at Jonah. He was ripping up boxes for recycling and scowling as he did so. His profile was guarded and cross, every inch of him warning people to stay away. Yet Allegra found herself remembering the compliment he had reluctantly given her during the game at Simon's house.

She wondered what emails from Jonah might look like. He would occasionally leave notes on the front desk of the shop, in serial killer handwriting, and they bore none of the wit and warmth of the emails. They made Allegra wonder about what went on under the water of him.

He was stubborn and always in a bad mood, but there were flashes of real character from him, the kind that Allegra couldn't stop thinking about. He was principled and honest. He would never showcase books that were ideologically lazy or too in favour of the status quo. He said what he thought. He was gentle with people who were intimidated by bookshops, and funny sometimes with the children who came in.

She slid her phone away, deciding to answer Simon's latest email later, and re-joined the others in the main part of the shop.

'So,' Simon addressed her with a familiar smile as she approached the other two booksellers. 'How are you finding summer in Lake Pristine?'

Allegra had to laugh. From people arguing in the line for ice cream to the floral garlands that were draped all over town, it was a wonderful departure. 'Love it. It's everything I've heard it would be.'

'You know we once ran a tattooist out of town because they wanted to open up a studio,' Simon said. 'I say "we", it was the elders. But I got one anyway, look!'

He rolled up his sleeve to show a small blotch of black ink.

'What is it?' asked Allegra, laughing.

'It was meant to be a rain cloud but my dad caught me under the needle and stopped the whole thing, so now it's just a blob. My family were mad but I remain one of the few tattooed individuals in town. They like it twee here.'

'They certainly do,' muttered Jonah, breaking apart another cardboard box.

'There's only one bar in town, hence why the arcade has become such a hellmouth,' Simon added. 'But the Arthouse is nice. And sometimes we drive into Mapesbury, the neighbouring town. It's still pretty small but it's the twenty-first century there. We were going to go tonight, actually.'

'Who's "we"? The town elders?'

'Me, Lucien, Skye—'

'I'll catch a ride with Grace and Kerrie,' Allegra said confidently. If they had not already been invited, they would be now. 'What's the plan?'

Mapesbury was not quite the bright lights of Paris nor the rainy chicness of London. It certainly wasn't the clinical mousetrap that was Los Angeles. It wasn't a city, but a slightly bigger town west of Lake Pristine. What was clear about Mapesbury was the fact that her new friends in Lake Pristine found it to be all the freedom that they needed from small-town life.

'Things stay open past six,' Grace said to Allegra, as they all made their way towards a laidback-seeming bar. 'Bliss!'

Once they were all inside, Lucien and Simon started seeing who could down a pint the fastest. Skye had elected not to come.

Allegra was looking at the mocktail menu with Kerrie when she felt the – unfortunately very common – feeling of being watched.

She glanced up and smiled uncomfortably at the two men in their twenties who were standing over their small bar table.

'Allegra Brooks!'

It wasn't a question. The man on the right had announced her name so loudly, a few of the staff behind the bar and a couple of waiters turned to watch.

Allegra wondered if she should try her occasionally useful trick of pretending that she was just a good lookalike. But before she could make a decision, Kerrie happily said, 'Yes! It's really her!'

Her sweet face quickly fell when Grace and Simon elbowed her from either side, but it was too late.

'Can you record something for my brother? You're on his list,' one of the men said, squeezing next to Allegra and opening his phone to take a picture without asking.

'List?' Allegra murmured.

'Of people he's allowed to sleep with apart from Lisa. That's his wife.'

'Oh. I—'

'She's eighteen,' Simon said with a tone of disgust. 'That's vile.'

'Say something from the show!' the man persisted, his mouth far too close to her ear.

'I'm actually just here for a bit of a break,' Allegra heard herself say, though in the smallest voice possible.

Suddenly she was seeing herself in the man's front camera of his phone. She looked rattled and bewildered and his breath was too pungent. It was probably nothing an allistic would notice, but Allegra could sense all of the layers to it: onions and pickle, hastily covered up with a barely chewed piece of peppermint gum. Someone else's phone flashed, too bright, the music felt too loud and the air had become thinner. She staggered up on her feet and started to make her way towards the exit.

'Can you just quickly say that line—'

A large hand was suddenly slapping the phone out of the man's grip. He exclaimed as it shot gracelessly to the floor and the screen cracked. The man's protestations had no effect on the newcomer, who said: 'What the fuck, dude?'

Allegra turned in astonishment to see Jonah Thorne looking disdainfully at the disrespectful fan.

'This is a bar, not a meet-and-greet,' Jonah told the man coldly. 'And even if it were, your behaviour would be cracked. So, go away.'

'Who the hell are y—?'

Allegra grabbed Jonah by the arm and used him to propel them both out of the bar and into the street outside. She kept walking until they were in a more secluded place, with the sun barely down and the air still warm. They found themselves in a far quieter street, behind the bar, where there were cherry blossoms on the cobblestones and fewer people around.

'Thanks,' she exhaled. 'You didn't have to do that.'

Jonah looked her up and down. 'You all right?'

'Yes.'

*No.*

'Are people always like that?' he asked, gesturing towards the bar they had just left.

'Oh, well. It's fine, really. Sometimes people just get . . .' The excuses Allegra normally made for other people faded away. 'Yes. Yes, they are. It's why I wanted a normal summer. There's only work and waiting for work in my life. I needed some freedom.'

She pressed herself against the outer brick wall of the bar. Even with her eyes closed, she could feel Jonah examining her.

'I couldn't do what you do.'

He said it harshly but Allegra was not offended. 'Okay.'

'Sorry,' he added. 'It just doesn't seem an easy way to live. But nothing is if you're . . . well. That doesn't matter.'

'What?' She opened her eyes and looked across at him.

He opened his mouth and then closed it again.

'What?' she pressed.

'Well.' He shrugged one shoulder and kicked a piece of glass on the ground with the toe of his boot. 'I'm autistic, so nothing is really built for people like me. But your world sounds particularly uninhabitable.'

For a moment, everything went away. 'What did you say? You're autistic?'

He glanced at her. 'Well, yeah. Did the sorting system at the shop not give it away?'

'I . . .' Allegra felt her voice dry up as she stared at him. 'I'm . . .'

'Please don't say you're sorry.'

'I would never,' she blurted out. *I'm like you. You're like me.*

'Anyway, I'm only saying it because I'm guessing you're feeling pretty vulnerable right now and it's apparently good to share with people in situations like this, so they feel less exposed. At least that's what my terrible ex-therapist used to say.'

Allegra laughed. A light, happy sound.

'Mind you,' Jonah added, oblivious to her inner sandstorm of emotion, 'the arts is probably a great place for a fellow autistic to hide. Lots of opportunities for escaping into imagined circumstances, characters, and stuff.'

'You think so?' Allegra said breathlessly. She shook her hands, drawing Jonah's eyes to them.

He studied her for another long moment before concern started to edge into his face. 'You sure you're all right?'

Allegra had a thousand answers to that question but she settled for the safest. 'I'm fine. Thanks again.'

There was silence between them for a moment before Allegra asked, 'Do you know any other neurodivergent people in Lake Pristine?'

'Hera, who runs the arcade? She's ADHD. But we're definitely part of a small pool.'

'Hera,' Allegra said with a smile in her voice. 'Such a great name.'

Jonah nodded. 'You like Greek mythology?'

'Dude. Of course. I'd say I was even low-key obsessed when I was fifteen. There were whispers about a full-blown adaptation of *The Odyssey* and I made a real nuisance of myself trying to get a meeting.'

Jonah laughed. 'Did it get made?'

'Nope. Greek mythology is so hard to get right on screen.'

'Yeah, I've noticed that.'

'What about you?' she asked him, as they walked side by side and at a slower pace along the backstreet behind the bar. 'Did you have a shrine to Persephone in the corner of your room or were you normal?'

He laughed once more. 'I definitely hyper fixated when I was younger.'

'Which story?'

'Well, all of them. I found this massive book in Brooks Books when I was twelve. Greek myths for teens. Great illustrations. The minotaur, Medusa, *The Iliad*. But . . .'

Allegra didn't push him. They both remained invisible to the rest of the world as they walked the hidden streets behind the main, bustling town.

'I loved Hephaestus.'

His words surprised her and so she glanced at him. 'Really? The blacksmith?'

'Well, yeah,' he shrugged, looking a little defensive. 'He— Well. He was the only god with a disability.'

Allegra's eyes widened in understanding and she felt a sudden piercing stab of vulnerability. 'Yes.'

'And he crafted the most amazing things for the Olympians,' Jonah added. 'Even though they cast him out. He made beautiful items they couldn't go without. Shoes with wings. I always liked that. The idea that, even though the people around you want to exclude you for what you are, you can be better. You can rise above. You can do things they can't do for themselves.'

Allegra suddenly felt short of breath. 'I think we should go back inside.'

A wave of guilt followed her as they both silently went back into the bar, Jonah radiating disappointment at the slight rejection.

But she needed the banality of the group. The bland normality of casual conversation and drinking games.

Everything she had just seen in Jonah was far too overwhelming. It raised questions she did not want to answer. It offered an alternative to a comfortable assumption and she didn't want to look directly at it any longer.

# Chapter Thirteen

Jonah opened Brooks Books the following day and took advantage of his solitude to check the email.

**westendgirl@gmail.com**
**to: shopfloor@BrooksBooks.com**
**RE: Not Myself**
Dear Friend and hopefully not so sad bookseller,
I totally know what you mean! I often find myself looking down, or back, at my own behaviour and wonder why I sometimes have this massive break of communication between what my brain wants to express and what actually ends up coming out. I wish people could hear and see intentions, as well as actions. I'm sure you are lovely. I know you are, because of these emails. You're being too hard on yourself.
I'm also sure the festival will be fine. I would like to meet you there. Maybe near the end of the run? That way, it won't ruin the whole experience for you if you think I'm not worth all of these emails we've been sending. I've been loving your pictures of the town; I can't wait to see it.
Feel better soon.
Friend.

Jonah felt a tightness in his chest as he read the objectively kind email. He hurriedly googled the address, hoping it might lead to a social media account or anything he could use to identify this joyous person who brought him relief during a troublesome summer. Nothing turned up so he began to draft another response.

**shopfloor@BrooksBooks.com**
**to: westendgirl@gmail.com**
**Subject: Who Are You?**

Dear Friend,

Your email pulled me out of a bit of a shame spiral. Even though you don't know who I am, and I don't know you, thank you for making me feel a bit human again. I've made so many stupid errors lately, I've not been my best self, and this was something I really needed.

Who are you? Are you an eighty-five-year-old lady who emailed the shop one day? Are you my age? Are you as great as you seem over email? As kind? I know we're both really enjoying this anonymity thing but I'd love to put a name to my friend. Who, right now, feels like the only friend I have left.

God, that sounds pathetic. I'm not actually that sad. Please let's meet. The festival is so soon, I could never be disappointed in you. There's always a party to celebrate the programme launch. It's next Friday. Pete's Cafe in Lake Pristine is very pretty. We could grab a drink there at seven and then head to the launch?

No pressure. Seriously. And if I'm too intense, that's fine. Ignore me. But don't stop writing. Your emails are the one thing I have to look forward to these days. Wish you were here.
Bookseller.

He sent it before he could start to doubt himself and as it swept from the outbox into the sent folder, Simon flew through the door.

'I'm doing the boring computer stuff this morning,' Jonah told him quickly. 'Can you do the click-and-collects?'

'Ah, yes, my favourite,' Simon said loftily. 'Trying to find that one copy of *Mrs Dalloway* that the online system is adamant we have, yet I can't find anywhere.'

Jonah ignored him, printing off the orders and handing them unceremoniously to Simon.

A reply pinged into his secret folder and his heart stopped for a moment.

**westendgirl@gmail.com**
**to: shopfloor@BrooksBooks.com**
**RE: Who Are You?**
Okay! Yes! I'll see you there on Friday. Seven? Can you put a flower in a book so I recognize you? Just kidding.
This is scary and exciting. Promise you won't be disappointed or mad?
Yours,
Friend.

Jonah was typing furiously, enough to make Simon look over at him.

**shopfloor@BrooksBooks.com**
**to: westendgirl@gmail.com**
**RE: Who Are You?**
I'll have a copy of *Middlemarch* by George Eliot. I know *Anna Karenina* or *Pride and Prejudice* would be more romantic, but you can't miss *Middlemarch*, especially with a flower inside of it. I'm actually not kidding.
Seven it is.
Bookseller.
PS Still wish you were here. But soon, you will be! I don't have a picture of it, but today's book cameo is *My Story* by Marilyn Monroe and you can picture it sitting on the cluttered shop desk with me. Maybe I should read it myself, so I can learn more about the glamorous arrival we have staying in town with us.

He dashed off the email and fled from the computer, as if it were hot to the touch. He raced to the little festival corner they had set up and he began to organize the books of the mostly confirmed authors. The Monroe memoir remained on the counter but he would reshelve it later, he told himself as he focused on the selection before him.

Quentin Morrison's books were notably absent. He had dropped out in an enormous huff and was apparently deriding the festival in one of the newspapers.

Simon moved to the computer, muttering about a missing book that he needed to find for a customer. He picked up the Marilyn Monroe book and turned it over to read the blurb. As he did so, the door to the upstairs flat burst open and Allegra appeared. Her hair was down, her face wore no make-up and yet she looked fresh and bright. A mixture of emotion crossed her face when she seemed to spot Simon at the computer, the book in his hand, and she gave the smallest smile.

'You can have a longer lie-in,' Simon teased. 'Meeting isn't until eleven.'

'I'm off to explore the town a bit more,' Allegra said breezily, peering towards the computer screen. Her eyes still appeared agitated and locked onto the book once more. 'Nice choice.'

'Thanks,' Simon said, putting the uncompleted autobiography of the Hollywood icon back down on the desk. 'Maybe I can learn a bit about you from it.'

Jonah sighed, slightly perturbed to have made the same comment in his email. For some strange reason, he wanted to grab her attention. He wanted her to acknowledge that he was also in the room.

'Have you seen the market?' he asked her.

Her head turned and she nodded at him. 'Yes.'

'The square?'

'Yes.'

'The dance studio?'

'Yes.'

'The actual lake?'

'Yes!'

'The Arthouse? The church? Main Street?'

'Yes, Jonah.'

'Then you've seen all of Lake Pristine.'

He expected Allegra to roll her eyes at him but she gave him a smirk and then headed for the exit.

'Thanks, Jonah. But I'm off to see how the festival site is coming along.'

Jonah watched the cogs turn in Simon's head and, for reasons he didn't fully want to examine, he said, 'I'll come with you. I need to check in with the board about volunteers.'

Allegra didn't object.

'I'll just stay here all by myself then!' Simon called after them.

The whole town was baking beneath the sun, which to Jonah felt oppressive and too intense. The early heatwave meant that townsfolk were walking around with sunburns. The air conditioning had broken in the post office, which had resulted in two mailmen fighting over a parking space. Everyone was either dashing to the water, pouring into the venues that served ice or growing crabby from the scorching heat.

Jonah glanced at Allegra. She had put on her oversized sunglasses. In her white lace dress and gold locket, she looked every bit the movie star.

'Are you wearing SPF?'

'Huh?' he said, dragging his gaze from her hands and waist and hair to her face. 'Sorry.'

'Are you wearing sunscreen? It's way too hot today. The sun's bearing down.'

'No.'

She opened the canvas tote bag that was neatly hanging from her elbow and took out a small white bottle of designer SPF. She opened it and put some on the back of her hand before tapping the cream with her fingertips.

'May I?'

He realized that she was asking his permission to protect him from the sun. 'Uh-huh.'

She gently massaged the small dollops of white cream into his face and jawline. He felt every molecule react to the touch. He noticed that she smelled of lemons.

His family and teachers had always lovingly teased him about his more emotional side. While he was prone to stoicism and terse responses, his demeanour had been occasionally shattered by the odd pretty face and the adults around him had always found it extremely amusing.

'Thanks,' was all he managed to say to Allegra. He avoided eye contact and held his breath, turning himself to hardened stone in the hope that it would conceal all of his blatant awareness of her.

'ALLEGRA BROOKS!'

A voice shattered the moment, and Jonah watched Allegra's face as she looked towards the intrusive sound.

Saffron, who worked in the newly opened Lake Pristine salon, was sprinting towards them with her phone already primed for taking a picture.

'You're the talk of the whole town,' she gushed, on reaching them. 'I didn't believe my sister when she said you were here for the summer.'

'Hello,' Allegra said, in a serene and unflustered tone that did not for a moment convey the strangeness of this stranger's presumed intimacy and familiarity. 'Nice to meet you.'

It was a jarring scene for Jonah to watch. Saffron had greeted

Allegra like they were old friends, or at least acquaintances. Allegra was warm and polite, but Jonah was waiting for her to address the truth of the situation.

Saffron did not know Allegra.

Social rules mattered to Jonah, as an autistic. Not because they made sense or felt natural to him, but because he had been punished so severely for breaking them, as a younger neurodivergent person.

He watched Allegra hold herself like a canvas, awaiting the colourful paint of another person's expectations and wants.

He hated it.

Saffron was taking pictures with Allegra without asking. Allegra smiled into the young woman's lens, but Jonah knew her well enough now to see that it was forced.

It was the kind of expression he had forced out of himself when the school picture photographer yelled, 'Smile'. It was a plea as much as it was a surrender.

A quiet, unconfident question knocked on the door of his mind. It was a question that examined Allegra's pleasing nature. The way she sometimes shook her hands in rapid motion when she thought no one could see. The way she was so particular about the texture of her food, the way she would sometimes repeat other people's words as she formulated a response, the way she seemed to glance away when she was speaking only to look intently into someone's eyes when they were replying and she was the listener.

Jonah watched her beautiful smile, forced though it was, and wondered.

When Saffron finally returned to the salon, Jonah watched as all of her colleagues moved away from the window. Presumably they had taken surreptitious pictures of their own. It was horrid to

Jonah, that creeping feeling of being perceived.

He was about to say as much to Allegra when her phone rang with imprudent urgency.

'Sorry,' she said quietly, as she checked the caller ID. 'Publicist.'

It was such a funny word to Jonah, so out of his normal vocabulary. He watched her answer the call.

'Hey, Nat. Everything okay? I'm not on emails.'

Jonah could hear the other woman's voice easily from the other end of the line. The publicist laughed as she spoke, but it was a hollow, stressed sound. 'Yeah, I know. Been trying to reach you.'

'Sorry,' Allegra said instantaneously. 'What's up?'

'I've forwarded you a big, long email about the screening. I've put an updated itinerary in as well.'

'Yes, about that,' Allegra said. 'I've invited a few Lake Pristine friends to come along. Can we add them to the guest list?'

There was a pause on the end of the call and while Jonah was not an expert at predicting human behaviour, he could still feel the surprise through the phone. 'How many people, lovely?'

'Lovely' was said with a sense of exhaustion.

'Um,' Allegra glanced at Jonah, clearly realizing in that moment that he could hear everything that was being said. 'Five, including me?'

She said it as if she was asking a question. She even looked to Jonah for non-verbal confirmation. He waved one hand frantically, freeing her from any invitation issued out of obligation. Simon's gloating and Grace's gushing had alerted him that a trip to the big city was planned.

'Names?' the publicist asked, with a slightly put-on sigh.

'Grace Lancaster, Kerrie . . .'

She looked quickly to Jonah, silently begging for his schoolfriend's surname.

'Rodriguez.'

'Kerrie Rodriguez. Simon Hannigan and Jonah Thorne.'

Jonah's head shot up in astonishment and he stared at her. He mouthed words of discouragement at her, trying to wordlessly communicate his total acceptance of not being invited.

However, Allegra stared back adamantly. 'Yeah, those four plus me.'

He could hear the publicist reciting back the names and then Allegra confirmed them. When the phone call was over, she set off walking once more, as though nothing had happened.

'You don't have to invite me,' he finally managed to say. 'I know we don't exactly get on very well.'

'Five is a good number,' she said matter-of-factly. 'And it'll be nice to have an entourage at one of these things for once.'

When Jonah did not know how to respond, she turned to him and quietly added, 'You genuinely don't have to come if you don't want to, though. Loads of people RSVP and then don't show. It's a screening, not a wedding. But if you want to tag along, your name's on the list.'

The open invitation was an olive branch that made him bristle and feel ashamed. He had been a nightmare to her, which had provoked her into becoming one in return. They had locked horns ever since she'd arrived in Lake Pristine.

Jonah had just assumed that she hated him.

Now he wondered if Allegra was capable of hating anyone. She was always making things easier for other people. She handled social hiccups with a deftness he had never seen before. She remembered everyone. Her patience for Simon and his overtly inappropriate overtures seemed to be a deep well of generosity.

She was not only defying his expectations.

She was starting to seriously unnerve him.

Later that day, Jonah distracted himself with tasks.

He had been charged with putting up some new shelves in the small travel section of Brooks Books. It was a task he had been putting off for an age and now that Simon, Allegra and the rest of his old schoolmates in Lake Pristine were making merry together on the town bandstand, he felt like getting it done. In peace.

He assembled his screws, the shelves, the supports and the old toolbox that George kept in his messy office. The shop was closed and quiet, everyone in Lake Pristine enjoying the summer breeze and the evening lights that looked like pale blue fireflies.

He hummed along to his playlist as he worked.

'Great song! I love Tom Waits.'

He swore at the new arrival's words and almost dropped his little pile of screws.

'Sorry,' Allegra said sheepishly. 'World of your own.'

'Yes, well,' Jonah grunted, returning to his work. 'Comes with the gig.'

He felt Allegra sit down next to him as he assembled the wood for the shelves. 'Need any help?'

It had only been a few hours since her polite invitation to the film premiere. Jonah had busied himself with stock and pre-orders and festival planning, while Allegra and Simon had laughed with one another. He had tried to suppress the unnameable feelings brought up by their flirting. It was like a terrible, emotional, jealous acid reflux.

He shook the word 'jealousy' out of his mind, knowing he had no right to it.

Yet, 'Why aren't you with Simon?' he asked. He couldn't help it.

'We're all having a nice time out by the bandstand, but I noticed you weren't with us,' she replied.

He scoffed. So, they had all been having a jolly time and, after one too many jokes, they had finally deigned to notice that he was still working. He hated how disposable he felt.

'Promised George I would do this months ago,' he said gruffly.

'Well, do you want me to bring you something to eat? We have burgers.'

'No,' he said, a little more sharply than he had intended.

He heard, and somehow felt, her sigh. 'Jonah. I'm trying here. I've really been trying. I know we had a rough start, you shouldn't have said what you said when we met, and I should have forgiven you for it. But can't we be friends?'

*No*, thought Jonah sadly. They couldn't be friends because he still thought about her fingertips on his face. He questioned why it had been so easy to tell her about his neurodivergence. He thought about her more than he thought about anyone. He was petrified about falling into some strange kind of limerence, where he would never be free of her.

The only difference between such limerence and love was uncertainty. While true love was supposed to be mutual, a bridge between two people, limerence was standing on the bank of the river, wondering if you would survive the deep water and the strong currents.

Jonah didn't know how the word 'love' had crept into his

tormented thoughts, just as 'jealousy' had, but he shoved it away, too. He thought about his email friend. The one who actually wanted to see him. The one who didn't make his blood roar in his ears or his heart rate accelerate. The one who was just as smart as Allegra and just as interesting.

'Sure,' was all he said when he realized Allegra was still waiting for a response. 'We can be friends.'

Even he could hear how icy he sounded, but it made Allegra laugh. A few minutes later, she was offering him a burger wrapped in tinfoil. He stared at it, her outstretched hand an offer of a truce.

He took the burger.

They sat in silence for a moment, while he worked on the shelves and took breaks to chew.

'Why did you think I was going to be stuck-up?'

She asked him the question without reproach but he felt shame at the memory of their first meeting. 'I don't know.'

He glanced at her and was surprised to see apprehension in her eyes.

'Did my dad say that I am?'

'God, no,' Jonah said, and he was so desperate to relieve her of her anxiety, he accidentally blurted out the truth. 'I googled you and – you were so beautiful, I got flustered and had to tell myself you weren't very nice to people in order to get control of myself again.'

She was clearly stunned at this revelation, as was Jonah. He didn't add that he had since learned how deep that beauty went. He was amazed by her memory, her varied reading tastes and her quick wit. He was astonished by her composure when confronted with boorish, bullish people with no understanding of boundaries.

'It wasn't from George,' he added. 'He was so thrilled you were coming.'

Allegra regarded her fellow bookseller as he worked away at his task. She had noticed how handy he was around her father's shop. While he and Simon had worked there in chorus, their employment time almost identical, Jonah was the one who knew everything. He fixed things. He found things. He knew every contact. He called Mary and Nick, the part-time booksellers, when George forgot. He took the deliveries. He checked the stock and the orders. He spoke to the wholesalers.

He was indispensable.

So she had often wondered about him. When the two of them fought, when it got messy, she wondered why no one defended him. Perhaps it was because he almost always started it. They would bicker and bite at each other and everyone watched as though they were hired entertainment. It made her feel like she was playing a part in some film, only she couldn't walk off set and leave it behind. When Jonah would storm off, no one followed. She wondered why a loyal employee, one who was integral to the business, was treated so coldly by her father. Especially when Jonah showed the man such loyalty.

'Do you like living in such a small town?' she asked him.

She watched him visibly consider the question, while he worked. He smelled incredible. He always did. Allegra was so used to adolescent men smelling of unwashed odour, it was something poor make-up artists often whispered to the third ADs about on set. Wardrobe, too. They would quietly beg the thirds to have a word with the actor, perhaps suggesting that the scene would be more comfortable for everyone to shoot if he were showered.

Jonah always smelled of a delicious cologne with undertones of soap, applied generously all over. His clothes were always fresh. She had seen him, during her second week in town, carrying large bags over to the launderette. He was, according to Simon, fastidious about cleanliness. He had criticized some of her dusting once. That had turned into the argument of all arguments, partly because Allegra was embarrassed to have been found wanting.

Now, as he worked with a hammer and screws and wood, there was the slightest sheen on his face. His shirt had ridden up slightly as he lay on the ground to fix the bottom shelf with supports. They were very close and she couldn't quite bring herself to examine what she was feeling. She didn't want to wonder why she was staying there, when she should be out having a perfectly nice time with Simon.

She shouldn't be here with the sullen one.

'I like it fine,' he said, answering her question while oblivious to her thoughts. 'It's a bit much, at this time of year. Population triples and all that. And people always know your business. But it's nice enough.'

'Don't answer if it's too personal,' she said quietly, 'but isn't it hard? Being autistic in a small town?'

His eyes lifted to hers for a moment while he pondered the question, and possibly her intentions. 'Yeah. Can be. But I don't know any different. I've always lived here.'

'Was school horrible?' It had been for her. In fact, it had been unbearable. Leaving for a film set, with homework in her trailer, had been so much better.

'Yes.'

There were a thousand stories in the one word he uttered. Allegra almost didn't need to know more. She could imagine. Or rather, she could remember.

'You said autistic.'

She frowned at him. 'Yes. Is that—'

'Most people say "with autism". I hate it. Makes it sound like I have a little hamster in my pocket called Autism.'

Allegra laughed at that. 'Autistic is much better. Sounds more . . . whole.'

'Exactly.'

They smiled at each other for a moment before Allegra looked away.

'Don't waste a nice summer evening in here with me,' Jonah said. 'I'm doing the boring stuff. Too hot out there, anyhow. For me, that is. Don't let the cold air out when you leave.'

Allegra wanted to say that it was too hot for her, too. She wondered if he would believe her. She wanted to tell him her secret. She flinched at the fluorescent lights, just as he did. They both asked people to explain things when they were choosing vagueness and politeness over direct communication. They both winced when the shrill landline rang. They stimmed. They took their breaks in isolation, to decompress from the overstimulation and the masking.

*Look at me*, she wanted to say. *We're so similar. Maybe that's why we have such friction. We're two stones scraping together and the sparks come off because we're just the same.*

She said nothing, though. She was meeting Simon. Their email relationship was about to come off the page.

# Chapter Fourteen

**shopfloor@BrooksBooks.com**
**to: westendgirl@gmail.com**
**Subject: Wish You Were Here!**
Dear Friend,
Today's book is *Middlemarch*, as promised. Here's a picture of it outside Pete's Cafe. I can't wait to see you. Sorry if I've been distant of late. Some strange things have been going on and I need to get over something. Nothing major, something small. Totally manageable. I'm trying not to dress-rehearse horrible scenarios in my head where you take one look at me and run away from Lake Pristine for ever.
Wish you were here as I need my brain to stop catastrophizing.
Your friend.

Allegra had one mirror in the small spare bedroom of her father's bookshop apartment and it was on the inside of the wardrobe door. She had spent longer than normal trying to find the right thing to wear. She loved fashion and dressing up, but this was the first time in years without a stylist on the other end of a text chain to approve and co-sign the ensemble. She had complete freedom of choice for once.

The silver lamé dress was a little revealing and perhaps too dressy for the launch of a small-town book festival, but Allegra was hoping that the date beforehand with Simon would ignite in person what was so natural and becoming over email. She hoped that he would apologize for his priggishness and attribute it to nerves or posturing.

Allegra wanted to be in love. She had read once that falling in love only happened when a person was ready for change in their life. She had fallen a handful of times and had realized, after bracing for impact and feeling the ground, that she had fallen alone. She had pulled herself up alone. She had waited out the fever of it all alone.

As an actor, she had watched others while they lived their lives. Halloween parties, school trips and wild weekends with their friends. She had known call sheets, early commutes to set with strange men driving black sedans and no one around her but adults who were telling her which plastic surgeries she should undergo in order to 'get ahead of the inevitable'.

She knew she was fortunate. She knew luck had touched her in a way that most people would never know.

But sometimes she just hungered. She watched her peers and she thirsted for a warm group chat and inside jokes. For joint eighteenth birthday parties and 'did you get home safe?' texts. She was watched from the moment she left her apartment for set until the second her bedroom light went off. The security detail were always quiet and quick; they didn't need to exchange words with her. Getting rid of them for quiet time in Lake Pristine had taken a great deal of persuasion but it had been worth it.

She appreciated their work but they inevitably always made her feel like a commodity that they moved swiftly and silently from mark to mark. It had been miraculous, escaping to Lake Pristine and shedding all of the control.

When the camera began to roll, she was allowed to come alive. She was allowed to live in the lives of people whose skin she could climb inside. Those moments of electricity were what kept her heart beating through the whole ordeal of it. The in-between moments, the constant shuffling and promoting and waiting, they were bearable because making the art was so wonderfully cosmic.

But she wanted some spontaneity. She wanted to taste the food on the table of life that the industry had promised was bad for her. She wanted to take a bite and hear their gasps of disbelief and horror.

Flavours became so mild when you were always tasting someone else's food for them.

She wanted a feast of her own.

She slid on the Manolos she had purchased with her first TV pay cheque and descended the stairs from the apartment to the bookshop beneath. The lights in the shop were switched off for the evening, everyone in town for the festival launch party. Only the computer was awake. Allegra opened up the inbox and checked the sent folder, smiling when she eventually found the latest from Simon.

*Wish you were here.*

She wondered if the spark from their emails would come to life when he finally realized that she always had been.

'God, Jonah, you look nice.'

Jonah swallowed and thanked Alice, as she showed him to

his empty table in the cafe she ran with her husband, Pete. It was abuzz with people, only a few other tables were empty. The whole room was adorned with flowers from the summer solstice and the chandelier brought occasion and pomp to the otherwise cosy cafe.

Jonah was wearing a black suit with the white opera scarf he had begged his mother for five Hanukkahs ago. He placed *Middlemarch* on the table and slid a rose between the pages.

His nerves were overpowering but the hope was even worse.

School had been tough. Jonah always asked why things were the way they were, and it had never gone down well with the teachers. If it hadn't been for Simon, he would have been a social pariah because he was always saying the wrong thing. His intentions were never bad, but his delivery could never assure people of that.

The bookshop had allowed him room to breathe but also to become even more tetchy, even more isolated.

Then came her emails.

In some careless, frivolous way, someone was actually amused by him. Intrigued enough to keep talking, despite the social niceties having been adhered to and the obligation no longer necessary.

Perhaps he hadn't told anyone about it because it would seem pathetic. He was so lonely that a stranger sending emails had become a lifeline for him.

'Who are you so dressed up for, son?' Pete asked the question as he brought a water jug to the table, as well as some menus.

'Kind of like a date,' Jonah admitted.

Pete's eyes widened and then his entire face broke into a beaming smile. Jonah instantly tensed.

'Alice!' called Pete, his voice frantic with excitement. His wife walked over to Jonah's table, expectantly. 'You were right. He's meeting someone!'

Jonah cringed. This was what George Brooks liked to call the Lake Pristine Tax. Your business was never your own, everybody took an interest in your life as though it was a long-running television show.

'I've always said you're the most handsome young man in town. You should be out every Friday night!' Alice said and while the words were complimentary, they were accompanied by a pat on the cheek that spoke to her almost familial bias.

'Thanks,' Jonah said, coughing on the water he was trying to sip from.

'So, what's their name?' The question came from Pete.

Jonah thought very hard about whether he should just lie. 'I don't know.' But he had always been terrible at anything other than the pure truth.

'You don't know?' Alice blinked down at him. 'Is it . . . some kind of internet thing?'

Pete and Alice still refused to have Wi-Fi in the cafe so the suspicion in her voice as she asked him the question was unsurprising, and it made Jonah smile.

'Kind of. Got talking via email. Tonight's our first meeting. She's from out of town.'

'Oh, that's actually quite romantic!' Alice said, her whole attitude transforming in an instant. 'Like lonely hearts!'

'Well,' Jonah bristled slightly at that description. 'I'm not sure—'

'I'm going to get you a candle for the table,' Pete interjected. 'And, Alice, dim the lights a little more. Set the mood!'

Jonah grimaced as they fussed, suddenly feeling a stabbing pressure for the whole thing to go well. He wondered if he would have to apologize to his email girl for the antics of the Lake Pristine elders.

'Good luck, darling,' Alice whispered as she finally returned to the counter. 'You look wonderful, it will be great. I bet she'll be beautiful!'

A flash of someone else coursed through Jonah's mind at Alice's words but he quickly slammed that lid shut. He couldn't think about her. She was from a different story, one that had no room on the call sheet for someone like him.

She was too special. Too much of everything.

He just needed someone nice and normal.

'I just hope she likes me,' Jonah said quietly, more to himself than to anyone else.

Under all of the blunders, the faux pas, the unintended offences, there was one single, steadfast flame that never went out.

He wanted someone to like him. Someone special.

He could live with being an irritant to so many other people if he could just be a balm for one.

Lake Pristine looked like a dream as Allegra walked along Main Street. The summer sun was cooler and night was starting to gently cut in. There were flowers everywhere, roses, hydrangeas and marigolds wherever it was possible to hang them. The air was warm and the people all around her were untouched by worry. The festival site stood up ahead, fully mounted marquees ready to hold audiences of readers and authors from all over the world. People were already exploring the exterior of the site, looking with interest and asking volunteers about the programme.

Allegra spotted Grace leaving the ballet studio and the other girl's eyebrows shot into her dark hairline as she laid eyes on the actress.

'Allegra!'

Allegra smiled, feeling delighted and shy all at once. 'I have a date. This isn't all for the book festival.'

'With Simon?' Grace asked, filling in the story for herself and taking in Allegra's ensemble with unguarded wonder. 'He's going to pass out when he sees you.'

'I just hope . . .' Allegra glanced ahead at Pete's Cafe. 'I hope . . . we connect properly now. When he finds out it's been me, you know, writing to him.'

'Okay,' Grace said, 'maybe he's just making an ass of himself every now and again because he's so nervous around you. He obviously likes you. I mean, every guy for a hundred miles does.'

'Well, all but one,' Allegra said, but Grace didn't hear her.

'My brother used to make such a fool of himself around Jasper. Now they're the most in-love people you'll ever meet.'

'You're being nice,' Allegra said gently. 'I know you don't think that highly of Simon.'

'I think neutrally of Simon,' Grace corrected. 'But I think highly of you. And if you think you're getting something else from his emails, then he deserves a chance to prove that to you.'

'I think . . .' Allegra looked up at the sky which was like a mess of paint colours all spilled across a dark table. 'I was someone who struggled for so long with expressing how I really felt. With showing people who I really was. It's why acting felt so freeing. But I don't want to struggle any more. I want people to have good faith and patience and see the best in me, even if I say the wrong thing. So, I need to extend that to him.'

Grace regarded Allegra. Allegra could feel the chasm that fame created between two people. Grace could only offer advice from her own lived experience. One that was so different from Allegra's.

'I hope it works out for you both,' was all Grace said, but it was enough to make Allegra smile.

'Thank you.'

'Want me to check that he's in there before you go in?'

'God, yes.'

Allegra hovered as Grace moved to the cafe window.

'We were supposed to meet at seven. I'm a little late,' she said, when Grace did not immediately confirm Simon's attendance.

When Grace's shoulders stiffened, Allegra knew something was wrong. She stared at her new friend's back, her eyes scanning and searching for any sign of an answer. But when Grace turned, her face was ashen.

'What is it?' Allegra breathed.

'Um.' Grace looked so sorry, it made Allegra want to panic. To flee.

'What?'

'It's . . .' Grace cast a glance back at the cafe and then stepped towards Allegra. 'It's definitely a bookseller in there. But it's not Simon.'

Allegra stared at the other girl before pushing ahead to the window and looking for herself. The cafe looked almost Parisian with its beautiful lighting and its calm, composed atmosphere. She spotted the book first, perched on the end of a small table for two in the middle of the main floor. A waitress was blocking her view of the book's owner. She spotted the rose, crushed gently between the pages of *Middlemarch*, exactly as promised. She stared at the spine of the large book and tried to control her breathing.

When the waitress moved away, the owner of the book, the person dressed in a black suit with combed hair, was not the person she had anticipated. It was the person who had always been in her periphery, an unwelcome thought, a 'what if' every time she had told herself that it *had* to be Simon.

Her eyes took in the scene with a tight breath and a deep feeling of shock.

Jonah Thorne.

# Chapter Fifteen

'Are you just going to leave him there?' Grace asked softly, as Allegra backed away from Pete's Cafe and set off towards the book festival site, now built up and put together in the middle of town. Multiple great white tents, just waiting for everything to begin.

'Yeah,' Allegra said sullenly. 'I am.'

But she stopped. She hesitated. If she left for the festival site, she would be standing him up. He wouldn't know it was her, but it was still unkind. A little cowardly.

Jonah Thorne, she thought bitterly. It had to have been Jonah Thorne.

'Confirmation bias,' she said, her words barely audible; a sad admission from a girl in a town that did not have room for movie stars. 'I just assumed it was Simon . . .'

A million little coincidences. The shared language, the jovial tone, the same books from the pictures. Allegra had had the narrative so ready to go in her own head, she hadn't looked properly at other factors.

Other booksellers.

'Go in and see if you can both find the funny side,' Grace suggested.

Allegra stimmed and stumbled, caught between two places and unable to find even a drop of humour in anything.

'I'm so stupid,' was all she could conjure up. 'So, so stupid.'

The stupid girl, who had watched as national newspapers printed a countdown clock to her eighteenth birthday, who had wanted to come to a small town and fall in love.

'Stupid,' she repeated.

She began to walk away once more, her heels clacking against the cobblestones. She heard Grace make a noise of disbelief.

'You can't leave him alone in there, Allegra.'

'I can, Grace,' Allegra said without looking back. 'He can sit there all night for all I care.'

'Allegra!'

She stopped at that, shocked by Grace's sharp and forceful tone. 'What?'

Grace was staring her down with steely disapproval. 'Jonah Thorne is like his name. Prickly and spiky. But he's a good guy. He's my friend, even. You are, too. But you're not going to leave him there, wondering and worrying about you. Go inside. Explain.'

Allegra's eyes drifted back to the cafe and she felt a flood of fear and humiliation. 'I can't, Grace. I can't go in there and face him.'

She had auditioned for some of the most terrifying directors in the business but this was something else completely.

'Yes, you can,' Grace said firmly. 'What are you even upset about? Really? You love those emails but you were lacklustre about Simon. No, you were! Come on, be honest. The only thing he had going for him in your eyes was the possibility of being this mystery pen-pal.'

'Well, it's not him,' Allegra said. 'It's not Simon. It's the guy who said I looked like a snob and who has barely said a nice word to me since.'

Even as she said it she knew it wasn't the whole truth, but she was feeling tripped up and scared.

'Because you're not at all intimidating?'

'Grace, stop.'

'No, you stop. You're not in your big, fancy city now. This is Lake Pristine. And we don't ghost people here. It's too small. So be a big girl and get inside.'

A smile flickered on Allegra's lips as she regarded her friend. 'You know, no one speaks to me like this.'

'Well,' Grace shrugged unapologetically. 'Maybe they should. Friends tell their friends when they're being dicks.'

Allegra's small smile wobbled. 'Grace.'

'I know, babe,' Grace said, her voice almost sisterly in its softness. 'It's okay, you're okay.'

'Why does it have to be him?' she asked the universe as much as she did her new friend. 'Him! The guy who yelled at me over movie tie-in covers!'

'Just give him a chance,' Grace said.

Allegra shook her head, too shaken by the prospect. They had argued too often, snarled at each other one too many times. He thought she was a joke. One or two nice moments did not erase the many that had made her humbly aware of what he really thought of her. She didn't care if her mind had occasionally replayed those nice moments before going to sleep. She didn't want to think about the pang of relief she felt that her pen-pal was not Simon. She couldn't focus on any of that. She needed to escape.

But she turned and dashed to the cafe entrance.

'Good girl,' Grace called.

As Allegra stepped inside, the smell of burning candles welcomed her. The lights were dim and the chatter was muted. It was a perfect meeting point for two autistics. She just wished they had each known about the other.

She approached Jonah as if in a trance, and when he looked up, her own panic was suddenly evident on his face. He stared at her, his eyes raking up and down her body, as though seeing her for the very first time.

'Allegra?'

And Allegra Brooks, having learned to hide so well, was unable to give up this little piece of herself. It was just too hard. Vulnerability is the chip one has to play into the game if one wants the cards to come out right, but Allegra held her chips close and refused to bet.

She had disguised herself so well within the emails: some girl from out of town with a job in social media. She had been careful to cover her tracks.

She acted quickly.

'Are you here to meet some girl?' The words sounded ugly. She wished them undone as soon as they were said.

Jonah stared up at her. 'Yes.'

'Well,' Allegra was good at improvising. Actors had to be. 'We just got a call at the bookshop. Sounded like a young woman. Said she was meeting one of the booksellers at Pete's Cafe. Or she was supposed to. She got stuck, out of town. Something to do with her job and a client. Asked me to apologize on her behalf, but she has to reschedule.'

She expected to see relief in Jonah's face, she knew she was the last person he would want as his mystery girl, but he gave nothing away.

'Are you who she meant?' Allegra asked, her voice shaking but her gaze unblinking. 'Or is that message for Simon?'

A part of her wondered if she had still somehow got it wrong. She hoped against hope that he was here by some strange accident.

'No, it's for me.' He said it in his deep, hard-to-read voice and they stared at one another. Allegra couldn't even begin to identify her emotions.

She just knew it stung.

'So, you have an out-of-town girlfriend?'

He scowled. 'No. More like . . . a pen-pal.'

'You've never met each other?' She made her face look casual as they stared each other down.

'No.' Jonah looked on edge as he answered her rapid-fire questions. 'Tonight was . . . going to be the first time.'

'Why have you never mentioned her?'

It came out far more accusingly than she meant it to.

'Because we're just two people who have been emailing. Why would I mention it? It's not like you and I are friends, Allegra.'

Allegra knew this was the perfect moment to bow out, to wish him well and then head to the launch party without even an afterthought.

Instead, she sat down in the seat across from him.

Allegra looked like a goddess. A surprisingly angry one.

Jonah had been wondering what his mystery girl would sound like when the actress had walked through the cafe door. He had been too stunned by her appearance to be embarrassed by the fact that she had stumbled across his would-be date with a stranger. He was taking in her dress as she told him that his friend was unable to make it. Her long hair, the breeze of her perfume and the way the dress was cut. He had barely a moment to process what she was saying.

When she sat across from him, disorientation turned into familiar prickliness.

'You don't need to keep me company,' he snapped.

'Oh, I know,' she snapped back. 'I'm curious, though. How long have you been conversing with this . . . person?'

'A while,' he answered stonily. 'Not that it's your business.'

'So, that's why you and Simon are so possessive of that ancient computer. Exchanging romantic correspondence with anonymous strangers.'

'Simon can't draft our press releases, let alone love letters.'

'And yet he was the one I expected to find here.'

The words startled both of them.

'After receiving her message,' Allegra added quickly. 'She wasn't able to say which one of you the message was for. But I thought it would be Simon.'

He glared. 'You assumed it would be Simon?'

'Yes,' Allegra snapped defensively. 'He's . . . always by the computer.'

It was a weak justification and they both knew it.

'I don't know who she is,' Jonah admitted, his tone contemplative. He peered up at her. 'What was she like?'

Allegra blanched. 'Sorry?'

'What did she sound like? How did she seem?'

'I don't know,' she answered, avoiding his gaze. 'Normal, I guess. I wasn't really taking notes.'

He watched her sigh with a heaviness that surprised him. Frustrated with himself for being defensive and cantankerous, he extended an olive branch.

'I'm sorry for being short,' he said.

'You've been short all summer,' she fired back, symbolically snapping the branch. 'You've been rude and stand-offish and judgemental since the moment I came into Dad's shop. You sneer at what I read. You chase away my customers. You treat me like a stack of orders you can't be bothered to process and you roll your eyes when I speak.'

Jonah swallowed. He couldn't deny any of it. And the real reason for his frosty, flinty feelings stared at him with indignation, wondering why he wouldn't address them.

He wanted to apologize. However, the fear of vulnerability, the terror of being perceived . . . it was a terrible chaser to a cocktail of pride.

'Some of us aren't slumming it here for a summer, some of us care about the store all year round.'

The words were the perfect disguise.

He could keep his secrets. It just meant being an ass.

He regarded the disappointment on Allegra's face. There was nothing guarded about it; her dismay was etched into the atoms of her perfect features. She sat back in her chair and exhaled, taking him in.

'I suppose,' she finally spoke with resignation, 'I just thought that coldness was your nature. But whomever you've been emailing . . . they've been getting a kind person. Right? A funny person. Or they wouldn't want to come tonight.'

Jonah didn't say anything.

'So, you *can* be nice, I guess,' Allegra continued. 'Just not to me. You know, Simon once said you think of people as books. So, here.

To me, you're like the pretentious novels you love so much. Just a story that nobody wants to hear.'

The words landed like a spark on a line of powder and it ignited something in Jonah.

'Why did you come to this stupid little town?' he fired back. His voice was loud enough to cause a few bystanders to glance over at the two of them. 'In all the years George has lived here alone, you've never visited.'

'Don't talk about my dad to me.'

'Why now? Why a summer in Lake Pristine? You have everything. You're loved all over the world. People write *essays* about how in love with you they are. They sleep in the street to catch a glimpse of you at a premiere. You have more money than my whole family combined. What more could you possibly want? Why come here? Why do you have to conquer this small town when you have the whole world, Allegra?'

He blurted out the last word just as he realized his private thoughts had broken free and hit her like a defiant spit in the face. They stared at each other and he was horrified by the shimmer of moisture in her eyes.

'That's my cue to leave,' she finally said, her words a whisper. She rose to her feet with the posture of a dancer and the serenity of an empress. Jonah felt his insides clench.

'Allegra—'

'I don't see my father, or any of my family much, because I'm on back-to-back ninety-day shoots,' she told him calmly. 'Often in countries I don't live in. I don't have friends, just co-workers. My Christmas card list is my agent, my publicist, my estate agent, all of their assistants, my accountant and my managerial advisory board.'

She took a shaky breath and smiled sadly. 'A journalist wrote a horrible, snarky article about me and I felt tired. I needed to escape. To have a normal summer, like other eighteen-year-olds.'

She made to leave and then stopped.

'And you know something? One of those I-Love-Allegra-Brooks essay writers, as you call it? He broke into my apartment and held a knife to my throat.'

She said it so matter-of-factly that it made Jonah feel ill.

'I was sixteen. It didn't really feel like love, you know, a blade on your skin. I'll have to take your word for it. I don't really know what love is. Just what it feels like on the cinema screen. And in the romances you hate so much.'

She was already gone from the cafe before Jonah was able to process what had happened. He felt so ashamed. For someone who struggled with naming emotions, this one was so astutely easy to identify. Shame – and regret.

He wanted to chase after her, but she was already on the other side of Main Street, heading towards the large festival tent. The launch party was about to begin and, as the last of the light died, electricity and anticipation came alive in town as people flocked towards the first event of the Lake Pristine Book Festival.

Jonah felt as though he had been shoved from a moving train. He had been fantasizing and fixating on this meeting, hoping that the charming, loveable person on the other end of those emails would come and ease the ache in his chest – the one that had been growing and groaning since Allegra Brooks blew into town. He should be thinking about her, his friend, but he was consumed by the girl who had just stormed out.

Her words had wounded him. Maybe she was right and he was

a book nobody wanted to read. He floated through Lake Pristine, more tolerated than he was wanted.

It was painful for him to admit that witnessing a person with such explosive charisma made him only capable of small, ugly words. Such sweetness brought out bitterness; in a light so bright, you had to cower away and find respite in darkness.

He had to put a stop to it.

'What was that about, pal?'

The question came from Nick, one of their part-time booksellers. He was with his partner at the table by the window and they were looking at Jonah with concern.

'Nothing,' Jonah said, sounding less broken than he felt. 'Professional disagreement.'

'About the festival?'

'Sure.' He despised the Lake Pristine Tax. 'Something like that.'

'Don't let anything spoil your last year with the festival.'

'I won't – what?'

Jonah turned in his chair to look properly at Nick. The man looked surprised by the follow-up question, or perhaps by Jonah's slightly indignant tone.

'I just meant,' Nick scrambled for words, 'you'll be going to uni or to the city after the summer, won't you? Like Simon? Getting out of here.'

Jonah felt like someone had tied a piece of wire around his neck. People kept making comments like this to him. To his mother in the bakery as she worked. To him at the market. George, a few months after Christmas, had also mentioned it a lot. Jonah had finally grown tired of it and told the older man that he had no plans to leave town.

'I . . .' Jonah spoke around the invisible wire. 'I don't know what I would do. Or where I would go.'

'That's the fun of it, isn't it?' Nick said gently. 'Finding out?'

'Maybe,' Jonah said, staggering to his feet. 'Sorry, Nick, I have to go.'

He fled, leaving *Middlemarch* and the rose in his wake.

# Chapter Sixteen

Allegra stood among a crowd of volunteers, authors, book lovers and curious townspeople while her father made a welcome speech and she tried to smile through it. She had endeavoured to shed the shock of finding Jonah instead of Simon, hoping to leave it lying on the steps of the cafe like an old newspaper.

But it was all still with her.

She was soaked in feelings. So she did what her job had taught her: she beamed and clapped during all of the correct pauses and focused on other people.

All great actors made everything about their scene partners. They did not indicate or become consumed with their own performance. They fixed all of their attention on other people and reacted accordingly.

Strangely, she felt his arrival. She didn't look behind her, or even away from her father onstage, but she knew from the little fish swimming up and down her spine that he was in the tent. She was insanely aware of him.

'This year, we have a very special festival programme for you. But before we start celebrating the incredible authors we have visiting Lake Pristine this year –' George spoke warmly to the crowd, a warmth he seemed to reserve for strangers; for eccentric older gentlemen who wanted to buy travel books for cities they had no intention of visiting; for opinionated women who wanted to debate political non-fiction with him; for children picking out their first independent read; for young men browsing memoirs and hiding from novels written by women.

He had all the time in the world for books and the people who made or loved them.

'This summer is extremely special because my daughter, Allegra, is taking a break from being the biggest superstar on the planet to do some work experience with us.'

The room laughed and applauded and Allegra turned a little pink at the praise. She winced internally at the kind, if not hyperbolic, description. She was intensely aware of how many people were bigger stars than she. It was impossible to avoid such knowledge in her industry. The pecking order was not written down anywhere, but it was understood.

Nevertheless, she smiled at all of the faces that were staring at her. She tried to ignore the anxious clawing of common sense. Her father shouldn't be drawing attention to her presence in town, but it would break both of their hearts if she made him stop.

'Ally's mother and I are so proud of her and it means a lot to have her here, working with her old man, this summer.'

When some patrons of the festival began to make speeches, Allegra moved towards the other side of the tent. She could see Simon and Kerrie with some of the festival volunteers.

'Hey,' Simon greeted her with such open cheeriness, it made her all the more deflated over her pen-pal's unmasking. 'I haven't seen you all night.'

'Had to deliver a message to Jonah,' she said, seeing no reason to be dishonest. 'And it ended in our usual.'

'A massive argument?' Simon surmised.

'Yes.'

'Poor Jonah,' Kerrie said. Allegra sensed something mournful in the other girl's tone. 'He gets so muddled up. He means well.'

'Nah, Kerrie,' Simon said, picking up a paper plate from the catering table. He loaded it with meat cuts, grapes and cheese without asking if anyone else would like any. 'He's weird with Allegra. Different.'

'Well, she *is* a beautiful movie star,' Kerrie said, turning to beam at Allegra.

'Well, Beautiful Movie Star. There's an after-party to this rather dull launch party at my house in a bit, if you want to spend time with the rest of the under-fifties.'

Allegra smiled at Simon, in spite of herself. She found herself suddenly at ease with him, now that he was just the nice guy she worked with and not the architect behind the emails she would reread over and over again. 'Sounds good.'

As he stuffed food into his mouth, Kerrie leaned a little nearer to Allegra.

'Jonah really isn't a bad guy.'

'I know,' Allegra said, a touch defensive. 'We just don't . . . gel.'

'He's very guarded,' Kerrie said, with the authority of a person who had known Jonah for a long time. 'His dad left him and his mum for a whole second family when he was tiny. Just after he was diagnosed.' Allegra winced at this, feeling a shot of guilt burn her throat as she listened. 'He takes such good care of Viv, and he used to be a lot more fun. Your dad really relies on him! George is like a mentor to him.'

This piqued Allegra's interest, merely because her father always seemed a little distant and cold with Jonah. If they had shared a warm bond at some point, it wasn't there now.

'He also doesn't know or appreciate how hot he's become in the last few years,' Kerrie added, casting a furtive glance over to the subject of their quiet conversation. Allegra did not join her in looking but her heart pounded. '*And* he doesn't realize that the frostiness just makes him a bit more intimidating.'

Allegra smiled very softly. 'Got a crush?'

Kerrie's eyes flashed to Allegra's and the latter could see her considering whether to deny it or not. 'Yeah. A little bit.'

Ordinarily, Allegra would tell the other girl to 'go for it'. Yet in the festival tent, surrounded by so many people but with only one person on her mind, something made her stay silent.

The after-party at Simon's house left Jonah emptier than being stood up at Pete's Cafe. It was full of enthusiastic book festival volunteers, most of whom were people he had gone to school with, who had suddenly, out of the blue, the year that Allegra Brooks was in town, discovered an interest in literature.

'Jonah!' One of the volunteers called him over to a group who were gathered around the stereo. 'I need you as back-up.'

Kerrie was with the group, smiling at him with an unreadable question in her eyes. He gave her a tight nod and then turned to the boy who had hollered at him. 'What?'

'Tell Kerrie what you told me.'

'About what?'

'About romance books.'

Jonah paled. This loud conversation had caught the attention of Allegra and Grace, who were getting up from their spots on the couch. Allegra was watching him coyly.

'I can't remember what I said,' Jonah murmured, and it wasn't a lie. He could barely remember this volunteer, let alone what he might have blabbed about to them during their orientation.

'I'm guessing it wasn't very complimentary, knowing Jonah,' Kerrie said gregariously.

Jonah watched Allegra as she arched an eyebrow at that and whispered something to Grace. They began to leave the room.

'I'm coming around to them actually,' he said loudly. 'Think I was probably being a bit of a snob before, to be honest. Some books are about the journey, not the destination. Just because there's a contract between author and reader when it comes to certain genres, it doesn't mean there can't be invention. Or something really beautiful.'

He watched as Allegra's shoulders tensed and she stopped walking for a moment. He felt his breath catch, but the moment passed as quickly as it had come. She moved into the hallway with Grace, and didn't look back.

He felt his phone start to vibrate.

He excused himself gruffly and made his way to the kitchen, which was quieter than the *rumpus room*, a term only used by the obnoxiously rich of Lake Pristine. He answered his phone.

'Hey.'

'Hi, darling,' his mother's voice said from the other end of the line. 'You okay?'

'Fine,' he lied. 'At Simon's. You all right?'

'I'm at Auntie Shosh's, darling. I've had far too much wine, I can't drive myself home so I'm sleeping over. Will you be okay on your own tonight? Got your keys?'

He smiled, in spite of the nightmare evening. 'I'm eighteen, Ma.'

'I know, I know. I can get a cab—'

'You're fine. Say hi to Aunt Shosh.'

'I have done, darling. Be safe and have fun.'

From his spot by the kitchen door he could see Grace Lancaster and Allegra chatting on the stairs.

'I'm finally experiencing proper teen parties,' he heard Allegra tell Grace. 'I want to see all of the staples. Couple making out. A fight. And some girl crying on the stairs. Right here. On this spot. Don't even care if it's me.'

Grace grinned and then said something too quietly for Jonah to hear. Allegra laughed and the sound caused many people to glance quickly at her. She was always being observed, whether she realized it or not. Someone at the dining room door took a sneaky picture of her on his phone and Jonah wanted to snatch the thing out of his hand.

As she and Grace ascended the stairs, he spotted Kerrie coming towards him.

'You look really nice tonight,' she told him, shouting over the extremely loud music.

'Thanks,' he answered, glancing at the stairs again. 'You doing okay?'

She looked disappointed for a brief second, glancing down at herself a little self-consciously, but then she said, 'All good. Want a drink?'

'I'm fine,' he said. 'Think I might go upstairs a minute.'

She started to say something else but he was already moving away, needing some darkness and some quiet.

\*

Grace led Allegra into a completely dark spare bedroom. They climbed over the large bed to lie down on the floor next to it, so as not to muss the expensive sheets Simon's mother had no doubt picked out. As they lay side by side on the carpeted floor, Grace whispered, 'Are loud parties a lot for you?'

'Yes,' Allegra said, wondering if she should disclose just how much. 'I've had major fear of missing out over house parties, but I also find them really overstimulating.'

'We'll be fine in here,' Grace said, squeezing her arm.

They grasped hands in the dark and stared up at a ceiling neither of them could really see.

'Grace, I'm autistic.'

Allegra said the words quietly.

'Like Jonah?'

'Yeah.'

'Cool. Thank you for telling me.'

No prodding remarks. No demands. Nothing intrusive. Grace took in the information, honouring her name and making Allegra feel more at home than she ever had in her own apartment.

'You know,' Allegra heard herself saying. 'My life is so lonely. I was in my apartment once, reading a script, and a line in it said that scientifically, we all lie at least once a day. And I realized it was almost midnight and I hadn't spoken to a single soul that day. So I had broken the rule. Except, I guess, I was lying to myself.'

The other girl's hand did not loosen or edge away. 'You've got us now.'

The words were the breaking of a curse and Allegra felt tears start to fall.

Before she could tell Grace how much her words meant to a

confused movie star, the bedroom door opened and closed. Light filled the room for the briefest moment from the hall before whomever it was shut it out again. The bed creaked as someone flung themselves onto it and Allegra and Grace had to cover their mouths to keep from alerting the new person to their presence on the floor next to the bed.

They could hear the person tapping on their phone. They typed steadily and without interruption for a while, as if sending a long message – or, Allegra considered with her heart in her throat, an email. Then, when they were finally finished, the room was completely black again as they tucked away their phone. They exhaled and Allegra finally did, too.

Allegra knew, from the faint smell of neroli, that it was Jonah.

Her urge to laugh was suddenly gone. She became as still as the expensive art on the walls.

'Thought you were lost.' It was Kerrie, from the doorway. She slipped inside and Allegra and Grace both tensed as she climbed onto the bed next to Jonah. Grace squeezed Allegra's hand in a vicelike grip, as if to say, '*Do you think they're about to . . . you know?*'

Allegra hoped not. The idea made her inexplicably furious. Anger that she had no business feeling started to pulse inside her head. She and Jonah were not even friends, she had no right to get jealous about what Kerrie wanted to happen.

'You really do look nice tonight,' Kerrie said softly, clearly reiterating an earlier compliment. Her voice was hushed and sensual, and it made Allegra's eyelashes hurt and her heart feel too big for her chest.

'Thanks.' Jonah's voice was deep and gruff. Uninviting, Allegra thought. She heard one of them, probably Kerrie, shift on the bed.

'Yeah, parties are just a lot,' he added, as if trying to fill the gap in conversation.

Grace's touch was ghostlike but definitely there.

'Jonah.'

Kerrie's voice was almost wheedling, but still quiet.

'Don't, Ker. Let's just—'

'You look so good.'

And then the sound of kissing was all Allegra could hear, and her eyes closed in horror. Even the music downstairs seemed to cease.

It made sense, she told herself over the sound of Kerrie pressing her mouth to Jonah's. They were schoolfriends, old friends even, and Kerrie had openly told Allegra about her crush.

Still, when she heard Jonah pull away, Allegra opened her eyes.

'Sorry, Ker. I'm all over the place at the moment. You're great. I – I've always thought so, but I'm . . . I'm just . . .'

Grace's body was shaking with silent laughter. Allegra knew it wasn't born from nastiness, the girl was just beside herself with discomfort at being trapped in this situation. Grace was completely overcome by awkwardness. If it had been anyone else making out above them, Allegra would have been the same way. But something was needling her.

She heard Kerrie kiss Jonah again and even though she was lying in darkness, Allegra could picture it. The gentle force which wore Jonah down, just enough for him to join in with a little more enthusiasm. Then, a sigh like a record scratch:

'*Allegra.*'

# Chapter Seventeen

Jonah saw Kerrie as a friend. A good friend. He didn't want to hurt her, or take advantage, or let anything go too far.

But it had been an awful night, a confusing summer, and he was lonely. The girl in his inbox was out of reach, the girl he thought about more and more with each day thought he was a story no one wanted to hear, and everything felt impossible. So, when Kerrie kissed him a second time, he allowed it. He kissed her back.

She shifted so that she was about to straddle him, rubbed the waistline of his jeans and slid her other hand under his black tee. He let the physical sensation carry him away. His imagination joined the two of them on the bed and, as their kiss became deeper, he began to picture a different face in his mind. It belonged to a person he had struggled to stop thinking about since her arrival in town. She had become a fixture in his mind. And, before he could bring sense along with fantasy:

'*Allegra.*'

Kerrie's hand froze on his stomach and her lips stopped moving against his. He pulled back, horrified.

'Kerrie. I'm . . . fuck, I'm sorry. I'm an asshole. That's – that's just, I'm sorry. I'm so sorry.'

'It's fine,' she said, in a tone that categorically confirmed that it was not. 'Honestly.'

'I'm sorry. It's nothing. I just, Allegra and I – we had another argument earlier, she's in my head. Not like that. I mean, yes, like that, but I'll get over it. I'll get over *her*. I'll get through it. I will.'

'Who are you convincing, you or me?'

'I didn't mean to think of her, it just happened. It happens a lot, it's a problem, but I—'

'I don't want to hear you talk about how you were thinking about some other girl while kissing me, Jonah.'

'I know, that sounds bad. Sorry. It just came out.'

'Jonah!'

'Kerrie, I'm sorry.'

'It's fine, Jonah.' She sat back and sighed.

'I'm sorry,' he repeated, sick of hearing himself say it but incapable of stopping.

'Everyone's in love with her. You know that, right? Simon is. He's going to ask her out once the festival is done. It's practically official. Plus, she's dated a rockstar. She's probably got a bunch of boyfriends in the city.'

Jonah said nothing.

'*I* get silly around her, for God's sake,' Kerrie said, spluttering out a disbelieving laugh. 'She's amazing. She's beautiful, *and* she's sweet. She's stupidly, annoyingly perfect. But . . . but she's not one of us. She never will be. And I . . . I don't want you to get hurt. She's like a cold. We're all going to get it at some point. You'll be immune once the summer is over and she goes back to dreamland.'

Jonah almost believed her.

'But still,' he eventually said, 'it doesn't excuse what I just did. I'm sorry, I didn't mean to.'

'Of course you didn't,' she said gently, swinging her legs from the bed and sitting up straight. 'It's fine. Um . . . I'm going to go home, actually. I'll see you at the festival tomorrow?'

'Okay,' Jonah said, also sitting up. 'I'm . . . I'm sorry, Kerrie. Let me walk you home.'

'No, it's fine. Honestly. I'm good.'

'Kerrie . . . can you . . .? No, never mind.'

'Can I not tell anyone about this?'

'Yeah.'

'You really think that I want people knowing about this, Jonah? Do you know how human beings work? Like, at all?'

He flinched as if she had hit him and waited in the dark as she moved silently out of the room.

He waited for at least ninety seconds before getting up and doing the same.

Allegra couldn't move. She didn't release her breath until Jonah had left the room. There was a beat of silence once he was gone and then Grace sat up.

'Fuck.'

'Yeah,' Allegra whispered, her voice hoarse. 'That was a ride.'

'What happened in Pete's Cafe?' Grace asked with urgency. 'What on earth went down between you two? Obviously enough to make him groan out your name when another girl is kissing him.'

Allegra suddenly felt like crying. She smacked her hand to her lips, as they trembled and her jaw grew painfully tight.

'I was really mean to him,' she said. Grace's sympathetic silence gave her room to breathe out all of her regret. 'It wasn't like me. I was so mad about getting it all completely wrong . . . But I wasn't mad that he wasn't Simon.'

'Mm hmm,' Grace said softly, a touch of something mischievous entering her voice.

'Should we find Kerrie?'

'I'll do it,' Grace said. 'The sight of you might be a bit raw for her right now.'

While Allegra knew it was true, she couldn't help but feel dejected, as though she had done something wrong. She would hate for Kerrie to feel as if this was all some sort of cruel joke.

So she said to Grace, 'We were never here.'

'Yup,' her friend said, with a tone of complete and utter concurrence.

'Grace?' Allegra sat up and Grace mirrored her.

'Yeah?'

'I didn't tell Jonah the truth. About me. He still thinks he was stood up.'

Grace didn't say anything for a moment then sighed. 'So, I'm still keeping that secret?'

'Please.'

'You owe me.'

'Sure do.'

Allegra made a hasty exit, leaving the party without saying goodbye to Simon. He was in full host-mode and Allegra always felt acutely different from her peers when it came to goodbyes. She liked slipping away without a word. She was also worried that he would spot her unease and ask about it.

The night air was a cool stroke of the cheek to Allegra, as she slipped out of Simon's little mansion. She made for town, scrolling through her mess of messages (completely ignoring her email inbox) only to find a text from her father, informing her via his new (and first) mobile phone that he would be late at the festival site with some authors. He asked if she had her keys.

She confirmed that she did, just as she reached Main Street, with Brooks Books ahead and in her sights.

She missed walking. She didn't get to do much of it in the city, she was ferried from location to car to location to plane to hotel or apartment. She was never allowed to spend more than a few seconds on the pavement at a time.

Natalie and Allegra's agent were worried about her being in Lake Pristine without a security detail; both convinced that her new location would be leaked. Her father's speech from earlier in the night had left Allegra with a bad taste in her mouth. The daughter in her was thrilled but the actor was afraid. Allegra had assured her team that the town was discreet, and that most of its population did not understand social media, let alone partake in it. That service wasn't great. That town gossip was considered as ubiquitous as groceries, but most residents had very little interest in communicating with the outside world.

She let herself into Brooks Books, turning on a couple of lights but making sure to check that the 'Closed' sign was facing out towards the street. She moved over to the front desk, hoisting herself up onto it and opening her inbox.

There were countless emails, most of them chains that ended in Natalie saying, 'Leave it with me, kid!' in her adorably harried fashion. There were people reaching out for meetings and self-tapes. There were lunch invitations.

Then she saw one, sent recently, and it stopped her breath and her heart.

**JonahThorne@gmail.com**
**to: westendgirl@gmail.com**
**Subject: Hello**

Hi. I hope this isn't alarming. It's me. Disgruntled bookseller, or shopfloor@BrooksBooks.com. I thought I would email from my personal account – even though you didn't show. If this is unwanted, please tell me or just block accordingly. I just felt like being brave because I've been a bit of a coward tonight.

I wish you had come. I don't really know what you told Allegra when she answered the phone at the shop and took your message. Did you know you were leaving a message with a supernova? Probably not. 'Why didn't you ask Allegra?' I hear you ask. Because I can barely speak to Allegra. And that inability to speak in her presence eventually comes out as meanness. And I hate meanness. I hate people who try to make others feel small, but I tell myself that I'm not doing that with her. It's self-defence, it's protection, whatever. She can give as good as she gets, but she's entitled to hate me. I'm an embarrassment around her. She takes away all of my sensible qualities and puts me in fight or flight mode. And I always pick fight because flight would mean no longer being around her.

Anyway. I was alone, waiting for you, when she delivered your message. It's me. I'm Jonah. The bookseller you've been emailing. I hope we can meet one day. I hope I'm not a huge disappointment.

I hope, I hope, I hope.

Have a great evening. Wish you were her.

Jonah.

Allegra stared at the last sentence before his name and then a PS suddenly appeared in the thread.

PS SORRY ABOUT THAT, STUPID FINGERS, WISH YOU WERE HERE. HERE. I WISH YOU WERE HERE.
JONAH.

She was typing before reason could take hold.

**westendgirl@gmail.com**
**to: JonahThorne@gmail.com**
**RE: Hello**
I'm so sorry, Jonah. I should have been there.

She pressed SEND on her phone but before the small notification sound was even over, a knock on the bookshop window jolted her out of her reverie. She looked up to see Jonah and for one mortified moment, she foolishly wondered if he had worked out what she was doing. She shoved her phone away. He nodded to the door and she nodded back, silently telling him that it was unlocked.

He moved inside and she finally allowed herself to concede that he was extremely handsome, tall as he was with his dark curls and long lashes. She felt the tension in the room settle into something serious. It was the same way, sometimes, with a scene partner. Sometimes, just sometimes, the arduous setup, the rewrites, the blocking and the rehearsal were all finalized and then they dissipated to leave her and another actor with nothing but the beauty of making art together.

When Jonah walked towards her with an intensely focused expression, she knew that this was not their usual play. He eyed her appearance with a hint of hunger and Allegra didn't trust herself to speak. They were terrible and full of bluster when they spoke to each other. Two eighteen-year-olds who were ahead of their peers in so many ways, and so guarded and afraid of adulthood in so many other ways.

She slid off the desk and he came to stand in front of her, the two of them surrounded by tables of books in a dimly lit shop with no one else around. He was still in his suit and she in her dress, which suddenly felt like liquid that could be pulled away very easily.

'I'm sorry,' he said quietly, before she could think of a thing to say.

'What are you sorry for, Jonah?' she asked, barely a whisper.

'Everything. The way I spoke to you when you first came into the shop. And every day since.'

Allegra had kicked off her heels on reaching the front desk and so he had a few inches of height on her. She looked up into his face, marking the tiny dark circles under his eyes and the beauty of his mouth.

'It's okay,' she said. 'People get . . . weird around me.'

He was very close now. If anyone walked by the shop window they wouldn't be able to see her. She was eclipsed by him.

'I know they do,' he said. 'But I don't want to be one of those people to you. The strange weirdos who want the interaction to be over so they can go and call someone about it. I want . . .'

His fingers were lightly brushing her forearms and he was almost pressed up against her. He smelled incredible.

'What do you want, Jonah?' she asked, mimicking the formal way he always spoke, that formality she had strangely started to crave. 'What everyone else wants, right?' It wasn't bitterness, really, it was regret.

'No,' he murmured, looking briefly into her eyes and then back down to where his hands were touching her skin. 'You. I want you. And I want you more than anyone else.'

The words were said so matter-of-factly, Allegra almost laughed.

He shook his head as he looked at her, as if trying to break free of a trance. 'There's something different about you.'

Allegra swallowed. 'Jonah—'

'You're not like everyone else. And not because of movie contracts or glamour or any of the crazy things you left behind to come here. There's something else.'

Allegra heard this often, usually with an accusatory tone. But Jonah sounded fascinated. Full of wonder. And it made her nervous.

'Someone said something true to me tonight,' he went on. 'They said, "everyone is in love with you". And it's true.'

'It's not, Jonah,' she said weakly. 'I could show you—'

'And so I gave myself permission,' he said, ignoring her frail protestations. His voice had changed, it sounded deeper and more full of heat. 'To stop being an asshole, to stop covering up what I want with unconscious meanness. And if you hate it, okay. If you don't feel the same in any way, I'll live. Not happily, and without much colour, but I'll survive. Rejection doesn't seem as horrible as regret. I'll lose you either way, might as well do it with the knowledge that I tried.'

'What about your email girl?' she asked, surprised by how breathless she was beginning to sound.

'I thought she and I might be kind of soulmates because of how we write, but she didn't come tonight. Allegra. Stop hiding. Look at me.'

She did.

'Reject me,' he said. 'So I can start getting over you.'

She glanced down at his hands which had now climbed up to her elbows. He was so close she could breathe in the smell of the night air on his body. He lifted one hand to gently move her long hair away from her face. He pressed his lips against the newly exposed skin of her throat and she closed her eyes.

'Tell me to go away and I will,' he said against her neck. Her hands had drifted up to pull him closer and his arms had encircled her. They were tightly locked together. Every part of her was humming.

Allegra's first kiss had been on camera. She had performed love scenes with other young actors, sometimes with an intimacy coordinator, sometimes the director would flatly refuse. Usually, the love scenes she shot were impossible to mistake for anything real. The other actor would be angling their face so that they were completely visible on camera. Nothing felt true. And it saddened Allegra, who had chosen the life of an actor because she loved the delicious cocktail of a fairy tale on the screen mixed with the truth of the human condition.

Jonah wasn't like any of those actors. Sometimes he was *too* truthful. It was why they caused one another to flare up so often.

He reminded her of who she had been before focus groups,

industry luncheons and award seasons.

She slid her hands into his hair, and his came to rest on her hips.

When he spoke, he sounded starved. 'Kiss me.'

She heard herself make a small noise of encouragement, and then everything caught fire.

His mouth came down on hers and she pressed her body against his until it elicited a groan from him. He hoisted her up so he was holding her flush against him, her legs moving automatically to drape around his hips.

Allegra kissed him back as he manoeuvred her to one of the shop tables. 'Not the paperbacks, the jackets will bend.'

She felt him smile against her mouth. 'Hardbacks it is.'

He shoved some expensive books from the table and laid her down on it. She bit his bottom lip, he licked her collarbone. She slid her tongue into his mouth. He dragged her hips against his once more.

'Fuck,' he groaned, as his hands found her breasts and hers found his belt.

She was about to respond when they both heard a noise, a scuffling at the front door of the shop. They froze in the near-dark, and then Allegra rolled gracelessly off the table. She crawled underneath it to hide, pinching the heels of Jonah's shoes until he did the same. As soon as they were safely hidden, the door opened.

They watched George's feet cross the shopfloor and listened to him as he whistled jauntily. He moved straight through the door that led up to his and Allegra's apartment, too distracted by his own thoughts to see their feet or the books on the floor. Before she could even process his arrival, Allegra felt her phone ringing.

There was no tone, just vibration, and it was enough to push her into sensory overload, given everything else that she was feeling. She rolled onto her back beneath the table of books and answered it.

'Hey. I'm almost home. I'll be up in a minute.'

She spoke very softly and Jonah leaned over to press his mouth between her breasts. She almost gasped and almost grimaced in a mixture of pleasure and anxiety.

'All right,' George said, his voice happily tired and oblivious. 'Be safe.'

'Yes,' she said, trying not to sound breathy as she pulled Jonah on top of her. 'Bye.'

She dropped the phone with a thud and pulled Jonah's mouth back to hers.

Jonah was finding it hard to breathe. He was living out the daydreams he had not even allowed himself to look directly at. The dreams that were logged away and unacknowledged, because coming out of them would be too painful.

Allegra was beneath him and she could no doubt feel how much he wanted her.

He wanted to apologize again, for letting his attraction morph into defensiveness. He wanted to tell her that he liked the pieces of her that she revealed when she didn't know anyone was watching. He liked the Allegra he saw with George over lunch. The way she would take the baby tomatoes out of his salad because she knew her father didn't like them. The way she read picture books when she was organizing the children's section. He liked so many things about her, things that the rest of the world knew nothing about.

He didn't want them to know.

'Go on then,' she said breathily, letting her knees fall to either side of her. 'Get your immunity.'

Jonah paused. He blinked at her beautiful face in the darkness. 'What?'

'Isn't that what this is? You're getting me out of your system?'

He was confused. And then he panicked, wondering if he had misread her. 'If you don't want this, Allegra, we'll stop immediately—'

'No, I do,' she sighed, pulling him back onto her. 'But let's not pretend it's something it's not. I'm like the common cold, remember. Just something to get over.'

Horror slowly took the place of desire and arousal. 'You . . . you know about that?'

'Grace and I couldn't help overhearing.'

'How?'

'Does it matter?'

'I told Kerrie not to—'

'She didn't, we overheard, like I said.'

'How much did you overhear?' He reached down to touch her face, his eyes searching her face for answers.

She looked into his eyes for a brief moment and then glanced away. 'Not much.'

Jonah tried to read her face. 'I don't understand.'

'If we're going to do this, let's do it.'

'Allegra, I want you but not on the floor of the shop. You can come back to my place.'

A flash of something vulnerable crossed her face and she looked up at him briefly. 'That'll just complicate things, Jonah.'

He felt his expression harden. 'I want to complicate things.'

'No, you want me out of your system. So, let's go.'

Jonah shook his head. 'I didn't – I didn't mean that.'

'Actually, you know what,' she wriggled out from beneath him and leapt to her feet. 'Better not. Your email friend might get jealous.'

Jonah was ashamed to admit to himself that he had barely thought of his pen-pal. Partly because he was still feeling resentful about sitting alone in Pete's Cafe without a real explanation. Mostly because as soon as he had allowed himself to think about Allegra in the way he had denied himself for weeks, everything else had gone away.

'Allegra . . .'

A light was suddenly switched on and they both blinked in astonishment, turning instinctively to the apartment entrance. George stood at the bottom of the stairs, glancing between the two of them.

'Jonah,' he finally said. 'Is everything all right? It's late.'

There was no retribution or even admonishment in the man's tone. Just bewilderment.

'I was just letting Allegra know that she'll be working with me on the main stage tomorrow,' he said, turning to eye Allegra with a silent promise. She glared back at him but did not say anything.

'Oh,' George said. 'Good. But—'

'See you tomorrow, Allegra.' Jonah's tone spoke of a refusal to return to their previous dynamic. 'We have a lot to discuss in the morning.'

And reluctantly, but with a newly found spring of determination, he left.

**westendgirl@gmail.com**
**to: JonahThorne@gmail.com**
**Subject: I'm Sorry**

Dear Jonah.

A longer email, now. I'm sorry. My clients kept me away from Lake Pristine. I know it's not an excuse. I'm sorry you were made to feel like you were alone. I'm ashamed you were stood up. I wish I could explain properly.

Who answered the phone at the shop? Who was she to you? You've hardly mentioned her in any of your responses. I know we've unofficially agreed to never share too much personal information via these exchanges but I'm curious.

Your friend.

**JonahThorne@gmail.com**
**to: westendgirl@gmail.com**
**Subject: Allegra**

Dear Friend,

Allegra. She was the one who answered the phone. She's eighteen, like me. She's an actress and George's daughter. She's an enigma. And she gave me some hard truths while I was waiting for you.

I wish you had been there. It might have spared me from a lot of humiliation and some other feelings I don't fully understand yet.

Jonah.

# Chapter Eighteen

As Jonah stood in the green room, checking authors in, he couldn't help but overhear other volunteers as they expressed doubts about Pamela H. J. Wilcox's arrival.

'She won't come,' one volunteer murmured to the other, as they arranged physical copies of the programme.

'She hasn't done an interview since the show came out,' said another, filling the mini-fridges with sandwiches and drinks. 'She's sick of people asking about the last *Court of Bystanders* book. She's definitely not coming. Courtney couldn't even get her on the phone.'

Jonah was starting to feel a little nervous himself. Allegra had promised to arrange the author's appearance when Quentin Morrison had dropped out – but Allegra had yet to appear. He was apprehensive about Pamela's presence, even without his gossiping colleagues.

A children's author suddenly marched into the tent, having just finished his story-time reading in the smallest venue.

'How was it?' asked Kerrie, appearing on Jonah's left. She spoke to the author warmly but he ignored her, going straight to the mini-fridge. He withdrew two bottles of white wine, shoving them unceremoniously into his satchel. Then he was off.

'I didn't know children's authors could be so thirsty,' Jonah mused.

'They write for kids, that doesn't mean they drink like them,' Kerrie said, as they both watched the author march to his car. Jonah met her gaze and they both shared a laugh.

'Are we okay?' Jonah finally asked her, keeping his voice low and his tone gentle.

'Yeah,' she said, just as quietly. 'We're good.'

'Great.'

'But only because you'll never get her,' she added, a little venomously, in a way that felt totally out of character. He saw a flicker of shame cross her face, but underneath it he could see she was hurt and embarrassed. He couldn't blame her. He watched her blink back tears as she walked away and he cursed himself for being so clumsy with her. Obliviousness did not excuse the fumbling of someone's heart.

Kerrie went to help with setting up the main tent, clearly determined to make it presentable whether Pamela H. J. Wilcox arrived or not.

'The whole event sold out in eight minutes,' the first volunteer whispered. 'That's never happened, in the history of the Lake Pristine Book Festival.'

Jonah did not need them to finish their thought. If Pamela did not show, after such a reception, it would fall onto the festival and they would have to give everyone their money back with a grovelling apology. The possibility made Jonah feel ill.

The invited authors were always told to arrive at least ninety minutes before the start time of their event, and so the green room was starting to fill up with literary figures. Some were nervous debuts, others regular guests of the festival. Jonah watched with interest as a face he recognized appeared at the entrance to the green room.

A young publicist was bustling one of Jonah's favourite literary fiction writers towards the table he was manning. The publicist smiled up at Jonah but he felt his heart deflate in weak disappointment at the rude manners on display from her companion.

'Food better be nicer than the crap they serve at—'

'Let's just sign you in, Rodger.' And then, turning to Jonah, genially: 'Rodger Altringham. He's here for his event at noon.'

Jonah's eyes drifted to the author, but the man was glaring angrily at his smartphone.

'Here's his pass,' Jonah said, handing the publicist Rodger's laminated name badge and lanyard. 'Welcome to the Lake Pristine Book Festival.'

Rodger did not even spare him a glance, heading for one of the green room sofas instead. His publicist offered up an apologetic smile, but Jonah continued to feel dejected.

'Oh, my God, here she comes!' The slightly hysterical chattering from the young volunteers alerted Jonah to Allegra's arrival. While the volunteers all wore bright yellow T-shirts with the festival name printed on them, Allegra had elected to wear a pale pink sundress with large dark glasses. She smiled at the volunteers and then nodded at their matching apparel.

'Mine didn't fit, I'm afraid.'

'We can get you a different size,' one of them said instantly, their words a little garbled and overly loud.

'She's fine,' Jonah said. 'She's perfect.'

Allegra finally looked at him and, for the first time since their initial unfortunate meeting, he dropped the mask. He let her see all of the things he had been terrified of anyone noticing – especially her.

The wanting, the pining, the curiosity and the hope.

She quickly looked away, but he refused to be dispirited. She had shown up, despite the way they had left each other the night before. Despite all of the things they had said and done to one another.

Jonah's mystery girl had stood him up, but Allegra was not hiding away.

George arrived moments later.

'Any sign of our big name?' he asked Jonah.

'Not yet, and Courtney can't get hold of anyone,' he reported, feeling strangely thrilled by his mentor's attention.

'It'll be fine,' Allegra said smoothly. She clearly had complete faith in Wilcox. 'She told me she would be here.'

'Yes, but that was a while ago now, darling, just after Quentin dropped out,' George said, speaking to Allegra as though she were eight and not eighteen. 'Authors are temperamental.'

'She promised me,' Allegra said, speaking of the novelist with deep familiarity.

After confirming Wilcox as a guest to the festival, Allegra had suggested that they invite a debut fantasy author to the event to act as chair. Melena Banks, said debut, had now arrived, entering the green room with obvious trepidation. Allegra moved swiftly to greet her.

'We might have to shove my daughter onstage to appease the Wilcox fans if she doesn't show,' George said to Jonah.

Jonah frowned. 'That wouldn't be the safest thing for her. It's unsettling that she's in town without security as it is. And that she was announced so publicly during the launch.'

He felt his boss glance at him. 'I was only joking, son.'

Jonah shook himself. 'Sorry. Yes. We will definitely need something to keep them calm if she doesn't show.'

'Funny you mention security though,' George went on, lowering his voice as they both watched Allegra chat to the young author on one of the sofas, putting her completely at ease. 'I've worried a lot about that. Her mother and I discussed it when she suddenly decided to spend the summer here.'

'It's a miracle everyone has kept her presence quiet,' Jonah acknowledged, thrilled that he and George seemed, at last, to be getting along again. 'Can't stop people staring like losers, but it's lucky that nothing has got out.'

'There are social contracts in this town,' George said, conspiratorially. 'People know to keep their mouths shut; they don't want even more outsiders descending on us. This is the only time of year that they tolerate it. But you're right, we have been lucky.'

'Maybe this could be her home in the long run,' Jonah heard himself say. 'If it's safer, quieter for her.'

George examined him, suspicion starting to bleed into his expression. 'But what about you?'

Jonah blinked. 'What about me?'

'Surely you don't want to stay here for much longer? What about an education? A life? A girlfriend?'

'I can have two of those things here. And higher education isn't for me.'

'Come on, Jonah,' George said, and Jonah was shocked by the irritation in his employer's voice. 'You're too smart to stay here and never see the world.'

'I work in a bookshop,' Jonah reminded him. 'The world comes to me. I don't need to find it.'

'And that's a nice, romantic idea. But you need to live your own life, have experiences outside of the things that you read.'

Whatever Jonah had been about to say next was swallowed up, because gasps could suddenly be heard all throughout the green room. Jonah and George looked over to the doorway and both were struck with silence.

It was Pamela H. J. Wilcox.

She was tiny and slender, wearing a clean but worn white cotton suit with one bright teal bangle on her left wrist and a pair of tennis shoes that were slightly scuffed. Her long silvery hair was tied back in a sensible braid and the only thing glamorous about her was her dark sunglasses, not unlike the pair that Allegra wore.

The famous recluse ignored people's stares and astonishment, choosing instead to survey the room, and when her sharp grey eyes landed on Allegra Brooks, her thin lips twitched into an almost-smile.

'There she is,' she said, her Irish accent full of warmth. She held out her arms and made her way towards Allegra, ignoring the small crowd of onlookers. Jonah and George watched the two embrace, Allegra towering over the small woman.

'So glad you could make it,' Allegra said, throwing Jonah a quick but triumphant look over her shoulder.

'Only because it was you who asked,' Pamela said in response, loudly enough for everyone to hear. She made her way over to the table of food, eyeing the mushroom tarts and the baked goods donated by Jonah's mother.

It was only when volunteers started to approach Pamela that Jonah realized she had come without an escort of any kind. No publicist or publisher. She was there, quite happily, by herself.

'This is really happening,' he told Simon, who had shown up to work at exactly the right moment. 'We need to get someone outside to corral the audience once they arrive.'

'They're already starting to queue, saw them on my way in,' Simon said. 'So, she's really here!'

'Yeah,' Jonah said dazedly. 'Allegra did it. She actually did it.'

'Well, let's be fair, Allegra has probably got one hell of a little black book.'

Jonah allowed himself to take in all of Allegra as she laughed at something Pamela was saying. Her long hair with its streaks of gold, her ears that stuck out just a little. Her left thumb and forefinger, which were often stroking together in a soothing motion. Stimming – if Jonah did not know better.

When Allegra had first come to Lake Pristine, he had been struck by how beautiful she was. Now, there was so much more about her that made him admire her. Her quiet confidence in saving the day and getting Wilcox to come. Her generosity in pledging to do so in the first place. Her interest in listening to other people. She was the greatest conversationalist he had ever witnessed – she remembered tiny details about people and spoke to them with such curiosity. It made him realize how closed off he had become.

He respected her intelligence – and her short fuse. Her occasional flashes of temper were always followed by a micro expression that conveyed her regret that he found endearing. He wished he could see it more often.

It had started to dawn on him, since being stood up by one person only to have his dream girl show up instead, that he denied himself a lot of chances. If something required vulnerability, Jonah would become avoidant. He had taken a risk, showing up to Pete's Cafe and letting all of Lake Pristine see him sitting there alone with a copy of *Middlemarch* and a red rose.

He didn't regret a moment of it. The sting of both his pen-pal and Allegra's rejection was far more bearable than the dull pain of wondering 'what if?'

Usually, he lived in the postcode of What If. It was a familiar, well-tended cul-de-sac with high walls and few visitors. The way out was always in view but the courage to walk out was far more elusive.

He suddenly remembered the picture of Allegra Brooks on the computer screen, the day he heard she was coming to Lake Pristine. He had seen the most beautiful girl in the world on that screen, and his instincts, years of trying to mask and hide and be invisible, had forced him to push down those feelings. The many allistic voices that had told him he was made incorrectly had merged to become a voice in his own head.

*Don't even look at that girl, she'll want nothing to do with you. She won't even want to breathe the same air as you.*

He wasn't going to sabotage his own happiness any more. He had entered into romantic entanglements before, as a boy. He was going to approach Allegra as a man.

'Simon,' he said to his friend, as they both stood by the catering table of the green room. 'I really like Allegra.'

He felt his friend go cold. There was a long silence between the two of them, while the room bustled and throbbed with noise and anticipation.

When Simon did eventually speak, it was with a voice Jonah had never heard his old friend use before. 'You could have fooled me. The two of you are always at each other's throats.'

'I know,' Jonah allowed. 'That was all my fault. I made a shitty first impression and then I doubled down because of pride.'

'You've been distracted a lot lately. I knew it was down to something.'

'I wasn't trying to keep secrets from you.'

'It's not that,' Simon said flatly, cracking his neck and shrugging with feigned indifference. 'You've never been big on talking about feelings.'

'I know.'

'You were just on your phone a lot. I knew it was someone. Just didn't think it was Allegra, because you're pretty rude to her.'

'There was someone else, and then they – then there wasn't. It's complicated.'

'Why are you telling me?' Simon said, his tone still frosty and curt. 'Are you asking my permission?'

Jonah was taken aback. 'No. Of course not.'

'Because I'm not going to stop trying to get with her just because you want to start, Jonah. That's not how these things work.'

It was happening. As it so often happened with allistic friends. Simon was a best friend to Jonah, but only when he was biddable. Only when he was in a supporting role, docile in his friendship and playing in the background. When Jonah played the neurotypical game, he was allowed to stay at the table. But neurotypicals could turn. They could move the goalposts and change the rules whenever it pleased them. Jonah's invitation could be rescinded at any time.

He was starting to wonder if friendship was always supposed to feel like this, if it was normal to walk on eggshells around a friend. If it was normal to feel tolerated instead of loved.

'Let's be clear,' Jonah said. 'I'm not trying to "get with her". I'm falling in love with her.'

Simon visibly cringed at Jonah's infamous formality. 'Oh, God.'

'Can you be a friend to me about this?' Jonah asked quietly. 'A real friend?'

Simon had protected Jonah from football players who wanted to shove him in school corridors when they were twelve, but in later years, he had repeatedly gone after the girls Jonah liked. Jonah had always written it up to unfortunate timing, but he was no longer convinced about any of it. Maybe other people had friendships that didn't feel like this. Maybe it didn't always have to be this way for him.

Something close to worry flashed across Simon's face. 'Jonah, she's a really nice girl. She's been a pal all summer and a big help at the shop, especially since you and George have been so weird with each other. Don't scare her off. Don't do anything to ruin this summer for her.'

Jonah flinched. 'Why would you think—'

'She's a good girl. Even Skye has given up trying to pick fights with her. She's a great person. She doesn't deserve to be messed about by you.'

Jonah felt a stab of jealousy and narrowed his eyes. 'As opposed to whatever it is *you've* been trying to do all summer?'

'I say, let the best man win,' Simon finally said.

Jonah regarded him for a long while and then spoke, in a cold, hardened tone of his own before walking away. 'She's not something to win, Simon.'

# Chapter Nineteen

Allegra hid in the green room during Pamela's event, watching it live on the monitor that had been set up. It showed what the viewers at home would be seeing. Allegra had suggested they provide online streaming for the event, as thousands of Wilcox fans would want to be involved, but unable to reach Lake Pristine.

When Pamela stepped onstage, her first stage in a decade, the entire room erupted. Allegra hugged her father and felt little-girl pride at seeing how wet his eyes were. The standing ovation lasted for four minutes before Pamela gestured for everyone to sit.

'So proud of you,' George whispered to Allegra, before he was pulled away to meet with the caterers.

'I just want to preface our conversation with a momentary acknowledgement,' Pamela said, when the audience eventually quietened enough for her to be heard. 'I am only here because one girl asked me. And if that girl wasn't the sweetest, dearest girl who took one of my characters and breathed life into her, in such a way that the whole world is now in love with her . . .'

The room began to applaud again and despite the kind words, Allegra winced.

'. . . The girl who never asks for anything. The girl who got hypothermia on set. The girl who is always early, last to leave and nice to the press and the fans, even when they didn't deserve it. She is the reason I'm here.'

The room exploded once more and Allegra, while grateful, felt her heart start to pound. She was safe in the green room, but she unconsciously backed up a little anyway, feeling as if the walls and ceiling were closing in on her as she fought to breathe.

A camera was petrifying enough. A stage was death.

Fortunately, Melena Banks, the debut author who was chairing, asked an opening question and the event began. Melena asked about how Pamela structured her novels and Pamela spoke eloquently. She was so inspiring, the green room fell into comfortable silence and all settled in to watch her event.

After forty-five minutes, Melena turned to the audience and asked if anyone had any questions.

'I will repeat them into the microphone so everyone can hear,' she said, looking about the vast crowd of people. Many hands were in the air and she eventually settled on a man of about forty.

'Is Allegra Brooks here?' he asked, bluntly. His voice was loud enough for him to be heard without amplification.

'Um,' the debut author smiled nervously, but shook her head once. 'Do you have a question for Pamela?'

'Next,' Pamela said shortly, and someone asked her about the process of her current draft.

'That man was old enough to be your dad,' Simon said, suddenly appearing by Allegra's side.

Allegra started at his arrival and felt a small twinge of protectiveness over the *Court of Bystanders* fan. 'The one who asked the question? It's okay, they're just enthusiastic.'

'He's a grown man asking for the whereabouts of an eighteen-year-old girl.'

'Because he likes the show I was in.'

'I don't think men like you in that show for your acting.'

The reply was so horrifying, Allegra was rendered momentarily speechless. 'What the fuck, Simon?'

'Sorry,' he said, clearly embarrassed. 'That was cracked.'

'Yeah.'

She saw him glance back towards the front desk of the green room. She followed his gaze. Kerrie had reappeared, wearing a yellow festival T-shirt. She had volunteered at the last minute and was now saying something to Jonah, something that was amusing enough for him to smile down at her.

Allegra felt a memory from the night before nudge at her mind and she grew hot as she remembered where the night had almost gone. She was back under the table, recalling every touch and every word.

'Jonah is such a prick,' Simon said.

Allegra jolted back into the room. 'What?'

'He's just so rude. I hate how crap he's been to you.'

'It's fine,' Allegra said. 'He's just . . . not a bullshitter.'

'That's not the medical term.'

'Simon!' Allegra turned to face him. 'What is wrong with you today? Why are you being such a dick?'

He looked, for one quick beat, like a little boy who was surprised at being scolded. But then he fixed his face quickly and scowled. 'He's just pissed me off. I don't like how he's treated you, Allegra.'

'I've given it right back to him, each time,' Allegra snapped. 'Don't talk about me like I'm overly precious. We've sparred a few times. Who cares? It's fine.'

'Let me take you out tonight,' Simon wheedled. 'We've hardly had any time, just the two of us.'

Perhaps it was the way Jonah leaned closer to Kerrie to hear her say something in his ear, or perhaps it was the memory of the two of them discussing her the night before as if she were an unfortunate ghost who had floated into the attic of Lake Pristine, but whatever the reason, she turned to Simon: 'Sure.'

Loud and vigorous applause alerted the two of them to the end of the event and volunteers leapt into action. The signing tent was next to the Pamela H. J. Wilcox event and Allegra watched from the green room as the author was hurried to her table by two volunteers, who turned into blurs of yellow.

Allegra smiled and, by the time everyone had met Pamela or had a book signed, and every copy they had ordered in was sold (including the movie tie-in editions), the author returned to the green room. She embraced Allegra tightly and said, 'Only for you.'

And then was gone.

Allegra regretted going with Simon to the Lake Pristine Arthouse the moment they were on Main Street. The Arthouse stood at the end of the street, shining and welcoming, but Allegra was increasingly aware of her lukewarm feelings for Simon, and also how busy the small town suddenly seemed.

'The population usually triples during festival time, but Pamela will have brought it up to quadruple,' Simon said.

Shuttle buses had taken plenty of visitors back to the city, as Lake Pristine had no hotels or bed and breakfasts, but it seemed that a lot had stayed behind to eat, drink and celebrate the beautiful summer.

And stare.

Allegra was aware of how much Simon was relishing that.

'The cinema has a nice little bar area,' Simon told her, though she already knew this.

'Grace's brother runs it,' she said, recoiling as one man came far too close, staring at her with such intensity, it felt like a pinch.

'Arthur, yeah.'

Someone snapped a picture of the two of them and then took off running with their companion, both of them giggling like children. Allegra felt her heart begin to hurt.

Walking in Lake Pristine had become something so soothing and freeing for her of late and now it was being spoiled by the outside world bleeding in. She tried to take a deep breath, but the tightness in her chest made her ache and for a moment she felt as if she were drowning out of water. She told herself that it was just a picture here, a murmur there. She was still safe. She was fine.

When they reached the Arthouse, she was pleased to see that it was relatively empty and quiet. The lights were dimmed in the seating area of the bar and the vibe was relaxed and seemingly discreet. The two of them found a quiet corner and Simon sat a little too close to her, which made her realize that when she and Jonah had been wrapped around one another the night before, she had felt as though he could never be close enough. She was constantly aware of Jonah whenever they were in a room together. She could feel herself putting on a show when he was looking at her while she spoke to someone else. She felt exposed every time they locked eyes.

She thought about the email he had sent, not knowing that she was the recipient.

*Wish you were her.* The words had made her smile. Even though they had been a mistake. She desperately wanted to attribute some deeper meaning to the typo, but she knew there probably was none. He was physically attracted to her, and a little intrigued because she was someone he had seen on a screen.

She felt none of those intense feelings with Simon. She couldn't muster up a single thing. Her initial interest in him had been because she was deeply amused by the person behind the charming emails. Once it had become clear that he had nothing to do with them, all that potential went away.

She would need to make it clear to him that they were only meant to be friends. He had spent the summer bringing her little treats, asking her about her day and pressing her for book recommendations. She hoped none of that would stop now that she was dancing around his thorny colleague.

'Is it the best thing in the world?' Simon asked. 'Having everyone know who you are? To be loved by everyone?'

Allegra smiled sadly at him. It was a common misconception, a fantasy that people dreamed up, a story they thought they knew, as if fame were the touch of a God or a romantic curse. She knew it was neither. It was actually something altogether plainer. It was a bargain, a handshake, a deal. An exchange. Only, you didn't know what you were giving up.

Money to buy yourself a home and keep your family safe would arrive, sporadically at first, and then hurriedly and in vast quantities. The worry of 'what if' would become something hidden behind a door. Then, slowly and intrusively, the dealmakers would start to call in their chips. The work was not enough, the interviews and the profiles. The art that was wrought from the vulnerable blue in your veins, none of it was enough any more.

They didn't want a likeness of the flesh, they wanted to feel your skin under their nails. Seeing and reading and hearing were no longer fulfilling. They hungered to touch.

'I'm eighteen,' Allegra would hear herself saying to people, multiple times a day.

'Cool, that's impressive. Sign here, kid.'

And the things you didn't know were worth holding on to were suddenly gone. Replaced by gold, by an image of yourself that you didn't know, but everyone else said that they did. They spoke words that they claimed were yours, said that they knew your mind and your dreams and your heart. Grew angry at a version of you that they had dreamed up inside their heads.

For a young autistic girl, who had always been alone in the world – not just felt alone, but *been* alone – the deal had seemed so freeing. It had felt like a chance to eat at the table with everyone else.

And, for the first few years, it had all been so wonderful. To be wanted. To be seen. To be listened to. She had been able to share parts of herself that the world had only ever told her were ugly and unnatural. She was no longer made of stone to the people around her.

And then they turned her new flesh into bronze and gold and copper. Her name on too many tongues had cast the spell, and she was stationary again, while the world moved and spoke all around her.

And there are sadder songs. There are crueller stories. There are many, if not mostly, harder lives.

To become an idol is to be safe from the wind and the rain and the cold.

But no one can love a statue. Not really. They can touch parts of it until it turns to gold. But it can never go home with anyone. It can never touch them back.

She was just a statue to Jonah, she thought bitterly. When he said, 'wish you were her' in his emails, that 'her' didn't even exist. He was intrigued by the statue, the idol, the thing that was skin-deep.

'It's a privilege,' was all she said to Simon, knowing that it was the truth and also what people needed to hear. 'I'm very lucky.'

She wanted Jonah, though. She wanted his gaze, which was always so unclouded by the things that other people deemed so important. He hated her fame, and she had thought he hated her.

He was like her. She remembered it every time they were close to one another. Had felt it with every breath and gasp when they had come together in the bookshop.

'Simon,' she said, overwhelmed by the realization. 'I have to go.'

He frowned. 'You okay?'

'Yeah, I just—' She suddenly realized that he wasn't. There was something distracted about him. He seemed fidgety and on edge. 'Are you?'

He looked surprised by the question. 'I'm fine.'

'You don't seem fine.'

'Just . . . Jonah. He's being difficult.'

Allegra almost smiled. 'Difficult how?'

Simon exhaled. 'He's usually pretty regular, you know. But lately, he's been acting weird. Different. More than the usual.'

Allegra wasn't sure what he was getting at. 'Are you worried about him?'

'No. I'm worried about everyone around him. Worried that

he's going to keep upsetting people. First you, now Kerrie. George barely speaks to him.'

Allegra felt a touch of protectiveness rise up. 'He hasn't "upset" me, Simon. I can handle myself.'

'I've always sort of looked out for him but sometimes he just can't act right.'

'Hey,' Allegra said softly, disliking the focus on Jonah. It felt too familiar to her, too similar to the language used by people who had judged her for her disability when she was little. 'He acts just fine.'

Simon gave her a look of betrayal, one that made her wonder about him. She knew about masks better than anyone. She and Jonah were autistic, they wore theirs to survive. She wondered if Simon's was perhaps a touch more sinister, if the niceness was skin-deep. A veneer that was employed as means to an end.

It didn't happen too often, but when neurotypicals revealed themselves to be two-faced or insincere or, at the very worst, ableist – it always made her feel like a person in a movie who had just discovered that their friend was concealing a zombie bite.

'I'm going to go, Simon.'

She had never been good at predicting other people. She expected him to look disappointed, but to understand. But that was not what happened. He leaned in and kissed her.

It was too wet and too firm and she pulled away at once, scowling at him in fury.

She knew that he, like so many before him, just wanted to say that he had conquered Allegra Brooks – that's why he was doing it in public. A few people were watching and pretending not to. Simon winced as soon as it was done, and said, 'Sorry, Allegra,' almost too quietly for her to hear.

'That was so unasked for,' she snapped at him.

'I know,' he said hurriedly. 'I'm sorry. Stupid. Shouldn't have done it.'

Allegra shook her head and her eyes slid to the exit doors.

But one person openly stared from his place by the Arthouse door. Allegra focused and her eyes widened as she stared back.

'Jonah,' she breathed.

His hand was on the door, as if he had only just arrived. He looked full of thunder for a moment, and then it disintegrated into disappointment and resignation, as if he had expected to find such a scene. He shook his head.

So, Allegra moved. She didn't care if anyone saw or gossiped about it. The whole world was a small town to her, full of opinions and discourse and tittle-tattle. She was sick of the confines of other people's judgements.

She chased Jonah out onto Main Street, blinking as she realized that the sun had set and a light fall of rain was coming down. It was warm, summer rain; the kind that was so gentle and easy on the skin, you didn't realize you were soaked through until it was over. Jonah was like that rain. He had infiltrated her heart with such slowness. The rain had set in without her noticing.

She had not even felt the fall.

And it was frightening. To be falling for someone who thought they liked a version of you that could never be real. It filled her with anxiety, the worry of being found out. That she would let him down and he would feel cheated. That he would end up cursing her for letting him fall in love with a lie, with a person who did not exist.

Not a statue. Just a mortal with a disability. Not any kind of creature from Olympus. Just someone who borrowed a little stardust now and then, when there was film in the camera.

'Jonah!'

He stopped on the cobbled stones up ahead and she recognized the disillusionment in his shoulders, the kind of weariness and wariness that aged neurodivergent children in comparison to their peers. That early knowledge of rejection and the constant choice between being guarded or being hurt.

'Allegra, it's all right,' he called back to her, as she closed the distance between them on the dimly lit road. 'You don't owe me anything, that's not . . . I didn't walk out because of that, you don't have to explain.'

*You're just like me*, she wanted to say. *I think we probably have so many memories that are the same. I think if we were both songs, the melodies would sound so similar. Or maybe they would be in harmony. And we would know the tune and the words straight away, we wouldn't need to rehearse it. The cadences are already inside us. I just need to know you see me, the real me, before I give you everything. Loads of people love her. The girl on the screen. But she's not real, she's the mask. I'm* what's underneath.

'Jonah, I don't like him. Not that way and, actually, not any kind of way, right now.'

She could never properly articulate what she felt. Instead, she wrapped her arms around his torso, laid her head against his heart and closed her eyes.

# Chapter Twenty

Jonah felt his arms slowly wrap around Allegra. His chin fit perfectly atop her head. The rain came down around them and he felt all of the noise stop. The sound that had always buzzed in his head, made worse by an unquiet world, suddenly turned to stillness. As a child, he had always loved stories. That was what had led him to bookshops, his hunger for stories and his need for patterns and order within the chaos of a neurotypical world.

The stories always spoke of true love. Of Gods and gathered flowers, of princes on horses and lonely men in large houses with no room big enough to hold a broken heart. To him, it had always seemed as far away as stories of dragons and wolves who could speak. Now, as he linked his hands together, he felt as though he were holding the whole world. The stories made sense.

Colour showed up in the world in ways it never had before.

'You don't need to like me back,' he told her as he held her. 'It's okay. But I don't think I'll ever stop liking you. So, maybe . . . maybe if it's you and him, I shouldn't be around you both any more.'

'Shut up, Jonah.'

He blinked. 'What?'

'Jonah, I don't like Simon. *He* kissed *me*, I didn't want him to.'

He felt himself scowl. 'Then I'll kill him.'

He felt her laugh against his lungs. Lungs she had robbed of breath from the first moment he saw her.

'I shouldn't even have come out with him tonight,' she said. 'I saw you talking to Kerrie, and I felt jealous. I'm so stupid.'

'Not stupid.'

'And lonely. I'm so fucking lonely.'

Jonah looked up at the stars that were always brighter in Lake Pristine than anywhere else he had ever been. Stars that couldn't be seen in the hellish smoke of the city, where everything was too much and all at once.

Allegra was just lonely. In Lake Pristine for a season and then gone like the fine weather. She wasn't staying. She just needed a new palate for a while.

He could be that for her.

'Come home with me,' he said against her hair. 'Please.'

He knew she was going to say 'yes' by the way she looked up at him, but before the word could come out, a strangled, excitable scream made both of them jump. They turned like two spooked animals to see Saffron Billingham and her older sister, Rebecca, staring at them in visible glee.

'This is too cute,' Saffron cried, her smartphone out and filming the two of them like they were two exotic flowers or a stag in the mist. As if they were something far more interesting than just two teenagers in the street with their arms around each other.

'Please don't film me,' Allegra said softly, and Jonah knew it was a plea she had made so many times before.

More people were gathering, most of them people Jonah did not recognize – out-of-towners who had come to see Pamela. Jonah felt a stab of fear as he looked into some of their faces. He was invisible to them, as they stared at Allegra, ravenous. It completely terrified him, especially as they started to edge closer.

He tightened his arms around Allegra. 'Back off her.' They ignored him. They progressed with terrifying intensity and Jonah saw the world, in a flash, through Allegra's eyes. People's individual natures, the parts that made them whole and loveable, gone in an instant as they formed into a mob. Their faces all looked the same. 'I said back the fuck away from her!'

He pulled Allegra with him as he started walking towards home, and she followed him, gripping his hand tightly. The crowd, however, moved after them like an amoeba. Jonah wondered if they would follow him all the way up to his apartment, when a jeep suddenly lurched into his eyeline, pulling to a stop before the two of them.

'Get in!'

Jasper Montgomery, Lake Pristine's twenty-three-year-old golden girl, was a sight for sore eyes. Allegra seemed hesitant but after noticing Arthur Lancaster in the passenger seat, and Grace in the back, she piled into the beat-up old car without a second thought. Jonah followed suit and, as he pulled the door shut behind them, the car tore off into the woodland surrounding Lake Pristine, leaving the unforgiving mob behind in the dust.

'Hoo, this is the getaway car!' cried the beautiful girl in the driver's seat.

Allegra stared at the back of her head, feeling dazed. She had to be Arthur's girlfriend, the one Grace always spoke about with such reverence. Arthur, the cinema manager, sat in the passenger seat and he watched Jasper with a look that made Allegra feel like giving them some privacy.

'You okay, sweets?' Jasper asked, throwing a quick look to Allegra through the rear-view mirror.

'Fine,' Allegra said, smiling gratefully at the stranger. 'But thanks. That's not the worst I've seen, but it can get a bit ugly when you've nowhere to go.'

'Not many places to escape to in this damn town,' Arthur muttered darkly.

Jasper flashed him a look. 'I know a place.'

Allegra glanced away. The looks the two of them shared felt so intimate that it smarted. They were poking a wound that Allegra was not prepared to bandage up just yet. She turned to give Grace a sideways hug.

'Thanks for the rescue,' she said, to everyone in the car.

'We should have prepped for this,' Jonah said, sounding frustrated. 'We should have known the fans would stay in town.'

'You didn't think Pamela would even come,' Grace pointed out, leaning across Allegra to glare at Jonah.

'No,' Jonah admitted. 'But . . . it wasn't a lack of faith in you, Allegra.'

'No, just past experience with temperamental authors?' She turned to smile at him as she asked the question. He slowly smiled back and they stared at one another for a moment, his eyes dropping to her mouth. They were incredibly close, side by side in the backseat.

'Anyway,' Arthur Lancaster's deep voice interrupted the moment. 'We'll drop you back home after they get bored, Allegra. And we're not going far.'

'Jasper, isn't this the ditch you crashed this car into?' Grace asked cheerfully.

'Gracie!' cried Jasper. 'You'll have them thinking I'm a dangerous driver.'

'I feel like I'm meeting a local legend,' Allegra said.

'You are,' Arthur, Grace and Jonah said all at once.

'No, you're not.' Jasper batted the compliment away while checking her mirrors. 'I'm mostly a chauffeur, these days. Driving her highness in the back to all of her auditions and callbacks.'

Allegra glanced at Grace, who was beaming.

The car was moving very smoothly now. Allegra watched Arthur's hand slip across and grasp Jasper's, the one that was not gripping the steering wheel. Their fingers interlocked. She knew they were long-time residents of Lake Pristine and she wondered how many drives they had taken together, with their hands laced together just so.

Jasper pulled up next to the large house by the actual Lake Pristine. It still looked like a sleepy little mansion from a holiday card. It sat alone by the glassy lake, making it seem like a fortress and a haven all in one. Jasper ushered everyone inside, after checking that they hadn't been followed. She grinned at Allegra and said, 'Any trespassers show up, I'll set my old cat on them.'

Allegra chuffed out a small laugh and followed her inside.

'No offence, Jasper, but this house looks a lot nicer than the last time I visited,' Jonah said bluntly.

'You've been here before?' Allegra asked. She realized everyone knew one another in Lake Pristine, but the Montgomery house always seemed so separate and intimidating.

'Yep. For the annual Montgomery Christmas Party.'

'I redecorated it all for Dad's birthday,' Jasper said. 'They're in Florida right now, but I'll pass on your compliments.'

'You're a decorator?' Allegra turned to Jasper again.

'She's a designer,' Arthur said firmly, the pride in his voice unmistakable.

Jasper invited everyone into the large, glossy kitchen and she poured some ice-cold water. Grace was immediately very at home, fetching a tin of tiny cakes to pass around. Allegra and Jonah stood beside one another by the breakfast bar and his fingers brushed against hers, out of everyone else's view.

'Did you grow up here?' Allegra asked Jasper, staring up at the high ceiling.

'Yes,' Jasper said, as she switched on a kettle.

'It's unbelievable.'

'Thanks. I think so, too.'

'Do you still live here?'

Jasper smiled. 'No. I live with this one now.'

She jerked her head towards Arthur, whose serious face softened for a moment.

'I'm going to build her a house on the other side of the water,' he said quietly, brushing his lips across her knuckles.

Jonah wandered into the small den area while Grace excitedly spoke to Jasper about another dance call-back for the conservatory she wanted to go to. Allegra followed him and they sat, a little away from the rest of the group, on one of the sofas, staring out of the ceiling-to-floor windows that looked out over the whole lake.

'You don't want to go to university when the summer is over?'

Jonah glanced at her, shrugging. 'No.'

'Can I ask why?'

'I don't do very well in educational environments. I always argue with teachers.'

'I think at uni, you're meant to kind of argue with the teachers.'

'No, everyone hates that guy.'

Allegra laughed. 'What do you mean?'

'The "this is more of a comment than a question" guy. The guy who challenges the person with a PHD and tenure. The guy who just wants to have his voice heard.'

Allegra arched an eyebrow. 'Are you saying going to uni will turn you into that guy?'

He smiled and she marvelled at his dimples. 'Maybe. I'm not sure. Don't want to risk it.'

'How long have you been at Brooks Books?'

'Started helping out when I was fourteen. Employed officially at sixteen. I wore your dad down.'

'Are you two close?'

Something appeared in Jonah's eyes for a moment but it was gone in an instant. 'I thought we were.'

'You did?'

'Yeah. But he's been super distant of late.'

'You probably know Dad better than me, but he's never been an amazing communicator.'

'Yeah, well.' Jonah released an exhale. 'Neither am I.'

'You want to work there for always?'

She was aware that she was interrogating him a little, but he didn't seem to mind.

'No, not always,' he said. 'But I want to stay in the world of books.'

'What about publishing?'

'Not many presses in Lake Pristine.'

'You could start one.'

He turned to stare at her, as if no one had ever offered up any kind of interest in this side of him before. She wondered if she had thrown him off the script in his head.

'Yeah, maybe,' he said softly, still staring at her.

'My mother works in publishing,' she reminded him. 'I could reintroduce you. In a professional capacity.'

He regarded her for a moment and then said, 'I want to write.'

Her expression did not change, she had to stop herself from saying, 'I know' because she had read his emails over and over again. All she did was nod. 'I can tell. You aren't . . . you don't speak like anyone else around here. And I think you see everything. It's why you have so many opinions.'

'Too many.'

'That girl you were writing to,' she spoke in a whisper, 'I'm sure she could tell you were a writer.'

'She was a good friend to me. Whoever she is.'

Allegra felt her chest seize. 'Yeah?'

'Yeah. This summer's been weird. Not just because of the arrival of a beautiful film star. Simon's not who I thought he was. I'm re-examining our whole friendship. Kerrie's been weird. George – your dad – has been weird. And every time I screwed up with you at the shop, I would write to her. And she would write back, telling me everything would be okay. She was a real friend.'

Allegra blinked rapidly, desperately trying to keep her eyes dry and her face relaxed. 'I'm sorry she didn't come.'

'Me too. It's . . . it's complicated. She must have had a reason.'

'She was really sorry,' Allegra breathed. 'When I spoke to her. Desperately sorry. She wanted to be there.'

'Yeah. Well. I've kinda got a small amount of tolerance for

people who don't show up.'

Allegra watched the regret mark up his handsome face and it was exactly what made her want to hold back her feelings. He was definitely cooler towards his mystery girl, clearly stung from being stood up.

So, she pushed a little, dipping her toe in the waters of something she had sworn she wouldn't do.

'How old is she? Your pen-pal?'

Jonah blinked. 'I don't actually know. We don't exchange super personal details.'

Allegra pretended to gape at him. 'Jonah!'

'What?'

'She could be ancient. She could be old enough to be your great-grandmother.'

Jonah's eyes widened a little but he shook his head, clearly dislodging any doubt. 'She's not old! She sounds my age. I think.'

'But you're a bit of an old man, Thorne.'

There was a pause.

'How old did she sound over the phone?' he asked innocently.

Allegra smothered a smirk. 'Not sure. She sounded stressed. But if she has a hotshot job in social media, she must be well out of school.'

*You're evil*, a voice in her head whispered. But another reminded her that she needed him to know exactly who it was he claimed to like. Not a goddess on the screen, not a saviour in an email.

A human.

Their eyes locked and she felt the full force of the electricity he always invoked. Palpable and overpowering, but she was no longer able to bury it beneath an argumentative tone or a squabble.

'Allegra,' Jonah spoke roughly, his voice deeper than before. 'I can't stop thinking about you.'

Allegra was held back by eighteen years of saying the wrong thing. She didn't have a script with stage directions in front of her. She had no way of knowing how the scene would go, how the other person would respond. It wasn't blocked or written down or rehearsed. It was live and unpredictable. And she was scared.

'You said you were lonely,' he said, too quietly for any of the others to hear. 'I know you're here for a summer. I know you'll be gone soon. Everything will turn back to pumpkins for me. But, in the meantime, I want to . . . I want . . .'

She watched him fight with how to word it. 'Yes?'

'I want you.'

She watched his pupils dilate as he looked at her. 'Lots of people have wanted me, Jonah. They don't want it any more, once they've come too close.'

He shook his head, moving closer. 'I'm not like that.'

'No one thinks they're like that, until the shiny thing in their head turns out to be a human. Just like everybody else.'

He was about to respond when Jasper appeared in the entryway, wearing a knowing smile. 'I can drive you back into town. Or you can stay here. We've got three spare rooms.'

'I get Christine's old room!' shouted Grace from the kitchen.

'Who's Christine?' Allegra asked.

'Jasper's sister,' Jonah murmured. 'Don't ask, it's impossible to explain her.'

'How about it?' Jasper asked Allegra, every inch the hostess. 'I can make you all some amazing eggs in the morning?'

Allegra liked her so much. There was something different about her. Something familiar. As if they had met in another life. She brought up feelings of déjà vu, despite Allegra knowing they had never interacted before.

'You can have the blue room upstairs, Allegra,' Jasper said. 'It has the nicest en-suite.' She looked pointedly at Jonah. 'You all right to sleep here on the sofa? No one's allowed in my parents' room, I'm afraid.'

Allegra grinned as he released a heavy sigh. 'Sure.'

Jasper led Allegra up to the blue room.

'It's the same size as my dad's apartment,' Allegra said, laughing.

Jasper smiled and Allegra was a little dazzled by it. 'Do you have your own place?'

'Yes,' Allegra said. 'An apartment in the city. I bought it when I turned eighteen. It's . . . barely furnished, I'm hardly there. Only room that is finished is the walk-in wardrobe.' She paused for a beat and then groaned. 'That makes me sound like a monster.'

Jasper regarded her with a warmth that made Allegra feel tearful. 'No, it doesn't. Makes you sound like someone who has had to grow up way too fast.'

Allegra didn't know if it was exhaustion from preparing for the festival, overstimulation after a full day of working in the sun, or frustration after the stress of Simon's unwanted kiss. Or Jonah's all-seeing eyes.

But Jasper's empathy released something in her.

And she started to cry.

# Chapter Twenty-One

**JonahThorne@gmail.com**
**to: westendgirl@gmail.com**
**Subject: Just Wondering**
Dear Friend,
I was thinking. How old are you? You have a big career in social media, which feels like a young person's game but it's far more impressive than anything on my resumé. I was just wondering. I know we don't talk too much about the personal stuff, but anyway . . .
Jonah.

**westendgirl@gmail.com**
**to: JonahThorne@gmail.com**
**Subject: Just Telling**
Let me guess. Someone close to you says that I'm ancient.

**JonahThorne@gmail.com**
**to: westendgirl@gmail.com**
**Subject: (no subject)**
Sorry!! No, that's not it exactly. I was just wondering.

Allegra smiled to herself as she switched off her phone. The emails were giving her a touch of lightness that she desperately needed after a tumultuous evening. Jasper had let her cry and had now gone to wet a flannel so Allegra could wash her face. On returning, Jasper spoke to her softly, so softly, about how Allegra deserved all of the good things she had earned. That sacrifices were a part of success and it was all right to feel a sense of loss when she looked at her achievements, as well as pride. She explained that imposter syndrome seemed to plague women who didn't deserve it more than it did the men who made money from their art. It was the speech Allegra had needed someone to make to her for years. While she knew twenty-three was not a big gap in terms of age and maturity, she looked at Jasper as though she were the wisest of women.

And Allegra knew. She just knew. This woman in her mid-twenties, who smiled at everyone and noticed who felt left out or too scared to talk, was like her.

'I'm autistic,' Allegra heard herself say. 'The studios don't know. The fans, my co-workers, no one. Only my team and my parents. And Grace.'

Jasper's smile did not falter, there was not a fleck of surprise in her face. 'Oh, really?'

'I'm not ashamed of it. But I can't always cope. I have these . . . I don't know, these hangovers after press junkets. When I have to speak to hundreds of people. Or do a talk show.'

'Your body is taking on more stimulation than its designed for,' Jasper said quietly. 'It's not a flaw in you. It's the infrastructure that's the problem.'

'If I tell the networks, it'll get out to the press. Then I'll be vilified and held up as some kind of spokesperson all at once.'

Something flashed through Jasper's eyes but she said nothing for a moment. And then: 'Your medical diagnosis is not anyone else's business. No matter their relation to you. It's yours to disclose. And I think you deserve some privacy.'

It felt like someone had finally given Allegra permission. She exhaled. She sat back and the claw that had been wrapped around her heart let go. 'I feel like I owe everyone my whole life. All of the time. To reassure them that their investment or their admiration hasn't been misplaced.'

Jasper squeezed Allegra's hand and smiled kindly. 'Well. Fuck that.'

'But there's also a small part of me that wants to stop hiding it. Maybe it would help some of the more well-adjusted people understand me a little better. Maybe journalists wouldn't jump to weird conclusions when they write about me. Maybe . . . maybe I could find, like, my own world.'

Jasper frowned. 'Your own . . .?'

'World. I . . .' Allegra hesitated, wondering if what she wanted to say sounded too childlike, too sensitive. 'I want to have my own little world, like a shelter from everything else. My life, my whole life . . . I feel like I've been watching other people live. Like they're the ones on the screen. I'm always this expert on things that don't happen for me. I'm like an academic on the topic of, I don't know – some ancient civilization I can never truly be a part of. Maybe that's what has helped me to act well. I can tell you everything about so much of life. But I don't know what it *feels* like. I'm almost like someone who knows every bone of a bird, every mechanism of flight – except what it actually feels like to fly.'

She knew she was monologuing, in a way that was unnatural to other young adults. She knew her difference was seeping from the edges of the mask, but she didn't care.

'So, that's what I want,' she concluded. 'My own little world, my own corner of something beautiful. I came here looking to find it and I just watched from the sidelines, like I always do. And I am just so sick of always meeting my old, comfortable self everywhere I go.'

The words stayed in the air. Jasper stared at the girl, clearly feeling the weight of everything that had been overshared. Yet Allegra could tell she was not uncomfortable. There was respect in her eyes. As she stood to fetch some water for the room, Allegra wondered why she had felt so open in front of this perfect stranger. Why the difficulties that other people often inspired were no longer there.

As Jasper went back downstairs, Arthur crossed the upstairs landing. He caught Allegra's eye through the open door and smiled dryly.

'You just got Jaspered.'

Allegra nodded, wiping her last tear away. 'Yes.'

He nodded, sympathetically. 'She can't help it.'

Allegra didn't know what to say so she said nothing.

'What's going on with you and Jonah Thorne?'

She was surprised by that. 'Nothing. Nothing, why?'

He scoffed, not unkindly. 'The way he looks at you? It's not nothing.'

Jasper appeared at the top of the stairs with a large glass of water. 'Arthur Lancaster, are you getting into other people's business? Keep it moving, Grumble. It's their private life.'

The pair of them disappeared into another room, closing the door firmly behind them. Grace popped her head in, toothbrush in hand, to say goodnight. Once Grace had gone, Allegra stripped down to her bra and underwear and slid under the duvet. She let the cool sheets caress her skin for a moment and then got up to open the window. She used one of the many new toothbrushes in the guest bathroom drawer and the unopened toothpaste. She splashed water on her face.

She looked back into the empty, quiet bedroom. One small bedside lamp lit the room, but it was dim and inviting. The summer rain was still pouring outside, a gentle whisper against the window. It provided a touch of coolness through the slightly open window.

She turned her phone off. It was full of people trying to reach her. None of them friends, none of them people who really knew her.

It made her all the lonelier.

So, she silently slipped on a robe and went downstairs.

Jonah had folded his clothes neatly and laid them on the floor by the large sofa he was going to sleep on. The lights in the den were still lit but the lake outside the nearly transparent room was in total darkness. Wearing only his boxers, he placed a spare sheet that Jasper had handed him across the leather couch and was about to turn off the lights when Allegra appeared in the entryway.

He took in her appearance and quietly said, 'Oh, God.'

She blinked. 'I'm not tired.'

'Me neither.'

'Have you asked your dream girl if she's seventy-four years old yet?'

His lips twitched. 'Maybe.'

'What did she say?'

'She wasn't happy about it.'

'Maybe you're onto something then.'

'Are you jealous of my pen-pal, Allegra?'

Her eyes danced for a moment and then grew serious. 'I just want you to be sure, Jonah. About what you want. About *who* you want.'

Her long hair was loose and wild. Her expression was determined. So Jonah, who had never claimed to read people well or know what they really wanted, finally felt as though he could communicate with someone in a perfect code. Her eyes raked over his bare torso and he reached out to wrap one hand around her wrist. He pulled gently. She moved until they were almost pressed together. Her hand ran down his stomach to the thin line of hair beneath his navel. He groaned and the sound made her back up a little, moving towards the long windows looking out over the lake.

Jonah hated that so many other people's opinions lived inside her head, making her question everything that she felt. He moved behind her as she shrugged out of her robe. He circled his arms around her middle, pulling her back to his front. Gentle but firm. The noise she made brought his mouth down to her neck.

'You have the most beautiful body.'

She brought her hands up to cover his. 'People write stuff every day, saying that's not true.'

'Those people are losers.'

He kissed her neck again and she moaned. She started to pull his hands further down her stomach.

Then she suddenly stopped.

'You okay?' he asked instantly.

'Sorry,' she murmured. 'Thought something moved out there . . .'

'Maybe a deer?'

'Yeah, maybe.'

She turned and kissed him, making him forget whatever it was he had been about say. He groaned and pushed her up against the window. She draped her arms around his neck and he lifted her up so she could wrap her legs around his waist.

'Take me upstairs,' she said against his mouth.

'You're sure?'

'Yeah.'

She led him upstairs, to the warm, darkened room with the rain lightly falling outside. He sat on the bed and she sat on him. He kissed her and tried to tell her through doing so that he wanted all of her. Bodies could only express and inspire so much. The soul she let him glimpse was far more beautiful. The part of her that had ignited that fear in him on their first meeting. The part that had created the spark between them, a spark they had turned into quarrelling; a stupid disguise for an obvious attraction. The confident parts, the anxious parts. The parts that were assured, the parts that doubted. The parts that he had yet to meet.

It was the simplest thing – something he had always thought would be messy and complicated. And it was so easy.

Allegra had always felt the world a little more than some. Lights were always brighter, sounds went through her ear and into the backs of her eyes. Smells and tastes and touch were electricity in the nose and mouth and fingertips. So when sitting in Jonah

Thorne's lap and kissing him brought pleasure, it came in a way that was intense and overwhelming.

After about half an hour of kissing without drawing breath, it was only a cough from Grace in the other room that made them both pause. Allegra smiled against his neck and whispered, 'I want this . . . but maybe not in a house with three other people.'

Jonah, who was a little out of oxygen, nodded. 'Yes. But please tell me the millisecond you change your mind.'

As they lay side by side, she threw one leg over him and rested her head against his chest.

'This is such a nice house,' she finally whispered.

'It is. The Montgomerys are a big deal in these parts.'

'Small-town royalty?'

'Exactly.'

'So, how did Arthur . . .?'

'How did he land Jasper?'

'Yeah.'

Jonah shrugged. 'Not sure. They've been together for years now. I thought they hated each other when they were at school.'

'Guess you never can tell.'

He grinned at her. 'Seems so.'

Allegra glanced across at her bedside table. She slid open its tiny drawer and withdrew a pink device, with two silver balls.

'What is that?' demanded Jonah, with a laugh in his voice.

'Possibly something very dirty. Oh, no, I know! I was sent three of these last year. It's a skincare thing.'

He eyed her dubiously and, as she pressed a small indentation on the pink body of the device, it began to vibrate which caused both of them to shake with laughter.

'That is not skincare, Allegra Brooks.'

'Yes, it is! Look, I'll try it on your face.'

'You will do no such thing!'

She slowly dragged the vibrating device up and down his jawline, causing him to grimace.

'It stings.'

'No, it doesn't.'

'It does! It's tingling.'

'Men are such babies.'

'What exactly is it doing for me?'

She smiled as she took in his beautiful face. The long, dark lashes fanned out on his flawless skin. Dark curls and just the smallest hint of stubble beneath the silly skincare aid.

'Not much,' she said honestly. 'You look pretty great already.'

They slept for a few hours. Allegra woke to find him spooning her, with his hand splayed out across her stomach. She normally hated people touching her middle but she didn't mind when it was him. She had done kissing scenes for work, and she had dated a few people, but nobody made her feel the way Jonah did. It was not just arousal, it was something deeper. She felt him stir, waking as she had done. He kissed her neck and gently turned her chin so he could kiss her face.

She rolled over to take his face in her hands and kissed him again. When she ran her hands through his black hair, he groaned again.

'You're going to kill me.'

She smiled and then both of them started as the shrill sound of a telephone from downstairs pierced the air. It rang and rang, an insistent new guest in the house. Jonah and Allegra listened as Jasper slipped downstairs, with light ballerina feet.

'Hello, Montgomery residence,' they heard her say.

There was a long, still silence after this greeting. A call late into the night, on a landline, signalled so many awful things.

But nothing could have prepared Allegra for what came next.

Jasper appeared on the landing, the phone in her hand. She registered Jonah's presence in Allegra's bed but said nothing about it. 'Allegra, your dad would like you to come home.'

Allegra shook her head, confused. 'I – how does he know I'm here?'

Jasper's face was a picture of confusion as she handed the phone over.

'Dad?'

'Come home, Ally. Now, please. Get someone to drive you.'

# Chapter Twenty-Two

Allegra didn't have to ask Jasper for a ride, the keys were already in her hand. Jonah got dressed and followed the two of them out to the jeep, not even entertaining the idea of staying behind. Allegra watched Arthur lean down to whisper something into Jasper's ear.

'No, stay here with Grace, I'll be back soon,' she replied.

Jonah and Allegra got into the car and Allegra tried to keep her heart steady.

'It's my mum,' she said quietly. 'Gotta be. I'm too scared to turn my phone on.'

'He would have said if it was your mum,' Jonah said softly. He knew her father better than she did. 'Don't do that to yourself.'

They were at Brooks Books in minutes, due to quiet roads and the size of the town. As Jasper turned off the engine, she placed her hand on Allegra's arm.

'Breathe. You haven't done anything wrong.'

'Tonight's been a whole mess. Everything with Simon—'

'Simon is a huckster. I may be the only person in this town who doesn't like him, but I'm glad you're seeing through him. He may turn out good someday, but he's a—'

Jasper suddenly remembered that Jonah was in the car and it stopped her from continuing.

'Don't worry,' Jonah said bitterly. 'I'm starting to see him more clearly.'

'This is an autistic canonical event, I'm afraid,' Jasper said. 'Some of us trust people's words a little too quickly because we forget that not everyone is like us. It's a rite of passage.'

'I have to go in,' Allegra said, her words staccato-like with nerves.

'Can I say something quickly?' Jasper pressed.

Allegra tried to calm her breathing. 'Yes.'

'You're eighteen. You're independent. You can't get in trouble. Not any more, schooldays are done. If he's cross or mad about something, you don't have to bow your head and take it. I know you're eighteen and being a young adult is weird, and you're never sure where the lines really are. They're not in a number or a birthday and none of the rules click into place. But you're allowed to stand up for yourself. Trust me. I've been there.'

If Allegra was not in such a hurry to find out why her father had sounded so ominous she would have spilled out all of the warm feelings she felt towards this woman. Instead she swiftly hugged her, before running to the bookshop door.

She unlocked it with shaking hands, holding it open for Jonah as the two of them dashed inside and upstairs. They found George Brooks in the kitchen and, to the astonishment of them both, there was a laptop set up next to him. It sat menacingly on the kitchen table.

Allegra watched her father scowl at the sight of Jonah. 'What's going on, Dad?'

'Sit down, Allegra.'

Remembering Jasper's words, Allegra elected to stand. 'No. Tell me. Is it Mum? Is she okay?'

'Can you hear us, honey?'

Natalie, her publicist, was on the laptop screen and she was wearing a robe. She looked haggard. Allegra would never usually use such a word to describe Natalie, but it was fitting. An assistant to her agent, Sam, was also present on the call.

'I can hear you,' Allegra said shakily.

'Okay, hon. You haven't been answering either of your phones.'

'No, they're switched off.'

'Okay. Well.' Natalie was clearly searching for how to begin, while her father would barely look at her. 'Did you go on a date tonight?'

The question completely threw Allegra. She felt Jonah's fingers brush her own, a silent reminder that he was there and on her side. 'Yes. Kind of. Not really a date, we just went—'

'But you kissed?'

'Is this about Simon?' Allegra asked, glancing at her silent father. 'He kissed me. I didn't want it, so I left.'

'Okay, hon,' Natalie said, trying to sound soothing. 'Well, some amateur pap got a photo of it.'

'Okay,' said Allegra, feeling her body starting to relax. 'But, that's okay. It'll blow over. Or we explain. I didn't want it.'

'Well. Then there were follow-up amateur shots of you and,' Natalie suddenly looked to Jonah, 'that young man.'

'Jonah,' Allegra said. Her voice sounded different in her ears. 'His name is Jonah.'

Natalie sighed. 'Well. Honey . . .'

Allegra watched her publicist fall silent. She watched as the agency assistant looked down at her lap. She watched her father's face, filled with rage, as he wouldn't meet her eyes. 'What? What is it? What's happening?'

Natalie looked like she wanted to cry, and that scared Allegra more than anything. 'Someone . . . some *scumbag* . . . got shots of you and Jonah tonight.'

Allegra shook her head, feeling slow. 'On the street? We were being mobbed.'

'No, sweetheart,' Natalie said. She sounded maternal. Sad. 'In the house by the lake.'

Allegra's whole world stopped. 'What?'

'Some parasite with a long lens, maybe,' Natalie said.

'Fuck,' Jonah said softly. 'Allegra. It wasn't a deer.'

Allegra squeezed his hand. 'Natalie. Do you – you have the pictures? They're up already?'

'Yes,' Natalie said. She pulled up the first one. It was Simon and Allegra, the unwanted kiss caught by a bystander. It was obvious, even to a person who had no context, that she did not return his attentions. In the picture, her arms were crossed and she was leaning as far away from him as possible.

'This one went up much earlier tonight. Someone on social media, as I said. It didn't worry me so much,' Natalie said, as if they were discussing rehearsed answers for a television appearance and not captured moments of Allegra's actual life. 'But these ones . . .'

She shared three professionally taken images and they made Allegra's knees give out. She released a noise of distress as she stared at the screen. She could feel Jonah's arms around her, trying to help her stand but she couldn't move, rendered immobile by the images she was looking at and the knowledge of what they would do to her reputation now that they were public.

The pictures had been taken by someone lurking on the beach by Lake Pristine. The den of the house was an almost transparent room, so it was like she and Jonah were in a goldfish bowl. The first image was him standing behind her, his face buried in her neck with his hands brushing the top of her underwear. Allegra's front was facing out towards the lake and, unbeknownst to her, the photographer. It was impossible for someone to believe the images showed a platonic pair.

The second image was Allegra with her back against the long glass window, legs wrapped around Jonah while they kissed passionately.

The third was the two of them kissing. It was, perhaps, the tamer of the three images and yet it was strikingly intimate. He was holding her head in his hands and her arms were draped over his shoulders, their bodies fused together.

A beautiful moment, tarnished. Turned to ash.

'I think I'm going to be sick,' Allegra breathed.

'So, by the by, the editor had Simon confirm his identity from the first photograph and he was only too happy to identify Jonah as well. Once they established everyone was over eighteen, they published,' Natalie reported, rubbing her eyes and taking a quick sip of something that did not look like coffee or tea.

'I'll kill him,' Allegra heard Jonah say quietly.

'Okay, look,' Natalie spoke, sounding so weary. 'If you were my client, Jonah, this would be the easiest fix in the world. In fact, it wouldn't need fixing. The world would throw you a parade. But, Allegra, we need to get detoxing. The anti-sex crowd will want your contracts dropped. So, we need—'

'Wait a second,' Jonah said, and he sounded far away to Allegra's ears even though his arms were still around her. 'Why is everyone acting like Allegra's done something wrong? We've done nothing wrong. Don't talk to her like she's been caught drink-driving or hurting an animal – she's got nothing to apologize for!'

'Logically, of course that's true,' Natalie said, exhaling heavily. 'Give me some credit, I'm not a schoolmarm! Most people aren't. Most people are going to be completely indifferent or neutral to these pictures. That's what any normal person would feel. But the people who hate women being happy or sexual or visibly enlightened are going to be *loud*, Jonah. They're going to come after her. In bad faith! We have to get our skates on now.'

'You shouldn't even be here,' George said quietly.

Allegra and Jonah looked at him.

'What?' Jonah said.

'You,' George repeated, looking up at his employee, with cold detachment. 'You're not needed here, you can go. You've done enough.'

'Here's my plan.' Natalie clapped her hands, as if to pull the focus back to the only person who was willing to be unemotional and practical. 'You're in love. Young love. Fell in love during a much-needed slice of normality for Allegra. Got a little passionate during a beautiful night by the lake, but did not go any further—'

'Stop,' Allegra said brokenly.

Natalie's eyes widened. 'What?'

'We're not going to lie. Spin some sanitized version. We're not going to say anything.'

She was not going to force Jonah into some charade where he had to pretend that he loved her in order to save her reputation.

'Darling, saying nothing just creates a vacuum for them to make up their own version.'

'Allegra,' Jonah spoke gently to her, his face open. 'Why can't we—?'

George suddenly got to his feet, leaving the room without any ceremony. Yet his exit was loud and a clear signal. He would not speak to Allegra with Jonah there.

'Allegra, I think you should post a picture of the two of you on your Instagram and we'll treat it as a hard launch. The leaked pictures were unfortunate but you're proud of your relationship and—'

'There is no relationship,' snapped Allegra. 'You're not pressuring him into pretending to date me so I can keep a few networks happy. I'm done with this conversation.'

She went to her room. Not her room, really; George's spare bedroom. The room she was currently sleeping in. It would go back to being spare when she returned to the city.

It was not her home. She did not belong there. The little world of sanctuary she had come looking for was no longer there, in Lake Pristine.

It had been a silly dream, she thought. Silly to want a world to yourself when the world had decided that it owned you.

Jonah walked home in the early morning daylight. He turned his phone on and it was instantly ringing. His mother.

'Hey,' he said on picking up.

'I'm still with Aunt Shosh but she saw something online and then we turned on the breakfast show—'

'So, you've seen the pictures,' he said, his voice flat and without feeling.

'Yes! Jonah, are you all right? Is Allegra all right?'

'I'm okay.' Jonah felt a lump in his throat, at both her kindness and her refreshing lack of judgement. 'Allegra's . . . not.'

Allegra had gone to her room and when Jonah had knocked, she had pleaded with him to leave. He felt completely disassembled. He knew what images like that meant for a young woman and he hated himself for not protecting her. He hated that she was distraught. He hated that she didn't think he was the person that could make it all go away.

And he couldn't stop thinking of how she had declared there to be no relationship, how adamant she had been about it.

He had taken a work number and an email address from Natalie, determined to put the whole thing right somehow.

'I'm scared for you, honey. Aunt Shosh is driving me back to Lake Pristine right now.'

'Okay,' Jonah said, on autopilot. 'I need some sleep.'

'Yes, get some rest. I'm so sorry, but we will fix this.'

He hung up as he arrived at his family's bakery. It was shut but there were a few people lingering on the kerb.

'Are you Jonah Thorne?' a woman in a transparent raincoat asked. 'Can we have a comment from you about Allegra Brooks?'

He said nothing, letting himself into the apartment without even acknowledging her. He jogged up the stairs to their front door, let himself inside and went straight to his bedroom. He collapsed onto the double bed and finally started to check his messages.

A voice note from Kerrie: 'Wow, Jonah, just wow. Couldn't wait five minutes. Screw you. Or not. Whatever.'

A few more reassuring messages of support from both his mother and Aunt Shosh.

Some gross texts of feigned sympathy from people he hadn't

spoken to since leaving school, followed up by invasive questions from them as they nosily pressed their faces up against the window of his life.

Plus a few random journalists, sending almost identical requests for comment. One voicemail from a woman with a very toffee-nosed voice.

'Hello, Jonah, Julie M. Atkins here, celebrity journalist. I wondered if I could get a quote from you about the young madam that is Allegra—'

He deleted everything.

As if under a strange spell, he opened YouTube. He started to type her name, but the algorithm had already anticipated his interest. There was a video from the official channel of a morning talk show called *Morning Tea*. The video had only thirty thousand views, but it was climbing rapidly. Allegra's full name was in the video title.

There were four women around a table, in front of a live television audience. There was a huge screen behind them, which showed the picture of Jonah kissing Allegra from behind.

'Can we even show this on morning TV?' asked the blondest of the three blonde women at the table, laughing loudly but with nothing behind her eyes.

'As a massive *Court of Bystanders* fan,' another woman said, 'we haven't seen this girl for months, then all of a sudden we get this? Good on you, girl, go get yours.'

'I don't know,' the only brunette interrupted, looking serious. 'I feel bad for her.'

'You feel bad for her?' shrieked the first woman. 'Estelle, she's debasing herself for the whole world to see—'

'She's been photographed without her consent in what looks like a private residence,' the brunette said, with enough force to stop the audience from laughing at the exaggerated outrage from the first woman. 'She's not "debasing herself", LeeAnn. She's with – probably with her boyfriend.'

'Then who was the guy she was with just hours before those pictures were taken?' the final blonde woman asked. 'I'm barely following this drama.'

'We have a statement from her team about that,' Estelle said, lifting a small cue card from the table. She read from it, seemingly verbatim. 'Allegra Brooks would like her privacy to be respected at this time. A member of the public took an unwanted photograph of an unwanted kiss from a work colleague and Miss Brooks would like to put the entire ordeal behind her.'

Jonah stared at the screen. He hadn't even been mentioned. The statement was deliberately vague. Natalie had kept him out of it completely. He should have felt relieved. Instead he felt dejected, useless. He wanted to claim the pictures. He wanted to be unapologetic. Proud, even. He wanted to take care of Allegra and physically fight anyone who had something nasty or self-righteous to say.

But he had been erased.

'We have a journalist on the phone,' Estelle said, turning to look into another camera. 'Julie M. Atkins, you've interviewed Allegra Brooks before, you are her most recent interviewer. What were your impressions of her?'

Jonah frowned, recognizing the name from the voicemail on his phone. He glowered as the same snobbish, disembodied voice began to speak.

'She's a real struggle to interview, I'll say that much,' Julie said, sounding utterly delighted to be on the air. 'She gives herself airs, so it's actually quite fabulous to see her being humbled like this.'

'She's a kid,' Estelle said, quietly and with a look of distaste, but Julie barrelled on.

'To be perfectly honest though, when I met her, I found her to be a tad . . . off. A bit of a cold fish. So these pictures were a surprise.'

'What was "off" about her?' asked LeAnn.

'Can't put my finger on it. Just something.'

'She was Little Miss Squeaky Clean before this,' LeeAnn added smugly. 'Not much of a role model any more, is she? And those lakehouse pictures were no unwanted kiss. That was far too steamy.'

'No, the kiss with . . .' Estelle checked her notes, '. . . Simon Hannigan was unwanted. Not sure about the dark-haired one.'

Jonah rolled his eyes. It was surreal to hear Simon's name on television.

'She's eighteen years old,' Estelle went on, eyeing her colleagues with a steely look. 'She's a baby. She's doing what millions of other young adults are doing, all over the world, except she has eyes on her at all times. People should leave her alone. If this were my daughter, I would be fighting all of you.'

'Your daughter would not do this, Estelle.'

'My daughter *has* done this, LeeAnn. Everyone at this table has. It just hasn't ended up in the tabloids. Let's move on.'

Jonah threw his phone across the room and swore. He buried his head in his hands. He wanted to take the last few hours and fight them but he couldn't. A reputation was a fragile thing that could not be handled or grasped or even rescued.

He pulled his ancient laptop towards him and he started to write, what he always did when he had too many feelings to process and the air wouldn't come. He wrote his friend an email. He poured out everything he felt. Everything that he knew was inevitable.

But for some reason, he didn't release it. His finger hovered over the 'send' button but he could not bring himself to do it. He saved it to his drafts and fell into a tormented sleep instead.

# Chapter Twenty-Three

Allegra couldn't sleep.

Her father had brought her a tray of food along with a disapproving aura, but they hadn't exchanged words. Her phone remained switched off. It was her first day off from the festival and she planned to spend it in hiding.

She knew what was going to happen anyway. Press would already be descending on Lake Pristine. So, Natalie and her management would have a car come to collect her. One with tinted windows and a surly, silent driver. It would spirit her away, back to the city. To her empty apartment.

Back to the glamorous grindstone.

Back to colleagues instead of friends.

Back to stone.

As late morning slipped into her room, her self-pity was interrupted by a knock on the front door. Her father was manning the shop downstairs, so Allegra slipped into the hall. She cracked the door open a little, just in case her father had unwittingly sent a journalist up to their flat.

It was Jasper Montgomery.

Her face was so full of empathy, Allegra feared she might cry if she had any tears left.

'May I come in?'

'Sure.'

Jasper stepped into the flat, her interior designer eyes landing on every piece of furniture in a sweeping survey of the room. She was obviously not too impressed but she smiled warmly at Allegra.

'This is fucking shit.'

Allegra laughed at the woman's bluntness. 'Yes, it is.'

'I can't believe they get to do this to you.'

'Yeah, well. Price of fame.'

'I'm checking the security tapes. If they even brushed at the borders of our land at the Lakehouse, I'm suing them to within an inch of their lives.'

'Thanks.'

They sat on Allegra's bed and Jasper took her hand. 'Have you spoken to anyone?'

'No. My publicist, briefly. She'll be putting a plan together. They'll have me out of here by tonight.'

Jasper scanned Allegra's face, as though trying to catch her tells. 'Is that what you want, though?'

'Doesn't matter what I want. I'm the one who fucked up.'

'You did not fuck up, sweets. You got preyed on by a horrible photographer and an unscrupulous editor.'

Hearing Jasper say it made Allegra feel like some of the curse was lifting. 'I— it's not just my reputation, everyone I work with will be worried about implication.'

'Well, if anyone gives you a hard time about this, they don't deserve to work with you.'

Allegra felt her breath quicken and her jaw start to tremble. 'I might have ruined Jonah's life. Those pictures will be online for ever.'

'Allegra,' Jasper said her name softly. 'Jonah will not agree with that assessment. You haven't ruined anyone's life, least of all his.'

One tear slid free before Allegra could stop it. Jasper quickly caught it, but made no fuss. Instead, she reached into a large Dior tote to remove what looked like a portfolio.

'What's this?' asked Allegra.

'Well, I'm actually here on business,' Jasper said, speaking with a brisk and bright tone. 'I wanted to pitch something to you.'

Allegra's eyebrows shot up. 'A pitch?'

'Yes. I wasn't able to stop thinking about what you said last night, about your unfinished apartment.'

Allegra stared at the sketches and colours Jasper was showing her. 'You – you want to design my apartment?'

'Well, I would have to see what I'm working with but yes, I would love to. I think your first home as an adult should be entirely to your own taste. Screw what anybody else thinks. I will literally just make your ideas happen.'

Allegra could have kissed her. Somehow, Jasper had known that she needed distraction. More than anything, she needed to be diverted from everything that people were thinking and saying about her.

'And, I'll waive my fee,' Jasper said, after showing Allegra samples and drawings and design ideas. 'Only invoice for furniture and trimmings. As an apology for letting that shit go down while you were under my roof.'

'Jasper,' Allegra shook her head. 'It's not your fault.'

'Well, it's definitely not *yours*,' Jasper said quickly. 'Now. Talk me through your apartment.'

Jonah was due to start his shift at the festival, but he was not looking for volunteers to direct or guests to usher in. He was searching for one person and one person alone. He showered, shaved and threw on a white tee and jeans, plus his boots, before jogging to Main Street and heading for the festival site.

Volunteers were guiding a mass of visitors through the hay bales that represented the opening gates. Children were coming out of a smaller tent, many of them wearing face paint. There were food carts and ice cream vendors set up. People sat in deck chairs, reading newly purchased books. Everything was as it should be and Jonah would normally take a moment to appreciate their hard work paying off.

Not this year.

When he entered the green room, a few volunteers were already there and setting up for a full morning. Kerrie was organizing the hot drinks station and when she saw Jonah, her face darkened.

'Come to meet your new adoring fans?' she asked him sharply.

'No, Kerrie,' he said, less sharply than her but still with feeling. 'You're being mean. I'm sorry if those pictures hurt you but you're not my priority. I'm not sorry I like Allegra, okay? Where's Simon?'

'Those pictures didn't hurt me,' Kerrie snapped, her cheeks flushing a deep crimson. 'I was stupid at that party. Don't flatter yourself.'

'Sure. Fine. Where's Simon?'

'He's taking the morning off. He's not loving the news cycle right now.'

'You mean the one he initiated? He gave both of our names to some leech and now we're all indicted. Allegra more than anyone.'

'She's a big girl, Jonah, she'll be fine.'

Jonah had been moving to leave the green room but that shifted something in him. He rounded on Kerrie, glaring at her. 'She's been nothing but nice to you, Kerrie. More than nice. Why the hell have you turned on her?'

'I haven't turned on anyone, her dramatic tendencies are obviously rubbing off on you. Probably when you were rubbing all over her!'

Jonah wished he could give Kerrie what she wanted. He wished he could even know what that was. He knew there was hurt bubbling beneath the disdain and the antagonism she was demonstrating. Her resentment was a sour perfume she was trying to spray over her pain, hoping no one could scent what was really the matter.

'Kerrie, I'm sorry if you thought I was leading you on.' Jonah tried to be understanding, despite the adrenaline pumping through him. 'I'm sorry for all of it. But I hope you don't take this out on Allegra.'

'God, the way you defend her,' Kerrie said, almost inaudibly. She suddenly seemed overly fascinated with her cuticles. 'She's a multi-millionaire, Jonah, she'll be fine.'

Jonah threw her a look of disgust and then stormed out of the tent. He was about to cross Main Street and head for Simon's house on the other side of town, when he realized that a small crowd had gathered by the Arthouse.

Jonah saw, a little too late, that the press had set up just outside of the retro movie house and were waiting to see if anyone would talk to them about Allegra. Mrs Heywood was saying something to a reporter with a camera but judging by his bored expression, it was probably nothing salacious. More likely local gossip about Virgil who ran the flower shop, a person Mrs Heywood famously hated.

Jonah stepped back into the shadow of a tall tree, making sure to stay out of their eyeline. Most of them looked fed up, which he supposed was a good sign. A large black Mercedes suddenly pulled up, parking near Brooks Books. The driver stepped out and went straight into the bookshop. Jonah watched with curiosity and a slight pang of worry.

Ten minutes later, the driver exited the bookshop carrying a pale pink suitcase. A few reporters spotted him putting it in the trunk of the car and they began to lurk a little closer. Jonah started to truly panic when they all suddenly rushed en masse, like a flock of pigeons to a handful of seeds.

Allegra emerged from Brooks Books. And, while she always looked beautiful to Jonah, in this moment she looked every inch a movie star.

Cameras clicked and people shouted, as she walked to the backseat of the car. Her long hair was piled into a neat updo. Her oversized Valentino shades covered most of her pretty face, but her lips were a dark cherry colour. She wore pink pearl drop earrings. A pair of Manolos. A simple white dress with no sleeves.

Her face gave absolutely nothing away as she opened the car door herself, shaking her head ever so slightly at the driver when he offered to do so.

Questions were barked at her but she had clearly dismissed them all. Jonah felt his heart drop in his ribs: she was about to leave. Possibly for ever.

He shifted forwards, almost involuntarily. As if sensing him, Allegra looked up. Her mask slipped for the tiniest moment. She tipped her shades down for a millisecond and let him see a whole world of emotion in her eyes. Apology. Appreciation. Something unnameable.

And goodbye.

Jonah felt his heart shatter. It cracked and then broke like glass.

As he watched the car pull away, the press momentarily wilted and sighed as a group – as if someone had thrown cold water over them. But then, before Jonah was able to make his own escape, he watched realization spark one reporter's face.

'Hey! Jonah?'

Jonah didn't know what to do. He wondered if anyone had ever sat Allegra down and taught her how to handle this strange intrusion. He set off towards the festival site. Then stopped. He couldn't lead this mob to his place of work.

'Jonah, have the two of you called off your relationship? Will you still be friends? Did you get to say goodbye?'

Jonah felt the cold, grasping anxiety of being chased. Corners and blockades felt more intense and he wasn't sure of where to run. He knew Allegra needed him to be silent.

He made for the Arthouse.

Grace Lancaster was behind the cinema bar and, on seeing Jonah, she immediately sprang into action. She ushered him into the back of the theatre, where the family's private apartment was, and shut out the press with a firm snick.

'They're such vultures,' she said as Jonah caught his breath.

Jonah sat down at the kitchen table in the middle of the room. He looked at the walls, all covered with pictures of the Lancaster family. Drawings that Grace had made as a girl. It was a home, completely made of memories.

Jonah wondered how it must feel to be part of a large family, rather than one of two.

'I'm never going to see her again.' Jonah said the words lifelessly.

'Well. That's not exactly true. I can watch her on the screen, like everybody else.'

Grace sat across from him, frowning in an unusually stoic manner. 'Did she say that?'

Jonah glanced over at her. 'Not exactly. But leaving Lake Pristine without saying goodbye doesn't exactly fill me with hope.'

'Don't do that.'

'Do what?'

'Start telling yourself a story about what someone else is feeling.'

Jonah winced. 'Ouch.'

'Unless she's told you she doesn't want to see you again, don't start telling yourself that you know what she feels.'

Jonah glanced away, unable to meet her stare because it felt like an X-ray. 'I don't want to be that guy, Gracie.'

'What guy?' she asked, crossing her arms and softening slightly.

'The one that can't take a hint. The one that pushes and makes things weird.'

'Sure, but you also don't want to be the guy that churlishly pushes her away. Believe me.'

'There's no way to push. She's gone. It's done.'

'Jasper has her phone number; she's working with her on her new apartment. She told me over breakfast. She'll be your go-between. If Allegra wants to talk to you, she will. But table that for now. Are *you* okay?'

Jonah was surprised by the question. It wasn't one he heard very regularly. 'I'm . . . fine.'

'Sure?'

'It's not the best feeling. Knowing those pictures are out there. Middle-aged men have been giving me approving looks all morning and it makes me feel ill. Knowing what people are trying to say about Allegra.'

'Can I say one more thing?'

'Yes.'

'We could all see how much you two were feeling each other. You were doing that weird dance thing. The kind two people do when they're getting up to stuff in private, but don't know how to label it. And, no offence, but judging by those photos, you two communicate perfectly well in one respect. So . . . just do the whole thing. Tell her. Use your words.'

'Well, that's always been the problem. Fine with writing things down. Terrible with speaking.'

'So, write it down,' she said, smiling softly. 'I feel very confident that she would like your writing.'

Allegra closed the car door and turned to smile sadly at Natalie, who was waiting for her in the backseat. They sat side by side for a few minutes, waiting for the car to pull out of Lake Pristine. Allegra threw a look behind her to gaze out of the back window. No one was following them.

She sighed in relief and then looked over to Natalie. 'Okay. Hit me with it.'

'It . . . could definitely be worse.'

'Bullet points?'

'Everyone your age is vehemently defending you. Millennials, too. In fact, a lot of millennial women are writing think pieces about the whole thing. *Bustle* and *Cosmo* have been so great, I can't even tell you.'

'But?'

'The morning shows have been kind of brutal. Lots of red-faced, right-wing men. Lots of heat on you, none on the boys.'

'That's good, I guess,' Allegra said quietly.

'It's not good,' Natalie shot back, sounding indignant. 'Allegra, that horrid weasel gave all three of your names to that editor. He doesn't deserve your sympathy.'

'But Jonah does.'

She could feel Natalie staring at her profile, as she looked ahead and out of the windscreen of the car. Nothing but woodland road ahead, barely a goodbye to her father. Lake Pristine fading away in the rear-view mirror and all of the invisible bindings of fame starting to tighten around her once more.

'You really liked him, didn't you?'

Allegra felt the bindings creep up to her throat, as if trying to stop the truth from slipping out. Her eyes itched and her chin trembled. 'Yes.'

'So, why not just go with Plan A? Owning the relationship? Ask people to be understanding?'

'Because,' Allegra rounded on Natalie and, for the first time in their long, professional relationship, her voice was raised, 'I want better for him. I want better for him than an embarrassing publicity stunt that he's only going along with because he's a good guy. I've had to fight for every fucking role in this industry, countless auditions and call-backs and meetings and readings and lunches. I gave up prom and school and sneaking out and having fun. Always auditioning. Always trying to impress, always fighting to be considered. I want him to choose. I don't want to have to convince him. I don't want to have to win him over. And hey, guess what, Nat? He's autistic, like me. You've always said I'm so good at auditions. Ever wonder why? Autism. When every fucking social interaction feels like an audition, a performance, you get really good at it.'

She took breath, anger melting away to reveal a deep sadness she had felt since leaving the house at the lake.

'Except him,' she breathed. 'Never felt like a performance with him. Suddenly . . . didn't feel like there was a camera inside my head any more. It felt easy. And hard. And natural.' She paused, wishing he was there. 'And *real*.'

There was a whole minute of complete silence and stillness between them. Then Allegra felt a tentative hand on her arm. She glanced at Nat, shocked to see the other woman, who was always so clipped and proper, looking devastated.

'Okay,' the publicist said softly. 'Hear you loud and clear. Your mother is at your apartment, we're going to debrief there and then let you get some peace.'

Allegra nodded but couldn't help glancing back at Lake Pristine, as it completely disappeared from view. It brought on a strange, emotional ache to leave the place that had so lived up to the imaginary version she had put together in her head. Now she was fleeing it. She was always fleeing – darting from a restaurant to a car, from a set to a hotel. From a meet-and-greet to a hastily scheduled doctor's appointment, where the doctor told her that her lungs needed rest, and she could only laugh and give him a pitying look.

She didn't want to flee Lake Pristine. She wanted to stay.

She had the strange feeling that she had left her chance at peace behind.

# Chapter Twenty-Four

By lunchtime, Jonah had had enough.

He was able to dodge the last of the remaining reporters, but he was sick of cars slowing down so Old Man Mason or his schoolfriends' fathers could lean out of the window to congratulate him, or try to shake his hand. He hated how Mrs Heywood quietly asked him if he was going to make an honest woman out of 'the actress'. He despised the looks, the stares and the whispers. He was used to the small-town experience of Lake Pristine.

But this was something else entirely.

He pushed through festival-goers and burst into the small tent reserved on site for festival employees and volunteers. Simon was standing up against the far wall with a bottle of water, talking with Kerrie and Skye. Jonah stalked towards his ex-friend without a second care and grabbed him by the neck.

'The hell?!' squawked Simon, spluttering and spraying water everywhere as Jonah shoved him against the flimsy tent wall.

'Give me a good reason not to maim you right now,' Jonah said, his voice dangerously quiet. 'Because I'm struggling, Si.'

'Let go, you lunatic.'

'No. You fucked up. What were you thinking?'

He could vaguely hear Kerrie and Skye demanding that he let Simon go, but he was too far gone. He stared at his old friend, a friend he had always made allowances for. Jonah had been forced to fight his way out of special needs classes, where his disability had been foolishly considered synonymous with unintelligence. Simon, who had struggled with reading, had been his lighthouse in the storm. They had made mischief together. Jonah had overlooked the exceedingly rare occasions where Simon had lashed out at him, and only him, attributing it to the idea he was a lot to deal with as a friend. After all, that was all he had ever heard as a kid. From teachers to absent fathers, he had been told he was 'a lot'. So he took Simon's sporadic flashes of meanness as the tollbooth fee on the road to having a friend.

But this latest act was too much for Jonah to unimagine. It was unforgivable. And Jonah was starting to realize that he had been the only one accepting Simon's weaknesses while everyone else got the sunshine. And then he had made a huge mistake with Allegra.

'You've fucked everything, Simon,' he snarled, and he couldn't quite manage to keep the hurt from bubbling up as he spoke. 'You've brought a shitty tornado down on her.'

The smallest flickering of shame passed through Simon's grey eyes before outrage took its place. 'Of course this is about her!'

'She's the one having her name and pictures splashed all over the world,' Jonah hissed. 'What did you think would happen? Do you have any idea what these people are going to do to her? What they'll print about her?'

'I wasn't thinking, Jonah,' snapped Simon, bitterly. 'Clearly! Clearly, I was not thinking. Some editor calls me in the middle of the night. Said there are pictures of me, someone put them on the internet and identified me. Asked for some confirmation. I didn't know what to do!'

'Say "no comment". Hang up! God, Simon, you've never had a

scam or cold call before? Just hang up the damn phone!'

'Why are you even mad?' Simon shoved Jonah, hard enough to dislodge his grip but not enough to unbalance him. 'You get to look like a hero and I look like a creep!'

'You *are* a creep, Simon. You paraded her around like an ornament and then backed her into a corner.'

'It doesn't make sense,' Simon said, staring into Jonah's face as though he were seeing his friend for the very first time. 'I've always had to make excuses for you. I've always had to teach you shit! And she picks you? It makes no sense.'

Jonah could tell that the confusion was real. While Simon wore sunny, affable masks for most of the town, he had always been honest with Jonah. He could tell that his old schoolfriend couldn't understand the supposed injustice of it all.

'You stole a kiss and then got pissed o—'

'Stole a kiss?' Simon laughed, a hollow sound with no humour. He threw a look to Kerrie and Skye. 'Listen to him. Loves to use his big words and stupidly formal phrases. To lord it over us that he's read everything in that shop. Fucking Cyrano right here.'

'Well, what can I say, Simon. Some of us actually read the books, we don't just use them to flirt with customers.'

'Do you even know what flirting is, you sad freak? Because let me assure you, that's not what Allegra was ever doing with you. And it seems like she's fled this place as fast as possible. Think she wants to get away from you. You and your weird little fucked-up brain—'

Jonah punched him right on the jaw and he went down like a house of cards in the breeze. Simon was momentarily disorientated, then rage and adrenaline took over his body. He tackled Jonah to the ground and they began to scrap, landing blows and cursing between hits. Jonah was doing more damage. He could hear Skye laughing and Kerrie shouting for help, but he had no intention of stopping. Neither, it seemed, did Simon.

They rolled on the ground and Simon even grabbed a fistful of Jonah's dark curls before the latter was suddenly and sharply hauled away from Jonah. The look of surprise on Simon's face was almost comical, but when both of them realized who had broken up the fight, they grew demonstrably more serious.

George Brooks stood over both of them with enough rage and disappointment to fill the entire festival site.

'Jonah,' he finally said. 'Come with me, please.'

'Shit,' whispered Skye.

'Damn,' another volunteer added, as Jonah got to his feet, a little uneasily. He followed his employer from the tent, only because he had a few things of his own to say. He threw a dark look back to Simon, who appeared to be dazed.

'Jonah! Jonah, I—'

Whatever Simon wanted to say, it was cut off as Jonah left the room. Jonah had a thumping headache and a few scratches, but Simon would have the majority of the bruises.

The festival site was made up of five tents: the main theatre, the smaller venue, the green room, the staff tent and the pop-up bookshop. The box office was a converted food truck. There were picnic tables and bunting. It was always thus, the whole town came together to make a good showing, even if they resented their population tripling for a month.

George was leading Jonah to Brooks Books. There were customers milling about, as Mary manned the register. She bestowed both George and Jonah with a look of bemusement as they went into the back office.

The room was disorganized and cluttered, always had been, so when George told Jonah to sit, he wasn't exactly sure where or how to do so. When he removed a delivery box of books that Simon had promised to return to the wholesaler, he discovered a spare office seat.

They faced each other in tense silence for a few moments, letting the sound of a busy, bustling town fill the small room.

'Once the festival is over, I think we should call it a day.'

Jonah blinked, stupefied. 'Sorry?'

He studied his mentor's face. Eyes that had once danced with kindness were now tired and testy. His once jovial tone was now waspish and short.

'I think it's time you moved on from Brooks Books, Jonah.'

'Let's just be clear,' Jonah said, adopting a cantankerous tone of his own. 'You're firing me? Don't use euphemisms, just say it.'

'Fine. I'm letting you go.'

'Firing me, George. You're firing me.'

'Yes.'

'But you want me to see out the rest of the festival.'

'I would appreciate it. Allegra is already a big loss to the team.'

There was real heaviness and regret in George's words, enough for Jonah to question him. 'That's what this is actually about, right?'

George cleared his throat. 'No. This is a necessary career decision, for both our sakes. And you were physically fighting in the staff tent. That will be the official reason, as it's completely unacceptable.'

'So, Simon's going, too?'

'No, Simon will remain.'

'That's bullshit!'

'I won't be spoken to like that, Jonah. I really will not be.'

'George, I'm sorry Allegra and I got seen like that. No one regrets it more than me. The photographer, that is, not . . . not what he was photographing – I don't regret that part at all. I'm sorry. I know it's the reason she's gone back to the city. But you can't punish me because I l—'

'It's not about Allegra. I can't have you starting fights.'

'How do you know I started it?'

George fixed him with a stern look. 'Jonah.'

'I'd say Simon started it by handing the press all of our names! Didn't you specifically order us not to do that, when Roxanne and Allegra first came here?'

He knew that he had spoiled his shot by saying Roxanne's name. There was always an unspoken understanding about that, she was not to be mentioned to George. Jonah's mother had warned him about it, before his first shift at the shop.

'*She left him long ago,*' she had told him, whispering as if the age-old gossip was dangerous. '*He's never got over her.*'

'Don't act like this is a decision you've been forced into,' Jonah added, deciding to go down in an inferno rather than a blown-out candle. You've been weird and cold with me all summer. Before you even knew Allegra was coming here.'

'Correct,' George acknowledged. 'This has been ongoing. And today I made up my mind.'

'Why has it been ongoing? You've been treating me like a bad draught for months! What's the reason?'

He thought, for a moment, George might tell him. Then his

now ex-employer merely shook his head and said, 'I've told you the reason for your termination. Will you serve your notice?'

Jonah stared at the older man, desperately trying to see a little of Allegra in him. If they had shared the same eyes or smile, he might have felt comforted for the briefest moment, as if he had her back.

But there was nothing of Allegra in her father.

Jonah thought about the years he had spent in the shop. The displays he had made, the countless emails and phone calls he had fielded, organizing the festival and chasing publishers on behalf of George. He thought about every moment of sweat he had given to the poorly paid job, just to get books to the right people and to support authors who needed his help.

All of it washed away because of a mystery grudge and one bad decision.

'Yeah, I'm done,' Jonah said wearily. 'No notice. I'll leave right now.'

He fished his keys and computer card out of his jeans and dropped them onto George's already chaotic work desk. He could tell by the astounded look on George's face that he had not expected this. Despite years of dedication and hard work, Jonah had to wonder what made the man think he would meekly stay and work where he was clearly not wanted.

'Jonah, look, I—'

Jonah gave him a half-hearted salute. 'Thanks for a few years of work and some serious retail-back-problems, I guess.'

'Jonah, let's discuss things a little more calmly, maybe when—'
'Nah. Bye.'

Jonah felt an undeniable, yet completely surprising, sense of relief as he left the office, and then Brooks Books. He gave Nick, the other part-time bookseller who had arrived, a warm nod but did not fill him in. He walked with an easiness and a sense of purpose.

Grace Lancaster was emerging from the Arthouse as he made his way home. She sprinted up Main Street to reach him.

'Jonah, what happened? Someone said you knocked Simon out!'

'Not quite,' Jonah said. 'Wish that were true.'

'So, what—'

'Let's go to the arcade, I'll tell you everything.'

Allegra was on her street, outside her apartment building. She waited until Cliff, the driver, gave the nod to signal that the street was clear. She slipped out of the car with Natalie and smiled at Mohammad, the building's doorman, as he held the door open for her. The marble lobby was just as sparkling and as clean as it had been in May, when she left.

She and Natalie entered the lift and rode up in silence. There was a small vestibule between the elevator and her front door. She took out her keys but it flew open to reveal her mother.

Allegra burst into tears.

Her mother embraced her and she could feel Natalie rubbing her back. The three women stood in the small vestibule, with its finely embossed wallpaper and prettily tiled flooring, and Allegra just cried. She let out every thought and feeling that had been constrained beneath the mask. She let the neurotypical gaze fade into unimportance.

'Everything went wrong,' she said into her mother's shoulder.

'It might feel that way now,' her mother said, her voice a cocktail of kindness and assurance with a zesty twist of no-nonsense: 'But we'll come out clean. Let's go and sit in your weirdly empty apartment, which has no furniture.'

There was a beat and then all three of them laughed.

The penthouse apartment had four bedrooms, one bathroom, three en-suites, a kitchen, a dining room, a small pantry, a walk-in wardrobe, a large reception room, a small study/sitting room, two storage closets and a wide balcony overlooking the rest of the neighbourhood. There was air conditioning, twinkling chandeliers, and secure locks on all doors and . . .

It had been the biggest undertaking of Allegra's life. She had purchased it the week after her eighteenth birthday. Anonymously, as sellers had tried to up their prices on hearing that an interested party was a movie star. It was in her name. Paid for with cash, and completely her own.

Yet it didn't feel like home.

'You are one lucky eighteen-year-old,' her mother said, as the three of them stood in the vast reception room. Her mother took in the high ceilings with amazement while Natalie made sure that the door was securely locked, and Allegra checked for her own peace of mind. It was a little routine of theirs.

'Very lucky,' Allegra acknowledged, gazing around at the empty rooms. 'Mum. I met someone really great in Lake Pristine.'

'I know, I did see the pictures.'

Allegra released a dry laugh. 'As well as him.'

'Oh?'

'Jasper Montgomery?' She turned it into a question, knowing that her mother had grown up in Lake Pristine and, while older than Jasper, probably knew her parents.

'The Montgomerys in the Lakehouse? Howard and Andrea Montgomery?'

'Must be,' Allegra said.

'Wow. They're a fancy-pants Lake Pristine family.'

'Fancy-pants,' Natalie repeated under her breath, laughing.

'Which one is Jasper?' her mother asked. 'They had two daughters, a sweet one and a . . . not so sweet one.'

'She's the sweet one. And an interior designer and she has the most amazing ideas.'

'Well, maybe if we can get her clearance, she can visit here and you guys can work together.'

Even though Allegra was technically an adult, and even though she had privileges and responsibilities that other eighteen-year-olds could scarcely imagine, she still ran ideas past her mother, as if asking for permission and advice all in one. Roxanne knew that Allegra needed her approval, even still, so she would always anticipate what Allegra wanted to hear before gently offering it up as a suggestion.

This was one such occasion. So, it was decided. Jasper Montgomery would be invited to the apartment, and employed as its new designer. It was a carrot dangled in front of Allegra. A reward waiting at the end of Natalie's battle plan.

'You're invited onto *Beckton's* tonight. Are we saying "yes"?'

'You don't have to,' Allegra's mother said, as soon as Natalie had asked the question. 'You've done nothing wrong.'

Allegra exhaled. 'Natalie's right. We need to shatter the void, or whatever. Fine. I'll do it.'

# Chapter Twenty-Five

Jonah and Grace sat in one of the arcade booths, underneath a large flatscreen. Jonah was on his third beer, Grace her second pink lemonade. The arcade was always a favourite haunt of young people in Lake Pristine. Hera was only strict when it came to stepping onto the bowling lanes.

'Grace, can I just check something?' Jonah asked. 'This, we're just friends, right?'

Grace spluttered out a delighted laugh. 'Yes, Jonah. We're just friends.'

'Sorry,' he said, meaning it. 'It's just . . . I thought me and Kerrie were just friends and—'

'I know,' Grace said soothingly. 'She's . . . she'll get over it, don't worry. She's a bit down at the moment. Mapesbury University put her on their waiting list. She's hoping to get a call every day and it just never comes.'

'I didn't mean for all of this to get so complicated. I didn't realize I was leading her on.'

'Aw, Jonah, you weren't leading her on,' Grace said. She glanced up at the TV screen and then around at the bustling arcade. 'The whole town knows who it is you like.'

Jonah felt himself flush but he downed another swig, wincing at the taste of hops and barley. 'Don't, Grace.'

'I mean, the whole world now knows.'

'Except Allegra.'

'What do you mean?'

'She doesn't know how I feel. We never got to even talk about it. Her team put her in a car and took her away from me. Her dad wants me dead, her publicist, too, I reckon.'

'Her dad? George. You mean George. Since when is he anything but George to you?'

'Sure. George who just fired me.'

He took another drink as Grace stared at him in complete disbelief. 'Are you kidding?'

'Nope.'

'Why?!'

'Fighting Simon. Almost having Allegra. Some other stuff he won't tell me about.'

'He's been weird with you all summer.'

'Agreed.'

'But I never thought he would . . .'

'Well, he did.'

They sat in silence and Jonah realized how restless and angry he was. Restless with Lake Pristine and its confines, angry with George for giving him a reason to leave. 'I have to get out of Lake Pristine.'

'Jonah,' Grace said sternly. 'Just drink your drink, okay? Feel sad, feel whatever you're feeling, but don't make any rash decisions.'

'It's not rash, it's overdue.'

'What's overdue?'

'Leaving! Getting out. There isn't anything for me here that's worth staying for. Nothing that won't be here when I come back to visit, that is.'

Grace, who he knew was also planning to leave, asked, 'What will you do?'

He had barely got that far in his mind. Or perhaps he had always known, so he had never needed to think about it. 'I want to write. So, I'll write. I'll sell books in the meantime, on the street with a wooden box if I have to. Earn pennies while I write and then earn possibly even less. It's better than having a boss.'

'It's normal to have a boss.'

'I've had one for years now, it's overrated. And Allegra? Stuck at the whim of those studio bosses? No. I'll make my own work, and then me and Allegra—'

He stopped speaking as Grace made a noise of surprise and pointed to the flatscreen above their heads. He glanced up and swore.

Allegra was on *The Late Show with Ellis Beckton*. Ellis was sitting behind his large, mahogany desk on the right side of the screen. He had black hair with dignified streaks of silver and a suit that probably cost more than what Jonah used to earn in a year. The interview had clearly just begun, as Allegra settled herself into the guest chair on the left side of the screen.

She looked otherworldly. She wore a floor-length dress of lamé fabric in the Grecian style. It looked like molten gold, hugging her and shaping her. Modest but stunning. Her hair glinted in the bright studio lights and she smiled at Ellis Beckton as if they were old friends.

'Turn it up,' Jonah said, to no one in particular, before jumping up to adjust the volume himself.

'. . . back again, friend of the show, so it's lovely to see you,' Ellis Beckton said, in his tone that was always brash and playing to the back row. 'So! Allegra! How's your summer been? Do anything interesting? Or anyone?'

Jonah frowned as the studio audience laughed uproariously at this pointed remark. 'That's not funny.'

'Shh,' Grace said.

Allegra merely smiled, in a way that completely beguiled her host. 'I had a very relaxing summer, Ellis. How about you, how's everything been here in the EBC building? I hear they don't let you leave.'

The audience laughed and Ellis joined in. He cast a quick look into the crowd and then quipped, 'Yep, I'm just stored in the back with a caffeinated IV.'

'And then they wheel you out every night at ten-thirty?'

'Wheel me out?! Wait, why are you clapping, don't turn on me!'

The audience roared as Ellis cartoonishly chastised them and Allegra smiled in victory. It was extraordinary. She had quickly moved the conversation away from the elephant in the room. Her long legs, her sparkling Jimmy Choos and her knowing smile – it was still Allegra, but it was like Allegra with an extra gear. She was a supernova.

'She's . . . so good at this,' Grace remarked, her voice almost inaudible. They both stared up at the screen in amazement.

'So, you've got a new movie coming out in a couple of weeks,' the late-night host said, continuing with the interview after the audience quietened. 'It's called *Maybe in Waiting* and it's – well, you tell them what it's about.'

'Sure,' Allegra glowed as she crossed one leg over the other. 'So, it's directed by Diego Charlotte—'

'Who just won the academy award for Best Director.'

'Yes, sure did—'

'For *Time in Tinseltown*—'

'—for *Time in Tinseltown*, yes. Anyway, so yeah, he's directing and it's about this cafe in Paris and like a lot of his work, his incredible work, it's very old Hollywood. And it's about this guy, played by the amazing—'

'Auden Bishop.'

'Yes, he's unbelievable. He plays this guy stuck in this Parisian cafe while it's raining and me, and the rest of the ensemble cast, are the, sort of, colourful characters he meets as they all wait for the downpour to stop.'

'Sounds great, here's a clip!'

As the show started playing a scene from *Maybe in Waiting*, Grace turned to Jonah. 'This is the one she's taking us to. The premiere.'

Jonah swallowed, as he watched this apparently amazing male actor and Allegra as they moved about the screen in the clip from their film. 'If she still wants us to go.'

'She will, Jonah, she's not mad at you. She just had to get out of this town.'

'I'm just,' Jonah stared up at her face, the face he had held in his hands, the face that had haunted him for weeks. 'I've never been good at knowing what to do or say in social situations, let alone unusual situations . . .'

'Yeah?'

'But when I'm with Allegra, it feels so easy. I just want to love her and tell her she's perfect. But that's not socially acceptable. So, I panicked and made so many stupid mistakes.'

'But it wasn't your fault that the two of you got photographed.

And she knows that. She's not stupid. Let her put out this fire. Then try again.'

As Jonah stared up at the screen, he knew he had to move. In the chess game of his life, he had to get to the other side of the board somehow. Lake Pristine stayed the same. It was a town in a beautiful painting or the inside of a snow globe. It was hard to change inside it. He needed to wake himself up from its comforting spell.

He didn't want anyone else's life. Not in Lake Pristine, anyway. He wanted a life that couldn't be found in a small place, with comfortable people.

He was not going to leave his teenage years, grow old and be that guy getting drunk in the afternoons and talking about the time he had almost loved a movie star.

He had to be something else. Something better.

Allegra had learned to smile broadly every time Ellis interrupted her. While most late-night hosts were now young men who had been comedy writers or cast members on *Saturday Night Live*, Ellis was more old-school. He was usually more famous than his guests, and he knew it. Allegra's fame was the kind he would find a little intimidating, so she anticipated some male foolery from him. His show was a small kingdom, where everyone fawned and bowed. Allegra had been reminded about how lucky she was to be squeezed in, lucky because they had bumped an up-and-coming comic until the following day so that she could have the slot.

Now, as Ellis smiled in a way that told Allegra he was about to turn, she braced herself. She was not afraid. She was playing a role. The mask had grown to cover her entire body. It was a terrible sort of armour, now necessary and employed like an octopus ready to ink.

Autistic girls were told they were their own worst enemies, but Allegra knew that was a neurotypical lie. She was her own ally. She was her own protector. She let her true self curl up into a ball inside a small room in her heart, a frightened eighteen-year-old in the foetal position, while *she* took over.

She. The person Allegra became when it was time to pretend. To seduce, to entertain, to convince. It was a choice so many actresses had been forced to make, autistic or not. Should I be her? she asked herself, whenever she stared at her own reflection in the dressing room mirror.

'Now, Allegra,' Ellis said, as the applause for the film clip died down, 'let's get serious for a moment.'

Allegra did not let her smile fade. 'Sure, Ellis, let's. That sounds fun.'

Murmurs of amusement met her answer, but the audience members were clearly anticipating the talk show host's line of questioning.

'Some pictures of you went viral recently . . .'

Allegra pushed her long hair back and feigned innocence. 'Was it the benefit for literacy I did back in May? Where we raised millions for children to have access to books?'

'Um, not exactly.'

'Ah,' Allegra sighed, playing up her disappointment. 'Damn! That stuff never seems to go viral, such a shame. So, what are *you* talking about, Ellis?'

The audience laughed and hooted.

*What a good sport she's being, isn't she charming, you'd never know the overhead lights are killing her and that she can smell everything and feel the springs of the seat beneath her thighs.*

'Yes, some pictures of me and my very good friend were taken against our will and published,' Allegra said, before Ellis could. 'We were both in a state of undress due to a broken air conditioner.'

More screams of laughter from the jackals, who looked to the people next to them to check that they were laughing as well.

'And we were actually having a fight, that's what the photos don't quite capture. If the pap had hung around, he'd have seen me pin him to the floor and get him in a headlock, but of course in this cynical day and age, everyone jumps to conclusions. I'm actually a Black Belt.'

Even Ellis smiled tightly at that, as the audience bellowed. Allegra felt her body silently begging her to wrap it up. The sensory overload was crushing her, but she told herself to persevere, she had minutes left. They had to make it through the fakery for a little longer. Yet as the audience cackled and shrieked, she breathed a small sigh of relief.

She had won. She had taken it back.

Albeit with shaking, frightened hands.

'Now, let's talk more about Diego Charlotte and his sensational movie. Out very soon!'

When the interview was over, Allegra took a quick photo with Ellis for socials, blew a kiss to the enraptured audience and swiftly power-walked to the guest bathroom where she promptly vomited all over the floor.

Her feet slipped out of her high heels and her knees hit the floor as she retched. Within a moment Natalie was by her side, whispering comforting things and rubbing her back.

'You were perfect!' she said, careful to keep her voice as low as possible. 'Just brilliant. It's over now, baby, it's done. That's buried it. You did it, you're the greatest. I've never seen anyone command a room like you when you want to.'

The other woman's words tumbled out quickly as Allegra staggered to her feet to grab some paper towels. Natalie poked her head out of the bathroom door and barked at someone for some water. Allegra pressed her forehead against the cold tile on the wall until Natalie pushed a glass of water into her hands.

People thought masking was something that everyone did. They thought it was like speaking 'corporate' or behaving differently for your in-laws. But it was so much more than that. It was the physical suppression of every natural, autistic instinct. It was mimicry. It was sunburn. It was a hand around your own throat. It was burying yourself while you were still alive.

Allegra felt the delayed reaction to the sensory overload and her body cried out, begging for mercy. She gulped down the water and splashed some on her face, hoping to disguise the salty tears.

Ellis Beckton was the only late-night show that went out live. Most others were filmed in the late afternoon. She took a moment to breathe, to try and pull herself together. She moved like a sleepwalker to her dressing room, where her two smartphones were locked away. She withdrew her personal phone and called the bookshop.

No one answered. She called again. Still nobody. She could picture the old landline ringing in the shop with no one there to answer it.

She wanted to talk to Jonah. But she didn't have a number saved for him on either of her phones. She was about to open her email inbox when—

'Everything okay? The car's outside. You good, baby?'

Natalie's words came from the other side of the dressing room door. Allegra locked eyes with herself in the mirror. She blinked away the redness. She grabbed some concealer and quickly got to work on her face. She brushed her hair. She stared at herself, commanding herself to be all right.

*Come on, we've done this before. We're back to work now. They want the golden goose so let's go. Time to sparkle.*

'I'm great,' she heard herself say. 'Ready to go.'

# Chapter Twenty-Six

**westendgirl@gmail.com**
**to: JonahThorne@gmail.com**
**Subject: Late Show**
Dear Jonah,
Your name is everywhere!! I saw the pictures!! What the hell is going on in that tiny town?!

**JonahThorne@gmail.com**
**to: westendgirl@gmail.com**
**Subject: Nightmare**
I'm so sorry. It's been a hurricane. Allegra Brooks is the glamorous visitor to Lake Pristine. I can't say much more about her, as I want to respect her privacy, but I didn't think about you seeing my name all over the media circus.
Jonah.

**westendgirl@gmail.com**
**to: JonahThorne@gmail.com**
**Subject: What?!**
Allegra Brooks!! That girl from that fantasy show?! I saw the pictures; I couldn't really believe that you're the same person as the guy in those pictures. Are you

okay? Has she ditched you? Is she a total diva? What on earth has been going on?

**JonahThorne@gmail.com**
**to: westendgirl@gmail.com**
**Subject: Allegra Brooks.**

Like I said, private. You work in social media. Do you have any advice? I'm not looking at what's being said any more, but I can imagine. What can I do to make it better?
Jonah x

**westendgirl@gmail.com**
**to: JonahThorne@gmail.com**
**Subject: Social Media**

Sadly, the one constant that I have seen in my professional life is that men always come out of the other side. Men's misdemeanours are overlooked while women are punished for assumptions and associations. *You're* going to be okay. You haven't even done anything wrong. Give it time. Let people move on to the next cycle. And just remind yourself that you haven't hurt anyone, you're just the subject of gossip. And continually tell yourself that it's weird for people to care so much about strangers.
Hope that helps.
A friend.

**JonahThorne@gmail.com**
**to: westendgirl@gmail.com**
**RE: Social Media**

It does help but I should have been clearer. I'm wondering how I can make it easier for Allegra.

Jonah x

---

Allegra stared at his latest email and felt a flush of something she couldn't label.

She put the phone to one side, deciding to deal with practical, less overwhelming things instead.

She had a few weeks left of her summer break, so to speak, before the premiere for *Maybe in Waiting*. Then, the publicity tour would need her for appearances. She hoped these pictures would be yesterday's news by then. She had made a date with Jasper to come and see the apartment, as she urgently wanted to get started on the bedroom. She loved that Jasper had a different way of working as a designer, and that she was keen to be deeply collaborative with Allegra.

There was a queen-size bed in Allegra's bedroom suite and nothing else. Her phone lay on the floorboards, charging, and it was the only light in the dark room. She lay back against the Egyptian cotton and closed her eyes. In the dark, she wished he was lying next to her.

Her phone flashed as a voice note arrived from Jasper.

When Allegra played it, the designer's voice could be heard saying, 'Hey, so, I have a slightly tipsy, lovesick man at my boyfriend's cinema right now and he won't stop talking about you. I was wondering if it would be okay (when he's sober) for me to give him your personal number? Totally okay if not, he doesn't even know I'm asking you so won't know if you said no.'

Allegra hesitated. She liked Jonah, even more than she wanted to admit. But she didn't want him to try and make up for what happened at the Lakehouse. She didn't want him to reach out to her from a place of guilt.

Now that she was back in the barren, isolated apartment in the city – it was hard for her to trust.

But she gave Jasper the okay. The heart wanted things, things that the head had been told were not possible.

Miles away in Lake Pristine, Jonah tried to slip into his bedroom without crossing paths with his mother. He had just fired off a risky email to a tiny press he admired in the city. They would often bring the bookshop their latest releases by hand, they had no money, but he loved what they printed. He hoped that, when they read his email in the morning, they would overlook the late hour of its arrival.

He quietly washed his face, brushed his teeth and he was about to slide into his bedroom when all of the apartment was suddenly bathed in light.

His mother stood in her bathrobe by the living room door.

'Hey,' Jonah said, trying to sound as sober as possible. 'Thought you were asleep.'

'Nope. Wide awake, worrying about you.'

'I'm fine, Ma.'

'No, you're not fine. Those pictures are everywhere. I heard all about what happened between you and Simon. His father told me in the checkout line. Said he's nursing a real shiner on his face.'

'Serves him right for what he did.'

'Jonah—'

'I applied for a job tonight,' he said, and at that, something changed between them, in their home, for ever.

His mother stared at him. 'You what?'

'Matuschek Press. In the city. One of their editors got stolen by a corporate publisher so there's an opening for an assistant. I applied.'

'You're eighteen! They'll hire someone with a degree, Jonah. Someone with more experience.'

He knew it was her worry speaking.

'Maybe not. They don't have a lot of money to play with.'

'Jonah,' she stepped towards him, looking afraid. 'What's happening? Everything suddenly has to change for you, it seems. These decisions seem to come out of nowhere, because you don't talk me through your thinking.'

'I can't talk through my thinking myself, Ma,' he said honestly. 'I – you know I can't. You know I don't think like you do. Or like most people do.'

'I know,' she said despondently. 'But this is all just . . .'

'It's time, Ma,' he said gently. 'I keep thinking about graduation. Sitting there, everyone heading off to bigger things. Teachers who told me I would never even pass finals asking where I'm going next. I'm staying at Brooks and working for George, I would say. And I believed it.'

'It's a wonderful job and it suits you so well,' his mother said and Jonah could tell by her tone that the news of his firing had not reached her. 'You love working there.'

'I do. I *did*,' he acknowledged. 'It *was* an amazing job. But I'm not supposed to be there any more. George never let me buy in certain titles, exciting titles. He never will. He can't stand books about relationships breaking down because his did. He's snobbish about new authors. So, if I can't fill the shop with the stories I want, I have to go out and write them myself.'

Vivienne Thorne exhaled and rubbed her temples. She looked around the small apartment they shared, the one they had lived in their whole lives.

'I thought you might want to take over the shop,' she said, her tone a little desperate. It wasn't a conversation they had even danced around before.

'You can't keep me here, Ma,' he said, seeing right through her. 'I'm running on empty. I know I'm never on everyone else's schedule, but it's now. I need to go.'

He moved into his bedroom, switching on the small lamp by his pillow and taking his shoes off. His mother moved to lean in the doorway, knowing that he was fixed on it and there was little she could say to dissuade him from his course.

'Is this about her?'

Jonah paused for the smallest second as he put his shoes away, his back to his mother. When he turned to face her, he wore a grim expression. 'Yes.'

'She's very special, Jonah. I know it, I see it. The whole world does. But that's the whole problem. She's—'

'Too good for me.'

'No! Not at all. She's just . . .'

Jonah couldn't blame his mother for having trouble with words. Allegra was not 'just' anything. He had felt so as he was emailing his elusive pen-pal, the one who seemed further and further away every single day. It was impossible to describe Allegra. He knew the human. The girl with the mole on her neck. The girl who would only say 'bless you' twice – if you sneezed a third time, she was silent. The girl who picked at her lips when she was nervous. The girl who carried her own hot sauce around. The girl who stared off into space, sometimes for minutes on end. The girl who only made eye contact when she was listening to you, rarely when she was speaking to you. The girl who loathed smelly cheese. The girl who unconsciously mimicked people's accents. The girl whose entire face transformed when she laughed.

His Allegra. The one millions would never know. The one he had earned through one summer of working with her, and one night in a glass house.

'She has people all over the world chasing her down, Jonah,' his mother said, and she sounded sadder than he had ever heard her. 'How can anyone compete with that?'

'Because I don't want to chase her down,' Jonah said. 'I want to stand still with her.'

Allegra slept late and, on waking, felt an old wound twinge. Her chest felt as though someone had casually placed a piano on top of it during the night. Each breath she took felt laboured and painful.

It was how her lungs had felt when she was ill with pneumonia.

She fired off a text to Jasper, who was due at the apartment for a consultation. It hurt to get out of bed, she realized, as she staggered to the bathroom. She brushed her teeth with great difficulty and tried to splash some warm water on her face, but it soon became clear that standing and walking were only making the problem worse.

She stumbled back into bed and must have slept for another

hour, as she woke to the sound of Jasper calling her phone.

'Hey,' croaked Allegra.

'God, you sound terrible,' Jasper replied, her voice full of concern. 'Listen, someone got wind that you're not well and . . . can I let him up?'

Understanding hit Allegra and she closed her eyes. Her hair was a long mass of unbrushed tresses, she had no make-up on, and she was wearing nothing but an old T-shirt and underwear.

But there was one person she had missed the most since leaving Lake Pristine.

'Yes,' she breathed. 'That's – that's okay.'

She tripped and clawed her way to the intercom as it buzzed with great urgency.

'Hey, Mohammad. They're good to come up once they've signed in.'

'Loud and clear, Ally,' he replied and then there was a click.

Allegra swayed on the spot in her vast and empty reception room, awaiting her guests. She cursed her own executive dysfunction, wishing she had just bought some basic furnishings so that they would now have something to sit on.

'The door's open,' she wheezed, as she heard Jasper's polite, and now very familiar, knock.

'Oh, my God,' Jasper gasped, as she gingerly entered the apartment. 'Allegra, get into bed right now, you can barely stand.'

Allegra glanced to the open door, happy to see Jasper but also confused and dismayed by her solitude.

'He's gone to grab something, he was very insistent,' Jasper explained, in response to Allegra's expression. 'Come on. Back to bed.'

Allegra let the designer walk her into the sparse bedroom. She climbed under the covers and coughed, a coarse and crunching sound.

'I'm getting you more water. And you need to eat.'

'Don't,' Allegra pushed out the words, 'worry about me.'

She closed her eyes for another little while and was vaguely aware of Jasper putting a jug of water and a glass on the floor by her bed. She was exhausted but her aching lungs made it difficult to get to sleep. She opened her eyes, about to call out and ask Jasper if she needed anything to work with, but stopped.

Jonah was standing in her bedroom doorway, holding a takeaway cup of something that smelled incredible. They regarded one another in silence, and Allegra felt what little air there was left in her lungs disappear. She had been thinking about him since the moment Lake Pristine became a speck in the distance. She had tried to script together what she would say to him, on the other side of the media circus.

She tried to say, 'Hey.'

But nothing came out because it was so hard to breathe. He moved towards her, looking twice as concerned as Jasper. Jonah was almost beside himself.

'You look like you're dying,' he said quietly.

'God,' she indicated a laugh, as she was not able to deliver a real one. 'Thanks.'

'No, I mean it. Jasper said it was a chest infection so I insisted on coming, and then I said I needed to get you this.' He gestured to the wonderful soup in the takeaway cup. 'But this . . . this looks so much worse.'

'Can I have some of whatever that is?' she asked him. 'It smells incredible.'

'Of course! It's my Uncle Reuben's chicken soup. It's pure, salty chicken broth. He runs a deli not far from here. I wanted you to have this. It's penicillin in liquid form.'

He handed it to her and she sipped from the cup, closing her eyes in bliss as she inhaled its aromatics.

'It's unbelievable,' she sighed after swallowing a few sips. 'Your uncle is a genius.'

'Yeah, it can cure the common cold,' he said, but then he frowned. 'But I'm not sure about what you've got. This is bad, Allegra. I'm . . . I'm worried about you.'

'I had pneumonia a while back. I was in cold water and got hypothermia during a scene and wasn't right afterwards. This is just a bit of a call-back, must have picked up a bug at the studio the other night. I wore a mask there and back, but they don't let you keep it on once you're on air.'

It took her three times longer to say all of this than it would have done if she was in good health. She closed her eyes for a moment, saddened by her own fragility, before taking another big sip of soup. 'Jonah, this is so good,' she said with a moan.

'Good.'

He glanced around the room and then slowly sat down on the beautifully varnished floorboards. 'This isn't how I pictured a movie star living.'

'Sorry,' Allegra chuffed. 'That's what Jasper's do-doing in the other room. Planning to turn this place into an actual ho-home where people can sit in chairs and stuff.'

Jonah smiled sadly. 'Don't speak if it hurts.'

*Everything hurts*, she wanted to say. *The sun hurts my skin during the day, the night makes it impossible for me to sleep. Everyone is too close, except you. You're the only one who was ever just enough. Just right.*

She sipped again and felt something close to peace.

'My dad,' she took it slow, 'was so weird about me coming back here.'

Something appeared in Jonah's face for a split second before vanishing again. Allegra had expected him to laugh but he looked almost forlorn. 'Well. George is weird about a lot of things.'

'He understood why I had to leave, but,' Allegra inhaled and waited for the pain to ease, 'but he also seemed so mad that it all happened in the first place. The pictures.'

'He was worried for you,' Jonah said softly. 'He doesn't understand computers or the internet or anything outside of Lake Pristine. But he knows it exists and he knows it can turn on people. He was scared for you.'

Allegra was so startled by his gentle understanding. She sipped a little more, still staring at him.

'And,' Jonah added, now looking full of regret, 'it wasn't just the pictures themselves that had upset him.'

'No?'

'No. It was because they were with me.'

# Chapter Twenty-Seven

Jonah was struggling to keep his composure. Allegra could elicit intense emotion in him just by looking in his direction. But seeing her in such a fragile state, with dark circles and barely-there breaths, it was incredibly unsettling. He was used to her being vibrant and bright. Now he was scared, afraid that he was somehow part of the cycle which had led to her becoming this unwell.

For the briefest moment, Allegra had looked excited to see him. Now, she looked haunted. His words had clearly unmoored her.

'I'm sure that's not it,' she said carefully.

'I'm not saying it to make anyone feel bad,' Jonah assured her. 'But I'm not the sort of person your dad wants you with. Not that we're, you know . . . with each other.'

'Well,' Allegra's words had a staccato feel to them. 'He's probably not the best judge of relationships.'

'I thought the split was amicable.'

'It was. It wasn't violent or nasty. He just . . . got complacent. At least, that's what Mum says whenever I really push her about it. And she wanted more than a small town and he is terrified . . . of,' she coughed and heaved a breath. 'Anything else, he's terrified of anything else.'

Jonah wanted to tell her everything. That George had fired him, yes, but mostly how he felt. He wanted that last little dam of fear to break. He didn't understand how love could be the most desirable thing, while also being something that commanded such fear and hesitation. Perhaps because it was so desirable. As she was. The idea of losing the stability they had in favour of a great love was the ultimate reward, but to risk it meant possibly ending up with none of her. And that, he found to be unbearable.

Being without Allegra had creepingly, and casually, become nothing less than unbearable.

She frowned and tilted her head, regarding him. 'Are you all right, Jonah?'

*I wish you were her.* It was what he had inadvertently said to the kind person on the other end of an email chain, the anonymous friend who made him feel worthwhile as Simon flirted with Allegra and made her smile politely. Now he had to acknowledge that it was true. He would wish every face was hers. If he protected this flame out of fear of it burning out, he would keep a little light in his life.

It might have to be enough.

So, strike up another match. Make another friend. Take her home, fool around without a paparazzi. Have a whole box of different matches, be good to every one of them.

It would never be her. It would always end the same. Burned out and in the dark.

'I'm fine,' he said, trying to suppress everything. 'What do you need? I want you to feel better.'

She smiled, a little dazedly. 'This soup is amazing.'

'I'll get you more. I'll get you a bathtub full.'

She laughed and the sound sealed it up for him. He had lived his whole life being told that the way he saw things, felt things, reacted to things, was wrong and irregular and frustrating. That he was spoiling everyone else's great performance with his need to rehearse and analyse. He had treated Allegra with the same shortness and coldness that neurotypicals had always used on him and he hated that. He hated the distance he had forced between them.

Nothing about the overly neurotypical world had mattered much to him until she walked through the door of Brooks Books. Suddenly, the songs were for him. The love stories were for them. The poetry sparked memories rather than intellectual detachment. The curse of overstimulation that the world had always pressed on him suddenly promised pleasure beyond understanding. He knew what many didn't, that a mind that so many had been taught to fear could connect to a heart with more love than the average brain could feel.

If autism meant being in one's own world, why couldn't someone else become that whole, entire world. They could live in each other.

She leaned forward, as if reading the many emotions in his face.

'I'm fine,' he reiterated. The last thing he wanted was to cause her any discomfort. She would want to be kind and make him feel better, if he broke the dam and told her what he had come to feel. 'Don't worry about me. Do you need some heartier food? Painkillers?'

She smiled at him, in a way she had never smiled at him before. 'Will you lie next to me and just talk?'

'Yeah?' he said, almost balking. Lying next to her on a bed, even though he was fully dressed and on top of the covers, still sounded incredibly intimate. 'What do you want to talk about?'

'Can you just talk? I like your voice. It's deep and even and it relaxes me. When – when it's not yelling about book returns.'

He smiled, despite the small jab. He slid onto the bedspread beside her and she nestled a little closer, shutting her eyes and trying to take a deep breath despite her lungs insisting on shallow ones.

He talked nonsense for her. She pulled him a little closer, her head on her pillow and her hand clutching his black fisherman's knit. He lay on his back, she on her side. He spoke slowly and softly, deliberately trying to lull her into a state of complete rest. When he knew she was out, he kept talking. He didn't want his silence to jolt her back into discomfort. He told stories of his first wooden sword at twelve. His favourite Greek mythology facts. The lyrics to 'Downtown Train'.

He talked and talked until she was completely at peace.

When he finally left her to sleep, he went into the kitchen and started to make a note on his phone. Jasper was sitting in the window seat, drawing on a tablet with a stylus. She smiled at him as he entered the room.

'How's our girl?'

Jonah raised his smartphone, showing her his list in progress. 'I'm cooking her dinner.'

Jasper formed an 'O' in delighted surprise. 'You are, indeed.'

'I'll make enough for all of us,' he added hastily. 'But most of it for her. Maybe a lamb ragu, something that'll stick to the bones. But I'll get some bread and eggs and cheese and spinach and stuff, all she has in here are bananas and oatmeal. I can do a veggie omelette or a grilled cheese, if ragu is too heavy right now. And Tylenol, she needs Tylenol.'

Jasper still wore a small smile as she watched him type. 'Okay.'

'I don't know how deliveries will work in this building, it's pretty airtight and I don't want randoms knowing she lives here so I'll go down and get it when it's here.'

'I'll keep guard.'

He knew she was teasing but he nodded anyway. 'Thanks.'

If she had any opinion about his prepping, she didn't express it. When the bags of groceries arrived, he fetched them from the lobby and thanked Mohammad for quizzing the delivery driver on entry. He took the brown bags back to the apartment and, after locking the door securely behind him, he got to work.

'Jasper, I know you're working and I hate to, like, use you, but could you ask her what she would like to eat? I can order in more if nothing here speaks to her.'

Jasper's smile widened as she obediently rose to her feet, with the grace of an ex-ballerina, and made her way across the apartment to Allegra's room where Jonah heard her speaking softly. She returned after a few moments.

'She says an omelette sounds amazing but you don't have to.'

'I do,' Jonah said quietly. 'I'm on it.'

'I didn't know you could cook.'

'I know some basics.'

Jasper sat back down. 'Arthur and I are both useless, we go out way too often to eat.'

'My mum's great at baking but she can't cook. It's too unpredictable for her, she likes to say. She likes measuring cups and stuff. I had to learn at twelve how to cook for two when I couldn't take it any more.'

There was silence from Jasper as he started to crack eggs into a bowl.

'That can't have been easy,' she finally said.

He shrugged, focused on cooking for Allegra. 'She felt so bad but we couldn't keep eating overly well done – sorry, *burned* – lamb chops and brisket.'

Jasper's phone rang, giving him an excuse to cook in comfortable silence.

'Hey, baby.' She was speaking to Arthur. The endearment was telling enough, and Jonah could hear the low murmurings of the cinema manager on the other end of the line. He threw a quick glance towards Jasper. She was leaning against the kitchen wall, smiling as she listened to whatever Arthur was saying. As her smile grew, Jonah felt a painful pang.

He wanted Allegra to look like Jasper did when he called her. He wanted her to light up and answer on the first ring. He wanted to make her feel as loved as Jasper felt. That intimacy, the quiet luxury of private love.

'I'm off the clock soon, but I'm also Jonah's ride home,' she told Arthur.

'That's okay,' Jonah told her, whispering in that way that people did when they were speaking to someone who was already on the phone. 'I can get the last bus or something.'

'Uh-huh,' Jasper said, spluttering out a laugh. 'Sure. I'm your chaperone as well, young man.'

A voice spoke to them both from the doorway. 'No paps on the twelfth floor, don't worry. This building is super secure and off the grid. Even my most obsessive fans don't know about it.'

Both Jonah and Jasper turned to see a very weak-looking Allegra.

'You shouldn't be up, you need rest,' Jonah said. 'Get back to bed.'

Her eyes danced with amusement. 'No. I'm watching you cook.'

'Back to bed, Allegra.'

'It smells great.'

'Allegra!'

Jasper made her way to the door. 'Well, if you're sure about that bus, Jonah, I've got to get back to my grump. You're both okay?'

'Yes,' Allegra said. 'Thanks for everything, Jasper. I can't wait to see what you're ma-making.'

Her words were earnest but clumsily delivered, a cough fighting its way out of her as she tried to thank her new designer. Jasper reached across to squeeze her arm and needed no words as she said goodbye and closed the front door behind her.

They were alone.

Allegra watched as Jonah flipped the omelette onto one of her many unused plates. They were pristine and untouched and she had a sudden wish. She wanted to see them chipped and scorched; blemished by a life lived with someone else. Meals made and shared, without worrying about perfection.

'Go back to bed. Now.'

She watched tendrils of heat rise from the omelette on the plate he was holding. 'Looks so good.'

She wasn't speaking purely of the food, but he was too busy ushering her back to her bed to notice any hidden meaning. He pulled the covers over her and only once she was still and breathing a little more steadily, did he give her the food. She ate slowly but intently. It was a comfort to her throat, now raw from coughing.

'Thank you, Jonah.'

He was perched on the edge of the bed, keeping a respectful

distance as he watched her eat. He took the empty plate from her when she was done and they looked at each other.

'Everything is so easy with you,' Jonah told her softly. He sounded incredulous and her face must have shown bemusement because he clarified. 'It's rarely that way with allistics.'

'Ah,' she said, smiling. 'Well . . .'

'I'm always having to explain myself,' Jonah said and his sadness seemed bone deep. 'They don't get that it's a disability. I can't read between their lines unless I have a million miles of energy. Which most of the time, I don't. Because I'm fighting off sensory overload or trying to keep my scripts in order. They never say what they mean and if I ever stand up for myself, I'm the asshole. And I was an asshole to you. Horribly. But I wasn't always like that. I used to be really open. I – I used to be softer. You know that there's this whale in the ocean that sings at a different frequency from all the others? So, it's always alone. The others never hear it. That was me. For so long. It's why I overlooked Simon being an ass to me. He never was to other people, they wouldn't believe me if I ever told them about his darker moments.'

'I believe you,' Allegra breathed.

'I know! That's what's so wonderfully jarring about you. You're nothing like the rest of them.'

Allegra reached out a hand to caress his face. She held it in her hand. 'Jonah . . .'

'They've never understood,' he said, almost to himself. As if finally realizing something. 'They'll never understand.'

'No,' whispered Allegra, who had met this truth long ago. She and that truth were old friends. They would sometimes clink glasses and laugh about how naive she had once been. But she knew Jonah needed this. Perhaps he was shedding the mask more easily now that he was away from Lake Pristine.

'They will make me explain myself and explain myself until I've no breath left in me,' he said. 'They will never see what I see. They won't even try to look, even though I've memorized every colour of their lives. They'll never see the disability because it makes them uncomfortable. They'll tell themselves they're just tougher. Built stronger. But they'll never know what that whale knows.'

Allegra brushed his cheek with the pad of her thumb.

'Jonah, I have something to tell you,' she heard herself say.

She had so many secrets. The one that was directly tied up with him, and pages of online letters. She was afraid of that one. Terrified that she was some base attraction to him, a warm body, while the girl in the emails was an imaginary girl on a pedestal. A fantasy that wasn't based in reality. It was a frightened, whispered thought in her head. It made no logical sense but eighteen years of feeling othered let self-doubt dig its claws in deep.

But there was one secret she needed him to know now.

'Jonah, I'm autistic, too.'

# Chapter Twenty-Eight

Allegra had been diagnosed for a few years. Her mother had fought for it on behalf of both of them. When it was finally granted, her school had done nothing to help her. Ear defenders were not allowed, aids in the classroom were sneered at and labelled 'special treatment', with an extra dose of callousness in the first word. Her school reports were written in venom.

So, leaving it all behind for *Court of Bystanders* had been a ship leaving the harbour with no glance back.

Since then, no one had heard the word from her. It was her private information to bear. She turned down the occasional script with a 'disturbed' character whose mysterious, unnamed neurodevelopmental disability made them a savant or a burden or a plot point. A neurotypical actor would gladly take the role and lament at parties when the awards never came.

All of that felt far away as she watched Jonah take in the new information.

'You . . . you're . . .'

'Yes.'

He blinked in astonishment and then pressed his forehead to hers. She felt her eyes fill but more than anything, a weight had been carefully lifted from her soul.

'I knew you weren't like them,' he said, his voice full of something like worship.

'I don't tell many people. Not ashamed of it, I just don't have a lot of control over privacy any more. And that's why I'm so sick. The masking, the work, the last few years – it's all reached a bit of a breaking point.'

She watched everything pass in front of his eyes. She could see him applying this new knowledge to the memories of the two of them, to everything he knew about her. She wondered, for the quickest of seconds, if he would wear the usual look of discomfort that people donned when she brought up her neurodivergence.

Instead, his eyes filled with something she was too cowardly to put a name to and he said her name with a desperate mix of reverence and pain.

'Oh, Allegra.'

And she was crying. At least, she thought she was. She wanted to slap the back of her own head; furious that she had cried more in the last few days than she had for a year. She felt the wetness on her face and the tremble in her stiff jaw but she didn't make a sound. She supposed that she knew, deep inside, that he would understand in an instant. Neurodivergent people always did.

She never liked to waste her time, explaining to neurotypicals. She occasionally read articles or memoirs from other autistic women, where they laid out their condition for their allistic readers. She would give them no such patience. She would not let them entertain themselves for a train journey with the authenticities of her less examined life. For they would only put it down and return to a world that was crafted for them, with the accomplishments of autistics vital but not visible. Seen but not heard. They didn't get to have that part of her. They didn't get the meltdowns on bathroom floors or the splitting headaches from masking. They also wouldn't get the joy. The heightened senses from a life lived in fuller colour.

'You've done all this,' Jonah said brokenly, looking around at the apartment, the result of her labour, 'without telling anyone. Or asking for help. Allegra, your lungs! The masking has made them give out. Why is no one helping you?'

'I'm not interested in a free ride.'

'We give them free rides every day! All of the time! Why can't you have one sliver of understanding?'

The break in Jonah's voice as he looked at her, at all of her, was too much. She bowed forward, her head pressing against the cool sheets. She turned her head to look at him and he stretched out next to her so they were face-to-face.

'It makes a strange sort of sense.'

'What does?' Allegra asked him.

'When your dad hired me, years ago now, I asked if there was a room somewhere in the shop for employees to step into if things got overwhelming. I had one at school, it helps to—'

'Delay a bad spell.'

'Yes. Exactly.' He started stroking her open palm with his fingers.

'What did he say?'

'Before he could answer, I told him. Said I was autistic. Wanted to let a potential employer know, maybe I was curious to see what he would do.'

She touched his foot with hers. 'What did he do?'

'Said it was completely fine, I could use the office or the stock room whenever I needed. No questions, no pushback. It was . . . it was cool of him. That's when I started liking him.'

'He knows. About me, I mean. Mum told him after the fact.

But we never spoke of it.'

'That's George, though. Reads thousands of words a day, speaks only a handful.'

She laughed. 'Yes.'

He stared into her face with such devotion, she felt completely exposed.

'Allegra, you're like me.'

Like a prayer had been answered.

They talked into the night. Allegra felt wobbly but content. She had just enough strength to occasionally push Jonah's dark hair out of his eyes. When she said she wished she could get a manicure without someone trying to sneak a picture, he went to the drugstore on the corner and came back with an assortment of her favourite colours. He painted polish onto her toenails with sweet precision. He blew on them. They talked about books. She told him about scripts. He asked about her co-stars.

She didn't remember falling asleep. But she slept through the whole night, without waking in pain.

Jonah woke the next morning, still fully dressed, to the sound of his phone vibrating. He quickly excused himself, though Allegra was dead asleep. He slipped into the kitchen and answered the call before noting that it was coming from an unknown number.

'This is Jonah.'

'Hey, man. Sorry to call early, it's Charlie Matuschek, from Matuschek Press.'

'Oh, yes, hi,' Jonah said, fixing his bed hair even though the man on the other end of the line couldn't see him. 'Thank you for calling.'

'That's okay.' Jonah could tell that the man was occupied with something else while on the phone, but not completely distracted. 'You wouldn't happen to be free for an interview today? We can do online, if it's too far from where—'

'That would be great. I'm in the city, so in person is fine.'

'Ah, excellent. Cool. Um, we're on Upper Oak Street and—'

'I know where. By the movie house with the ancient coffee machine.'

'Noon too soon?'

'Not at all.'

'Great. Easy! See you there then, Jonah, thank you for being so flexible.'

Jonah had to smile. It was not a word often used about him. He slipped back into Allegra's bedroom, ready to ask her what she wanted for breakfast. He found her getting dressed in her walk-in wardrobe. She was wearing pink satin trousers and a soft pink jumper and she looked marginally healthier than the day before.

'I can't face a bra just yet,' she told him conspiratorially and he blushed.

'I've got a job interview. At noon.'

His whole body filled with heat as she stared up at him in complete delight. 'Jonah, that's fantastic! Where?'

'A small press downtown. They're great.'

'What about Dad? What will he do without you?'

She said it teasingly and Jonah still did not have the heart to reveal what had happened.

'I want to bring you breakfast,' he said instead.

'I'm fine.'

'Properly fine or autistic-won't-realize-she-needs-to-eat-until-much-later fine?'

She laughed heartily at that. 'First one.'

'Okay.'

'It's after ten, you should go. If it's at noon.'

Yet neither of them moved. Jonah stared at this cosmic person who, as it turned out, was so much more like him than he could have known. Her mask had been so impenetrable, he had never suspected.

He could imagine the cost of it. The weight of it. Maybe they were both too afraid to say how they felt because they had been communicating with neurotypicals for too long, and become protective of their hearts in a way that only the outcasts do.

'Eighteen! You're only eighteen! I thought by your cover letter you were an old man!'

Jonah sat across from Charlie Matuschek and tried to find the right response. 'The resumé didn't tip you off?'

'Well, if I'm honest, I've interviewed nine people fresh out of graduate school and their resumés are nicely padded, but I'm not sure they've ever read a book published after the Hindenburg.'

'Ah.'

'You know the type?'

'I like the classics.'

'Sure, but you're not allergic to the Women's Prize or the Newbery?'

'No, but shortlists can be very dry and trauma-dependent. I've recently found my impatience for people who overlook genre fiction and commercial writing.'

'Not exactly what we publish.'

'Right,' Jonah acknowledged, unbothered. 'But maybe you should.'

The publisher who owned the small press was in his forties. He wore corduroy trousers and old T-shirts. His teeth were slightly yellow, possibly due to his coffee habit, he was drinking from the largest mug Jonah had ever seen. His hair was thinning but a nice colour. He was affable but clearly looking for someone to engage the parts of his intellect that had become as comfy and soft as him.

'I love your poetry anthologies,' Jonah said honestly. 'And the essay collections. But you should publish more women and marginalized writers. The literary writing you promote is all a bit . . . samey.'

This was met with stunned silence.

'I'm autistic,' Jonah said, feeling emboldened by Allegra's earlier courage. 'Your job description said someone who isn't afraid to say what they think and push the envelope when it comes to editorial direction. Now, if that's neurotypical code and you actually just want someone to boil a kettle, file things and take minutes, fine. But that's what I think. And your relationship with bookshops is pretty legendary. But you have to engage with the internet, too.'

Jonah forced himself to make eye contact with the publisher, who was regarding him with an unreadable expression.

'Are you a writer?' Charlie Matuschek eventually asked.

'I,' Jonah hesitated and then decided to be brave. Like Allegra. 'Yes, I am.'

The interview continued for an hour. When Jonah was finally allowed to leave, there were two other candidates sitting in the main part of the Matuschek Bookshop, where the press also had their offices. Both interviewees looked disgruntled at having to wait and, as Jonah walked back to Allegra's building, he felt the timid glow of certainty, the kind one felt after acing a test or excelling in front of a group of strangers.

And no one had brought up the pictures.

It had gone well. He had experienced enough occasions where things had not gone well in his life. That was how he knew the difference.

Perhaps it had all come to a point.

# Chapter Twenty-Nine

Photographers followed Allegra to a hot yoga session. She ended up hiding in the bathroom for the entire hour, too anxious to brave the class and face the irritable faces of the people who had been forced to push their way past paparazzi to get into the studio. She emailed Natalie, who reminded her about a style consultation for the premiere.

'We need to talk about our narrative for press on the movie, post photos,' Natalie added in a voice note.

Jasper texted, asking if Allegra needed a pickup from the back of the building. Allegra felt horrible asking, but Jasper would hear none of her apologies. They drove to the cast recording of *Sunday in the Park with George* for fifteen minutes before Allegra was able to relax, knowing that no one had seen or followed them.

'Ready to be back in Lake Pristine?' Jasper asked.

'Yes,' Allegra said. 'I don't like how I left things with Dad, I took off like I did something wrong, and I know I didn't.'

'Parents have a way of making their kids feel guilty over stuff they would never dream of judging others for.'

The words suspended time for a moment and when Allegra glanced at Jasper, she noticed a touch of melancholy on the woman's face. She wondered, not for the first time, what it must have been like, growing up autistic in a tiny town. To have everyone witness your worst days, and your disability before you were even able to give it a name.

'So, how are things with Jonah?' asked Jasper, in what could only be described as a big-sister voice.

Allegra let out one final cough of indignation, as her chest was almost clear, and gave Jasper an affronted look. 'We're . . . friends.'

'You're friends?'

'Yes. Former work colleagues, now friends.'

'I don't have pictures of me and my friends like the ones that leech took of the two of you.'

'Low blow, bringing up the pap.'

'Then don't lie to me, kid. Friends? Please.'

'We are.'

'Allegra,' Jasper said her name with exasperation, and it made the actress laugh. It was fun. It felt like being in a scene from a sweet movie, where the emotional stakes were high but there were no nasty plot twists. It was the kind of movie she wished her life could be.

She kept laughing, enjoying their play. 'We are, Jasper.'

'That boy cooked for you. He looked ready to yell at me if I didn't tell you that he wanted to see you. He almost killed Simon because of what he told that editor. Never mind that kiss.'

Allegra's smile faded and she winced. 'Yeah, that's . . .'

'He is in love with you, Allegra.'

Allegra blinked. 'Don't be silly.'

'He is. I've watched enough old movies to know.'

Allegra was momentarily distracted. She smiled. 'You like old movies? Me, too.'

'My new favourite is *Shop Around the Corner*. Jimmy Stewart. What a mensch.'

'I'll have to watch it,' Allegra said.

'You should. But yes. He is hopelessly in love with you, girlie.'

Allegra shook her head and tried to be composed. 'He is not!'

'No, he is. Jonah Thorne has always been a beautiful loner, who tolerates other people. But you, he more than tolerates.'

'We're friends. All of yesterday and last night, he was a good friend, nothing more.'

'Exactly what kind of person would make advances on someone who has a chest infection, made worse by the threat of an autistic shutdown?'

Allegra made a noise of derision but she was smiling. 'Okay, a bad friend would do that. So he was being a good friend. Like I said.'

Allegra didn't know why she was denying anything. It was obvious she and Jonah were on a pathway that did not lead to friendship as a final destination. She just needed to bide time until it was her, the real her, he really liked and not some imaginary girl on the computer or film screen.

'Like I said.' Jasper turned the music up and sped the car into a long, easy sprint down the country road leading to her small hometown. 'No pictures of me and my friends like the ones of you and him.'

'I think the whole aftermath scared him off.'

Jasper's lips twitched but she kept her eyes ahead. 'I'm not so sure.'

They drove in comfortable silence as Mandy Patinkin sang. When Jasper spoke, it was with a musing tone.

'Lake Pristine is a funny place. It sort of freezes in time, when you leave it. You can go for, like, ten hours, ten days. Ten years, even. And when you get back, everything is almost exactly as you left it. People haven't moved on. They haven't forgotten the version of you that they knew when you left. They're not interested in who you've become while you've been away.'

Allegra glanced at Jasper. 'She says with experience?'

'Yes.'

'Maybe that's why my dad is so weird.'

'With you?'

'Yeah. Acts like I'm still twelve. Which, to be fair, was when he last saw me.'

'That's a dad thing, as well as a Lake Pristine thing.'

They discussed Allegra's home and interior design for the rest of the drive, but Jasper's words about her small hometown returned to Allegra as the *Welcome to Lake Pristine* sign appeared ahead of them. When Allegra had called the shop, her father had answered. Thrilled at the news of her return, he had promised that there were no more paps lurking about.

As Jasper and Allegra had watched the original swarm of reporters from her father's flat, the day she left Lake Pristine, the only respite from the tension and anxiety had been when a local woman had almost run the reporters down with her Range Rover.

'My sister,' Jasper had said, with a wince. 'Christine.'

Now, as the town came into focus, Allegra understood exactly what Jasper had said. Everyone waved at the two of them in Jasper's car, as if nothing had happened, as if Allegra had just gone on vacation for a week and returned with no news for anyone. She spotted Vivienne Thorne outside her bakery, with two members of her staff. They were handing out free samples of what looked like some kind of brownie. When Vivienne spotted Allegra, she smiled and waved, but there was a clear look of worry in her eyes.

'Mothers and sons,' Jasper said, observing the reaction. 'Scary.'

'She's really nice.'

'She is, but Jonah's getting way too independent for her, I think. Not sure she's going to take it well.'

'I'm just here to talk to Dad, and then gather everyone up for the premiere.'

As Allegra said the words, she realized something.

'Jasper?'

'Yes.'

'I . . . really don't feel comfortable inviting Simon any more. Would you like to come instead?'

'To a fancy premiere of a Hollywood picture?'

'Yes.'

'Red carpet?'

'Yes.'

'Photographers?'

'Yes.'

'Pretty clothes?'

'The prettiest. Natalie, my publicist, is sending a car this afternoon and we're doing style options tonight in the hotel suite.'

'You won't mind an ancient twenty-three-year-old chumming along with you teenagers?'

'No, happy to have a responsible adult.'

Allegra had gone through a few premieres and screenings, plus one high-profile ball, in her career. Hotel suites full of colleagues and social media interns were fun, but she had always envied people who brought tons of their friends along. Polaroid photos of fun and friendship, the kind Allegra desperately wanted but sometimes didn't know how to cultivate. She made a great first impression. She could say, 'let's get lunch' as easily as anyone. But securing and maintaining friendships had always been hard for her. She didn't know the steps to that dance, and a childhood in film and television had not helped her in that regard either.

Gathering new friends together and whisking them out for champagne, pizza and a Cinderella night of Hollywood glamour was the scariest thing she had attempted in a while. It felt like being six years old again and wondering why no one had come to her birthday party.

Jasper dropped Allegra at Brooks Books, promising to meet her there again at three o'clock for the glamorous pickup. Allegra watched her go, feeling a type of gratitude that was reserved for only the most special people in her life. The ones that accepted all of the fingerprints on her canvas, the kind that spoke to a life lived with challenges and human mistakes. The ones who found it all the more beautiful.

She stepped into Brooks Books to find Simon there alone, packing up returns by the front desk. They stared at one another for a long while, Allegra watching with fascination as shame fought with defiance on Simon's face.

'Hey,' he finally said.

'Hi, Simon.'

She took note of the slight black eye he was sporting on his left side. 'Did Jonah give you that?'

'Yeah.' His voice was bitter. 'You're a sore subject for him, it seems.'

'Good. *I* wanted to hit you for what you did to me. If you ever do that to another girl, I'll make you regret it. The one good thing about fame is that there is always a journo willing to listen. You touch someone else without their consent, I'll make your whole world go away. It's what you did to me.'

'I'm sorry, Allegra.'

'You hurt him, too, Simon,' Allegra added. 'Putting him out in the public eye like that. It's not what he wants. It's a burden for anyone, let alone those who don't actually choose it.'

'He wants to be a writer, Ally. This will make a hell of a story for him. He should be grateful.'

She deliberately stayed silent, allowing her disapproval to fill the air like smoke.

'Sorry,' he finally mumbled. 'I'm sorry, Allegra. I really am. I didn't know what the pictures actually were. They asked about you and me and when I confirmed it was me, they pressed about the guy you were with as you left Main Street. I gave Jonah's name. I didn't know about the photos. I swear, I didn't. That . . . I had no idea about it.'

Allegra reached out to touch some of the books in her father's shop. 'Okay.'

'I – I'm really sorry. I am. I'm going to give Jasper my spot at the premiere, too. It will be too hard for Jonah to see me there.'

She still said nothing, the silence speaking volumes.

'I bought into your surface act,' Allegra said softly. 'Everyone around here thinks you're great. I believed the reviews. But you've got a nasty streak. You show it to Jonah, more than anyone. Don't you?'

'Allegra, I didn't know you liked him. I knew he liked you. God, I've never seen him like that around anyone. You were the name we could never bring up around him, and Jonah has always been indifferent or oblivious to everyone. So, it was weird. I worked it out pretty early on.'

Allegra wanted what he was saying to be true. 'I think he was rightly annoyed at an actor slumming it for a summer, at a job he took very seriously all year round.'

'Nah,' Simon said softly. 'You know how some people, when they trip? They get really mad? They get scared and embarrassed and then they look around to make sure no one has seen them fall?'

'Yes,' Allegra said, unable to suppress a smile. 'It happens to me on the regular.'

'You fall and your first instinct is what? To look around, act mad. Put on a show and let the world know that you are no faller. Something sabotaged you.'

'I suppose. But I'm dyspraxic. We fall a lot.'

'That's what Jonah did. He fell and then got mad about falling.'

Allegra felt colour rush to her face. 'Well . . . I'm not so sure—'

'That's what all that gruffness and bravado was,' said Simon matter-of-factly. 'He fell and he didn't see it coming. So, he acted stupidly. *She's not making a faller out of me*, all that nonsense. But I saw it. You would have, too, if you two had stopped fighting for two seconds. But . . . I mean, those pictures looked like the two of you figured it out.'

He said it without any bite but it still stung.

'I think the photographs going viral and appearing on morning television might have killed any feelings he had,' Allegra said, unable to keep both the pain and reprimand out of her voice.

Empathy flashed through Simon's eyes. 'Hey, no way. Thing about Jonah? He's all or nothing. He's yours for ever. If you want him. Trust me.' There was a beat of awkwardness before he added, 'I just hope he can forgive me. You, too.'

Allegra regarded him and then said, 'I might forgive you, Simon. Someday. But I'm not as concerned about making everyone else feel comfortable all of the time now. So don't be surprised if it takes a while.'

# Chapter Thirty

Allegra's father didn't return to the shop from the festival site until fifteen minutes to three.

'Hey, Dad.'

'Ally.'

He struggled to speak but she could see it all on his face: the guilt, the regret, the uncertainty and the love. She hugged him. She told him it was all going to be okay, that she was off to have a fun night with her friends before her movie's premiere the following day. She tried to show him, rather than tell him, that everything had worked out for the beautifully strange girl who was given a diagnosis but no help. Who found that she could only be her true self in the arts. She was a natural in a creative job, one that so many could never reach. The ordinary was too difficult but the extraordinary came easy.

*I'll be okay*, she told him through their embrace. *I will. They tried to tell me I was nothing, they wanted me to feel like I wasn't worth remembering. But I am. I'm going to find people like me through my art and they can print as many slut-shaming headlines as they like, they won't make me afraid. They can call me odd and cold and strange. But they can't do what I can do.*

'You can't be mad at Jonah, Dad,' she told him as they hugged. 'He's the only one who's been taking care of you.'

At first she wondered if he had heard her, but he eventually murmured, 'I know.'

They spoke softly until a large black car pulled up to the kerb. George kissed her quickly on the head and went into the shop, possibly hoping that she hadn't caught the gleam of tears. She watched him go, Simon inside to greet him. She could see them through the bookshop window and she wondered why they both looked so grave as they spoke.

Jonah was still in the city, hopefully riding high after his job interview, so he would meet them at the hotel suite. Allegra could see Jasper and Grace in the distance, walking arm in arm. Jasper wore dark glasses, just like Allegra, and Grace waved enthusiastically.

'I have never been more excited for anything!' Grace gushed as she and Jasper reached the car. 'Allegra, this is, like, the greatest night of my life.'

Allegra laughed warmly. 'Tonight's just playing dress-up, tomorrow is makeovers and the actual party.'

'I know, don't, I can't contain myself.'

Allegra had asked them both to message Natalie about their measurements and style influences so that the stylist could pull some specific choices. As a curvier girl, Allegra was used to the stylist complaining about having fewer options but Allegra always found something beautiful. She wanted Grace and Jasper to feel the same. Jasper had also sent over stills from an old movie called *What a Way to Go* as her inspiration.

'Is . . .' Allegra felt like a child again as she asked Grace the question that had been bothering her all morning. 'Is Kerrie still coming?'

Grace's smile slipped. 'I told her that she would have a lot of nerve.'

'No,' Allegra cried. 'No, I . . . I don't want her to be mad at me. Or think I'm mad at her.'

'It might be a little awkward for her,' Jasper pointed out gently. 'Seeing you and Jonah.'

'We're just friends,' insisted Allegra.

'And you're meant to be an actor? Very unconvincing.'

'There's no bad blood on my end. I want her to come. If she feels like it.'

'Well, there's a whole other thing,' Grace said with a sigh. 'She got waitlisted for Mapesbury. Ages ago, apparently. I was just telling Jonah the other day, that's why she's a bit sensitive at the moment.'

'Ouch,' Jasper whispered while Allegra frowned.

'What's that?'

'Mapesbury is, like, the university that every kid in this town goes to after high school,' Grace explained. 'My older brother went there, Jasper went there—'

'For eighteen horrible months,' Jasper interjected.

'Simon's going there in the fall,' Grace went on. 'Skye is going, too. And Kerrie was desperate to join them, but she didn't get in. She got waitlisted. She thought someone might drop out over the summer so she could get the call, but the call never came. So, she's a bit bitter right now. Best to be left alone.'

Kerrie and Skye appeared on the corner of Main Street to watch the three of them get into the car. Their expressions were stern and unforgiving as they watched the small, merry party pull away. Allegra felt a deep sense of foreboding as she stared into Kerrie's face as the Mercedes brushed by them. The other girl looked so young. Allegra knew they were the same age but there was something raw and rare in Kerrie's face, as if Allegra had turned the entire classroom and playground against her.

Allegra knew how that felt, and she hated seeing it on Kerrie's sweet face.

'Stop the car!'

The vehicle stalled and Allegra slipped out of the backseat before anyone could question her. Kerrie and Skye were shielding their vision from the bright, baking rays of the sun over Lake Pristine as Allegra made her way towards them.

'Hey, slut,' Skye said in greeting, with a sickly sweet and contemptuous tone.

'I don't use that word,' Allegra replied quietly. She turned to Kerrie, who looked mortified by Skye's words. 'Can I talk to you?'

'No, you can't talk to her,' Skye barked but Kerrie made a noise of frustration.

'She can talk, Skye.'

'Did you get all of the attention you wanted?' Skye ignored her friend and berated Allegra with a gleeful gleam in her eye. 'Do you know how few decent boys there are in this town? You had to have both of them.'

'I haven't "had" anyone,' Allegra said coolly. 'Kerrie. I'm sorry. Everything with Jonah happened unexpectedly and stupidly fast. We both should have considered your feelings more.'

Kerrie waved away her words, looking embarrassed. 'It's not, it's okay, Allegra. I've been a bitch. But, it's not what you think.'

'Is it about the university?'

Kerrie looked surprised. 'How did you—? Never mind, small town. Yeah. My whole family have gone to Mapesbury. It's a sort of Lake Pristine tradition. Kids go, they graduate, they come back here. Except I didn't get in.'

Allegra felt a brush of sympathy for her. She knew, as an actor, what it felt like to be ghosted by people who could change your life.

'Come with us tonight, like we planned,' she said softly, ignoring Skye and her evident disapproval. 'We'll get you a great outfit, we'll have fun.'

'Not ready to face Jonah yet,' Kerrie said, but it was with an appreciative smile. 'But thanks, Allegra.'

Allegra ached for the girl. She looked so forlorn and Allegra found it impossible to forget how sweet and kind she had been to Allegra on her arrival in Lake Pristine.

'Can I do something else for you then?' she asked.

'You've done enough,' snapped Skye, which caused Kerrie to round on her friend.

'Skye. Shut up. You don't even like me that much, you just want to take the famous actress down a peg. It's gross. Stop.'

Allegra smothered a smirk, while Skye's mouth made a perfect 'O' of shock. Kerrie turned back to Allegra with an exhale of relief.

'What did you have in mind?'

'Just a picture,' Allegra said gently. 'Taken by me, this time.'

Kerrie looked bewildered, but Allegra took a smiling selfie of them, side by side. Allegra wrote a quick caption, which she showed to Kerrie, who nodded in consent. Allegra posted it.

'Give it a few days to percolate,' Allegra told her. 'And if you change your mind about tomorrow, just call Grace and I can get you in.'

Kerrie watched the actress get back into the car, smiling in a way she never had before. Her hands trembled as she checked her own social media feed. There the two of them were, she a small-town girl with a handful of followers and the movie star who was sent death threats. They smiled defiantly at the camera lens.

This is my very good friend @KerrieR2008. Mapesbury University have, quite stupidly, waitlisted her. If anyone else knows a good thing when they see it, she'll make a great addition to your campus come fall. Love, Allegra Brooks.

She watched the car leave Lake Pristine, grateful to her new friend and ashamed of how she had behaved.

Inspired, too. By someone who had taken pain and refused to turn it into poison.

'May she never come back,' Skye said scornfully, as they watched the car become a speck in the distance.

'Skye,' Kerrie said, her voice matter-of-fact. 'I have so utterly outgrown you.'

Allegra felt her spirits soar as Grace took in the Parfumerie Suite at the Garland Hotel. It was on the top floor, with stunning skyline views. The reflection of the sun on the river was dazzling and the warmth filled the dustless rooms, where make-up stations were set up and racks of clothes waited to be chosen.

'I've died and gone to unattainable heaven,' Jasper said, as she walked towards one particular clothing rack that had her name attached to it. 'Is this Temperley?'

The stylist, a fun woman in her forties named February, glanced over at Jasper with an appraising look. 'Oh, work. Yes, it is.'

Allegra soaked in the second-hand delight of watching Jasper browse the sensual gowns February had pulled out for her. Grace was marvelling at sparkling tuxedos and some two-pieces that the stylist had sourced. She selected a Ralph Lauren suit and started to change at once, seemingly unbothered by the strangers in the room.

'I have a silk shirt for it here,' February said, getting to work and joining Grace by her clothing rack.

Allegra's dress was couture and would be the last thing to try. She didn't have a rack, she had a beautiful golden gown of dreamy fabrics and her trusty Manolos, the ones she had worn to her first ever premiere. She threw a look to the quiet rack of men's clothing in the corner. She felt only too aware of his absence and wondered what he would make of all the dressing up.

Maybe he would find it all trivial, and her by extension. She was still so unsure of where they stood. She liked him, far too much, but they hadn't discussed their status. Nothing was pinned down or written. It was all unspoken, which she was never great at analysing.

'Something smells amazing,' Grace said.

There was an ice bucket of something delicious and vegetarian pizza. Natalie gave Allegra a quick sideways hug, one that silently told Allegra that the publicist was proud of how she had handled the fallout. Music played while a social media manager filmed just about everything.

Allegra tried on the gown and it fit splendidly. The glamour team was clearly pleased, and that allowed Allegra to feel calm. She stepped out of it and watched February handle it with such dexterity, treating it like precious liquid gold. Once it was hung up, Allegra slipped into a hotel robe and tried to relax.

Then a knock on the suite door.

February, Natalie and Clark, the social media manager, were gathered around a laptop, as if the hotel suite had become a war room for fashion. Jasper was taking pictures of Grace in her suit, both of them also oblivious.

So Allegra went to open the door.

She and Jonah stared at each other for a moment. She could sense something different in him and it both thrilled and frightened her. He was standing taller. He looked a little older. There was something settled inside of him, something that had been undecided before.

'Hey,' he said, staring at her as though she were the one thing he wanted more than anything. It was so potent, Allegra felt frozen in the doorframe. He took in the sprinkling of gold around her eyes and the dusting of shimmery lotion across her decolletage.

'Hey.'

He leaned towards her, prompting her to lift her chin as their faces moved together. The same pull that they had felt in the bookshop on the day they' first met, the stardust that randomly chose to materialize between two people, it was almost physical now. A magnetized force that made her constantly aware of him when he was in the room, and painfully in tune to his absence when he was gone.

Not just friends. It had never been like this with a friend. But she was too scared to say it.

'Is this the young man of the party?' February's voice called from within the hotel suite.

It caused both Allegra and Jonah to pause, but they did not leap apart as if they were doing something wrong. Instead Jonah ran the pad of his thumb along Allegra's bottom lip, a silent promise that they would talk about it all. Later.

When the 'looks' were locked in, and the pizza was gone, February and Clark said their farewells and left the suite. Natalie gave the three teenagers a somewhat matronly look and said, 'There are two bedrooms . . . Have we decided who is sharing with who?'

Jasper, who was free from Natalie's gaze, smiled at Allegra and arched an eyebrow in a silent question.

Allegra pushed her ego and its fear of rejection out of the way and answered frankly.

'I'm sharing with Jonah.'

Her tone was casual on the surface, but it had steel underneath. She was not debating the matter. Jonah's hand gripped hers in solidarity.

'She is. You two good with the other one?' he asked, sporting the same tone as Allegra.

'Oh, yep,' Jasper said, fighting a smile as Grace did the same. 'No arguments here.'

Jonah had been offered the job at Matuschek just before arriving at the Garland Hotel. He had accepted over the phone, without a moment's hesitation, before asking if they intended to follow up on any references. He was slightly nervous that one grumpy phone call from George Brooks could make it all go away.

'No, we've had a glowing review from your former employer already. You can start a week from Monday.'

Jonah had stopped walking at this news. After ending the conversation with Charlie, he had dialled the shop. A part of him was ready for Simon to answer, though he had no idea what he intended to say to his once friend.

But George had picked up the phone.

'Hello, Brooks Books!'

Jonah had paused and considered hanging up before finally saying, 'Hey, George, it's me.'

There was just the faint buzz of the phone connection for a second. Then, 'Jonah.'

'I just wanted to say thank you for giving Matuschek Press a good reference. They've just offered me the job.'

'They'd be stupid not to.'

There had been an awkward silence. A beat of regret from both of them.

'I'm so sorry, Jonah. I made a mess of everything. I acted foolishly. I have . . . complex feelings about how I've not been there for Allegra and I projected a lot of it onto you. And pushed away my best employee.'

The neurotypical critic who liked to live in Jonah's neurodivergent head and tell him how he should act whispered to let it go, but Jonah wanted an answer.

'It wasn't only about me liking Allegra. It started before she came to Lake Pristine. What did I do? You were my mentor and you started treating me like a travelling salesman you couldn't wait to get out of the shop.'

'Yes. I know. It's . . . it's complicated, Jonah.'

'Okay, but you were the only person privy to those complications, George. I was in the dark. It's pretty uncomplicated when you're the one being treated badly. It's incredibly simple when you're on the receiving end.'

'I pushed you away because . . . because your life is going to be so much bigger than Lake Pristine and I didn't want to be responsible for holding you back.'

And George hung up.

Jonah stood in the street, unmoving, for five whole minutes as he processed George's words.

And perhaps the words had not hurt him because, ultimately, he knew they were true.

# Chapter Thirty-One

The bedroom they shared was cosy, warm and dimly lit – just how two autistics on the verge of becoming lovers liked it. Allegra climbed into his lap and he held her for thirty minutes without either of them speaking. Every electrified nerve that was tried each day by the neurotypical world started to quiet. Their jaws unclenched. The masks loosened and floated away, cast to the floor with the rest of their clothing.

'I have something important to tell you tomorrow,' Jonah said as the night ticked over into early morning.

Allegra had seen him glancing over his emails as she had brushed her teeth. She felt the secret like a stone, and regretted leaving him in the dark. It had gone on long enough now that she was almost too afraid to tell him the truth. Whatever important matter he had to discuss with her, it couldn't be as revealing as the truth of who was really writing to him in those emails.

Allegra pressed her check against his neck. 'Tell me now.'

'Can't. Has to be in public. Just before the movie starts tomorrow.'

'Why?'

'I'll be able to keep it together. Can't do it now. Want to say everything, just right.'

'Is it something bad?'

'No.'

She thought about her secret. She couldn't predict what he would do. When she tried to rehearse the scene in her mind, it disintegrated into mist every time she got to her confession. She was petrified he would be angry.

Or that she would lose him.

'How did your interview go, Jonah?'

'I got the job.'

She pulled her head back a little to stare at him. 'What? Jonah! That's amazing!'

'It is.'

'Have you told my dad?'

'Yes.'

'I bet he was happy for you. He's proud of you underneath it all, I know he is.'

'He fired me, you know.'

She wondered for a second if he was kidding. But, despite the darkness within the room, she could see a touch of sadness in his face. She brushed her hands across his jawline, as if she could somehow smooth away the sudden regret.

'Why didn't you tell me?'

'You were unwell. You were dealing with enough.'

He was rubbing her upper arms in a soothing motion and Allegra was reminded once again that she could never be just a friend to this person. As ever, when her mind wandered to romantic idealistic daydreams of the two of them, she wondered if he was still infatuated with an imaginary person on the other end of an email. His kisses and touches had spoken of desire, without question, but she couldn't forget the frustration on his face as she had found him in the cafe with a book and a flower.

That felt like another lifetime now.

'I can't wait until tomorrow,' she said, pressing a kiss to the corner of his mouth. 'Tell me now?'

'Nope. I had two things on my to-do list. Get a great new job, and tell you this thing. Did one today, gonna do the other tomorrow.'

'Can I seduce it out of you?' she asked teasingly.

'You are definitely welcome to try.'

They listened to the braying sounds of the city at night for a few minutes before Jonah asked, 'Does everyone who came tonight know you're autistic?'

'Yes. February, because I can't do certain fabrics and textures. Clark, so he knows if he ever does anything ableist on my socials stuff, he's out. And Natalie has known since the beginning. Apart from my agent and my parents, that's it.'

'And you don't want to go public?'

Allegra hesitated. 'I don't know. Telling people that you're autistic doesn't magically transform an intolerant person into an understanding one.'

'Preaching to the choir.'

'Well, even the choir needs to rehearse.'

He laughed at that.

'I don't know,' she said, listening to the beat of his heart as she spoke. 'I think a big part of me just wants to blurt it out. Then never talk about it again until I want to.'

'You should be able to do that.'

'Not in my business.'

'Allegra, you're grown. You're in charge of you. No one can get you into trouble any more, you don't answer to anyone.'

Allegra absorbed the words, which were spoken so casually. Another ode to the strange period of transition between childhood and adulthood. She was still playing by the old rules sometimes.

'Maybe,' she spoke softly. 'If I felt really safe. If I felt like I had something more to lose than my career, I would say. Just to be proud for once, instead of careful.'

When he didn't say anything, she looked into his face. He smiled sadly at her.

'You're so beautiful.'

Every time he told her that, it was gold paint between the cracks of the vase. 'You say that a lot.'

'You need to hear it.'

'Yes,' she said, surprising herself. 'You wouldn't believe how many people like to tell women they follow what they think of their looks. "Oh, if you just fixed your nose". "Have you gained weight, Allegra? Is it for a role?" "Your hair looks dry right now". It's constant. I can't hear my own voice sometimes, just everyone else's. It's why I like hearing yours.'

His fingers massaged her temples and she closed her eyes in bliss.

'People don't know,' she breathed. 'Having a disability . . . everything I did was wrong. When I was young, I mean. I would fail at things that seemed to come naturally to other people. The exasperation, the eye-rolling, the "you're just not getting this, are you?" It was inescapable. I always felt like an alien. Nothing I do comes naturally. I just wanted to be like other girls. I wanted to be like everyone else. I would lie awake and pray for it.'

So when the boy she liked called her beautiful, it felt like antivenom to the snake bite that was the world calling her imperfect. Jonah saw through everything.

'You're not an alien to me, Allegra,' he said, almost too quietly for her to hear. 'I want to write everything down. Everything about you. Everything you've ever said.'

A writer. His emails.

This unleashed in her an idea. The sketched outline of a plan for tomorrow. And as her mind wandered, Jonah kissed her and held her until she fell into the kind of sleep you can only reach when you're completely at home in your mind and body.

Jonah allowed February, Allegra's stylist, to suit him and boot him. He liked how he appeared in the tuxedo. As a tall, broad-shouldered person, shopping for clothes was never a favourite pastime. Yet he enjoyed how he looked in his reflection. As she doused him in Tom Ford, he wondered if he was finally starting to look the part.

The part of someone who could stand next to Allegra and belong there.

He was putting on cufflinks when she emerged from the bedroom. Jasper and Grace had already been dressed and were dancing in the living room of the suite, while Allegra changed and filmed content with Clark in the bedroom. He took in her golden gown and her sparkling eyes and the smile that she now seemed to reserve for him and he felt his breath leave his body.

'You – you look . . . Allegra, you're just—'

'Yes, she's stunning, but she's also late!' Natalie called from the front door of the hotel suite and Jonah inwardly wished everyone else could just vanish for a frozen moment in time, leaving him alone with Allegra.

'Thanks,' she told him softly, squeezing his elbow as she passed him. 'You look really hot.'

He caught her by the waist and pressed a kiss into her hairline, not caring a bit about everyone seeing them. The whole world had taken a look at one of the most private and precious moments of his life, but he didn't want that humiliation to stop him from showing Allegra how he felt about her.

He held her hand in the car, perfectly content to gaze out of the window while the three girls sang along to Cyndi Lauper and filmed themselves in the back of the limo. They shared a look before stepping out into the city square where the red carpet for the premiere was laid. Jonah blinked and winced at the size of the crowd and gripped Allegra's hand as they were ushered out of the car and towards the guest entrance to the carpet. Jonah watched as the mask slipped effortlessly onto Allegra's face as she greeted the associate at the gate.

'Just the VIP on the carpet and one guest,' the man said, shouting over the din of the crowd. Jonah could tell the exact moment that Allegra was spotted on the large screen erected nearer the actual movie house, as the crowd began to rumble and a few young women shrieked her name at a startling pitch and decibel.

'I'll take Jonah,' Allegra said.

Jonah stared at her in astonishment. 'Not . . . not your publicist?'

'No,' she said with a small smile. 'If you're okay with the carpet?'

'Allegra—' Natalie began to object, but Jasper swept her away with all the grace and decorum of the Lake Pristine royalty she was.

'We'll head straight in,' Jasper said, as if she had worked film premieres her entire life. 'See you after the carpet, Allegra.'

Jonah and Allegra, still holding hands, stepped onto the red fabric laid out like a brick road to a land he had never known before. The roar that greeted them was thunderous. Jonah winced as flashes began to take over his vision, as they moved from one step-and-repeat to another on the long, winding scarlet path. He moved back to allow Allegra her moment alone in front of the cameras.

He watched, both in awe and in disgust, as photographers yelled things at her.

'Over the shoulder!' one bellowed at her.

'Over here, whore!'

Jonah thought he must have imagined it, but when the female pap repeated the order, he was about ready to slap the camera from her hands. Allegra caught up to him and she gently steered them further down the carpet.

'They do it to get a reaction,' she told him, without needing to know his question. 'There are so many lenses to look into so sometimes they say horrible shit to get their shot.'

'I hate them.'

She looked as though she was about to be reasonable about the whole thing and then she peered up into his face and smiled, conspiratorially. 'Yeah, you know what? Me too.'

When they reached the final stretch of the carpet, fans threw their hands towards Allegra like zealots to a god.

'Allegra, please!' one woman screamed. 'You're the reason I'm alive, I love you!'

'Allegra, I have a tattoo of you!'

'Allegra, please! PLEASE!'

Jonah watched as Allegra brushed people's desperately outstretched hands with her fingers. She took a couple of selfies and when one man suddenly grabbed her, as if overcome by her nearness, Jonah intervened. He pulled her free and stood between her and the crowd so that his body shielded her from the grasping hands.

He was vibrating with rage. The entitlement that people felt over her! He wanted to fight every last one of them.

'Thank you,' she told him, sounding surprised.

'Don't mention it.'

'No one's ever done that before. I usually have to wriggle free myself.'

'Allegra,' the man who had snatched at her yelled, still trying desperately to seize her. 'You don't respond to me, how am I supposed to get in touch with you now?'

'You don't!' Jonah replied, glowering down at the shorter man.

'She knows who I am,' the man whined. 'She knows I need to talk to her every day.'

'Enough of this. You ready?' Jonah asked Allegra.

She nodded, taking his hand once more. They left the carpet for the movie house, leaving shrieks and shouts in their wake.

'Did you know him?' Jonah asked as they gave their names at the door.

'No,' Allegra said, shrugging. 'But lots of people think you're communicating directly to them. It can make things a bit parasocial.'

'Disgusting.'

'No,' she said firmly. 'Some people are just lonely.'

The din of the crowd could still be heard as they milled about the foyer of the cinema. Allegra air-kissed some producers and introduced Jonah to the slightly scatter-brained director. Natalie, Jasper and Grace waved as they made their way to the upper circle of the cinema auditorium.

'They're upstairs, but we're down in the stalls,' Allegra told him.

Jonah dazedly followed Allegra to their seat near the front.

'I like to come in early while it's still quiet,' Allegra said. She smiled earnestly at him, as they sat in two large reclining chairs in front of the biggest cinema screen he had ever seen. 'What did you want to tell me?'

'Oh, yes. That reminds me. Need to send an email really quickly.'

He fished out his phone and went straight to his inbox. He opened up his drafts and pressed 'send'.

'Your pen-pal?' Allegra asked, something strange crossing her face.

'Yes. Saying goodbye.'

'Goodbye? What do you mean, goodbye?'

'She's the best. She's great. But she's not real. She's not here. She's words on a page and while the words have changed my life, I can't waste time on an imaginary friend. One that I've built up in my head, from some perfect words. I need the whole human. Not just the great, edited parts. I wrote this letter after the pictures were published. I never sent it. I'm sending it now. Because I'm where I need to be.'

Allegra's eyes shone. 'You don't . . . wish she was here instead?'

'No. But you're right, I did have something to tell you.'

'Okay?'

Jonah took in her face. A face so perfect to him, without lights and retouches. The exterior of a soul more beautiful to him than any other he had known, even more so than the friend in his inbox. 'Nothing big. Just that I love you.'

Her eyes widened and her mouth formed a perfect 'O'.

'You don't need to say anything back,' he told her, meaning it. 'But I love you. Like how Pip loved Estella. My whole life, I was told I couldn't have the things I read about in books, the things I saw neurotypicals having. They said I wouldn't be anything. Education, speech, friendship. All of it wasn't what they saw for me. But I did it anyway. I'm done listening to them. Whoever "they" even are. I love you and I always will.' He said it all so matter-of-factly but it was because he wasn't afraid any more. Love wasn't supposed to be selfish. 'People get embarrassed after they fall – that's why I was such an arse. It's no excuse. But I fell a while ago and I've not been able to get over it. I love you. And it's been you. All along.' He loved her, no matter what the next scene held. It was a fact, not a conditional offering.

'Allegra!'

He didn't look away from Allegra when the studio employee hissed her name from the aisle of the cinema, and she didn't look away from him.

'Allegra, can you come backstage a sec? They want to do a line-up for the Q&A. We're doing it before the screening now, Anya has to catch a flight.'

'Go,' Jonah told her softly. 'Go be great. You always are.'

'Allegra?' the employee pushed.

'I want to stay here with you, though,' Allegra finally said.

'I'll be right here. Whatever you need, I'm here.'

When it seemed as though the employee might actually become physical, Allegra moved. She floated towards the small room that was considered 'backstage'. The rest of the cast had been assembled, along with the director.

'Phones off, everyone!'

Allegra moved to turn hers off, almost on autopilot. In doing so, sudden curiosity struck her and she opened her personal email address.

There he was. Waiting for her.

Dear Friend, it said. He still didn't know who he was truly writing to.

Dear Friend,
I think I'm falling in love. In fact, I know I am. I may already be all the way there. I think about her all of the time. I've always had a mind that either fixates or wanders and now it does both, over her. My thoughts always lead back to her.
And she's been hurt. Badly.
And it's my fault. Or rather, it wouldn't have happened at all if it weren't for me. I don't think she'll ever be able to separate me from this horrible hurt. I need three wishes now, more than I ever have, and I'm so aware that I don't have them. I can't fix it for her.
I'll spare you the details. You've seen it on the news. Sell them this email, if you like. My ex-best friend certainly sold me out, I don't expect loyalty from anyone now.
That was unfair, I'm sorry. You can probably tell I'm a mess.
How do I convince the girl that the whole world wants a piece of that she's my whole world? And that I want all of her?

Anyway. This is a thank you, and a goodbye. Your wonderful friendship got me through the denial stage of love. But I'm not in denial any more. You deserve better than a lovesick bookseller. I'll always be here if you need a friend. But I have to start writing something else now.
Love,
Jonah.

She stared at his letter and suddenly the clouds that had been gathering for so long were gone. The rain stopped. The way ahead cleared.

She had come to Lake Pristine to find her own little slice of the world. But what if that didn't have to be a place or an event or a moment in time?

Her search for something better could be another person, one just like her.

What a waste. Years of her life, the latter parts of her precious childhood, spent living through emails and meetings and screen tests. No friends, no holidays, just pats on the head from executives who needed a bright little product. The only truthful moments of her life were a few seconds of magic per day, captured on a camera that could go from being a dear friend to an invasive stalker within minutes.

She loved her job. But it couldn't love her back.

So when she and her colleagues were ushered onstage to rapturous applause, Allegra found his face in the crowd. It was a lighthouse, an anchor. She felt so much lightness where weight and heaviness had once resided.

And she suddenly knew that, for the first time at one of these events, she was going to tell the truth.

'Allegra, what inspired you to take on this project?'

The question came after numerous others had been put to the rest of the cast and crew. The script had been praised, the greenlighting process discussed. A couple of the actors with larger roles had waxed lyrical about the filming and their co-stars. It was all very polite and shiny and wonderfully fake.

While the others had been talking, Allegra had taken in the audience. Her heart had almost stopped when her gaze had landed on a smirking Julie M. Atkins, seated two rows behind Jonah. When she met Allegra's gaze, the columnist gave a snarky little sneer and Allegra was back in that restaurant once again, feeling on trial. But she steadied her nerves. She would not let Julie have the last word. No one was having the last word on Allegra Brooks any more.

The question was a generic one, asked by a friendly but shallow radio presenter called Matteo, who was hosting the talkback session. Allegra smiled, regardless.

'It's a love story. We need more of them. Maybe fewer stories about individuals saving the world, and more about people saving each other.'

The answer was clearly too short for the presenter's liking and he chose to expand with a rather daring additional question. 'You were recently the victim of a rather opportunistic photographer, has that made doing all of this a little trickier? Are you feeling all right? That's obviously the worst part of the job, but what's maybe the best part? Getting to talk to audiences like this? All of this?'

There were murmurings from the thousand people in the crowd.

She knew she should just shrug and say that the invasiveness was the price of a very special job. The overly familiar faux concern from strangers was always jarring and, under normal circumstances, she would brush over it efficiently and find her way back to promoting the project.

But something had changed. She looked back at Julie, who was assessing her with sharp little eyes.

Everything had changed. She was not the same person Julie had interviewed in that car crash of an article.

'That's funny,' she said softly, into the microphone she was holding. 'The way you phrased it. "All of this". What even is all of this?'

There was an awkward silence. The atmosphere in the audience instantly shifted. Allegra looked out at all of their faces. They stared up at her with a mixture of earnest engagement and curiosity. A few studio executives looked bored and bemused. Some fans looked decidedly worried. Only Jonah watched her, with eyes that told of real acceptance, no matter what came out of her mouth.

'That's not the worst part of the job, actually,' she said, her tone deceptively casual. 'The photographers? Not the worst part at all. No, the worst part is the dying kids.'

The stillness in the room made her want to laugh but the noise that came out of her mouth was a choked sound.

'So many kids who are sick and dying. And all their parents can do for them is get their favourite actor to come and see them in hospital. So you go. How can you not? You fall in love with them. You take pictures. You ring the bell with them. Then months later, the call comes. They're gone. And you can't mourn. Because it was never about you.'

The words had poured out without consciousness. She could still feel the grasping fingerprints of the strangers from outside bruising her arms. Years of characters who she had been praised for playing, who she knew better than she knew herself, standing in the room with her like ghosts who wanted to rest.

'I've been doing "all of this" since the age of fourteen. I've had stalkers. I've had people searching through my garbage. I've had people pretending to be my friend. I think I'm maybe better equipped for it than a lot of people.'

'And why is that?' pressed the presenter, despite the evident disapproval radiating from the rest of the panel, all completely mortified by the kind of honesty that should never be allowed in a press conference or preview screening.

Allegra smiled. 'Because I'm autistic.'

And the spell was broken. The words rushed like an enchanted wind through a dusty, locked-up castle. The thorns no longer had the power to wind and climb over the garden wall. The dragon that always relied on silence and secrecy didn't need a sword in its belly, just for her to reach out with one hand and touch the thing she had walked with since birth and only recently decided to learn to understand. They would step into the sun together.

'Because you're . . . did you say—'

'Autistic. Not artistic. Well, I'd like to think I'm that, too. But fame is manageable when you're an autistic woman, you see. Because you're so used to separating parts of yourself. You're used to keeping yourself safe. I think of the girl I have to be during things like this as a different person. A *her*, rather than a *me*. She does all of the work and yes, I pay the price, but that would be the same if I were working in an office or a restaurant.'

The audience was stunned but when she caught Jonah's eye, he was smiling up at her. Proud of her in a way she had never thought someone else could understand.

'I don't like these silly dances we all have to do to make great art,' Allegra continued, completely uncaring. 'I don't like that people in newspapers feel that it's okay to write pages and pages about me and my love life rather than my work. I don't like the fakery. Did you catch that, Julie?'

Julie, who had lost her smirk during Allegra's confession, turned as white as chalk dust and started to sink in her seat as a few people followed Allegra's direct gaze.

'I'm sorry I didn't give you anything juicy to write about,' Allegra told the reporter. 'I'm sorry your questions were so surface-level and boring, you had to write a tirade in order to get clicks. But I guess one has to get desperate. My mother told me you once got caught plagiarizing. So I guess you struggle with ideas.'

Julie sputtered and croaked, while people gasped. Some industry employees near the back whooped and clapped in appreciation of Allegra's attack. Perhaps they, too, had been victims of Julie's bile.

Allegra returned her focus to the wider room.

'So, I went to my dad's small town for a summer. And I fell in love.'

'Well, that brings us back to the film,' Matteo interjected frantically, but Allegra ignored him.

She glanced out to Jonah. 'Hey, you know what?'

He looked back, eyes wide but full of something beautiful. Allegra felt her own welling with tears as she smiled down at him. 'I got all of your emails. I loved all of them. I was there the whole time. And I love you, too.'

He made an unconscious noise of surprise, putting the picture together with the quickness of his truly brilliant mind, the one she had come to love so fiercely.

She smiled out at the audience. 'I hope you all enjoy the movie. I worked really hard in it, we all did. They've all done such an amazing job. You'll see it on the screen, you don't need us to spell it out for you. Wish I could stay but I have somewhere I need to be.'

Ignoring gasps of protest and loud commentary from the audience, she neatly jumped down from the platform and moved to the cinema aisle. Jonah met her there, after pushing by people's legs. He grasped her face with his hands and stared down at her in complete awe.

'It was you? All along, it was you?'

'I wish I were her, too,' she told him, completely indifferent to all of their onlookers, some of whom were taking pictures – even when the cinema ushers demanded that they stop. 'That girl on the screen, that's where she lives. She's not real. I only get to borrow her sometimes. I can't be her all of the time, Jonah, I hope you know that.'

'I know,' he told her. 'You're you. The one who picks out tomatoes and has to have the last word with me no matter what. That's the you I want.'

He kissed her and smatterings of applause burst out across the vast room, with one older woman loudly asking, 'Is this part of the movie?'

# Chapter Thirty-Two

The two of them fled the auditorium, hand in hand, and burst out into the long cinema corridor, leading to smaller screens and the lobby that would open out into the jaws of the press and the fans. The walls were adorned with movie posters, scribbled on by actors who had suffered similar screenings.

'It was you,' Jonah said, catching his breath as he stared down into Allegra's beautifully made-up face.

'Yes,' she replied, her euphoria diluting a little as she studied his reaction. 'I'm sorry. I thought it was Simon at first. Until that night—'

'At Pete and Alice's cafe. With the rose and *Middlemarch*?'

'Yes.'

She watched him replay their entire summer. 'You thought it was *Simon* writing to you?'

'He used a few of your expressions. I caught him at the computer right after an email arrived. The Oscar Wilde book was at his house.' Allegra could hear herself making excuses, so she cut off her own words and took a breath. 'I think, in the beginning . . . we were so mad at each other. I didn't consider it could be you, because—'

'Because I was such a dick.'

'Well—'

'No, I was. Especially during our first meeting.'

Allegra couldn't bear the touch of resignation that had materialized in him. His body language was slightly stiffer and his focus had shifted.

'I'm sorry I'm not Simon,' he finally said. 'Or someone like Simon.'

Allegra draped her arms around his neck and smiled as his cheeks turned just the lightest shade of pink. She pressed up against him and put her lips against his jawline.

'I don't want someone like Simon. The Simon I thought I knew wasn't even real, anyhow.'

She felt him swallow and his arms laced around her hips, pulling her closer.

'Simon makes people's mothers laugh,' he said. 'He buys the right gifts for the dinner host. He likes being on social media. He is, and always has been, the more obvious choice between the two of us. He wears lots of faces. I'm not surprised you wanted Dear Friend to be him.'

'I didn't want that, I just believed it. I want you. Since the moment I saw you up that stupid ladder, being such a prick.'

She felt him laugh.

'We're so similar,' she added quietly. Thoughtfully. 'I've never felt that before. I've never been around someone who feels and sees things almost exactly like I do. And I love you, Jonah. So please stop talking.'

His mouth came down on hers and everything else went away. Being with him was like playing music or falling into a really great scene. It banished all of the immaterial. It made all of the good things in life come sharply into focus.

He deepened the kiss and then let out a groan when she

responded with as much fervour. He pulled away to say, 'We need to get out of here. I can't do the things I want to do with loads of photographers lurking around.'

She smiled against his mouth. 'If you don't mind sneaking out the back way, we can go to my place.'

'Oh, great,' he said teasingly. 'We can roll around on the floor with no rugs and no furniture.'

She burst out laughing and playfully slapped him on the shoulder. 'I'm working on it!'

'Let's go then,' he said, clasping her hand with a firmness that promised he would not go anywhere, as long as she wanted him around. 'I'll make you something to eat when we're home.'

Home. For the first time to Allegra, it really did have the potential to be that.

They fled the cinema, sending Grace and Jasper a message to explain, and grabbed a cab once they were safely concealed in a back alley outside. They made out in the back of the taxi in a way that obviously annoyed the driver, as he eventually cleared his throat in a disapproving manner.

When they were alone in the darkened apartment, they danced slowly to music on Jonah's phone and Allegra felt, for the first time in years, like all the pieces of her were collectively assembled into one peaceful place. There was no division. No wishing that some parts were awake while others were stretched thin. She was thrillingly and miraculously all in one place, in one moment, with one person.

'You technically broke up with me tonight,' Allegra said, as they swayed to 'Downtown Train' by Tom Waits. 'I read your lovely email before I went onstage.'

'I did not break up with you,' smarted Jonah, which made Allegra laugh. 'I broke up with the invisible person who had weirdly started avoiding questions about her age.'

Allegra screamed at that, as he eyed her accusingly. Amusement lit up his face.

'Look,' she said, still laughing, 'I had to see if you really liked *me* or just some imaginary person on the other end of an email chain.'

'I'm glad that while I was pining and lost and feeling guilty, you were playing games.'

'I'll make it up to you.'

'I liked the you I was speaking to before you realized I wasn't Simon. And I love you. The pain in my ass from the bookshop.'

Allegra smiled. 'Good. Ditto.'

She rested her head against his shoulder while they moved.

'I don't know how you do your job,' he said quietly. 'All those people, all of those opinions.'

'Well, you can't ask people what they think. Or look it up. Someone gave my performance on IMDb one star once because they said I looked like someone who was mean to them once.'

'Excellent criticism.'

'It's not my business what people think of me. Especially now, people treat art like it's dishwasher liquid they ordered and didn't like. "Didn't meet expectations, wanted something else", et cetera. It's not real. Only the work is real.'

'I'm noting all of this before entering the publishing industry.'

'I fear for the authors who will have to put up with your notes, Jonah Thorne.'

He smirked and then grew serious. He stared at her with eyes full of so many unspoken thoughts, all she could do was hold his face in her hands.

'I know,' she said gently. 'I know, baby.'

'It's like . . .' He looked at her with incredulity. 'It's like coming home. Like I've been walking on some barren, empty planet and I've not been able to see through the toxic haze. And then suddenly, there you are. And you're everything.'

Allegra smiled, feeling wetness on her lashes. 'You're like me.'

He kissed her, a long languid one that made everything all right and then pressed his mouth against the place where her neck met her shoulder.

'Jonah?'

'Yeah?'

'This is so much better. So much better than everything I ever saw on a screen.'

'I know.'

And it was.

# Chapter Thirty-Three

It was the last night of the Lake Pristine Book Festival after a successful three weeks, and there was going to be the annual firework show to celebrate the summer. Everyone began to gather on the beach of the lake in Lake Pristine. Families carried wicker baskets full of food. They would all inevitably have prepared too much, so people passed things around for others to sample. The sun was already setting, autumn now waiting to step in and take over.

Allegra sat near the edge of the water with her sandals next to her tote bag. Only her personal phone sat beside her. She knew there were huge reactions happening online, all to do with her performance at the screening, but she didn't care. It was not her business. Her business was to watch the fireworks and have a wonderful time.

'Allegra!'

She looked up at the sound of her name and grinned as she saw Kerrie bounding over to her, almost knocking an elderly couple to the ground as she weaved chaotically through the crowd of townspeople who were settling on the beach.

Allegra was about to call out a greeting when the other girl threw her arms around the actress. She could feel tears on Kerrie's face as she pressed it into Allegra's neck. The touch was intense, a lot without warning and all very close, but Allegra hugged her back.

'Allegra, I've got six university invites!'

'What?'

'Yes! Your post, it lit everything on fire! Mapesbury called me at once, saying we could set up an interview. Then a bunch of other places, ones I was too scared to even apply for. I've been in virtual meetings with everyone!'

'Kerrie, that's awesome. I'm so happy for you.'

'It's all down to you! My dad says he's never been prouder of me!'

Allegra smiled, the warm breeze from the water and the twilight over Lake Pristine making everything about the present and nothing urgent or serious. 'That's amazing.'

'I just wanted to say thank you. And I'm sorry. You deserve the world and I'll never be able to—'

'Don't mention it.'

'I have to go and tell everyone. I don't even know how to choose!'

Allegra laughed and watched the other girl scamper over to what looked like her wider family, all of whom were sitting at the far side of the beach. As she approached, they cheered uproariously and her father raised a bottle of champagne into the air with a triumphant cry.

Allegra smiled and turned away. Her phone chirped. It was one of those notifications that she knew would be important, though how she knew that she couldn't say. She checked it. Her agent.

Hey, kiddo. The spin-off we were hoping to see greenlit has been cancelled. I'm sorry, bub. I know we were hopeful about this. More soon, lots of other irons in the fire. Call me.

\*

A year ago, it would have levelled Allegra. She had buried herself in ambition in the hope that someone would finally anoint her and tell her that she was enough. Little autistic girl, you finally proved to the world you were useful. You finally got them to look at you like a person and not some strange alien who crash-landed all over their well-made plans. She would have pulled her hair out and bartered with the universe and searched the lines in her palm and other people's emails for an answer as to why she was never enough for anyone.

Now, things were different. And as she saw a once sullen bookseller making his way towards her from the distance, she knew with complete certainty that the girl from before, the one who worried about approval and popularity, was gone.

She reached her arm back and hurled the phone. She watched it soar through the air and hit the lake like a star falling from the sky. She imagined it sinking, with all the opinions and unsolicited feedback drowning with it. They could sit on the bottom of Lake Pristine for evermore.

She would have her career. She would prosper and flourish. But not for the price of sacrificing love. Or sacrificing home.

Maybe all of the validation she had needed from those faceless people was the ghost she could finally give up. Perhaps she could forge something real from the people who looked at the true Allegra and loved her completely.

Jonah reached her spot by the edge of the water and sat next to her, pulling her into his lap. 'Hey, you.'

'Hey.'

'Did I just see you throw your phone into the lake?'

She grinned and pulled his mouth to hers. 'Maybe.'

He kissed her and then said, 'They say there's a mermaid in there.'

'Well then, she can deal with all the barracudas for me.'

'Speaking of barracudas, I spoke to Simon.'

'Oh, yeah?'

'He apologized. I said he has to order every single book Matuschek Press publishes and put each one in the window.'

'Seems fair.'

When the fireworks began, Allegra and Jonah were more interested in each other, the fireworks between the two of them finally directed in the right path. As Jonah kissed her, he caught sight of a pair of girls filming on their smartphones. He drew back and cleared his throat.

'Don't want you getting on any more morning shows,' he said quietly. 'That Julie woman might explode.'

Allegra rolled her eyes and then smiled at him. She pressed her lips to his once more and spoke softly against his mouth.

'Let them look, I don't care.'

# Chapter Thirty-Four

*Eight months later*

The reporter from *Architectural Digest* walked around Allegra Brooks's apartment with the photographer and openly marvelled at the decor.

'This is not the apartment of a regular nineteen-year-old,' Madison Swayne told Allegra Brooks, who was dressed in loose Levi jeans and a vintage crop top. Her boyfriend had his arm around her waist and wore a discerning expression. His protectiveness radiating from him like a warning to strangers.

Any disrespect would earn them a sharp word and an order to leave.

'All thanks to Jasper Montgomery,' Allegra said, handing the designer's business card over. 'She's available to answer any questions, probably with better detail than me.'

Madison took in the reception room of the classic apartment. The wallpaper was a fine teal with flecks of foiled gold. The chandelier was vintage and not too grand. The room was not designed around a television, as though it were a nucleus dictating the rest of the furnishings. There were shelves of books everywhere and the sofas and chairs were all turned to face the coffee table in the middle of the room

'And you met your designer on holiday last summer?'

'Sort of. She's a good friend now.'

Madison cast another quick glance at the boyfriend. 'And you're an editor, yes?'

'A junior one. I'm still learning.'

Madison knew a lot about him from her own internet sleuthing. He was young but his first poetry anthology had been reprinted multiple times, helped along by Allegra posting a picture of it to her millions of followers on publication day. A small subsection of her fans were dedicated to learning more about him. Madison had looked over their messages on a forum. They liked how publicly grumpy he seemed, only ever smiling if Allegra was speaking to him. He avoided the limelight and it only made him more enticing to his new online fans.

'What's it like going out with one of the most in-demand actresses of our time?'

Ever since Allegra's speech at the *Made in Waiting* premiere had gone viral, she had been in extreme demand. Her schedule was full for the next few years and she had written some essays on neurodivergence in film that had started numerous industry conversations. A hashtag about disability representation in media had caught fire as a result, and she was now in a position to be very picky about her projects.

Jonah Thorne merely smiled at the question, before nodding to the coffee table. 'We got that for five pounds at a flea market.'

Both the subtext and the remonstration were clear. She was not in their home to hear about their private life.

'Do you,' Madison had no idea of how to phrase her question so it fell out rather bluntly, 'want to talk at all about being autistic?'

Something unnameable passed through Allegra's eyes and then

she smiled and gave a small hiccup of a laugh. 'No, not really.'

Madison was both taken aback and a little embarrassed. She had hoped that maybe Allegra would share some secret about interior design and autism. Not that Madison knew anything about the latter, hence why she had asked.

A boundary made clear.

Allegra showed them the kitchen and a few of the smaller rooms but the bedroom remained unseen, another boundary the young actress was very clear about. Madison couldn't help but notice the pair as the photographer took shots of the apartment. They were always touching, in small almost unnoticeable ways. He was always checking on her and she was always throwing him reassuring smiles. It was as if they were communicating telepathically.

Madison took notes with only the slightest feeling of envy and bitterness.

'Do you two have any plans for this evening?' she asked, as they were packing up their equipment to leave. When the pair looked reticent to answer, she added, 'Off the record.'

'Nothing's ever off the record,' Allegra said, but she was smiling. 'Our friend Grace has a dance showcase with her conservatory peers tonight. We're going to see that.'

When Madison was gone, the pair breathed a sigh of relief and started to laugh.

'Why do neurotypicals stare so much?' Jonah asked gruffly, as they kicked off their shoes and collapsed onto their sofa.

'Because we're weird aliens to them, even if they don't exactly know it,' Allegra told him, putting her feet in his lap. He immediately began to stroke them soothingly.

'Hey, that Zoom I had booked in for tomorrow got moved to next week,' Allegra told her boyfriend. 'Want to do something normal tomorrow?'

'Absolutely.'

'Book shopping then the park?'

'Plus vanilla ice cream.'

'Perfect.'

And so they sat, just the two of them, in a private slice of the universe that no one else was allowed to access.

For autism means, *in one's own world.*

And that's what they were: each other's whole world.

## The End.

# Acknowledgements

This book is for the real ones who yes, love *You've Got Mail* but also know all about *Shop Around the Corner* with Jimmy Stewart. You are my people. See also, *She Loves Me*.

Thank you to the entire First Ink team at Pan Macmillan, from editorial to sales to marketing and to the social media crew.

Thank you to Emma for letting me pitch you this story after a presentation at the Barbican where I had to talk about making out with people in front of a Booker winner and the founder of the Women's Prize. And thank you for lots of other reasons that are less funny.

Thank you to Eileen and the entire US team at Wednesday Books.

Thank you to RV for the amazing cover.

Thank you to Beth who did so much brilliant work on *Some Like it Cold* before escaping to Oz.

Thank you to Louisa for being an absolute rock. We have an inside joke about crowd sizes that must, sadly, go to the grave but I appreciate you so much.

Thank you to every single person who read, reviewed and wrote about *Some Like it Cold*.

Thank you to everyone who has ever given me a gig.

Thank you to Peters and Books Are My Bag for making me an award-nominated Young Adult Author. It was very validating. I'm not embarrassed to admit it.

Thank you to all of the assistants, from the agency to the publishers, who work so hard to keep things running.

Thank you to Lauren, Paul and Callen.

Thank you to the booksellers. I remember how hard your job is and I'll never forget what you do.

Thank you to author friends, who are kind and don't scan the party for more advantageous connections.

Thank you to Josh and my family.

To all of my colleagues at *A Kind of Spark* (TV). You are the best. I'm so glad we have fun together. From many award show wins to tortoise wrangling or changing the world one frame at a time. Before Brooks Books, there was Do Good Books. Love you all.

And to Lola. Congrats on being (I think) the first openly autistic actor to receive an EMMY NOMINATION for playing an openly autistic character (Addie in *A Kind of Spark*, season two). You are extraordinary and you have given a voice and strength to thousands.

Thank you to ███████ for teaching me all about being a celebrity's plus one.

And maybe a bit of an acknowledgement to me, five years ago. I was so scared. I wrote a little book about being autistic and then everything became a rollercoaster. I did my best. I always try to.

And thank you to you. If you've come to an event and been kind. Said something nice on social media. Or just understood and empathized with the fact that being a young autistic woman in the public eye, especially after starting out when there were basically none of us, has been a learning experience and sometimes very overwhelming. All of the tweets/DMs in this story have been said to me. If you've been kind, you're one of the reasons I'm still here.

# About the Author

Elle McNicoll is a bestselling and award-winning novelist and screenwriter. Her debut, *A Kind of Spark*, won the Overall Waterstones Children's Book Prize in 2021. It was also voted number 75 in The 100 Greatest Children's Books of All Time in 2023. She is a five-time Carnegie-nominated author and was also honoured in the US with the Schneider Award, 2022. Her first novel has also been adapted for television by the BBC, and McNicoll was head writer on the project. The adaptation was described in the press as 'groundbreaking' for its inclusion of autistic actors and crew.

She is Scottish, autistic and an advocate for better neurodiversity representation in publishing. Writing romance stories has been her dream for most of her life. *Some Like it Cold* and *Wish You Were Her* are her first novels for YA readers. She lives in North London.